LEGENDS OF
THE RIFTWAR:
BOOK II

D0048053

NEW YORK TIMES BESTSELLING AUTHOR

RAYMOND E.
FEIST
& JOEL
# ROSENBERG

MURDER IN LAMUT

U.S. $7.99
CAN. $8.99

ISBN 978-0-06-079291-6

50799

"MIDKEMIA IS ONE OF THE MOST RICHLY DETAILED AND FULLY REALIZED WORLDS IN ALL OF FANTASY LITERATURE."
Syracuse Post-Standard (NY)

Also by Raymond E. Feist

Flight of the Nighthawks
Into a Dark Realm
Exile's Return
King of Foxes
Talon of the Silver Hawk
Magician
Silverthorn
A Darkness at Sethanon
Faerie Tale
Shadow of a Dark Queen
Rise of a Merchant Prince
Rage of a Demon King
Shards of a Broken Crown
Krondor: Tear of the Gods
Krondor: The Betrayal
Krondor: The Assassins

With Janny Wurts
Daughter of Empire
Servant of Empire
Mistress of Empire

With William R. Forstchen
Honored Enemy

MURDER IN LAMUT

LEGENDS OF THE RIFTWAR: BOOK II

RAYMOND E.
FEIST
& JOEL
ROSENBERG

An Imprint of HarperCollinsPublishers

This book was originally published in Great Britain in 2002 by Voyager, an imprint of HarperCollins Publishers.

EOS
An Imprint of HarperCollins*Publishers*
10 East 53rd Street
New York, New York 10022-5299

Copyright © 2002 by Raymond E. Feist and Joel Rosenberg
Excerpt from *Jimmy the Hand* copyright © 2003 by Raymond E. Feist and Steve Stirling
Map by Ralph M Askren, D.V.M.
Cover art by Geoff Taylor
ISBN 978-0-06-079291-6
www.eosbooks.com

First Eos paperback printing: July 2008
First Eos trade paperback printing: August 2007

HarperCollins® and Eos® are registered trademarks of HarperCollins Publishers.

Printed in the U.S.A.

10 9 8 7 6 5 4 3 2 1

For
Fritz Lieber
&
Donald E. Westlake

ACKNOWLEDGEMENTS

I'd like to thank Felicia, Judy and Rachel, for the obvious; Eleanor, for the usual; and Ray, for letting me bring some of my own toys for us to play with in his backyard.

Joel Rosenberg

As usual, I'm in debt to the original designers of Midkemia and thank them one more time.

I'd also like to thank everyone who kept me going over the last two years, you know who you are.

And I'd like to thank Joel for cloning three of my favourite characters from his universe and transplanting them into mine. They aren't exactly the Three Musketeers, but they are three of the most entertaining blackhearts to stick in a story.

Raymond E Feist

Contents

ONE

Night

It was a dark and stormy night.

That was fine with Durine.

Not that the goddess Killian, whose province was the weather, was asking his opinion. Nor were any of the other gods – or any mortals – for that matter.

In more than twenty years of a soldier's life, both fealty-bound and mercenary – as well as during the dimly-remembered time before he took blade and bow in hand – few of those in charge of anything had asked Durine's opinions before making their decisions.

And that was fine with him, too. The good thing about a soldier's life was that you could concentrate on the small but important decisions, like where to put the point of your sword next, and leave the big decisions to others.

Anyway, there was no point in objecting: complaining didn't make it any warmer, griping didn't stop the sleet from pelting down, bitching didn't stop the ice from clinging to his increasingly heavy sailcloth overcoat as he made his way, half-blinded, down the muddy street.

Mud.

Mud seemed to go with LaMut the way salt seemed to go with fish.

But that was just fine with Durine, too. Wading through this half-frozen mud was just part of the trade, and at least here and now it was just this vile slush, not the hideous sort of mud made from soil mixing with dying men's blood and shit. Now, the sight and particularly the smell of that kind of mud could make even Durine gag, and he had seen more than enough of it in his time.

What wasn't fine with him was the cold. It was still too damn cold. His toes had ceased to feel the cold and the pain, which wasn't good.

Locals were talking about the 'thaw', something they apparently expected any day now that Midwinter was behind them. Durine glanced up at the sleet smacking him in the face, and decided that this was an odd sort of thaw. To his way of thinking, there was far too damn much of this half-frozen stuff falling from the sky for a reasonable thaw, or even an unreasonable one. Yes, before the current storm they had had three days of clear skies, but there was no change in the air; it was still too damn wet, and too damn cold.

Too cold to fight, perhaps?

Well, yes, maybe, in the view of the Bugs and the Tsurani, and that was a good thing. They had fought Tsurani and goblins and Bugs in the north, and now, it seemed, they had run out of Tsurani and goblins and Bugs to kill – at least around here – and as soon as things thawed out enough, it was time for him and the other two to be paid and to be going.

A few months of garrison duty until then was just fine. Actually, as long as they were stuck here, Durine preferred the idea of garrison duty to being paid off today and having to spend his own coin to eat and lodge. Durine's perfect situation would have been to have the Earl pay for everything except drink and women until this hypothetical thaw – and he included that limitation only because he didn't think that even Pirojil could conceive of a way to cadge ale and whores from the paymaster – then pay them their wages the day they rode south for Ylith and a ship heading somewhere warmer.

Which made this, despite the mud and the cold, pretty close to perfect.

The heavy action was supposedly at Crydee these days, which meant that the one place they could be sure the three of them were *not* going was Crydee. Come spring, the privateer *Melanie* was due in Ylith. Captain Thorn could be counted on for a swift conveyance and be relied upon not to try to murder them in their sleep. That would be bad for one's health, as Thorn's predecessor had barely realized in the instant before Pirojil had stuck a knife in his right kidney while the late captain was standing, sword in hand, over what he had thought was Durine's sleeping form. Given that Thorn owed his captaincy to Durine and his companions' suspicious natures, he should be willing to transport them for free, Durine thought.

Away where, though?

Still, that wasn't Durine's worry. Let Kethol and Pirojil worry about that. Kethol would be able to find them somebody who needed three men who knew which part of the sword you used to cut with and which part you used to butter your bread; and Pirojil would be able to negotiate a price that was at least half again what the employer thought he was ready to pay. All Durine would have to do was to kill people.

Which was fine with him.

But until the ice broke the only way they would be leaving Yabon would be by foot, horse, or cart, overland to Krondor. Their only other choice would be heading back up north for more fighting, and right now they had earned enough – when they actually got paid, of course – that their cloaks would be so heavily laden with gold coin and their purses with silver coin that more fighting wouldn't appeal to any of them.

Enough.

This stint had left him with a new set to add to his already burgeoning collection of scars; a missing digit on his left hand from the time when he hadn't pulled back quite quickly enough while dispatching a Bug with his pikestaff. He now judged he would never play the lute. Not that he had ever tried, but he always had it in mind that he might like to learn, some day. That wound, and a long red weal on the inside of his thigh, reminded him with every step that he wasn't as young and nimble as he used to be.

Then again, Durine had been born old. But at least he was strong. He would just wait. Let the days drift past doing little chores, and it wouldn't be long before the thaw started and the ship was in port, and he and the others would be out of here. Somewhere warm – Salador maybe, where the women and breezes were warm and soft, and the cool beer was good and cheap and flowed freely as a running sore. About the time they ran out of gold, they could ship to the Eastern Kingdoms. Nice, friendly little wars. The locals there always appreciated good craftsmen who knew how to efficiently dispatch the neighbours, and they paid well, if not quite as well as the Earl of LaMut. And, from Durine's point of view, the best thing about fighting in the Eastern Kingdoms was there were no Bugs, which was even better than the absence of this horrible cold.

Or if they really wanted warmth, the three of them could head back down to the Vale of Dreams and make some good coin fighting Keshian Dog Soldiers and renegades for Lord Sutherland.

No, Durine decided after a moment, the Vale of Dreams wasn't really any better than frozen, muddy LaMut, no matter how it seemed on this cold and miserable night; last time they were down there he was almost as miserable with the heat as he was today with the cold.

Why couldn't someone start a war on a nice balmy beach somewhere?

Ahead, bars of light coming through the outer door to the Broken Tooth Tavern were his marker and guide, promising something approaching warmth, something resembling hot food, and something as close to friends as a mercenary soldier could possibly have.

That was good enough for Durine.

For now.

He staggered up from the muddy street to the wooden porch outside the entrance to the inn.

There were two men huddled in their cloaks under the overhang just outside the door.

'The Swordmaster wants to see you.'

One pulled his cloak back, as though in the dark Durine would be able to see the wolf's head emblazoned on his tabard, that Durine knew must be there.

They had been found out.

Looting the dead was, like most crimes, punishable by death (either outright hanging if the Earl was in a bad mood, or from exhaustion and bad food as you tried to get through your twenty years of hard labour in the mountain quarries) although Durine had never seen any harm in looting, himself. It wasn't as though the dead soldiers had had any use for the few pitiful coins in their purses, any more than they had for their cloaks. Durine and his two friends had more than a few coins of their own secreted about their persons – sewn into hidden pockets in the lining of their tunics, or the hems of their cloaks, in purses worn under their clothes, bound in shrunken rawhide, so that they wouldn't clink. A nobleman could put his wealth into a vault or strongroom, and hire armed men to watch it; a merchant could put his wealth into trade items that couldn't be easily walked off with; a wizard could leave his wealth in plain sight and trust that where sanity and self-interest wouldn't protect it from thieves, the spells on it could and would – Durine had seen a man who had tried, once, to burgle a sleeping magician's retreat.

Or, at least, what *had* been a man . . .

But a mercenary soldier could either carry his wealth with him or spend it, and Durine didn't have a good explanation for what a detailed search would reveal in his possession right now.

A nobleman would have just brushed past the two men – for they wouldn't have dared to stand in his way – but Durine was no nobleman. Besides, the number of people Durine would willingly allow within easy stabbing range of his broad back were very few, and two grey shapes in the dark were hardly likely candidates.

One on two? That wasn't the way he had planned to die, but so be it, if that was necessary, although he had taken on two men at a time many times before, without getting killed.

Yet.

It was getting to be too cold and wet and miserable a day to live, anyway.

He pretended to stagger on the rough wood while his right hand reached inside his cloak to his nearest knife. They would hardly give him time to draw his sword, after all.

At the movement, each man took a step back.

'Wait–' one started.

'Easy, man,' the other said, his hands outstretched, palms out in an unmistakable sign of peace. 'The Swordmaster says he just wants to *talk* to you,' he said. 'It's too cold and mean a night to die, and that goes as much for me as it does for you.'

'And big as he is, it would probably take both of us to put him down, if we had to,' the first man muttered.

Durine grunted, but kept his thoughts to himself, as usual. It would probably take more than the two of them. It would also, at the very least, take the two others who had come out of the darkness behind Durine, the ones he wasn't supposed to have noticed.

But bragging was something he left to others.

'Let's go,' he said. 'It isn't getting any warmer out here.'

He straightened. But he kept a hand near a knife. Just in case.

It was a dark and stormy night, but that was, thankfully, outside.

Here, inside, it was warm and smoky beneath the overhead lanterns, so that it was both too hot and too cold at the same time.

A mercenary soldier's life, Kethol often thought, was always either too lively or too dull. Either he was bored out of his skin, trying to stay awake while waiting on watch for something to happen, or he was wading through rivers of Tsurani troops, hoping that he was cutting down the bastards quickly enough that none of them would get past him to Pirojil or Durine. Either he was parched with thirst, or he was drowning in a driving rain. He was either crowded too close to other unbathed men, smelling their stink, or he was all by himself, holding down some watch-post in the middle of the night, hoping that the quiet rustle he heard out in the forest was just another deer, and not some Tsurani sneaking up on him, and wishing for a dozen friendly swords clustered around him.

Even here, in the relative comfort of the Broken Tooth Tavern, it was all or nothing.

In any tavern, on any cold night, there was no such thing as just right – he was always either too close to the main fireplace, or too far away. Given the choice, Kethol preferred too close, his back to the hearth, for it was hard to think of himself as being too warm in winter, even though he would regret it later, when he went out into the cold night to make his way back to the barracks at the south end of the city, with the wind cutting through his sweat-dampened clothes like a knife.

And there were better ways to work up a sweat.

Some of the other mercenaries were doing that at the moment – spending their hard-earned blood money in the sleeping rooms above, and the incessant creaking of the floorboards gave witness as to *how* they were spending their hard-earned money, but while Kethol didn't mind dropping the odd copper or two on a quick roll with one of the local whores, the cold shrivelled his passions as much as it did the relevant portions of his anatomy, and he couldn't see the point of spending good money on a soft itchy bed when there was an equally-itchy rope bedframe waiting at the barracks, for free.

Kethol watched closely as the placards fell. This game of pakir, or whatever they called it, wasn't something that he was familiar with, but a game was a game, and gambling was gambling, and all it would take would be enough familiarity with it to avoid the traps that drunken men would fall into, and then he could play.

Men took up the sword for any number of stupid reasons. Honour, family, country, hearth and home. Kethol did it for the money, but he didn't insist on earning *all* of his money with the edge of his sword, or even the point.

In the meantime, a few coppers spent on the particularly thin, sour beer of LaMut were coppers well spent. With an abundant supply of good dwarven ale nearby – Kethol was never sure if there was some magic involved, but it was consistently better than any humans brewed – it was clear that the local human brewers had only one mandate: make the beer as cheaply as possible, treating such things as good barley, unrotted hops, and washing out the vats in between batches as unnecessary fripperies. So when someone else bought, Kethol ordered dwarven ale; when he paid for it himself, he took the cheap stuff. It wasn't as if he was going to drink a lot of it, after all. He was only going to look as if he was drinking a lot of it.

It was an investment, as Pirojil would say. A small investment to make his opponent think him slightly in his cups, perhaps not as attentive to the game as he might be. A sip now and again, spilling most of the vile brew on the floor from time to time, and when he sat down to gamble, several empty ale jacks would testify to his being ready to be taken in a game. Then he could indulge in some serious gambling. Yes, it was an investment.

As much of an investment as their three swords. Blades that would chop through leather and flesh and into bone rather than chip and bend had proven their worth more than once. Saving money was a good thing, but just about the worst place Kethol could think of for economies was in the tools of the trade.

In his mind's eye, he could still see the widened eyes of the Tsurani whose blade had shattered on his shield, moments before he had slid his own sharp point under the enemy's arm, and into the soft juncture under the armpit that was protected on the sides by the pauldrons. He didn't have anything personal against the Tsurani, but then he had never had a personal grudge against any but a small percentage of the men he had killed. Besides, he had a lot in common with the Tsurani – they had invaded Midkemia for metal, so the strange story went, and a man who made his living killing with steel to earn gold and silver could understand that. If Kethol had a choice of metals, he would choose steel ten times out of ten – steel, in his experience, could get you gold more reliably than gold could get you steel.

Besides, his skills were useful here.

Blending into the scenery was a skill that a man who had started life as a forester's son could use on other grounds, as well.

The trick was not to overdo it, not to try to be *too* local, and be spotted as a phoney, arousing suspicion. Just add a little of the thick accent, throw in an occasional use of the local flick of the fingers that meant never-mind-it's-not-important, taking care to be friendly and smiling but not trying to be too comradely, and they wouldn't even notice that they barely noticed him.

It had worked when he was fist-boxing in that small village outside of Rodez – before Pirojil had killed that annoying little sergeant, and the three of them had to take to their heels, again – and it worked when he was learning how to roll dice in Northwarden.

Just learn the game, learn how to blend in, and be sober while seeming less than sober, and they would only notice that he had beaten them after it was accomplished and he was gone.

Somebody had to win, after all.

Why not Kethol?

Three beefy Muts, one with a fresh set of corporal's stripes on his sleeve, leaned over the rough-hewn table, examining the placards in front of them, while four others looked on. All wore the greyish livery of regular Mut soldiers, and all talked amongst themselves in the thick LaMut accent that Kethol could imitate without thinking about it.

'Nice play, Osic,' one said, as another scooped the pile of coppers toward him. 'I was sure I had you beat.'

'It can happen,' Osic said. He turned to Kethol. 'Kehol,' he said, mispronouncing the name in a way a prouder man would have taken offence at, 'you want to get in on the next hand? Only a couple of coppers to see some placards, but it can get expensive after that, truth to tell.'

Kethol had watched long enough, he thought, to have some idea about the ranking of combinations. More to the point, the Muts had been drinking long enough that a sober man wouldn't have any difficulty working out who thought, albeit in a drunken stupor, that he had a good combination, and that should be good enough.

In the country of the drunk, a sober man was at least a landed baron, and on a good day, an earl.

'I may as well,' Kethol said, emptying a judiciously small heap of patinaed copper coins out of his pouch and onto the table. He had considerably more on him, of course, but it was best not to seem rich.

'Your money's as green as the next fellow's,' one of the Muts said, and the others chuckled along with the jest that had been ancient when the Kingdom was new.

It was probably a risky idea to get into a game with regulars, but there were times for taking a risk.

Over in a far corner, near where the smell of roasting mutton oozed out of the kitchen, a game of two-thumb was going on between two Keshian mercenaries: the mad dwarf, Mackin, and a skinny, balding, puffy-faced fellow who called himself Milo, but who Kethol was certain had a price on his head under another name, and probably a local price, at that – why else would he make himself so scarce whenever the constable appeared? – and that's where Kethol should have been playing.

If one of *them* took offence at Kethol's winning, the odds were small that another would want to interfere. You could win a lot in a night when most of the time you appeared to be taking a deep draught of your beer you barely swallowed.

Here there was more risk, but there was also more profit to be had. It was just another field of battle, as far as Kethol was concerned. All he had to do was obey the same set of rules: protect himself and his friends; be sure not to draw too much attention to himself; and be sure to be one of the men standing when it was all over. And just as the best time to attack was before dawn, when the enemy would all be sleeping, the best time to gamble was late at night, when the others' minds would be clouded with too much drink and too little sleep.

And if that seemed ungentle and unsporting, well then, that was just fine with Kethol. He was, after all, a mercenary, serving his betters for pay, and like the whores upstairs he tried to be as well paid for as little service as he could manage.

So he nodded, sat down, and threw a couple of coppers in the middle of the table, and received his placards from the dealer's heavy hands.

He was just about to make his first play when the fight broke out at the table behind him.

You would think that men who made their living fighting would have better things to do in their time off than recreational brawling.

What was the point of it, after all? If it was practice, it was stupid practice. Neither the Tsurani nor the Bugs nor anybody else Kethol had taken up sword and pike against would have gone at it with bare fists if there was something sharp or blunt or big to hit the other with. And if it was really worth fighting over, it was worth killing over, and if that made you an outlaw, well, Midkemia was roomy enough that you could be declared an outlaw in more than a few places and still be able to earn a living, something that Kethol knew from personal experience.

Usually it was about one of three things: money, a woman, or I-just-feel-like-acting-like-an-idiot. Often it was all three.

Kethol had no idea what this fight was about, but grunts quickly turned into shouts and shouts were followed by the meaty *thunk* of blows landing.

He saw something out of the corner of his eye, and ducked quickly enough to avoid the flying chair, but the motion brought him into full contact with the burly regular on his right, and instinctively the Mut responded with a backhanded fist that caught Kethol high on the right cheekbone.

Lights went off in Kethol's right eye, but reflexes worked where vision couldn't; he lowered his head and lunged, catching the Mut around the waist in a tackle that brought both of them to the hard wooden floor. Kethol landed on top, hoping he had knocked the wind out of the other. He bashed his fist into the soldier's midsection, just below the ribcage, for a bit of insurance. Hope was a fine thing, but certainty was better. He had nothing personal against the man he was fighting, but he was used to killing people he had nothing against, so just roughing up one didn't count. Then he slammed his knee into the other man's groin and rolled away. This brawl was a matter of self-protection, not anger.

That was the thing about other people that Kethol never had understood: other people – even Pirojil and Durine – often got angry during a fight, letting their anger fuel them. For Kethol, it was all a matter of doing what you needed to. You got angry over other things – cruelty, or cheating, or incompetence or waste – not combat.

A few miscellaneous blows landed on his back and legs as he rose to a crouch – the wildly flailing feet of two other combatants as they rolled about the ground – but they didn't slow him down, and at least no knives or swords had come out, not yet. It was just a tavern fight, after all, and it was unlikely that, even drunk, the soldiers would escalate it into something more.

Off in the distance, somebody was ringing an alarm bell frantically. Most likely the tavernkeeper, calling for the Watch, for the alarm bell was quickly echoed by the Watch whistles. Clearly the Watch had been nearby, supplemented by a squad of regulars assigned from the garrison for the purpose of keeping order in the city. The Earl of LaMut might be young and new to his position, but it would be no surprise to him or his captains that garrisoned soldiers tended to fight with each other when they couldn't find anything else to do, and the best of the Kingdom nobility were used to accepting and dealing with the inevitable.

Neither was it a surprise to Kethol; he was always half-expecting a fight to break out, and while he hadn't been counting on it, he had been hoping for it.

He made his move.

In a fight, a man being knocked down was nothing to be surprised about, so as he grunted and fell to the floor, nobody would take particular notice that his fall hadn't been preceded by a blow. The fact that he fell to the floor where under a table several dozen of the coins had scattered was simply a matter of convenience.

He quickly scooped up a handful of coins – not worrying about the sound of clinking metal carrying over the shouts and grunts; everybody else would be too busy to notice a small thing like that – and made certain to pick out the silver reals first, before bothering with the coppers. All of the coins went into a hidden pocket sewn into the inside of his tunic, and he stuffed a rag in on top of them before pulling the pocket's drawstring tight.

Then he was on his hands and knees, making for the door as quickly as he could: he had already taken his pay for this fight, and it was time to be going.

A tavern fight had a dynamic of its own: after a few moments of free-for-all, some men would be down, hurting; others would have paired off, working off new or old grievances of their own with their fists.

Yet others would soon be doing what Kethol was busy doing: not hanging around for the fight to turn bloody, and particularly not waiting for the arrival of the Watch, but making themselves scarce. Unsurprisingly, that Milo fellow had been the first man through the door and out into the night, and others had followed. Kethol wouldn't be the first, or the last, and that was just fine.

Kethol launched himself through into the mud-room and through the mud-room to the entryway, brushing aside the thick sheets of canvas hung up to keep the chill air out of the tavern.

And stopped in his tracks.

They were waiting for him outside: a squad of regulars, led by a mounted corporal whose massive dark horse pranced nervously on the hard-packed snow, pawing at it with the strange clawed horseshoes that Kethol hadn't seen anywhere except in LaMut.

A lance pointed in his direction.

'You'd be Kethol, the mercenary,' came a voice out of the darkness.

There was a sharp point on the lance, and no point in denying it. If there was a problem, he would have to talk his way out of it now – or, more likely, think, talk, or fight his way out of it later.

'Yes,' he said, his hands spread in a question. 'Is there some problem?'

'Not for me. The Swordmaster wants to see you.'

'Me?'

'You. All three of you.'

He didn't have to ask what the corporal meant by 'all three of you'.

'So let's be on our way,' the corporal said.

Kethol shrugged.

With the stolen coins warm in his hidden pocket, he had nothing else that he needed to be doing, including dying in the street.

At the moment.

It was a dark and stormy night, and if there was such a thing as a barn that wasn't draughty, Pirojil had never seen one, so he wasn't surprised at the bitter cold ripping through the place as he rolled another bale of hay down from the loft, letting it fall onto the hard-packed earth below.

The horses were used to the *thunk* made by the bale hitting the floor, although the big bay gelding that was reserved for the use of the Horsemaster himself nickered and clomped in his stall.

Pirojil didn't have any particular objection to doing his share of tending the horses – all of the stableboys had been pressed into service as message runners during the last-but-one battle, and all of them had been cut down either by Tsurani or Bugs

– but he didn't particularly care to be doing it in a barn that was so cold and draughty that the sweat on his nose kept freezing.

It was a trade-off, as most things in life were. The less you complained about having to muck out a few stalls, the more likely it was that your name was not going to come to the top of the captain's mental list when he needed to send a patrol out to see if there really were Tsurani lying in ambush in the forest ahead. And if you could improve the job with more than a few swigs from a bottle of cheap Tyr-Sog wine that the late sergeant – may Tith-Onaka, god of soldiers, clasp him to his hairy, hoary breast! – didn't have any use for any more, well, then what was the harm?

It was lousy work, but it was easy.

You just slid a hackamore on the horse, led it to an empty stall, being sure to close the animal in properly, and then forked out the old, shit-and-piss-laden straw, then spread out some of the fresh. The old straw went into the wheelbarrow, and the wheelbarrow went up the ramp and through two sets of heavy swinging doors, to be dumped onto the back of the midden wagon, after which it was no longer Pirojil's problem. Somebody else would have to haul it out of town, and dump it. It was said that the dung of LaMut horses was why the local potatoes grew as big as horseflops, but growing vegetables was something that Pirojil didn't know much about.

Or care.

Pirojil knew that he was capable of being as complex a man as there was, which was why at times very simple things appealed to him. As did not thinking about things that didn't concern him. There was no point in employing his mental capacity without a good reason, after all. He had another swig of wine, gargled with it to clear the accumulated phlegm from his throat, and carefully re-stoppered the bottle before setting it down on the floor next to the ladder. The ladder could be used for getting down to the floor, but there was also the rope. And, just a short step away from the loft, a well-varnished pole stood invitingly.

Pirojil slid down the pole easily, his thick leather gloves warming only a trifle from the friction, and landed lightly. That was the trick of it, he had decided. You wanted to stop just at the floor, by your own friction, not drive your boots into the hard earthen floor.

It was a silly thing to be concentrating on, but there were worse.

Like the way women looked at him. Even the whores.

He shrugged. An ugly man was an ugly man, but an ugly rich man was a rich man, and some day he would be at least a moderately rich man, if he wasn't a dead man first. You had to keep building up your stake, and waiting for the right moment, and in the meantime –

In the meantime, you could amuse yourself with daydreams about wealth, while you waited for the predestined spear to run you through the belly, the fated sword to find your heart, or the inevitable arrow to seek your eye.

Willem, the last of the stableboys, had gone to war with his father's shield, and come back upon it. In his memory, the shield had been hung on the wall of the stable with the rest, and polished to a ridiculously high gloss by somebody who should have found something better to do with his time.

Thankfully, though, even as highly polished as the shield was, he couldn't see his reflection in it. He had no particular need to see the misshapen forehead hung heavy with bushy eyebrows, over sunken, tired eyes, and a nose that had been broken enough times to flatten it against the face, and turn him into a mouth-breather.

Pirojil fingered the scraggly beard that covered his jaw. It never did fill in, and he never would permit it to grow long enough for an enemy to grasp.

You couldn't always tell about people by looking at them. There were ugly people in this world, but many of them were good and kind. Pirojil had long ago decided that his own face was a mirror to his soul. It took something other than a gentle soul to decide to make most of your living sliding a sword into another man's guts, and the rest of it waiting to slide a sword into another man's, or any of the hundred other different ways of killing Pirojil had used to earn his pay.

A *skritch*ing sound sent his hand to his belt as he spun about.

He forced himself to relax. Just a rat, off in a corner up against the oat bin.

An ongoing problem, and one you'd think that the magicians would take time out of their busy schedule to handle. Couldn't they . . . wiggle their fingers or mutter their spells or whatever they did and keep the rats out of the horses' oats and carrots and corn? Well, it was none of his business. He wasn't sleeping in the cold stable, and, besides, nobody was paying him to kill rats.

Something whipped past his ear and *thunk*ed into the wood of the oat bin, accompanied by a short squeal.

'*Got* it.' A tall, rangy man stepped out of the shadows, tucking a second knife into a sheath on his right hip. A basket-hilted rapier hung from his belt – the narrow, precise weapon of a duellist, not the broader, longer sword that a line soldier would carry into battle. Tom Garnett chose his weapons with care.

It didn't much matter that Pirojil's own sword was a good six paces away, hung on a hook while he worked. Captain Tom Garnett, the oldest of the captains fealty-bound to his excellency the Earl of LaMut, was, even in his late forties, a far better swordsman than Pirojil could ever hope to be. Whether it was the result of innate talent or more than thirty years of spending half his waking hours with a sword in his hand – or, most likely, both – in a swordfight, Garnett could easily have carved Pirojil into little pieces.

And, apparently, he had a way with throwing knives, too,

although Pirojil would have thought better of him, for Pirojil had never heard of a thrown knife actually killing anybody, and it was absolutely silly to spend the gold to acquire a properly balanced throwing knife.

Pointless, really.

So Pirojil kept his hands from straying near where his own throwing knife was concealed under the hem of his tunic. Yet although he had never heard of a thrown knife actually killing anyone, he had seen one distract a man long enough for him to be killed some other way, and besides, there was always a first time; he just refused to pay enough gold for a good one, and even if he had, he wouldn't have risked it dispatching vermin. Letting his thoughts run, Pirojil stood silently as Tom Garnett walked over and retrieved the knife, displaying the rat that he had neatly skewered.

It was already limp and unmoving in death; Tom Garnett flicked its body off his knife and into the wheelbarrow with the straw and shit, then stooped to pick up a handful of fresh straw to clean his knife with before replacing it in his sheath.

He stood a head taller than Pirojil, who himself was of more than average height, but while Pirojil was built almost as thickly and solidly as Durine, Tom Garnett was even more rangy and gaunt than Kethol. His hair was coal-black, sprinkled with silver highlights, and except for a thin moustache and tiny, pointed goatee, his face was clean-shaven, revealing a wealth of scars about his cheeks and forehead. You would expect such a tall and gangly man to seem awkward in motion, but he moved like a dancer, seemingly always in balance.

'I seem to have taken you by surprise,' the Captain said, making a *tsk*ing sound with his teeth. 'I would have thought better of you, Pirojil.'

Pirojil ducked his head. 'The Captain is kind to remember me,' he said.

'And unkind to criticize? Ah. That could be.' Garnett gestured at the rat. 'You object to me killing a rat?'

Pirojil shook his head. 'Not at all, Captain,' he said. 'I might have done it myself.' He shrugged.

'If you'd cared to.' The Captain's tone was ever-so-slightly mocking.

'If I'd cared to.'

'And why didn't you care to, Pirojil?' Garnett asked, perhaps too gently.

Pirojil shrugged again. 'I didn't see any point. You kill one rat, there's another score of them where it came from. It wasn't bothering me, and I don't remember being ordered – or paid – to hunt rats.' He leaned on his pitchfork. 'Do you want to pay me to hunt rats, Captain?'

Tom Garnett shook his head, slowly. 'Not me, Pirojil. The Swordmaster, on the other hand, may have some rats for you to hunt, or at least to watch out for. I've sent for your companions; they should be at the Aerie by now. Would you very much mind coming with me?' he asked, politely, as though it was simply a request.

Pirojil shook his head. 'Not at all,' he lied. He didn't really have a choice.

Tom Garnett smiled. 'Relaxing to the inevitable is always wise, Pirojil.'

'That wasn't what you said when we were almost overrun by the Bugs, Captain,' Pirojil said. 'I seem to recall you shouting something about how we were going to die, but die like soldiers. Is my memory mistaken?'

Tom Garnett grinned. It wasn't a pleasant smile, being reminiscent of a wolf baring its teeth. 'Since we weren't overrun, it wasn't inevitable, now was it?'

The Captain turned, not waiting for a reply, expecting Pirojil to follow.

Pirojil elected to accommodate the Captain's expectations and silently trailed him out of the barn.

Glancing through the open gate on the other side of the marshalling yard, Pirojil caught a brief glimpse of lights from the buildings lining the road down the hill into the city proper, and considered the wisdom of building the castle on the bluff overlooking the original city. It was a fine defensive position, as long as you didn't have to run up and down the hill in this miserable weather. Then again, he considered, those who design castles are not usually the ones sent up and down the road in the middle of a storm. That was just the sort of task set aside for people like Pirojil, Durine and Kethol.

Damn. Now he wished he hadn't said anything about that Bug attack. Putting aside his own musing, he trudged after the Captain.

TWO

Concerns

Vandros noticed something.

A hint of Lady Mondegreen's scent of patchouli and myrrh still hung in the air of the Aerie, although probably nobody else would have been able to detect it over the sulphuric stink of the breath of Fantus, the green firedrake, who had just belched with satisfaction after arriving from his evening meal in the kitchen below.

The Earl of LaMut and his swordmaster exchanged glances as the creature settled in before the fire. The Swordmaster hadn't been amused by the firedrake's presence, and even less so by the fact that Fantus had selected the Aerie as his residence-of-choice, probably for its ease of access through the old Falconer's roost.

Vandros was still uncertain how the creature contrived to get the door open between the Swordmaster's quarters and the loft above where previous rulers of LaMut had housed their hunting birds for decades. It now held what Steven Argent thought was a thoroughly inadequate assortment of messenger pigeons, under the care of Haskell, the pigeon breeder, to whom Steven Argent sarcastically referred as 'the Birdmaster' – although not in Vandros's direct hearing.

Haskell was *supposed* to keep the firedrake up in the loft, but the only doors he was careful about locking were the doors to his charges' cages, each one labelled 'Mondegreen Keep' or 'Yabon' or 'Crydee' or wherever the occupant bird's raising and instinct would cause it to return to when released; Haskell was much less reliable when it came to the door to the loft.

Even when Swordmaster Steven Argent himself bolted the door, the drake managed to get down the narrow stone steps and gain entrance to the Swordmaster's bedchamber. But in the last few days Argent had apparently resigned himself to the creature being his lodger until the Duke of Crydee returned from his council up in the City of Yabon and collected the drake in the spring.

Fantus sighed in obvious satisfaction, extending its long, serpentlike neck, and let its chin rest on the warm stones before the hearth. Large wings folded gracefully across its back, the reflecting flames gave crimson and gold accents to the green scales of its body.

The firedrake had arrived a week earlier with Lord Borric's court magician, Kulgan, and when the Duke of Crydee and his entourage had departed two days before for the general staff meeting at Duke Brucal's castle in Yabon City, Fantus had stayed behind.

No one was quite sure what to do about it; most of the staff and household were too frightened by the small dragonlike creature to do more than get out of its way on its daily forays to the kitchen for food; though a few, like the Earl, were amused by it.

If Vandros was put off by the smell, he was discreet enough not to say a word about it, and neither did the habitually glum servitor who placed a tray down on the table and then poured each of them a glass of wine before setting the bottle back on the tray.

'Is there anything else required, Swordmaster?' Ereven asked Steven Argent instead of Vandros – and quite properly so, for while Vandros outranked the Swordmaster, and the entire castle was his residence, as the Earl of LaMut, the Aerie was the Swordmaster's quarters, and the housecarl was officially helping Steven Argent, as host, entertain the young Earl, it being the host's duty to see to the comfort of his guest.

Steven Argent smiled his appreciation to the servitor; the Swordmaster appreciated the fine points of hospitality, as well as of any other craft.

'Nothing at all, thank you, Ereven,' he said, after a quick nod from Vandros. 'Consider your service over for the evening, and do give my best to Becka and to your daughter.'

Ereven's already-gloomy face darkened slightly, although he forced a smile. 'I'll do that, Swordmaster, and bid you and his lordship a goodnight.'

Vandros didn't quite raise an eyebrow at that; he held his peace until Ereven had closed the door behind him. Not that he would have commented anyway. The Swordmaster's dalliances were legendary, but to take note of them at the moment would be impolitic, whether or not the rumoured dalliance was with the housecarl's very pretty young daughter (not true) or with Lady Mondegreen (true). Steven Argent was both a soldier and a lady's man, and his success in both fields of endeavour had propagated envy and enmity from many important men in the region. Several times in the last two decades the fact that Argent had merely exchanged polite conversation with a minor noble or rich merchant's wife had resulted in confrontation, and once in a duel. That duel had been the primary reason he had abandoned a fast-rising career in the King's army in Rillanon to come to the west twelve years ago, first as a captain in Vandros's father's garrison, then as Swordmaster. Although Vandros usually came across as a straightforward, uncomplicated warrior, he had spent most of his twenty-eight years studying to become the Earl of LaMut, and he could be as subtle as he needed to be: he knew when not to make a comment.

When the door closed, he said, 'I still find it hard to believe that there is a traitor among us. But . . .'

'. . . but there have been too many accidents of late,' Steven Argent finished. 'And I find myself uncomfortable assuming that all is well. Things have been too quiet in the north – and one of the things I learned when you were still in swaddling clothes was that when things seem to be going too well it's time to look for a trap.'

'But how could the Tsurani even identify and locate a traitor? It's not as if one could put on Kingdom clothing and wander into Ylith pretending to be a merchant from Sarth. Do they even have the capacity for that kind of plotting?'

Steven Argent shook his head. That was, it seemed, the part he didn't understand, either. 'I don't know,' he said, 'but I am concerned. Of course, if there is a traitor, he isn't necessarily employed by the Tsurani. If they were trying to kill someone, it would hardly be a baron, albeit an important one. They would be hunting earls and dukes, I'd wager. No, when it comes to sponsors for murder, we've too many other likely candidates to ignore. I've little fondness for Baron Morray – the feud between his and Baron Verheyen's families should probably have been settled by duel a generation ago, and he's made more than enough other enemies as well – but I think it would be best to make sure that he is not killed while in our city. It would tend to irritate the Duke.'

Vandros smiled at that. 'Nor, I can say with some greater authority, would it please the Earl.'

'To be struck down in battle? We could live with that; that's a risk we all take. But . . .'

Vandros sighed. 'I find it hard to believe that Lord Verheyen would countenance such a thing. He's hot-blooded and hot-headed, of a certainty. But suborning murder? That doesn't sound like him.' He shook his head.

Vandros's father had appointed Morray as the LaMutian Military Bursar at the beginning of the war, and Vandros had ratified his father's choice when he inherited the title two years earlier, since the man was good at the job. And as Earl, Vandros knew better than most that both an earldom – particularly during wartime – and an army, lived on gold and silver as much as on meat and grain.

If Steven Argent had had his way, the Earl would have sealed Baron Morray up in the Tower with his books and accounts and moneybags until every last Tsurani was driven from Midkemia, but that wasn't politically possible, and even keeping him resident in the City of LaMut was starting to look like a bad idea.

Time to get him out of town, at least for a while.

'It could be a coincidence. But there's an old saying, my lord,' the Swordmaster said. '"The first time is happenstance; the second time is remarkable coincidence; the third time is a conspiracy."'

Vandros grinned. 'I think my father should have chosen a good LaMutian as Swordmaster rather than some effete Easterner. Rillanon may be a good place to learn the fine points of swordsmanship, but I think that there is something about the Court that breeds not only conspiracy, but the suspicion of conspiracy, whether one exists or not.'

'There are always conspiracies, my lord, somewhere.'

Vandros's face darkened for a moment, and even though it remained unspoken, Argent knew what had passed through his mind. The rift between the King and the Prince of Krondor probably threatened the Kingdom in the long run every bit as much as the Rift through which the Tsurani had invaded. Rumours were running rampant: that the King had ordered his uncle the Prince imprisoned; that Guy du Bas-Tyra's viceroyalty of the city was simply a pretext to install Guy as the next Prince of Krondor; and lately, that Prince Erland was in fact dead at Guy's hand.

All official communication between the Armies of the West

and Krondor passed through Brucal and Borric's hands, and Vandros knew only what he was told, and as a matter of policy didn't believe the half of it.

At least that is what he had told his swordmaster. Steven Argent didn't know whether or not to entirely accept the Earl's scepticism, although he knew better than to voice any doubts. After all, rumours were often the first harbinger of uncomfortable truth. But that was not something that the young Earl would want to admit, openly or otherwise. Bad blood was the way of the nobility, particularly in such unsettled times, when an heir apparent – to a barony or a duchy – might well die in battle, leaving the succession unclear. Steven Argent had seen it when hunting wolves: when you killed the leader of the pack, the lesser males would spend the next few weeks fighting over dominance while you hunted them down. But that was not a comparison that would have much appeal to Earl Vandros, despite the wolf's head on his family's crest. And bringing up matters of succession even in a general way would probably irritate the Earl, given that he was unaccountably touchy on matters concerning his own likely future as Duke of Yabon, once he finally married Duke Brucal's daughter, Felina.

So Steven Argent changed the subject. 'I think those of you in the West –'

'You have served my father – and now me – for more than a dozen years, and to you still it's "those of you in the West"?' Vandros interrupted with a laugh.

'– those of you in the West tend to underrate Easterners. We have our share of able soldiers and more than a few exceptional fighters, as well, for that matter.'

'Perhaps.' Vandros appeared unpersuaded. He was playfully taunting the Swordmaster. There had always been a rivalry between the Eastern and Western Realms of the Kingdom. The Earl knew that historically the constant border struggles with the

Eastern Kingdoms had produced some of the best and most able commanders in the East, and some exceptional fighters, as well. It was the route to fast promotion and political opportunity, which is why ambitious soldiers often went east. For they would be fighting neighbouring armies under the gaze of barons, dukes, and kings, while most of the Western garrisons spent their time putting down bands of goblins and chasing outlaws under the supervision of swearing sergeants or the occasional officer. But seven years of constant warfare with the Tsurani had given the Armies of the West a hard core of blooded veterans, and new recruits every spring were quickly educated in warcraft or they were killed.

Or, often, both.

The Tsurani were harsh teachers in combat – tough enough that Vandros had been forced to hire mercenary companies to bolster his levies for the first time in the war – he just didn't have enough able-bodied men to meet his commitment to the Duke of Yabon without hired swords to replace the dead and wounded. No, the Tsurani were harsh teachers in warfare, but LaMut's soldiers had learned their lessons well; Earl Vandros would match his best company against the best from any Eastern garrison.

With a sly grin, Vandros said, 'We both know our own worth on the battlefield.'

Steven Argent raised an eyebrow. 'After you return from this next patrol, would you care to discuss this further on the training floor?'

There was an art to acceptably threatening a member of the nobility, one that somebody could either be born with or learn from study, and Steven Argent had spent much of his adult life studying it, so he was not at all surprised when Vandros's smile broadened.

'I think not!' Vandros laughed. 'I've got bruises enough from you, Swordmaster.' He sobered. 'But back to the business at hand:

Morray. You don't think it's a coincidence that he's come so close to being killed?'

The Swordmaster shook his head. 'A pot falling from a building, possibly – although there were none home in those flats at the time, as I understand it . . .'

'Which argues that it might just have been the wind.'

Steven Argent nodded. 'And the ice on Baron Morray's step could have been from a spilled pitcher, and his horse's saddle-strap might merely have been worn through from neglect, although I'd not care to suggest that to the Horsemaster.'

He walked to his desk and fingered the end of the strap that he had, himself, taken from the saddle for a close and careful examination. Yes, it had appeared to have been worn through, rather than cut, but he had been able to duplicate that effect himself by rubbing the strap against a sharp piece of stone.

'It's entirely possible that it's just a coincidence. But it's unlikely,' Argent said.

'But Verheyen? I know that there's bad blood between the two, but assassination . . . ?'

'I'd doubt it, but I wouldn't say it was impossible.' Steven Argent shook his head. 'I'd think that treason, somewhere, was more likely. I just have no idea as to who, or how, or why.'

'I want this kept quiet,' Vandros said. 'We're still at war, and that's not a time for accusations to be wildly flailed about, not with the Council of Barons meeting here as soon as they can be gathered. I think it would be a good time to clear the air on these matters, among others.'

Steven Argent nodded. 'That thought had occurred to me, as well. I think Baron Morray should be dispatched with a company of good men for the daily patrol, while I ask some discreet questions and see what I can find out.'

Morray had not particularly distinguished himself in the war, but he was not an embarrassment either, and it was a good idea to keep common soldiers under the eye, if not technically under the command, of a member of the nobility.

Vandros frowned. 'Should we send him off to Mondegreen with the lady, and to help escort Baron Mondegreen back for the Baronial Council, perhaps? We're about due to rotate baronial troops from both Mondegreen and Morray into LaMut – so sending him out to supervise that sounds to me like an even better idea.'

'My lord is most wise. I'd venture a suggestion that it would be even better to keep him out of LaMut during the council as well, but –'

'No. That would make me appear to take sides against him in his feud with Verheyen.'

Steven Argent nodded. 'True enough, my lord.' He knelt to scratch at Fantus's chin. The skin of all dragonkind was tougher than good leather – he had to dig in with the massive ring he wore on his middle finger before the firedrake arched its back and preened itself.

Vandros nodded to himself. 'Baron Mondegreen's presence might well act to keep things calmer.'

'Yes, indeed – he's a sickly old man, but a gentle one,' Steven Argent said. 'Although there's some steel under the surface, I'd say.' He scratched at the firedrake's neck again. 'Nice, Fantus. Good boy.'

'You have good men?' Vandros asked.

'All those who wear the tabard emblazoned with the crest of the Earl of LaMut are good men, of course.'

Vandros shook his head in irritation. 'I mean, particularly good men? For this?'

'I figured on Tom Garnett's company,' the Swordmaster said. 'With three of the mercenaries along, as bodyguard for Morray.' He bowed his head perfunctorily. 'Assuming, of course, the Earl finds my suggestion suitable. It would be better, I think, if the orders came from you.' Steven Argent was a soldier, and used to taking orders, but giving orders that involved the nobility was something he avoided, when possible.

Vandros nodded. 'I will, and then I'll have to leave this matter and all of LaMut in your hands; I've got to join Duke Brucal for the general staff meeting in Yabon next week, so I must leave today.'

'You'll bring back messenger pigeons?'

Vandros laughed. It was an ongoing by-play between them. Every time the Earl went somewhere, Argent would remind him to bring back messenger pigeons, as though he would have forgotten without the nagging. The Earl thought that Steven Argent was overly worried that there wouldn't be the ability to get the word out quickly enough, should something of importance happen in LaMut, and the Earl had just dispatched what Steven Argent was sure were the last of the pigeons, confirming his imminent departure for Yabon.

'Yes, I'll bring back pigeons. And a few good bottles of wine for your legendary thirst, as well. You can play host to the fractious barons in my absence. Putting Mondegreen in charge of the meeting in my place might be a wise move. Both Morray and Verheyen respect the old man – as does every noble I can think of, except perhaps for that prancing fool, Viztria – and that should put them on their good behaviour. As for the possible assassin, I can trust you with this matter?' the Earl asked.

Steven Argent nodded. 'Of course, my lord,' he said.

With the patrol sitting motionless in the middle of the road, it occurred to Kethol that he would have objected to Lady Mondegreen accompanying them, if he'd thought anybody would have listened to him.

But she and her two maids were due in Mondegreen, to minister to the ailing baron and accompany him back to LaMut for the Baronial Council – or, at least, she was due to stay out of noble beds in LaMut for the time being – and Baron Morray had insisted that the patrol might as well swing north to guard her on her way home. Which made sense, perhaps. A company of cavalry was due within a day or two from Mondegreen, and this way they could be pressed into service around the city itself, relieving the Earl's troops.

The trouble with what Pirojil called 'a creeping mission' was just that: it crept, and grew, and crept and grew, until it was increasingly unmanageable.

What had at first been a routine patrol which was to swing north and west and then back to LaMut had become an escort for those bound both for Mondegreen, as well as those to be escorted back from both Mondegreen and Morray. Sandwiched between the front and the back of the column were easily two dozen civilians: Father Finty and the young boy that he called his altar boy but whom Pirojil suspected to be his catamite; three of those rare tame Tsurani – former slaves who surrendered meekly after their masters were killed – who had been hired as tenant farmers in some Mondegreen franklins' holdings; Lady Mondegreen and her claque of ugly maids. An assortment of servants, porters, and lackeys rounded out the company.

Not that Kethol would have minded the lady's company, under other circumstances: she was companionable and more than a little pleasant on the eye. Some women seemed to bloom in their late teens and early twenties, but were clearly past their prime, jowls and breasts already beginning to sag, hair going limp, by their thirtieth year. Not so for Lady Mondegreen. Except for one white streak that only added character to her long, coal-black hair, she could have passed for her late teens. Perhaps that had something to do with her childlessness, or her relationship to the conDoin family – they tended to age well.

Those who didn't die in battle, that is.

Her face was heart-shaped, with a strong if pointed chin that would have seemed almost masculine if it weren't for the full, ripe lips above. And even in her riding outfit, with layers of clothes underneath the short jacket, her breasts seemed perky enough to make the palms of his hands itch. Long, aristocratic fingers, nails bitten short in a lower-class touch that Kethol found utterly charming, gripped the reins with practised ease, while her slim thighs, encased in tight leather riding breeches, gripped her saddle tightly when her huge red mare pranced nervously while they waited. Ladies usually rode in a coach for long journeys, and she likely would have preferred that, but the most direct route from LaMut to Mondegreen went through some rough country, and she had taken to horseback with good grace, riding like a man, astride her mare rather than sidesaddle.

Behind her, on what appeared to be a matched pair of remark-ably spavined and mottled geldings, her two maids huddled nerv-ously into their cloaks, clinging tightly to the cantle, clutching their reins without actually communicating to the horses. They seemed content to follow along behind the mounts in front, which Kethol decided was probably the reason the Horsemaster had picked out these two hayburners for this journey. Occasionally, those behind would have to flick the rumps of the two geldings, moving them along when they stopped to crop at the side of the road. Perhaps, thought Kethol, they might even have some sense of how to ride by the time they reached Mondegreen.

It was hard for Kethol to tell Elga from Olga – was Elga the one with the slight moustache and large potbelly, or the heavy moustache and slight potbelly? He thought it important to correctly identify which was which. Women as poorly favoured as those two needed any consideration available; somebody who partnered with Pirojil should understand that, and Kethol did.

'Easy, girl, easy,' Tom Garnett murmured to his big black mare. Kethol never understood why somebody would want an animal that edgy – 'high-spirited', to use the accepted term – when perfectly decent, placid mounts were available. It seemed foolish. And Garnett's mare appeared to be as hot-blooded as any horse Kethol had seen; the Captain had picked her for beauty and speed, he assumed, which was as stupid a choice as a mounted soldier could ever make. Now, a trained warhorse, *that* he could easily understand. He had seen more than one such trample infantry underfoot in battle, and while they were fractious, they were worth the effort; it gave the rider an extra weapon – four, if you counted each hoof separately, five if the horse was a biter. But a horse that was just plain nervous made no sense to Kethol under any circumstance. Well, at least the Captain had the good sense not to pick an uncut stallion as his mount, unlike that idiot they had served under in Bas-Tyra. That would be the last thing that anybody ever needed – a stallion going crazy because one of the maids was in her monthlies or a mare was in heat.

Tom Garnett had not liked the look of the stand of elms that guarded the far side of the clearing, and had sent a trio of horsemen ahead to scout for a possible ambush. The Tsurani were expected to be behind their lines for the winter, at least some twenty miles to the west of here, but Kethol had seen more than one corpse with a surprised expression on its face because things hadn't turned out quite as had been expected.

The scouts were a sensible precaution. The Tsurani were no match in forestcraft for the likes of the Natalese Rangers or for Kethol himself, granted, but they were learning quickly. Too quickly.

That was the trouble with making war on people without eliminating them to the last man: you killed the weak, stupid, and unlucky, leaving the strong, smart, and fortunate to face later on. If it was up to Kethol, the war would end with the Tsurani pursued to whatever vile pit they'd emerged from, and slaughtered right down to the last infant – despite the obviously preposterous stories about how many of them there were on Kelewan – but, at least for now, that issue wasn't even on the table.

All told, it was more than a good argument for Kethol, Pirojil and Durine getting their pay and getting themselves out of here, just as soon as this council of barons was over, and the ice had cleared in the south.

Warm winds and soft hands . . .

Soon, perhaps. Although . . . He sniffed the air. He couldn't have said how he knew, but there was a storm coming. Not soon, not right away. The sky to the west was clear and blue-grey, only the puffiest and most distant of clouds scudding across its surface. But there was a storm coming, and of that Kethol was sure.

Kethol glanced over to where Baron Morray waited, motionless, on his equally motionless mottled bay gelding. He was a big man, who would've seemed more pretty than handsome, if it wasn't for a certain calculated ruggedness in his plain-cut greatcoat and the utilitarian dragonhide grip of the great sword that hung from his saddle in counterpoint to the short rapier that hung from his hip. His features were just too regular, too even, his clean-shaven face too smooth, his movements too fine and precise, when he moved at all.

His look at Kethol was filled with disdain.

'As you can see, there was no reason for you to fear,' he said, his voice pitched low enough to carry only as far as Lady Mondegreen and Captain Tom Garnett.

Kethol didn't rise to the bait. What the Baron thought of him as he sat still while LaMutian regulars rode forward to scout was of no concern to him. He could more feel than hear Durine stirring behind him, while Pirojil's face held that studiously neutral expression that spoke volumes about his opinion of people who criticized professional men in their work.

Tom Garnett came to their rescue, his nervous horse taking a few prancing steps that Garnett managed with just the bare twitch of his fingers on the reins, and a tightening of his knees against the saddle. 'I'm afraid, I'm sorry to say, Baron Morray, that you misunderstand Kethol's reluctance to ride ahead.'

'Oh?'

Kethol shook his head minutely. Tom Garnett, too, eh?

As usual, it was for some reason incorrectly understood by people who really didn't know the three of them that he, Kethol, was the leader of the three. Durine was too large and too quiet, and Pirojil was grotesquely ugly; for some reason, that tended to make people think that Kethol was somehow in charge of the other two.

'I was with the Swordmaster when he assigned the three of them to *protect* you, Baron Morray,' Tom Garnett went on. 'I don't remember him telling them that they were in your service.'

Unspoken was the fact that the Swordmaster hadn't put Tom Garnett's company under Baron Morray's command, either; a distinction that seemed to escape Baron Morray more than occasionally.

Which was not surprising. Nobility tended to be punctilious about such things around other nobility, but less so around commoners, no matter what their military rank. That was one thing Kethol liked about working in the Western Realm of the Kingdom; while soldiers everywhere understood that nobility was no substitute for judgment and experience, out here you found the armies refreshingly free of ambitious office-seekers. Had Tom Garnett been back in the Eastern Realm, angling for a squire's rank or marriage to a minor noble's daughter, he'd have been kissing Morray's backside and asking politely which cheek he preferred smooched first.

The forest loomed ahead, all grey and stark. It would be spring, soon, bringing green life back to the woods. That was the nice thing about the woods: you could count on a forest to regenerate itself, both from the ravages of winter and those of invaders.

People were different.

Tom Garnett signalled for the column to proceed, and Kethol kicked his horse into a quick canter that put him ahead of Baron Morray, while Durine and Pirojil took up their places beside the Baron.

After years of working together, he could almost read the minds of his companions without the need for any word being spoken between them. Kethol would take the lead, not because he was any more expendable than the other two – any more than he was the leader of the three – but because he had been raised in forested land, and his early years had tuned his senses to the smells and sounds and the silences of the forest in a way that could only be learned from birth.

Off in the distance, a woodpecker hammered away, almost loud enough to hurt his ears. Apparently the clopping of horses' hooves on the hard, frozen ground wasn't threatening enough to cause the bird to go silent.

Raising his hand for attention, Kethol gave out a forester's shout, and the hammering desisted for a moment, only to take up again. Good. The bird was sufficiently wild to go silent in the presence of men, but sufficiently used to men to resume his work quickly; and that helped to verify that they were still alone in the forest.

He smiled as he rode. You could develop quite a legendary ability for being able to hear things in the woods if only you let the woodland creatures help you.

A cold wind picked up from the west, bringing a chill and a distant scent of woodsmoke, probably from some nearby franklin's croft. Birch mixed with the tang of pine, if Kethol was any judge of woodsmoke, which he was.

Morray kept up a steady stream of complaints about his franklins, which Kethol listened to with only half an ear, and then only because the Baron griped better than most grizzled cavalry sergeants.

By edict of the Earl, and probably the Duke himself, the borders of a franklin's croft were inviolable by the barons – who were always looking to increase their own holdings, and settle bondsmen on any vacant land – but the actual house itself was, in law and in practice, the property of the Baron, and while franklins were forbidden from expanding their wattle-and-daub buildings, the barons were required to make necessary repairs to 'their' property.

If you believed Baron Morray's complaints, not only had Tsurani troops put the red flower to every thatched roof in his barony last autumn, forcing the Baron now to spend sizeable sums for the hire of carpenters, daubers, and thatchers, but the mud and straw of LaMut invariably crumbled if a harsh thought was sent in its direction.

Arrangements would have to be made with Baron Monde-green, the earldom's Hereditary Bursar, for some loans of Crown money, no doubt, and Baron Mondegreen was as famous for being stingy with Crown money as he was for his own personal generosity, and it was likely that there was some other conflict between the two, given that Morray was serving as the Earl's wartime Bursar, if only because he was more mobile and healthy than Mondegreen was. His position would enable – and require – Morray to pay soldiers, fealty-bound or mercenary, as well as provisioning troops and suchlike; it would not permit him to dip into the Crown purse for repairs to his own barony.

For Morray to be tupping the Baron's wife while trying to get him to authorize a loan was probably not the wisest of ways to proceed, but Kethol had long since decided that wisdom and nobility seemed to go together only by coincidence.

The farming road they were using to make their way through the North Woods wound down into a draw, and then up and out through a shallow saddle between two low hills. The Earl's Road cut across the top of the hills, but it wasn't the fastest way to Morray, or from there to Mondegreen.

Lady Mondegreen left her maids behind as she rode up beside him. He nodded a greeting, and idly touched a hand to his forehead.

'I want to thank you for escorting me,' she said. Her voice was surprisingly low and pleasantly melodic, like a baritone windflute.

'You are, of course, welcome, my lady,' Kethol said.

And never mind that it was none of his idea, and he would have been perfectly comfortable leaving her to wait for the next company of Mondegreen cavalry to be cycled back to the barony. The larger the party, the better, sure – but that was only when you were counting fighting men, not when you added on baggage like noble women, no matter how pleasing to the eye they might be.

'There's something . . . frightening about a late-winter forest,' she said. 'When you look at the branches out of the corner of your eye, they sometimes look like skeletal fingers, reaching out for you. Add a few black robes, and you might think you had the Dark Brotherhood on every side.'

She rode almost knee-to-knee with him, letting the others lag behind.

'I guess that is so.' Kethol nodded. 'But I've always liked the forest. All forests.'

'Even when it looks so bare and desolate?' she asked, lightly.

'Looks can be deceiving, Lady.' His knife came to his hand without him having to have thought about drawing it; Kethol reached up and cut a twig from an overhanging branch. A blunt thumbnail cut through a grey bud on the twig, revealing the green hidden inside. 'No matter how dead it looks, there's always life hidden here,' he said.

Ahead, ashy corpses of burned trees told of where a raging fire had scarred the forest. Kethol remembered that specific fire, which had been started by fleeing Tsurani troops, and his jaw clenched at the memory.

'The winter trees are merely . . . sleeping,' he said. 'But, in fewer days than you care to think, if you'll probe with your fingers or a stick at the base of that burned oak, you'll see sprouts reaching out to the sky.'

'I see.'

'You will.' He smiled. 'Ten years from now, you won't be able to tell that there was a Tsurani bastard who lit a fire here like a dog puking over food he can't steal in order to prevent somebody else from eating it.'

He gestured with his twig at the top of the hill that rose up beside them. 'And right over there, maybe twenty or thirty years from now, there will be a nice little stand of oaks – short ones, granted, but real trees, and not merely saplings – drawing their sustenance from the ground below.'

She laughed, the sound of distant silver bells. Kethol normally didn't like being laughed at, but her laughter was in no way insulting.

'Why, Kethol,' she said, as though more in shock than surprise, 'one would think you were a poetic philosopher, not a soldier. Oaks, you say? Why oaks, rather than elms or pines or beeches? And how could you know that they'll grow there, and not somewhere else?'

'I could –' No. He caught himself, and forced a shrug. 'I guess there is no way that I really could know,' he said. 'But I believe it will happen. Tell you what, Lady: come back in twenty years and think kindly of me if you find a stand of oaks here.'

'I just might do that, Kethol,' she said. 'In fact, you may have my promise on it, and if you're still serving the Earl, I'll bet my silver real against your one copper that it will be elms or pines or something other than a stand of oaks, if you'd care to wager.'

He smiled. 'Well, I doubt that I'll still be in LaMut even come spring, but if I'm in the earldom twenty years from this day, I'll knock on your castle gate, and ask to collect that bet.'

'Or pay it.' She raised an eyebrow, and smiled. 'Unless you'd flee the earldom to avoid losing a copper?'

'No, I wouldn't do that, Lady.'

There was no point in mentioning that it was a safe bet, as the top of the hill was where he and Pirojil and Durine had buried the Tsurani Force Leader who had ordered the fire lit, scattering dozens of acorns over his bare chest before they had filled in the hole. The Tsurani's eyes had gone wide as they started to shovel in the earth. But gagged with a leather thong that held his acorn-filled mouth half-open, he hadn't said much beyond a few grunts, and hamstrung as he was at elbows, ankles, and thighs, he wasn't going anywhere. They had not packed down the earth very hard after they buried him; he probably had at least a few minutes to think over the wisdom of having burned down that which he could not conquer.

Kethol didn't mind the Tsurani having tried to kill him – that was business – but he took damage to a forest personally, and neither Durine nor Pirojil had raised a word of objection; they had just helped him shovel in the soil. He had no regrets, but burying a man alive wasn't the sort of thing that he really wanted to mention to a pretty woman, much less a pretty noblewoman, not when she was flirting with him.

Which she clearly was.

That was probably just to make Baron Morray jealous, but that was fine with Kethol. His sleep would be warmed by thoughts of her this night, and if she slept under Baron Morray that did Kethol no harm.

Still . . .

They broke at midday for a skimpy meal of cold bread and sausage, washed down with water and a gillful of cheap wine for the soldiers, while the nobles shared a glass bottle of something finer.

Pirojil would have had the Tsurani ex-slaves water and feed the horses – they seemed well-tamed, after all, and didn't quite get the notion that they were now free – but Tom Garnett had a different idea: as usual, one man from each squad was detailed to see to the animals of that squad, while the others ate and rested. There was little enough time to take your ease when you were on patrol, and it made sense to get what rest you could.

Pirojil didn't argue. He just let Kethol take his turn seeing to their three horses, while Pirojil ate his bread and sausage quickly enough to avoid tasting it, then drank his wine even more quickly. It warmed him a little, as he huddled in his cloak against the cold.

Even so. . .

'I'd best go see about watering something that needs watering,' he said to Durine, as he slung his swordbelt over his left shoulder, then stalked off over the crest of the hill to relieve himself.

Below, one of the regulars, a lanky man with a bald patch on his scalp where a Bug had nicked him, took out a set of pipes, and another a small drum, and soon off-key renditions of old martial songs filled the air.

'We are marching on Bosonia, Bosonia, Bosonia,

'We are marching on Bosonia, Bosonia, today . . .'

The Tsurani, as usual, seemed confused. Presumably, in the Empire, soldiers didn't sing or drum unless ordered to do so. They probably didn't fart unless explicitly instructed. These former slaves would find things much looser in service to the local nobles and franklins.

Pirojil's lips tightened. The Tsurani were even worse than were the Kingdom regulars when it came to showing individuality. What was there about a regular soldier's life that robbed him of any initiative?

He relieved himself quickly behind the broad bole of an ancient oak, while above a squirrel chittered at him. As he buttoned up his trousers, it was only a matter of reflex to check that the hilt of his sword was near his hand.

A twig snapped behind him, and his sword was no longer simply near his hand, but in his hand as he spun about to face –

Durine, a smile playing across his broad face, both hands up, palms out. 'Stand easy, Pirojil,' he said. 'I guess I should have cleared my throat instead of stepping on a twig.'

Pirojil had to laugh. Snapped twigs as warnings of impending attack were a staple of late-night, campfire stories. For the most part, twigs bent and didn't make any noise, except in the driest times of the year. Besides, in real life, an enemy was rarely considerate enough to give a warning before an assault: it kind of ruined the whole idea of a surprise attack.

Pirojil replaced his sword. They might be friends and long-time companions, but Durine's hand never strayed far from the hilt of his own sword until Pirojil finished resheathing. Some habits were hard enough to break that they probably weren't worth breaking.

'Excuse me,' Durine said, politely turning his back as he unbuttoned his own trousers.

A stream of piss steamed and smoked in the chilly air for an improbably long time.

'With all the places to relieve yourself,' Pirojil said, 'did you really need me to be a witness?'

Durine buttoned his fly. 'Well, truth be told, I always do prefer to have you or Kethol at my back when I'm occupied handling something this large and delicate, but no, I figured we ought to talk.'

'So, talk.'

Durine shook his head. 'I don't like any of this. Playing body-guard to an officer is one thing – you don't have to worry about your own soldiers trying to knock him off –'

Pirojil's eyebrows rose and he gave Durine a fish-eye.

'All right, you *usually* don't have to worry about your own soldiers trying to knock him off, just about enemy troops bothering him while he's busy running a battle. I like doing bodyguard stuff.' He patted his waist.

Pirojil nodded, though he did not meet the other's gaze. It wasn't that he was unwilling to. It was just a reflex for him, after all this time, with both Kethol and Durine: they automatically divided the world into fields of fire; it had saved their lives more than several times.

'I know,' Pirojil said. Bodyguard duty usually meant some extra coins, and the meals tended to be better, and while you were near enough the front not to get bored, you were also not so close that you had to worry about somebody leaping out at you while you were harvesting a bit of loot. 'Not the sort of thing I would have volunteered for, but I don't remember being asked to volunteer, do you?'

'So why us?'

'I don't know, although I have some ideas. For whatever they're worth.' Pirojil shrugged. 'I don't think it's because the Swordmaster thinks we're better than his own troops.'

'We are.'

Pirojil couldn't help but grin. 'Well, *I* think that, and *you* think that, and *Kethol* thinks that we're better than they are – but I'm willing to bet that the locals don't think we are.'

'Their problem.'

'No. *Our* problem. What we are is uninvolved, which is good.'

'Good?'

'Good for us. We're not expected to take sides in local rivalries, which means that we can expect not to have our throats cut for making the wrong move at the wrong time.'

'So you like this?'

'I didn't say that. The bad part is that we're uninvolved –'

'You said that was the good part.' Sometimes Durine was just too slow. Not that Pirojil would complain; Kethol was worse.

'It's good and bad,' Pirojil said slowly, patiently. 'Most things are. The bad has two parts: someone might try to cut our throats for just being in the way.'

'Nothing new in that.'

'And we're expendable.'

'Nothing new in that, either.'

'More so than usual.'

'Ah!' Durine nodded, finally understanding. 'Politics.' He said it as if it was a curse.

'Politics.' Pirojil nodded. 'Look at it from the political angle. If Baron Morray, say, falls down a flight of stairs and breaks his neck, the Earl can either treat it as an accident, or as our fault. If it's an accident, well then, there's no political problem, and Luke Verheyen isn't to blame – nobody is.'

'And that's a good thing, isn't it?'

'Sure. But if it's not an accident – if, say, the Baron was murdered – then whose fault is it?'

'The murderer's?'

Pirojil wasn't sure whether to groan or laugh. 'Sure: the murderer. And who is the murderer? Verheyen, the hereditary enemy, who is eyeing the earldom every bit as much as Morray is? Or the three freebooters who, upon a careful search, will of a certainty seem to have too much money on them?'

'So what do we do?'

'The obvious: we try to keep Baron Morray from falling off his horse and breaking his neck while we're on patrol, or falling down the stairs and breaking his neck when we're at Morray and Mondegreen. We get him back to LaMut intact and breathing, and hope to be relieved of this duty there. If somebody tries to kill him, we stop them; if we can't, we be sure to capture at least one assassin alive, and make sure he is able to tell who paid him, which won't have been us.'

'And if we can't?'

Pirojil just frowned at him. That was obvious. 'We kill everybody within reach, grab their horses and anything of value they have on them, and then we see if we can outrace the price on our heads.'

'And what do you think are our chances of that?'

'Sixty-sixty –'

'Optimist.'

'– on a good day.' Pirojil arched an eyebrow. 'If you have a better alternative, don't sit on it – trot it out and let's talk about it.'

Durine shook his head. 'No. I've no better idea, and that's a fact.'

'Then we go with –'

'*Mount up,*' sounded from below. Tom Garnett's voice carried well. '*We're wasting daylight.*'

'We'd better get down before they leave without us,' Pirojil said.

'Yes, I suppose so.' Durine nodded, and his massive brow wrinkled. 'But I see what you mean. Very clever of the Swordmaster, eh?'

'Eh?'

'I mean, if somebody does manage to kill Baron Morray out here, or if he does have a fatal accident, wouldn't the Swordmaster know that we'd be blamed and would have to run for it?'

'Well, yes.'

'So he wins either way.'

Pirojil had to nod. The Swordmaster would win, either way, at that. A dead baron wasn't an insuperable problem – the war had been almost as lethal for the nobility as it had been for the common soldier – but feuding barons getting the idea that assassination was acceptable was another thing altogether. Much better to blame the three freebooters, who had had no connection with any nobility faction. Someone would make it obvious they had just decided to kill and rob the Baron themselves – and whether Pirojil, Kethol and Durine were killed, captured, or escaped was immaterial; that's what the official story would be.

Maybe Durine wasn't really so stupid after all.

The Swordmaster surely wasn't.

Shit.

They were only an hour south of Mondegreen when the Tsurani attacked.

There was no warning, at least none that Durine noticed, not even in retrospect. Neither Kethol nor Pirojil had any, or they would have given a signal.

One moment the company was riding, in two ragged columns, down a farming road, a frozen, fallow field of hay on each side, and the next moment, dozens of black-and-orange-armoured soldiers were swarming out of the ditch where they had lain, hidden beneath a layer of hay.

Durine spurred his horse into the soldier who, broadsword in his hands, was making for Morray. The horse ploughed into the Tsurani, knocking him down, while Durine leapt to the ground on the far side.

That was the trouble with being mounted. You were too dependent on the movements of the horse, and with anything but a superbly trained warhorse under you that was hopeless. Durine needed solid ground beneath his boots if he was going to stay and fight, and he *was* going to stay and fight.

He leapt back to avoid a wild swing from another Tsurani swordsman, then lunged forwards, kicking at his deceptively fragile-looking breastplate while hacking down at another opponent.

There were shouts and screams of pain all around him, but Baron Morray was still on his horse, and Durine slapped the flank of the mare with the flat of his blade, sending the animal galloping down the road with the Baron clinging desperately, towards where Kethol and Pirojil were still mounted.

It was always tempting to underrate the locals – a professional mercenary, if he lived, survived far more fighting than all but the most seasoned Eastern soldiers, and far more than Westerners – but Tom Garnett was no green captain, eager to fall into a Tsurani trap: he was already leading the front of the column out onto the field, attempting to outflank the attackers quickly, and not simply galloping into the secondary ambush that almost certainly waited for the company down the road.

Durine found himself awash in a sea of orange-trimmed black armour. He lashed out with feet, sword, and his free fist, hoping to clear enough space to make his own escape before he was drowned in Tsurani.

He more felt than saw or heard Pirojil at his back, and moments later, Pirojil was joined by half a dozen lancers, who had apparently circled around to strike at the Tsurani from the rear.

One horseman impaled a screaming Tsurani on his lance, lifting him up and off the ground for a moment, until his lance snapped with a loud crack. Flailing wildly with the broken haft of his lance, the Mut managed to club several of them away before one leapt upon him from behind and bore him down to the ground.

Durine would have tried to go to his aid, but he was busy with two of the Tsurani himself. He kicked one towards where Pirojil had dismounted – Pirojil had just dispatched his latest opponent, and could handle an off-balance soldier easily – then he ducked under the wild swing of another Tsurani's two-handed black sword, and slashed in and up, into and through the smaller man's throat.

Blood fountained, as though he had pulled the bung out of a hogshead of crimson wine.

The look in the eyes of a man you were killing was always the same. *This can't be happening to me*, it said, in any language. *Not me.* Durine had often seen that expression on the face of a man who was facing the imminence of becoming a thing, and he didn't need to see it again; he kicked the dying man away.

Three Tsurani hacked at the legs of a big grey horse, sending horse and rider tumbling to the ground as the animal screamed in that strange, high-pitched horsy shriek that you never could get used to. But one of them miscalculated: as the horse fell, it fell on the Tsurani, crushing him in his black armour with a sodden series of snapping sounds.

It was all Durine could do not to laugh.

The Tsurani were, as always, determined and capable warriors, but they were outnumbered, and lying for hours in ambush in the bitter cold had slowed them down: it was only a matter of a few minutes until most of them lay on the ground, dead and dying.

The screams were horrible to hear.

Durine half-squatted, panting for breath. No matter how long you had been doing this, it still always took something out of you.

One of the Tsurani on the ground near Durine was still shrieking loudly. A wound to his groin that still oozed fresh, steaming blood onto the frozen ground. Durine straightened himself and walked over, then hacked down, once, at the back of the Tsurani's neck. The man twitched once, and was still, save for the flatulent sound as he fouled himself in his death.

Sudden death was rarely dignified.

'Wait.' Tom Garnett dismounted from his horse and braced Durine. 'We take prisoners when we can. That man could have been one of the slaves that the Tsurani keep, and be of no danger to us at all.'

Durine didn't answer.

'Well, man, did you hear me?'

'Excuse me.' Pirojil stepped between them. 'I think you might want to see something, Captain,' he said, kneeling over the dead man and turning him on his back. The Tsurani's head flopped loosely where it was still attached to the body.

Pirojil stood, toeing away a dagger from the Tsurani's hand. He waved at the dead Tsurani and said, 'Perhaps, Captain, you would not have wanted to have your last thought to be that your mercy had been misplaced.'

Durine hadn't seen any dagger, and it wouldn't have mattered. The Tsurani was dying, anyway, and it hardly made any difference whether he went on his way now, or in a few minutes. At least this way his screams wouldn't aggravate Durine's headache.

They would be bad enough to face in his dreams.

The regulars had two sullen Tsurani prisoners, their hands tightly bound and then leashed by the neck, under the care of a pair of lancers, although that was hardly necessary, as they weren't struggling. Captured Tsurani were either utterly intractable, and you eventually had to kill them, no matter how many times you beat them bloody, or how well you treated them while they were chained heavily enough to control them – or utterly tame. One of the locals had tried to explain to Durine that this was something to do with Tsurani honour: if captured, they assumed the gods cursed them or some nonsense like that; but Durine knew that once they gave up, they seemed resigned to spend the rest of their lives as slaves. Durine didn't understand, and he didn't particularly want to; where to put a sword in one was about all he needed to know. Though he did recall one of the Muts telling him the black-and-orange ones were called Minwanabi, and they were a particularly tough and evil bunch of bastards. Durine shrugged and walked away. He didn't plan on staying in the north long enough to discover what the other tribes were named or how evil they were. All Tsurani seemed tough enough.

The two tame ones were the only survivors among the Tsurani, though. Easily two dozen of the enemy lay dead on the ground, accompanied in death by four Muts and two horses. One soldier wept as he knelt over his horse, feeling at its neck to be sure that its heart had stopped beating.

Silly man. Getting so attached to something made of meat. Meat died and spoiled.

Lady Mondegreen and Baron Morray sat on their horses, overlooking the scene. Baron Morray's handsome face was impassive, if a little pale, but the lady's complexion was almost green, and she was distracted enough to wipe a trickle of vomit from the corner of her mouth with her sleeve instead of her handkerchief.

'I've . . . I've never seen a battle before,' she said, quietly.

'Battle?' Baron Morray shook his head. 'This was barely a skirmish.'

'What are they going to do with them?' she asked.

'Leave it to the landholder,' he said. 'It will be his responsibility.'

Durine nodded. Just as well it wasn't Durine's job to break the frozen soil and bury the bodies; that would be long and hard work, but it was somebody else's problem – disposing of the corpses would be for the local landholder or franklins to do, depending on whose field this was. The Mut soldiers would be wrapped in blankets and carried along to be given a proper cremation at Mondegreen. The Tsurani would probably end up fertilizing the fields.

It was all dirty work, certainly, but if the locals got to the scene quickly enough – and they would – there would be a couple of hundredweight of fresh horsemeat as payment for their work. An ignominious thing, perhaps, for a trusty mount to end up in a peasant stew, but that was the way of it.

Tom Garnett remounted his horse. 'I've got half the company chasing after the archers who lay in ambush, and I'm going to have to take the rest out after those who ran away here. We've got to run these dastards to ground before dark, or they'll be breaking into cottages and killing bondsmen. They're no military threat, not now, but . . .'

Durine nodded. 'But you still don't want them killing your people.'

That was the problem when dealing with an enemy so far behind his own lines. Retreat wasn't a practical option.

Durine didn't know much about what was and wasn't a military threat, but a scared man with a black blade almost as long as he was tall was the sort of thing he wouldn't have wanted to encounter unawares.

It apparently took Kethol a moment before he realized that the Captain had been talking to him.

'Yes, sir,' he said at last.

Tom Garnett indicated the two nobles and their coteries, huddling together further down the road. 'You three and a squad under Sergeant Henders will bring the civilians on to Mondegreen, and the rest of us shall meet you there.'

Kethol made a sketchy salute with his blade.

THREE

Mondegreen

Pirojil halted his horse. He paused to let the column catch up to him before kicking it into a walk next to the grizzled lancer sergeant.

'There's no need for outriders, Sergeant,' Pirojil said. 'I'd just as soon we keep everybody together.'

'That's very interesting, freebooter,' Sergeant Henders replied, his frown and tone in sarcastic counterpoint to his even words. 'I'll tell you again, I am always so very glad to have another opinion as to how I should run my squad.' He raised himself in the saddle. 'Hey, *you!*' he shouted. 'Yes, Sanderson, I mean you, you poxy son of a misbegotten cur. You and Scrupple take the point!' Then he turned to shout at another pair of riders. 'Williams! Bellows! You two are up as flankers – smartly now, or we'll see if you can run ahead faster without your horses. I said *move it!*' He turned back to Pirojil. 'Always happy to have advice, Pirojil, and particularly from a man as well-favoured as your good self,' he said, the sneer only at the edges of his mouth and voice. 'But I'd just as soon know if we're facing another ambush.'

'We're not going to see another ambush between here and

Mondegreen,' Pirojil said. 'Maybe a straggler or two, but more likely they'll be too busy running away.'

'If you say so,' the sergeant said, making no motion to recall the outriders.

Pirojil bit his lip, then decided to try again. 'Look, Sergeant, if there were more Tsurani within tens of miles of here, their commander would surely have used all of them for the ambush. The Tsurani commanders aren't stupid; they're just greedy. As it was, he split his forces too small, hoping the attack would drive the column into a killing zone for his archers.'

'I thank you much for that opinion, Pirojil,' the sergeant said. 'Now, if you'll excuse me, I've got a squad to run. Shouldn't you be off counting your high pay or wiping Baron Morray's backside or something useful?'

Pirojil shook his head. There was no point in trying. It was impossible to convince somebody who wouldn't be convinced, and while the three of them were in charge of the nobles, they hadn't been explicitly left in charge of the party, or even of the sergeant's squad. Now instead of having one rider away from the column, they had four, just because a sergeant got irritated at getting some good advice.

Tom Garnett should have been more direct and simply put the party under Kethol's command. The three mercenaries had understood that he had *meant* for them to be in charge, but the sergeant didn't, or affected not to. Pirojil could either live with that, or fight it out, with him, Kethol and Durine against the entire squad; and then they would have to make their escape rather than explain to Tom Garnett why they had killed all of his men – assuming that they could, of course.

Pirojil relaxed. So be it. For now.

It would probably be necessary to have Durine take the sergeant aside at some point and work this out, privately. He didn't particularly like asking Durine to do that, but he was used to doing things he didn't like. He'd had to do it a time or two before. That was the nice thing about having Durine beat somebody up: they didn't lose their comrades' respect by having Durine mess up their face just a little. Few men could stand up to Durine and no one – so far – could emerge unscathed from a fight with the big man.

He tried to be philosophical about it.

Relationships between regulars and mercenaries were always uncomfortable. Forget, for just a moment, that regular soldiers thought of freebooters as little more than land pirates, mostly because during peacetime, and around the fringes of war, they spent more time hunting them down than working with them.

Even when mercenaries were employed by the Crown, there were conflicts built into the relationship. The freebooters tended to report directly to an officer, who was expected to take a long view of things and understand that too many unnecessary fatalities among the mercenaries inevitably meant widespread mercenary desertion or revolt. It usually didn't work out when mercenaries had to answer to a sergeant, who would be much quicker to expend a mercenary than one of his own men, and while few mercenaries died in bed, even fewer wanted to spend their whole, short lives on point, or worse. The second or third time a mercenary company was ordered to be first over the wall, they started considering the wisdom of their employment choice.

Relations between the mercenaries and the regulars were unlikely to get any better in Mondegreen. The regular soldiers would be housed in the barracks at Mondegreen Castle. But Baron Morray would be housed in the Residence, and therefore Kethol, Durine and Pirojil would be as well, with the three of them sleeping in soft featherbeds, their every need being tended to by beautiful maidservants. At least that's what the regulars would think.

It wouldn't actually be that way, of course, but that was the way the story would be told around the barracks. Never mind that they would probably be bedded down on damp reeds in the kitchen, except for whichever of them drew the short straw and spent the night sleeping on the stone floor across the threshold of the Baron's bedchamber. And the maids were almost certain to be old, fat, ugly, or all three. But, the regulars would complain that the mercenaries were getting a soft assignment.

Pirojil slowed his horse to allow Baron Morray and Kethol to catch up with him, while behind, Durine trailed Lady Mondegreen and her maids.

Kethol arched an eyebrow; Pirojil shook his head. Kethol shrugged.

The Baron eyed them curiously. After a few moments, when neither of them answered the unvoiced question, he cleared his throat for attention. 'What was that all about?' he asked imperiously.

'Nothing for you to bother yourself with, my lord,' Kethol said, when Pirojil didn't immediately answer. 'Just a minor disagreement between Pirojil and the sergeant.'

'All that from a shake of the head?' Morray was visibly sceptical.

'Yes,' Pirojil said. But that wouldn't be enough to satisfy the Baron. 'Kethol and I've been working together for years; Durine's been with us only a little less. After so much time together, my lord, each of us knows how the others think.'

The Baron raised an eyebrow as if questioning the remark.

'You don't mask your thoughts to the man at your back, my lord. If a man insists on keeping his thoughts to himself all the time, well, you find somebody else to watch your back.'

The Baron scowled. 'I'm not overly impressed with the three of you,' he said. 'You distinguished yourself with bravery during the ambush, certainly more than one would expect from a bunch of freebooters, but your swordwork was clumsy – at least what I saw of it – and if Lady Mondegreen hadn't spurred her horse so quickly, she would have been brought down by the Tsurani without much trouble at all.'

Kethol started to open his mouth, but desisted at Pirojil's head-shake.

'We'll try to do better, next time, my lord,' Pirojil said. He had already had enough of arguing with somebody who would not be persuaded for one afternoon.

But you couldn't trust Kethol to keep his mouth shut about such a thing. Kethol would have to explain himself – it was one of his few weaknesses – and that would do nobody any good at all.

Pirojil pointed a finger toward the front of the column, tapped the finger against his own chest, jerked his thumb toward the rear of the column, and spurred his horse.

Lady Mondegreen's eyes held steady on Kethol as he dropped back beside her, replacing Durine. 'How soon do we arrive, Kethol?' she asked.

If he remembered right, and he did, the outer wall of Mondegreen Town was just beyond the next bend, across a stream, and then over a ridge. 'I believe we should be there within the hour, Lady.' Why the Lady of Castle Mondegreen wouldn't know the area around the keep better than a soldier who had only been through here once, during the war, he didn't know. 'We'll have you safe in your own bed this night, and may it be a comfort to you.'

'I've some comfort in my own bed, that's true,' she said. 'Though my husband is a good man, a gentle man, but a very sick man, and has been, for the past few years.'

Oh, he didn't say. *And is that why you spend your time warming other men's beds?* 'I'm sorry to hear that,' he did say. It seemed like the appropriate response.

She pursed her lips momentarily. 'Others suffer far worse than do I.'

'Is the Baron much older than you?'

She frowned. 'Yes, he is. And is there something wrong with that?'

'Not at all.' Kethol shook his head. 'But it must be difficult –'

'Yes, it's difficult.' She patted at her belly. 'It's difficult when you marry an older man, and are expected to produce an heir, and don't.' She started to say something more, then stopped herself.

'There's no need to watch your words around me, Lady,' Kethol said. 'I'm not loose of tongue, and I've got no stake in local matters.'

She didn't look at him. 'How fortunate for you,' she said, through tight lips.

They rode in silence for a few minutes.

'I seem to have something of a widespread reputation,' she said at last.

'Perhaps.' Kethol shrugged. 'I wouldn't know. The only gossip I get to hear is usually about how one sergeant is a glory-hound, or another officer will never send his men out in front of him if he doesn't have to – the private lives of our betters isn't a topic for barracks conversation.'

Which wasn't entirely true. It might not have been a topic for *Kethol's* barracks conversation, but some of the Mut soldiers gossiped like fishwives, and Lady Mondegreen was often a subject of their chatter. If you believed the gossip – and Kethol never either believed all or none of it – she flitted from bed to bed with wild abandon, looking for the satisfaction that her ancient husband couldn't have given her.

She looked at him, long and hard, as though trying to decide something.

A crow fluttered down and took a perch on an overhanging tree limb, and cawed down at them.

Well, as long as it didn't shit on him, he didn't mind.

Pirojil shook his head. Unless you knew how and where to look, the castle didn't look like the weapon that it actually was.

Castle Mondegreen rose, huge and solid and dark on its hill, looming above the town below. On top of its six towers watchmen stood, probably bored out of their minds, but even more probably happy to be bored. It didn't take much experience with battle to teach you that combat was far less romantic in real life than in all the tales, ballads and legends.

Of course, it wouldn't take long before the sights and sounds and particularly the smells of war would fade in the memory, and it wouldn't be long before young soldiers would be puffing their chests and strutting about, bragging of the great deeds they would do the next time the alarm horns sounded. Some of them would do very well. Some of them would die, and all of them would be changed, in ways many of them would not recognize until years later, if ever. A soldier's life gave you plenty of time for introspection, but many just pissed that time away.

Pirojil himself had pissed away many an hour that could have been spent just thinking about things. On the other hand, he had not wasted all his hours, and he had long ago worked out that it was dangerous to keep weapons too near you. Necessary, yes, but dangerous – weapons changed people, and not just enchanted weapons.

Like the castle itself.

Originally, Castle Mondegreen had been built by some cousin of the conDoin family, as a way to establish a permanent foothold in Yabon. While invited in to help drive out the Brotherhood of the Dark Path and their allies, many of the Yabonese had not expected the Kingdom to stay in Yabon once the enemy had been dislodged. Like neighbouring Bosonia, Yabon had been a far-flung colony of the Empire of Great Kesh.

Unlike Bosonia, which had many Keshian colonists living there, Yabon had been an administrated district with a few Keshian nobles and many Yabonese tribal chieftains and lords. The Kingdom's position was that once the Dark Brothers and their ilk were driven away, the natives were unable to protect themselves and therefore Yabon required a permanent Kingdom garrison. A rescue had turned into a conquest.

Some lords and chieftains had welcomed the Kingdom, and were rewarded with titles and lands. Other locals had, as locals did, resented their conquerors, and were primed for revolt in the early years. During that time, the remnants of the old regime would eye the new rulers, usually waiting and sometimes probing for weaknesses, ready to throw off the yoke of the newly-appointed Kingdom earl and his lickspittle barons.

And that was what the castle was for. Let the old regime raise an army in the countryside, let them gather together horses and men, bows and breastplates and swords, and let them rant and rave and fume as they would – so long as the new rulers controlled the castle.

Sometimes, the revolt could be put down by the Baron's troops riding out and dispersing the rebels. More often, the trouble could be stopped at the much smaller wall around the town, protecting not just the nobility in the castle, but those loyal to the new regime who were, during the early years, the only ones permitted to live in the town, directly under the protection of the Baron.

But sometimes, the occupying troops would have to retreat into the castle, and wait to be relieved by the Earl's troops. Stockpiled food and water were as much a part of the castle's armoury as stockpiled arrows and bolts. As conquests go, Yabon's was a relatively mild one, and by the third generation after the Kingdom annexed the former Keshian colony – which just happened to be Pirojil's generation – Yabonese and Kingdom were interchangeable, except maybe for a bit of a funny accent in Yabon.

And so, the castle stood: a monument to persistence, just as the tumble down wall of the town was a monument to mutability, to how things never lasted.

Pirojil couldn't tell how much of the town's wall had been destroyed in the war – the Tsurani had broken through into Mondegreen Town on their way to the castle – and how much had been cannibalized before the Tsurani invasion by locals seeking building materials. After a generation or so of peace, the wall around the town was more of an inconvenience than a benefit, and it took a wise ruler to remember that walls were important.

The wall around the keep itself, though, was intact, although as battle-scarred as the rest of the landscape. Ashes were all that remained of the siege towers the Tsurani had built against the western wall, and while the southern wall still stood firm, it was scarred by a patched breach in the stonework, above where Tsurani sappers had failed in their attempt to undermine its integrity. The slump in the ground at the foundation told Pirojil all he needed to know about the failed attempt. Nasty way to die, he thought, with tons of rock and earth suddenly falling upon you, crushing you in the darkness like a bug. The trick was to make the tunnel as large as you safely could, with just enough timber to hold everything above you in place until you were ready to fire the supports, collapse the tunnel – hopefully while you were a respectable distance away – and thereby collapse the wall above, forming a lovely breach through which your comrades could attack.

Pirojil had been in a mining party, down in the Vale, and the whole damn thing had failed to hold. He remembered the earthy smell as dust had been forced up his nose when the ceiling of the tunnel had come crashing down – on the heads of a few of his companions – leaving him and the rest of the sappers trapped with no way out but up out of the ground, emerging through the fire and rubble of a collapsed wall. They were half-blind, sneezing and coughing from dust and smoke, knowing full well that they had to kill all the defenders, who would fight – and die – like cornered rats.

As they had.

Once in a while, some captain or duke or prince got the wonderful notion that you should tunnel further so that you emerged inside the walls. Nice theory, if you weren't the idiots picked to be the first ones popping up out of the ground . . .

'I said,' Baron Morray reiterated, 'that you may take my horse to the stables, when I alight.'

Pirojil nodded, coming out of his momentary reverie. 'Of course, Baron.'

'I'll speak to the housecarl about your billets. Perhaps they can find room for you three in the barracks, rather than the stables.'

Well, they might as well have that out now as later.

'No, my lord,' Pirojil said, 'we're not staying in the stables. We'll all be staying in the Residence while one of us stands watch before your door.'

Baron Morray wasn't used to being contradicted. The reins twitched in his fingers. 'I hardly see the need. The barracks or perhaps the stables will be perfectly adequate for the likes of – for the three of you. If I find I need you in the middle of the night, I'll send a servant.'

Pirojil shrugged. 'Very well, my lord. If you'd be kind enough to put that in writing, I'll have a messenger send it to the Earl. If there's a fast enough horse available, it might reach Yabon before –'

'What?'

Well, at least the Baron was smart enough not to raise his voice.

'We've been assigned to protect you, night and day, by the Earl, my lord. If some accident or misdeed were to happen to you while we were neglecting our duty, it would be our heads into the noose. If I'm not to follow Earl Vandros's orders, I think he'll want to know why.'

The Baron started to say something, but Pirojil took the chance of speaking first. 'Please. We're assigned to protect you, my lord,' he said, quietly. 'Not just your body. We have been known to tell stories around the fire late at night, just like everybody else, but we don't gossip about what our betters are doing.'

If you're fool enough to have your dalliances with Lady Mondegreen under the very nose of her husband, then so be it, he didn't quite say.

The Baron was silent for a moment. 'I'm not quite the fool you take me for, freebooter,' he said. 'I take your full meaning, but I'd not dishonour even a churl under his own roof, much less a good man like Baron Mondegreen, no matter what you seem to think.'

'It isn't my job to think,' Pirojil said. 'Except about protecting you.'

'Then so be it. Protect me if you must, but don't bother me about it.' The Baron clucked at his horse, which responded by picking up a posting trot.

Pirojil sighed. It was going to be a long tour. He urged his own horse forward and followed the Baron.

A tall, slender and almost preposterously buxom serving maid brought a tray holding an enormous joint of mutton and an only slightly smaller pile of flatbread, still steaming from the oven. She was prettier than most, with nice, even features, her impressive breasts straining the ties of her blouse, her brown hair up in a simple knot that left her long, elegant neck bare. Tendrils of hair teased at the back of her neck as she walked, and Kethol envied them.

She didn't say anything, but looked from one to the next, barely avoiding sniffing in distaste, then set the tray down on the table without comment, leaving the three of them alone in the hall as she headed down the winding staircase, walking unselfconsciously, indifferent to the three pairs of eyes on her.

Kethol watched her go. You got used to being treated like garbage after a while, or so you told yourself. A soldier's life was full of lies.

'Hmm. I think I need a bath,' Pirojil said. 'Or maybe, better, a new face.'

'Bath sounds good.' Durine nodded.

'You take the first one, then me?'

'I can wait,' Durine said. 'Rather take my time. Looks like a good bathhouse outside the barracks. You can sluice off some of the road dust before you turn in, but as for me, soaking in some hot water sounds good about now. Just be careful to wipe your boots coming back in, eh?'

Pirojil looked at his boots, which were mud-free; the three of them had already received a thorough talking-to from the housecarl.

The west wing of the keep's second floor was dedicated to the use of guests. Of the dozen doors up and down the hall, all but two stood open, presumably waiting for their next occupants. The family residence was in the east wing, and on the floor below. Judging from the grumbling and dirty looks that the three of them had received from the soldiers on watch downstairs, the Baron's captain of the guard was less than pleased to have his master's care put in the hands of outsiders, and had placed soldiers on station on the floor below to drive home the point.

Pirojil's gaze followed where the serving maid had disappeared down the staircase, as though looking beyond to where Mondegreen troops were posted at the entrance to the family quarters. 'It's a sad day when people don't trust a trio of cutthroats like us.'

Durine laughed. Kethol shrugged.

While Kethol stayed outside, watching the entrance to the

Baron's rooms, Durine and Pirojil had gone through the chambers, emerging to report nothing out of the ordinary: no Tsurani assassin waiting in the bureaus; no covey of Dark Brotherhood killers hiding in an armoire, which wasn't particularly surprising.

You spent most of your time on this sort of job taking precautions that would turn out to have been unnecessary, but as certain as flies in summer, the one time you didn't check under a bed, that would be where the killers would be waiting.

Looking silly was the least of a soldier's worries, after all.

Behind the heavy oaken door, Baron Morray was probably already sleeping in the big bed, warmed by the fire in the small hearth and the metal trays placed under the mattress. If the bed was warmed by anything else – if, say, Lady Mondegreen had sneaked in through one of the secret passages with which all castles were rife – there was nothing that Kethol could do about it, and probably nothing he *should* do about it, so he decided not to worry about it.

Kethol hacked off a piece of mutton with his belt knife and chewed it. Old, tough and overcooked, but it was hot food, and probably better than whatever they were having in the barracks. On the other hand, there would probably be a dice game going on in the barracks, and it would be a shame to miss that, after such a hard day of travel. Bouncing on the back of a horse could tire the mind almost as well as strong drink.

'Hmm . . . you two mind if I take the first watch tonight?' he asked.

Both of the others shrugged.

'Sure,' Durine said. He rubbed at his lower back with one massive hand as he rose.

'Fine with me,' Pirojil said, rising.

For a moment, Pirojil looked as if he was going to say something more, but they each hacked off a huge chunk of mutton and carried it away on a bed of flatbread. Pirojil and Durine walked down the hall to the room where the three of them were billeted, Pirojil reappearing momentarily with his rucksack before disappearing down the winding stairs, presumably heading for the bathhouse as he popped the last bit of mutton and bread into his mouth.

Kethol was by himself, which was fine with him, although it felt a bit funny to have the first watch. You got into a pattern if you worked together long enough. The usual thing would be for Pirojil to take the first watch, then Durine and Kethol. Stolid Durine could will himself to sleep almost instantly, no matter what had been going on, and once Pirojil was down for the night, nothing short of an attack could easily get him out of bed.

Besides, Kethol liked watching the dawn, and the eastern window at the end of the corridor would have given him a nice view of the sun rising beyond the far wall.

But he just didn't feel like it, not tonight. Too busy wool-gathering, he supposed.

He walked over to the heavy oak door and carefully, gently, slowly, tried the knob, pushing the door open a scant inch, just enough to assure himself that it wasn't locked from the inside.

Any attack was unlikely, and one that could reach the Residence itself quickly even more so, but you had to take every precaution you could think of, and pray to a soldier's god that it would be unnecessary this time.

He sat down in the big leather chair next to the end table and nibbled at the mutton. Not enough garlic, and too much salt, but that was to be expected. Probably a little off, too, but the rabble could hardly expect to get the best cuts.

He was still nibbling away at what remained of the joint when Durine finally reappeared up the stairs, his hair damp and slicked back from the bath. After a quick nod, the big man disappeared into their room.

Kethol would have preferred that Durine stay up for a while to chat, but he wouldn't ask that of the big man. Sleeping time when you were taking a one-in-three was scant enough.

The trick when standing watch by yourself was always to stay awake and alert. Too much food would be a bad idea, and only an idiot would drink wine on watch. Kethol had known an old, moustachioed sergeant from Rodez who claimed that he was a bit sharper, a bit brighter on watch with a couple of skinfuls of wine in him, and if there was any justice in the world – always a bad bet – somebody had run a spear through his guts soon after Kethol, Pirojil and Durine had lit out, as they had not at that time been desperate enough to be serving under an idiot.

That was the good thing about being an independent: you could be a bit choosy, if you weren't *too* choosy. Kethol wouldn't much care what a sergeant's personal habits were – he could prefer that his bedmates be large-breasted blonde women, or slender brown-haired boys, or flaming goats, for all Kethol cared – but you stood enough chance of getting killed as it was without having to rely on somebody who made it easy for the enemy.

The distant sound of Durine's snoring came to his ears, a regular snorp-bleep, snorp-bleep that announced that the big man was resting for the night. Good. Kethol didn't know why Durine didn't do that when they were out in the open, when something as innocent as snoring could tell somebody where you were, but he didn't much care.

The trick was to not close your eyes on watch. Not ever; not for a moment.

Once, as a young man, he had decided to rest his eyes for just a moment on watch, and the next thing he knew, the sun was shining in his eyes in bright reproval. That he had got away with it, that nobody had known of his shame, then or ever, made it worse than if the sergeant had found him asleep and kicked him bloody.

The problem was –

He jerked upright in the chair. He'd heard something.

Damn! There were groans coming from Baron Morray's room.

'Pirojil! Durine!' he shouted, but Kethol didn't wait for them; he kicked through the door, careless of any damage to the jamb, and rushed in, sword in hand.

The room was dark, lit only by a flickering fire in the hearth up against the wall.

Two bodies were struggling on the massive bed up against the far wall. The simple thing to do would have been to stick a sword-point into the writhing mass, but –

'Stop.' Baron Morray, his torso bathed in sweat, was sitting up in his bed. His fingers clawed for the knife on the bedstand, but he had Kethol transfixed with a glare.

Durine and Pirojil were close behind Kethol; he more than saw them, knowing that Durine would move to his right, while Pirojil would guard him on his left.

But not from this.

A pair of eyes peeked out from under the blankets, accompanied by giggling.

'I'd ask what the meaning of this is,' the Baron said, 'but it's all far too clear, I'm afraid.' He ignored the giggling, and the way that his bed companion's struggles to hide herself under the blanket momentarily revealed a flash of a particularly shapely rump.

The Baron patted her on it and snorted. 'I don't see much point in hiding, young Kate,' he said.

She shrugged, and let the blankets drop below her shoulders, brazenly revealing the high young breasts that were every bit as firm as Kethol had imagined they would be.

Just as Kethol had suspected – too late it seemed – it was the serving maid who had delivered the food to the three of them. Easy for a young wench to turn up her nose at a trio of soldiers when she had what no doubt were more rewarding arrangements already made.

Beyond and to the right of the bed, a wooden panel in the inlaid wall had been swung wide open, revealing a dark passage behind it, through which the Baron's bedmate had apparently arrived.

'I apologize,' Kethol said, 'but –'

'Get out,' the Baron said. 'Just get out of this room. Now.'

It was a bad time to argue with him, but since the Baron wasn't raising his voice, and probably didn't want to raise a ruction now, maybe it wasn't the worst time.

'No.' Pirojil's voice was quiet, but insistent. 'No, my lord. Not until the door to the hidden passageway is secured.' He shook his head. 'It's no concern of ours who comes and goes into your rooms with your permission, but it's every concern of ours that nobody can gain access to your rooms without getting by us.'

Durine had taken a lantern down from the wall and was examining a piece of wainscoting on the far wall. 'There's another one here,' he said, grumbling.

And you didn't see it before? Kethol didn't ask. It was the sort of thing that they should have thought through, but this sort of bodyguarding was a new thing to the three of them, and they were bound to make mistakes, and Kethol didn't much like it. He knew enough to act as though the walls had ears, but the walls having doors that could swing open and shut more often than a whore's crib?

Bloody hell!

'Well, what do you propose to do?'

There was nothing vaguely unusual or remotely dangerous about a baron inviting a serving girl into his bed, but it was clearly not the sort of thing that Morray would want bruited about, particularly not around Lady Mondegreen.

Kethol walked to the open panel to the hidden passageway and closed it. There was some trick bit of lockwork hidden in the bric-a-brac, but he didn't trust it, so he slid a dressing chair in front of it, and balanced a clean chamberpot on top of the chair, leaning it against the panelling.

Somebody might still be able to get into the room, but not without making a lot of noise.

Durine had rigged a similar improvised alarm on the other hidden panel, while Pirojil leaned back against the door, his arms crossed in front of him.

'You've done what's needed. Now get out,' the Baron said. 'I can assure you that there will be some discussion of this in the morning.'

Kethol wasn't at all sure about that. He hoped the Baron would just let the matter drop, but he followed Pirojil's lead, and bowed his way out of the room.

Durine just shook his head.

Morning broke with Baron Morray off to the east wing of the keep to visit with the ailing Baron Mondegreen and Pirojil, along with Durine and Kethol, barred from the Mondegreen Keep's private quarters.

Which was about to be expected. Tom Garnett might have made it clear that Morray wasn't to take a dump without one of the three of them watching to see if some assassin would leap up out of the garderobe and spear his noble arse, but the Captain wasn't in charge in Mondegreen, and their warrant signed by the Earl of LaMut wasn't quite that specific; waving it in front of the face of Mondegreen's guard captain would do nothing more than cause a breeze.

Besides, most of the time, the law is what the most senior noble present says it is, and commoners were used to that.

So the three of them grabbed a skimpy breakfast of bread, onion and sausage in the barracks, and huddled in their cloaks against the cold as they headed across the outer courtyard to where the lackeys and stablemen were trying to prepare the Baron's carriage, despite the constant interference from the ragged bunch of castle boys in their endless games of tag and kick-the-ball.

It was far too cold for anybody sensible to be running around outdoors if they didn't have to. As they ran about, the young boys' breath puffed visibly in the cold air, and one or another would occasionally slip on an icy spot on the courtyard that hadn't been properly sanded over.

But perhaps the exercise kept them warm, and besides, it was at least something different from their daily chores.

'Sixthday,' one of the stablemen explained, as he beckoned at Pirojil to hold onto the reins while he fastened one of the big white geldings into its place in front of the carriage, then beckoned to his assistant to bring out another.

Pirojil didn't mind helping, although he couldn't help the way his eyes wandered to the large window in the east wing, across the courtyard, where he assumed that Baron Morray was explaining to Baron Mondegreen, over their own late breakfast, about how three ill-mannered freebooters had interfered with his sleep.

'Sixthday?'

'In the old days, they'd have only Sixthday afternoon to waste their time frolicking about like a bunch of ninnies, but things have got sloppy during the war, and the good Baron's been . . . occupied with other matters,' he said. 'What was the Sixthday afternoon seems to begin earlier every Sixthday morning.'

Other matters. Like dying of some wasting disease that neither clerics nor wizards could touch, apparently – although that was none of Pirojil's concern.

The lackey fastened a loop to a fitting, and pulled it into place with a loud grunt. 'A few more blows with a cudgel,' he said, 'would do the stableboys a lot more good than additional time to run about like a bunch of squirrels, if you ask me, but the Horsemaster seems to be far more interested in old Cedric's opinion of which animals are ready for the knacker than he is in my thoughts about which of the boys would learn better with more than a few clouts and a little less time to do whatever they take it in their heads to do.'

Pirojil wasn't terribly interested in the problems of the stableman, or in the beating up of young boys, but it didn't hurt to listen politely, at least for a while.

It wasn't as if he had anything better to do at the moment, unfortunately.

They should already have left. If Pirojil had been running things, the return trip to LaMut would have left the castle during what they called the 'wolf's tail' down in the Vale – the grey light well before dawn, which hid all colours if not shapes.

On the other hand, the delay had given their betters a good enough opportunity to get their poles greased, apparently, and got Kethol and the other two a good two-thirds of a night's sleep. *Not bad, all things considered*, he thought, yawning against the back of his hand. He wondered if there might be a mug full of hot tea in the battered iron pot simmering on the stove in the barracks, and whether it would be tannic enough actually to fry his tongue; of a certainty, it would be hot enough to warm his belly.

Kethol and Durine had set their weapons down under the care of a claque of the castle girls who were busy chatting among themselves while pretending to ignore their young male counterparts.

The two mercenaries had actually joined in the boys' game.

There were times when Pirojil was more than vaguely suspicious that the two of them had been dropped on their heads as children.

A pair of young ruffians, no more than half Durine's size, actually tried to tackle the big man, and he fell to the ground, releasing the leather ragbag with what probably looked to the others like an honestly-come-by slip.

Pirojil took a quick glance beyond the carriage into the stables. He reckoned it would be at least another hour before the Mondegreen detachment was ready to ride, and who knew how long they would be waiting for the nobility to –

'You are Kethol?' A soldier in Mondegreen livery had come up behind him without his noticing. Pirojil stopped himself from reaching for his sword. That was Pirojil's fault, and he tried not to let his irritation at himself show on his face. He was getting old.

'No. I'm Pirojil. Kethol's the one under that wriggling pile of boys over there.'

'The Baron will see him now. Will you pull him out of the pile, or shall I?'

'Baron Mondegreen?'

'Yes, Baron Mondegreen.' The soldier frowned in disgust. 'And in these walls, who else would *the* Baron be? Now, are you going to get him?'

'I'd better do it.' There were some risks involved in interrupting Kethol when he was distracted. The Mut would probably just grab Kethol by the collar or the foot, and the touch of a hand stronger than a boy's might set Kethol off.

'Then be quick about it.' The soldier spun on the ball of his foot and set off toward the keep.

Pirojil shook his head as he walked toward where Kethol was rolling around on the ground.

Lady Mondegreen was attending her husband as he lay propped up with pillows on the massive, brass-railed bed. She smiled a greeting to Kethol, and beckoned him toward the chair next to the bed.

Kethol stood and waited. He hadn't been told to sit, after all, and you could never tell when some noble would decide that you were being presumptuous.

The room smelled like old death, or maybe it was just the Baron himself. Mondegreen had, so legend had it, been a big and physically powerful man in his youth, but the wasting disease had turned him into a shrivelled relic of what he had been. Before Kethol lay a barely-living object trying not to pant with the exertion of sitting up.

'Please – remove your cloak,' the Baron said, 'or I fear you'll find yourself sweating furiously.' His voice was weak, but he was forcing himself not to pause for breath until he completed each sentence. Death would claim Baron Mondegreen sooner rather than later, and it would come as more of a blessing than a curse, but he would not go down without fighting it.

Kethol removed his cloak, and after looking around, folded it over the back of a chair.

Even without his thick cloak, the room was too hot. Castles were famous for being draughty, but somebody seemed to have taken great care in the mortaring of the cracks in these walls, and the huge, floor-to-ceiling tapestries blocked any flow of air that remained.

The hearth, on the opposite side of the chamber to the bed, held a fire with a nice glow to it, and it warmed the room enough that Kethol couldn't understand how the Baron could stand being under his thick pile of blankets.

'Please sit by me, Sergeant Kethol,' the Baron said, indicating the chair beside the bed. 'I trust that you have breakfasted?'

'Yes, my lord,' Kethol said, seating himself. It happened to be true, but the smell in the room would have taken away his appetite, anyway.

'I understand that I have you and your two companions to thank for my wife's safe arrival here,' the Baron said. 'I thought that it was only right that I thank you in person.'

Kethol didn't quite know what to say. Lady Mondegreen seemed nice, was pretty, and was far more pleasant with the hired warriors than she had any need to be, but if he'd had to watch her spitted on a Tsurani sword while he protected Morray from a scratch, he would have done just that, and would have let it bother him later.

'You're welcome, of course, my lord,' he finally said. 'But I don't think we actually did very much.' That, at least, was true.

The Baron smiled knowingly. Kethol didn't like the way the old eyes watched him. It reminded him too much of the eyes he'd seen in a mottled mirror.

'Yes,' the Baron said, 'and a thousand tons of thanks will buy you a pint of ale, as long as it comes with a bent green copper, eh?'

'Well, yes.' Kethol nodded. 'But the thanks are welcome, none-theless, my lord.'

'Yes. I'm sure that they are, Sergeant Kethol.' Baron Mondegreen broke into a fit of coughing, and stifled it only with an effort, then turned to his wife. 'My dear, would you be so very kind as to get me a half cup of that wonderful tea that Menicia has been brewing? I'd have the servant do it, but you always seem to add just the right amount of sugar.'

'But –'

'Please do it as a favour to a devoted husband,' he said, gently. 'And, if it would not dishonour you to do so, I think that Sergeant Kethol might well like to sample some, so perhaps two mugs?'

He might as easily have just come out and said that he wanted to talk to Kethol alone, but she smiled, nodded, and patted his hand before she left, shutting the door behind her.

'And you may be in need of more than some thanks,' the Baron went on, 'given, as I understand it, the likelihood that Baron Morray will make some complaint – perhaps only to Steven Argent, but perhaps to the Earl himself – about your supposed bad manners last night in interrupting his . . . rest?'

Kethol wouldn't have said something clever, even if he'd had something clever to say, so he just sat and waited for the Baron to go on.

'Sick old men usually are ill-tempered,' the Baron said. 'I'm that lovable exception.' A smile flickered over his thin lips. 'I'll have words with both the Swordmaster and the Earl on your behalf,' he said. 'Which might save you some embarrassment.'

Not that embarrassment was an important matter to the three of them, but . . .

Besides, how would he *have words* with them? The Baron looked as if he was about to breathe his last.

Well, it was a nice thought, anyway, even if it was an empty promise.

'That aside,' the Baron said, producing a small leather pouch from beneath his blanket, 'it's been said that gold is always sincere.' He handed the pouch to Kethol. 'I've written a letter to the Earl, and another to the Swordmaster, praising you for your service, and explaining that the little . . . disturbance in the castle last night was entirely my fault, not having discussed Morray's . . . ways with the serving girls.' He looked Kethol straight in the eye. 'It's one thing to have some sport with a willing young girl. It's another to do so far from one's own field, and be unwilling to provide for a bastard.' His lips tightened. 'You wouldn't think of it to look at me now, but I've sired a few bastards in my younger days, and I can say that I've made arrangements for them all, and probably for some that other men sired, as well.' He patted the pouch. 'The letters are in here. I've put my seal on my signature, rather than using it to seal the letters shut.'

Well, that would save Pirojil the trouble of carefully warming the wax so that he could read them without breaking the seals. Kethol was sure that this baron was as good as his word – he liked and trusted this man – but Pirojil was more cautious by nature.

But letters? 'Then you're not accompanying us back to LaMut?'

Other than getting Morray out of town and away from the putative assassin, getting Baron Mondegreen to LaMut had been the main purpose of this expedition. The rest of it could have waited. Yes, rotating the Mondegreen troops would have been necessary – the barons didn't like to have their own troops spend too long away from their own lands lest they form unlikely attachments to the wrong people – but there was no urgency. . .

'I think you've worked out that that's unlikely, at this point.' The Baron shook his head. 'Old Father Kelly says that I'm unlikely to survive an overland trip as far as LaMut, or even to survive many more days simply lying here,' he said, as though commenting on a minor problem. 'Duty compels me, yes, but it can not compel the flesh to be stronger than it is.'

Then why haul the lady out here and back? Kethol didn't understand, but the Baron's manner, while certainly unusually friendly, didn't seem to invite that kind of familiar inquisitiveness.

Kethol hadn't picked up the pouch. The Baron pushed it towards him with trembling fingers. 'I'll expect you to watch out for my wife on the trip back, as well.'

Pirojil would have said something to the effect that they would try to do it as well as they had done it on the trip out, but there was something about the Baron's manner that made it hard for Kethol to lie to him, even by indirection.

Damn.

There was nothing for it, so he picked up the pouch and looked inside – it was heavier than it looked; gold, not just silver – and stashed it inside his tunic.

The Baron smiled.

What was this really all about? Kethol was busy trying to work out a way to ask around the question – damn it all, why hadn't the Baron called for Pirojil? Pirojil was good at this sort of thing – when the door opened, and Lady Mondegreen entered, two steaming mugs on a tray. She set the tray down on the bedside table, and then sat down on the bed next to her husband, helping him prop up his head so that he could sip at his tea.

'I see that the carriage is being readied,' she said. 'But I know that I most clearly heard Father Kelly say that you're too ill to travel.'

The Baron seemed to draw himself straighter. 'Obligations, my dear. It's important that Mondegreen be represented at Council, and –'

'And –' she stopped herself with a look at Kethol. 'If you would excuse us for a moment, I would –'

'Please, be still, my dear. It would be ungracious to ask someone who has done us such a service to leave as if he were merely a servant.' He gestured at the mug of tea. 'He hasn't even finished his tea yet.'

Her lips pursed stubbornly. 'Very well, then. Embarrass me in front of this man, if you will.'

'Embarrass you? How could I do such a thing?'

'Very well: I want you to let me represent you at the Council. There's precedent, rare precedent . . .'

'I couldn't ask that of you, my dear,' the Baron said. 'You're tired from your trip.'

Kethol sat motionless. At least if they didn't notice him he wouldn't be getting involved in an argument between a baron and his wife. What the argument was really about Kethol wasn't sure – the Baron had just as much as said that she was going back to LaMut –

'If you don't trust me, then so be it,' she said. 'Who would you have speak for Mondegreen at the Council? Lord Venten? Benteen?'

Kethol didn't recognize the names – staying out of local politics was always a good idea – but the Baron frowned and tried to shake his head. 'Well, I suppose that my cousin Alfon could –'

'Alfon is an idiot, with an eye on the barony.'

The Baron reached out and patted her belly. 'I'd hoped that that would not come to pass,' he said. 'But . . .' he sighed.

'I'll ask this of you one more time, my husband,' she said. 'Send me to LaMut, to the Council, to represent your interests, our interests.'

The Baron sighed, and nodded. 'Very well, my dear. As you wish.' He turned to Kethol. 'I've great faith in my own troops, but I will expect that you will keep an eye on my wife, as well.'

Kethol was beginning to understand why the purse was so heavy.

'Yes, my lord,' he said.

'He wants us to *what?*' Durine shook his head.

'Bodyguard his wife.'

'And Morray?'

'He didn't say. I don't think, though, that he much cares one way or another.'

Durine snorted. 'Yeah, but Tom Garnett and Steven Argent do. We don't need another noble to babysit. If we get jumped by some more Tsurani, we'll have enough trouble trying to keep Morray alive, and we'll have the Captain and the Swordmaster to answer to if we don't.'

'I'm not telling you what we *should* do. I'm just telling you what he *asked*.' Kethol balanced the pouch on the palm of his hand. 'And what he paid good gold for.'

'Gold is a fine thing, but it doesn't make a sword any sharper or a wrist any faster,' Durine said. 'If it all goes to shit, I say we protect the Baron, and let Lady Mondegreen fend for herself.'

Pirojil stood silently for a moment, watching the carriage being loaded. The crates of messenger pigeons being loaded on the top of the carriage and the troop of relief soldiers would have been required in any event. The wagons would have had to be loaded with the sacks of grain for the horses; the canvas bags and oaken hogsheads containing supplies for the troops would have been necessary, as well.

It was entirely possible, of course, that the lady's travelling clothes had never been unpacked, and that a fresh set of dumpy maids had instantly been made ready; but the chests being loaded into the carriage boot and the presence of a second wagon suggested some degree of preparation.

Why? The lady was enough of a horsewoman to have preferred to travel on horseback . . .

He didn't like it, any of it.

'I'm with Durine on this,' Pirojil said, finally. 'You didn't swear any oaths, did you?' Kethol had strange ideas about keeping promises.

'No, not really. But I didn't empty the pouch out on his bed, either.'

'Shit.'

'Hmmm . . .' Durine felt at the hilt of his sword, his index finger idly tapping at it. 'I'm beginning to think that we might want to see if we can draw our pay as soon as we get to LaMut, and see if we can hole up in Ylith until the ice breaks.'

Pirojil nodded. Politics. The Baron's obvious heirs were dead, and unless there was another one in Lady Mondegreen's belly, there was sure to be some contention for the barony, once Mondegreen died.

Damn fool, to have let his last son and heir, presumably the son of a previous wife, ride off to be skewered by a Tsurani spear, but Kingdom nobles were like that. It would be hard to command men once you'd seemed too craven to lead them in battle.

'So,' Durine said, 'what say we get the caravan back to LaMut – keeping an eye on the Baron, not the lady – then draw our pay, and watch the ice floes breaking in Ylith from some seaside tavern?'

Kethol started to say something, then stopped.

'Go ahead,' Pirojil said, knowing what he was going to say.

'I like this baron,' Kethol said. 'He didn't have to intercede for us over last night's . . . embarrassment, and he didn't have to load us up with gold. All he's asking is that we do our best . . .'

'Yes. *Our* best. Which suggests,' Durine said, 'that he's got some reason to worry about the loyalty of at least some of his own men.'

'Or maybe he has some idea about how good we are at what we do.'

Their survival was proof enough that they were not just lucky, but good. The Tsurani were tough opponents, singly or *en masse*, and there were few soldiers, regulars or mercenaries, who had survived half the fights against them that the three of them had.

Durine shook his head. 'No. Have you ever met a noble who wouldn't be happy to tell you that his own troops were the best there ever were? I think that what makes us so attractive to this baron is our political connection – we don't have any.'

Pirojil nodded. 'I think you're right.' It had been just what he was thinking.

Kethol frowned. 'I think can we watch out for the lady, too,' he said.

'Yeah, and we can –'

'Shh.' Pirojil waved the two of them to silence. 'If you two can shut up for a moment and let me think . . .'

If the Baron was as near death as Kethol said that he seemed, whoever was next in line for the barony would certainly not mind if, say, Lady Mondegreen broke her neck in a fall from a horse, leaving the succession open.

But that only made sense if . . .

. . . if she was already pregnant, and if the child was Mondegreen's.

And from what Kethol said, it was unlikely that her husband was up to the task . . .

Which began to explain that Lady's reputation.

She wasn't some insatiable noblewoman, intent on riding every stallion. She had been, perhaps even with the connivance of her husband, trying to get with child. He tried to remember all the men with whom the rumours had associated her. Were they all, like Morray and Steven Argent, dark-haired and grey-eyed like her husband? Perhaps she picked out her paramours for their physical similarity to her husband, hoping for a match.

Wheels within wheels within wheels.

From the Baron's and his lady's point of view, it seemed that this trip home had been engineered entirely to place Lady Mondegreen in her husband's bed, at least one last time before he died, making the child the unquestioned heir, rather than throwing the barony into a succession dispute. That was the last thing that was needed anywhere in the Kingdom, even more so here in the West with the jostling already underway to see who would replace Vandros as Earl in LaMut when he became the next Duke, and of course, all those damn Tsurani running around trying to add to the gaiety.

It all sounded reasonable, if devious, and nobility anywhere was nothing if not devious.

Damn, in just a few minutes, this Baron Mondegreen had won over Kethol, and the last thing that the three of them needed was dissension between themselves.

Pirojil nodded. 'We protect both of them – but the priority is Morray, understood? He wears that sword for more than just vanity, I'll wager, so he might be foolish enough to draw it and start flailing about if we're not close by. So, make sure there are two of us with him, one with the lady, whoever's closest, if things turn dodgy. And if it's a choice between them, save the Baron first.

'You win on us watching out for Lady Mondegreen, Kethol, but Durine wins on us taking our pay and getting out of LaMut as soon as we can. No more waiting for this thaw – we settle them in at the Earl's castle in LaMut, and then we head south to Ylith. Are we all agreed?'

Kethol nodded and Durine, after a moment's hesitation, did, too.

It was a plan he could live with. Yes, garrison duty paid, but getting involved in local politics didn't, and it seemed that the three of them were up to their entirely-severable necks in local politics. Besides, the extra gold from Mondegreen would more than compensate them for the few extra bits of copper they'd earn freezing on the ramparts in LaMut during the next storm. The worst of the winter storms was likely over, and they could make their way south and enjoy the renewal that spring brought.

He shivered.

Kethol shook his head. 'I tell you, there's a storm coming.'

'When?'

'Not today, and not tomorrow, but soon. Too soon.'

Pirojil shook his head. With any luck, they would be out of LaMut with their pay warm in their pockets, but he had the feeling that luck wasn't going to be with them.

Not this time.

Shit.

FOUR

Cold

The sky was clear again.

The air seemed to have warmed a little – Durine could no longer quite feel the snot freezing in his nose – but it was still far too damned cold as they rode away, accompanied by both the Morray and Mondegreen relief troops destined for service in LaMut.

Maybe this 'thaw' was actually coming. That would be a good thing.

It was a much larger party than the one that had ridden out to Mondegreen, and would have been even without the Morray contingent: half again as many Mondegreen troops were being sent into the earldom's capital as had been rotated home, although why that was, Durine didn't know.

None of his business, really.

His business was to keep an eye out for Baron Morray, and prevent Kethol's and Pirojil's intention of guarding Lady Mondegreen from screwing that up, if they ran into trouble.

At a fork in the road they met up with Lord Verheyen and a company of his own soldiers, accompanied by a trio of

Natalese Rangers, several hours out from Verheyen's keep.

The Rangers were, as always, dressed in their traditional dark grey tunics, dark grey trousers, and equally dark grey cloaks. Durine never quite understood how legendary woodsmen would not want to adapt their clothing – their cloaks, in particular – to their surroundings. While he and Pirojil and Kethol travelled light by necessity, he had always accepted Kethol's notion that a cloak was more than just protection from the cold, more than something to sleep in, more than the basis for a stretcher to carry a wounded comrade, if you had that inclination and luxury: the three of them always made it a point to procure cloaks that were suited to the season. Even somebody as big as Durine was practically invisible in wooded country, if he was standing motionless and wearing the right cloak.

On the other hand, since it was almost impossible to see a Ranger unless he wished you to, they must know something Durine didn't. He turned his attention back to the approaching noble.

Luke Verheyen drew his horse to a halt. 'Hail, Ernest, Baron Morray,' he said formally.

Verheyen was a powerfully-built man, his hair and beard blond almost to the point of unhealthy whiteness, in stark contrast to his sun-darkened skin. His lips were twisted in a smile, and the creases along the side of his mouth and around his eyes suggested that he smiled often and much. He and his soldiers had thrown back their cloaks to reveal brown tabards quartered by a red cross, the only other device visible being a golden falcon on the upper left quarter, over the heart. Durine noticed the sword at his side was well cared for and well used, the hilt more suited for fighting than being a decoration. This was in keeping with his reputation as one of the deadliest blades in the West.

Morray nodded back. 'Hail, Luke, Baron Verheyen,' he returned. 'A cold day for travelling.'

'That it is.'

You might have thought that the two men were, at worst, friendly acquaintances from the amiable way they were chatting, but only if you didn't watch their eyes. Durine was carefully watching their eyes, until the leader of the three Rangers rode to the front and attracted his attention. The Ranger was a tall, slender man, who cut an almost absurd figure on his small pony, which from the easy way it moved under him, was surely sturdier than it seemed.

The Ranger greeted the Baron, then let his eyes slide past the soldiers in Morray, Mondegreen and LaMutian livery and settled on the three men who weren't in uniform.

'Hail, stranger,' he said, his eyes fixing on Kethol: as usual, there was something about the way Kethol looked that had made the Ranger think he was in charge. 'I am Grodan of Natal. I recognize the livery of the others, but I don't recognize yours.' His eyes indicated that 'yours' meant all three of them.

Despite their formal use of language, Natalese Rangers had, during his few encounters with them, always reminded Durine of constables – they watched everybody sceptically and pried for details that were, in any reasonable sense, none of their business.

'My name is Kethol,' Kethol said, pulling back his cloak to reveal his plain green tabard. 'I'm in the employ of the Earl of LaMut, as are my companions, Pirojil and Durine.'

Grodan nodded. 'Strange times make strange acquaintances.'

'So I hear,' Morray put in. 'As for us, we're accompanying the Lady Mondegreen to LaMut, for the same baronial council that Baron Verheyen is going to attend. Conduct of the war is important, but the earldom still has its own needs, and we're required –'

'Really?' Verheyen's smile broadened. 'I thought, perhaps, that I'd be of more use at the general staff meeting in Yabon City, but . . .' He trailed off with a shrug.

'Well, if you feel that you'd be welcome in Yabon City,' Morray said flatly, 'then you should point your horse north and west, rather than south. With these Rangers here to guide you, I'm sure you'll only be a few days late, if you ride hard.'

'I think not.' Verheyen spread his hands. 'I've always found that when my opinion differs from the Earl's as to what is best, it's better to do as he wishes.'

'Excuse me.' Grodan arched an eyebrow and leaned forward. 'Did I correctly hear you say it's the Lady Mondegreen in the coach? Not the Baron?'

Kethol shook his head. 'The Baron –'

'The Baron,' Morray interrupted, shutting Kethol up with a quick glare, 'is indisposed, and unable to travel at the moment. I'm not entirely sure why that's any concern of yours, Ranger.'

Durine didn't see any point in trying to keep Baron Mondegreen's fatal condition a secret. The old man would probably be dead within weeks, if not days. But nobody was asking him.

'No offence is intended,' Grodan said. 'As I said, strange times make for strange alliances.'

The Rangers were eyeing the LaMutian soldiers with expressions that were not particularly friendly, despite the fact that they were allies. Granted, it was a necessary alliance, not one born of brotherly love; after all, it had been the present Duke of Crydee's grandfather who had sacked Walinor and laid siege to Natal while attempting to conquer what had once been the Keshian province of Bosonia. Many in the Free Cities viewed the Duchy of Crydee as lands lost in that war. Durine knew that memories were long and people who felt a grievance normally could not be counted on to make distinctions between one duke or another, or one generation and the next. A curse of history, he judged. Sometimes it was better not to know things.

Durine could see there wasn't going to be a fight, grudging or otherwise, but if there were, it would be interesting to see how many of the locals the Rangers took down before they were over-whelmed. However, as the Ranger had said, war made strange alliances. This one would probably hold at least until a solid two or maybe three days after the last of the Tsurani were eliminated – if that ever happened. Or maybe for an entire week; Durine liked to look on the bright side of things.

'Well, then,' Grodan said, 'I think we had best accompany you all the way to LaMut.'

Morray nodded. 'I'll be grateful for your company, of course, and more grateful if the three of you will scout ahead. We had some minor trouble with Tsurani stragglers on the way out to Mondegreen, and it would be good to have some warning if there are any more such about.'

Good for him, thought Durine.

Kethol had never seen LaMut so full of soldiers – or nobles, or just plain people, for that matter. Everywhere he went, there seemed to be a plethora of baronial tabards, each bearing a different crest, although he knew that there were only a dozen or so barons that were fealty-bound to the Earl of LaMut. And everywhere you went, there seemed to be some noble or his lady, each with his or her own personal guard. For every landed baron, there appeared to be a couple of court barons, which meant there were dozens of squires, pages and other servants hurrying from one place to another, each wearing a mark or badge which he considered worthy of deference, but which was summarily ignored by everyone around him. He saw one scuffle between two young men who should have known better over who got to walk through the door of an inn first. The LaMutian constables walking by were more amused than annoyed and took evil delight in cuffing and kicking the two young 'nobles' to their feet, if not their senses.

Kethol made a point of staying out of their way; he had already had more than enough exposure to the nobility and their self-important servants for a lifetime, and all in a single week.

Just to complicate matters, Second-day was a full market day in LaMut, and the lull in the war had filled the markets, despite the bitter cold. The lower city was crowded with merchants selling everything Kethol could have imagined – except for mercenary services and fresh produce. The latter would have to wait for spring and if there were any good LaMutian citizens who needed to hire people like Kethol, Pirojil and Durine, the city markets were hardly the place to find them.

Near where a travelling farrier had set up his stall, a chicken-seller hawked his wares, clucking in protest against the cold in their wicker cages, already plucked and gutted and hanging from hooks where they were quickly freezing; or by the piece as they roasted on a hot spit over a fire. He was doing a brisk business with these, for the meaty, garlicky smells pried open pouches as quickly as a good pickpocket, and only iron self-discipline and the certain knowledge that hot food waited for him in the keep kept Kethol himself from parting with a few coppers.

Others weren't being quite so restrained. One stocky soldier, his cloak thrown back to display the Verheyen crest on his tabard, pushed to the front of the crowd, elbowed aside a pair of Benton men, and if the Watch hadn't been in the market in full force, it was just the sort of thing that would have degenerated into a brawl, despite the cold.

But the Watch moved quickly, so that the Verheyen man eventually passed on up the street, munching on a chicken leg, while the Benton men went down the street with a pair of roasted breasts and two baskets filled with eggs, suggesting that they had been on an errand for somebody.

Kethol was recognized at the keep's gate, and after a quick check of a list – mercenary soldiers did not come and go as they pleased within the walls of the Earl of LaMut's castle, but usually resided in a barracks in the city below. He was conducted into the court-yard surrounding the keep itself, made his way across the parade ground that occupied much of that inner courtyard, through the mud-room and into the foyer of the residence's west wing.

The sergeant in charge of the guard detachment there blocked his passage. 'I've been waiting for you – you're late,' he said.

'Yes, I know,' Kethol said. 'I'm due to relieve the others, at the Bursar's quarters. But that's a matter between me and Pirojil and Durine – meaning no offence, but it's none of your concern, after all.'

Like most of the barons fealty-bound to the Earl of LaMut, Morray maintained a small residence in the earldom's capital. Even in peacetime, the barons were frequently coming and going, doing whatever they needed to do in the capital besides working out a way to squeeze more taxes out of the peasants and franklins – which Kethol reckoned consumed most of their time and effort, although that probably wasn't fair. Kethol tried to be fair, at least within the confines of his mind. There were other attractions in LaMut. While two of the three playhouses in the city had been shut down early in the war, LaMut was still the cultural capital of the earldom, as well as the political one, and it was under-standable that the nobility would want to spend time in the capital for any number of reasons.

In addition to his house on Black Swan Road, Morray also had been assigned a small suite of rooms in the Earl's keep itself, probably both because of his status as the Bursar, and because he was one of the few people who knew the secret of the lock on the strongroom door. Gold and silver were sticky things, and if there ever was a noble fool enough to let just anybody have access to either the strongroom or the accounting books, Kethol would definitely have liked to have heard of him. He'd be first in line to stand guard all night at the strongroom door. For one night.

The sergeant shook his head. 'The other two can sit around with their thumbs up their arses watching the door for a while longer while Baron Morray takes his rest.' It seemed that the three of them were quickly becoming as popular with the keep's soldiers as they had become in Mondegreen. 'The Swordmaster wants to see you,' the sergeant went on. 'Weren't you told that at the gate?'

There were, Kethol decided, many wonderful times in life when it was best to keep your mouth shut. *If I had been told that at the gate, I wouldn't be here right now, would I?* he didn't say. You made enough enemies in this business as it was, and Kethol had no wish to add another. 'No, I wasn't,' he finally said.

The sergeant frowned. 'Hart, you'd better guide the freebooter up to the Aerie,' he said, turning to a gangly soldier with shifty eyes. 'He seems to have some trouble finding his way around to where he is supposed to be.'

Kethol followed the soldier down the hallway and up the winding staircase to the Aerie. The three of them couldn't be in serious trouble, he decided, or a detachment of troops would have met them at the front gate.

The soldier knocked briefly at the door, then opened it without asking.

'Ah,' Steven Argent said, glancing up from some paper in his lap, 'the tardy Kethol is finally here.' He grinned. 'I was thinking that I was going to have to send out a search party for you.'

Steven Argent glanced down at Fantus. The firedrake had stretched out in front of the hearth, spreading his wings to absorb what heat he could. The whole castle was probably far too draughty for the creature's tastes, but he had found himself a comfortable spot, at least for the moment, and a comfortable spot was something that Kethol envied as he stood not quite at attention.

'Fantus, here,' the Swordmaster went on, 'is quite the opposite of you; he's far too easy to find, underfoot, in front of my hearth. He keeps contriving to get himself down from the falconry loft where he belongs, and I never seem to manage to keep him out. If he weren't the Duke's wizard's pet, Fantus would find himself out in the forest, and quickly, never mind how cold it is.'

The drake stirred briefly, as if understanding the threat, fixed Argent with a baleful eye for a brief moment, then closed it, obviously contented with his lot. Kethol was now convinced Fantus had been some rich woman's pet cat in a previous life.

Argent allowed himself a rueful smile. 'Or how he seems to grow on me.' The Swordmaster looked up. 'You weren't quite so easy to find.'

Kethol didn't quite shrug. 'I'm sorry that the Swordmaster was put to any inconvenience,' he said.

He hoped it was the right thing to say, and he relaxed a trifle when Steven Argent waved the matter away.

'Not at all. Just give me a moment,' Steven Argent said, gesturing Kethol to the other chair next to the hearth. 'I'd better finish signing off on this report before it all flees my mind.' He bent over the papers in his lap again. 'It's a sad thing when an honest swordmaster has to take up all the bothersome details of running an earldom. I'll be almost as happy to see the Duke and Kulgan return to pick up Fantus as I will to see the Earl is back and I can return to my normal duties.'

Kethol slowly lowered himself into the indicated seat, nervous around the firedrake.

'He likes it when you scratch at his eye-ridges,' Steven Argent said, not looking up from his papers. 'You'd think he almost purrs.'

'If you don't mind,' Kethol said, 'I'll just keep my hands to myself.'

'I don't mind,' Argent said, still not looking up, 'but Fantus may have other ideas.'

As though he had heard and understood the Swordmaster,

Fantus slithered over to Kethol and presented his head for scratching.

Kethol had never been this close to a firedrake before. Once, years before, he had caught sight of a flight of new hatchlings. It had been another war, not as cold, but muddier, and he had enjoyed the moment of bright colours in the sky, if only as an early sign of spring. Dragons, large or small, had always made Kethol nervous, and he had no inclination to get any closer than a long bowshot. Their eyes seemed to see too much: some people claimed dragons could speak like men, but Kethol didn't care to engage one in conversation as an experiment. Even if they couldn't, Kethol was pretty sure they were smart; certainly this one was smart enough to have wormed his way into the Swordmaster's affections and into the Earl's kitchen through a cold winter.

Fantus craned his long neck to give Kethol a quick glance, then went back to spreading his broad wings in front of the raging fire.

Kethol narrowed his gaze at the creature. Then he reached out a tentative hand and scratched where the Swordmaster had indicated. The drake stretched his neck a bit, then relaxed into a satisfied, almost blissful expression, which fitted with Kethol's theory of feline reincarnation.

Steven Argent finally set his stack of papers down on the small table to his right – away from both the firedrake and the fire – and sat back in his chair. 'Well, I'm told you have a letter for me, and one for the Earl.'

Told? Who would have told – Oh. Lady Mondegreen, of course. He tried not to sniff the air for her signature scent of patchouli and myrrh.

'Yes, I do,' Kethol said.

'Well, out with them, man.'

Kethol stopped scratching the firedrake so that he could open his pouch and handed both of the letters over. That one was addressed to the Earl rather than to the Swordmaster was something that the Swordmaster and the Earl could work out by themselves, after Kethol, Pirojil and Durine were gone, he thought.

Steven Argent spent a suspiciously short time reading them. Either he was a very fast reader, or he already knew the letters' contents or, most probably, both.

He set the letters down in his lap, patted them, then nodded. 'It appears Baron Mondegreen has taken a liking to the three of you – and you in particular.' He smiled slightly. 'I can't say quite the same thing for the Military Bursar, though, although this letter from Baron Mondegreen puts some perspective on Baron Morray's complaints about the three of you interrupting his sleep.'

'I –'

'We'll just let that matter drop.' Steven Argent smiled. 'I'll tell Baron Morray the same if he brings it up again. Likely he won't –'

He was interrupted by a knock at the door. Steven Argent waited, as though he expected it to open, then said, 'Well, come in then, Ereven.'

The housecarl had a tray heavily laden with small loaves of bread and a huge wedge of blue-veined cheese balanced on one hand, a bottle of wine and two glasses in the other, and a glum expression on his face.

'I thought you might want some refreshment, sir.'

The Swordmaster nodded. 'I'd rather be working up a sweat on the training floor, but I should eat something.' He gestured at the low table between the two chairs. 'And if Kethol here will turn down an offer of good food and wine, he'll be a unique one.'

Ereven set the tray down and poured wine for both of them, while Steven Argent, disdaining the plate, set his papers in his lap, tore off a hunk of bread and took a bite before cutting a piece of cheese to go with it, beckoning at Kethol to do the same.

Kethol did so, tearing into the still-warm, thick crust. It had been too long since he had eaten. He knew that the fresh bread served to his betters in the castle was of a higher quality than the plain, thick brown loaves that were issued to the troops, but this was absolutely marvellous, beyond what he could have imagined. As his father had often said, hunger was by far the most pungent and effective of sauces.

The housecarl stood patiently, his hands folded in front of him.

'Ereven,' the Swordmaster said, 'we can manage to feed ourselves – there's no need for you to linger.'

The servitor almost smiled. 'As you wish, Swordmaster,' he said, bowing. 'Will there be anything else that you need before supper?'

'I think I can manage. Please give my best to Becka, and to your daughter, as well,' Steven Argent said, dismissing the servitor.

He turned to Kethol and shook his head after the door had closed. 'His daughter, Emma, is starting to show,' Argent said softly, as if the housecarl might overhear. 'The father must be one of the guard, as young men of the household staff are in fear of Ereven and a nobleman would already have stepped forward to make arrangements for the bastard. Which will make it my problem when the soldier is named.' He sighed. 'The girl won't talk about it, but I'm not inclined to press her, just yet. The Earl will know how to do that better than I can. When he tells me what he wants done, then I'll find out who the brainless lout is and see he does the Earl's will.' He scowled, then took another bite of his bread and cheese, and then drained his wine glass with one long draught. 'Well, that hits the spot on such a day, eh?' He looked at the door again, like a man who couldn't help himself from rubbing at an insect bite. 'The rumour is that I am the father.' He sat back and let out a slight sigh, and it occurred to Kethol he was in the unusual position of being told things he'd rather not hear by someone whose only reason for telling him was that he was inconsequential to the Swordmaster – much as soldiers talk to barmen, barbers and the stranger sitting next to them moments before they go over the wall. Depending on time and circumstance, Kethol would be inclined to tell the man to take his story elsewhere, or to pretend to listen politely while completely ignoring the fool, but given his present company, Kethol decided the best course was to nod occasionally and keep his mouth full of bread and cheese so that he couldn't make an inopportune remark.

Argent continued, 'And that irritates me more than a little. You'd think even these Westerners would know that an Eastern gentleman would take responsibility for the girl and his bastard.' He shook his head.

Kethol didn't say anything. Noble responsibilities were the problems of nobles, not his; besides, his mouth was full of bread and a particularly pungent and delicious cheese. Seeing that the Swordmaster was now expecting some sort of comment, Kethol quickly chewed and swallowed. Gulping the last bit, he said, 'You were speaking of Baron Mondegreen when the housecarl interrupted.'

'I was.' Noting that Kethol had almost hurt himself gulping his food so that he could answer, Argent softly said, 'Drink your wine. It's not as good as you'd find in Ravensburgh or Rillanon, but it's a fair enough companion to that cheese.'

Kethol forced himself to sip at his wine, rather than gulping it down, as he would have liked. It was worth the tasting, certainly, but to Kethol's way of thinking, the purpose of drinking wine in the middle of a cold day was to warm him from the inside, and the quicker it went down, the quicker it would start getting to work.

Steven Argent was still waiting for Kethol to speak.

'I . . . liked Baron Mondegreen,' Kethol said. 'He seems a kind man.'

Steven Argent nodded. 'True enough. Though those who failed

to notice the steel behind his smile have regretted the oversight. How did he appear?'

'Dying, my lord,' Kethol said.

Steven Argent sighed. 'Yes, he is.' He tapped at the letters in his lap. 'These are hardly the only letters brought back from Mondegreen, as you've undoubtedly concluded. Father Kelly is of the opinion that he'll be dead within a few weeks, even if he remains in his bed, and that if he had been fool enough to travel in this weather, you would have only delivered a body to LaMut.' He didn't wait for a comment. 'You managed to keep Morray alive, and that's what you were told to do.'

Kethol nodded.

'Other than the Tsurani attack, did you see any evidence of anybody trying to harm him?'

Kethol shook his head. 'None at all. He and Baron Verheyen seemed almost, well, chummy, and –'

'They despise one another. Just because they are both vying for the earldom doesn't make them fools.' Argent paused, then softly added, 'Quite the contrary, in fact.'

'The earldom, my lord?' he asked. 'Has something happened to the Earl?' Surely he would have heard about that.

'No.' Steven Argent shook his head. 'Earl Vandros is fine. It's an open secret, though, that he's certain to marry the Duke's daughter, Felina – although I wouldn't bring it up with him; he's unaccountably touchy on the subject. As the Duke of Yabon is without a son and heir, Vandros will end up being Duke of Yabon. The King will name his successor, here, but Vandros will have quite a say in the matter. Morray is Bursar, he enjoys that advantage, but Verheyen has distinguished himself in the war – there's no more deadly blade in the West – so as a military leader, he enjoys another edge. So, Morray and Verheyen are desperate for the Earl's favour. Starting trouble is not the way to earn Vandros's favour.' His brow furrowed. 'I'm surprised you didn't know that.'

Kethol forced himself not to shrug. 'I've never been much for barracks gossip.' Which wasn't quite true; you could learn a lot from barracks gossip, but Kethol had always been far more interested in everyday issues of, say, how eager a given captain was to expend men, or which serving girl was especially friendly, than he was in more lofty matters of noble succession.

Yes, everybody heard rumours about the court, about feuds between Guy du Bas-Tyra and Duke Borric, whispered stories about the King being stone crazy, or about Prince Erland being at death's door, or dead already at Guy's hands – but that didn't have much effect on you when your real concern was whether or not the Bugs were going to come over the next ridge and cut you into tiny bits. It was enough to know that those who were deciding things were meeting at Yabon. As serpentine as the politics were here in LaMut, it was probably worse there, and Kethol had always thought that the distinction between bad and worse was far sharper – and much more likely to get him killed – than that between good and better.

'And I assume,' Steven Argent said, 'that you'd like to be returned to Tom Garnett's service?'

'My lord?'

'Tom Garnett – I take it you want to go back to his company?'

To Kethol's way of thinking, the three of them had never quite left Tom Garnett's company; they had just been given a particular assignment, much like the time when Tom Garnett had sent them out to scout ahead during a lull in the fighting with the god-cursed Bugs. Come to think if it, that was probably the time when Tom Garnett had concluded that Kethol was the leader of the three of them – and actually, on that sort of thing, he was, by virtue of having been raised a forester's son.

'Actually, my lord,' Kethol said, 'we've talked it over among the three of us, and what we've decided is, well, we've decided that we'd like to be paid off now, and head south for Ylith, to wait for the thaw there.'

The Swordmaster arched an eyebrow. 'In this weather?' He frowned. 'It's bitter cold, and it's likely to get even worse. I've spoken with Grodan – he says that there's another storm coming – worse than the last – and Rangers have even more of a feel for such things than magicians. My guess is that it's not going to be as bad as Grodan suspects, but I'd not like to bet heavily on that. Certainly not enough to be out on the road when it hits.'

'But –'

'If Grodan's right, you might find yourself caught in a blizzard halfway to Ylith, and not thaw out until spring.'

Kethol didn't wonder how Steven Argent knew they were going south if paid – it was the logical choice if you had finished fighting and were seeking warmer weather.

'Gold and silver are fine things,' continued the Swordmaster, 'but you can't burn them to keep you warm. Better to have a warm bed and hot food safely inside the city's walls until spring, right?' He frowned. 'Besides, I'm still concerned about Baron Morray, and even if I didn't have specific instructions from Earl Vandros to see to his safety, I'd still like the idea of having you outsiders watching over him.'

Yes, Pirojil and Durine had pointed out, in great detail, why the Swordmaster would prefer that. But Kethol could hardly go into the politics of that here and now, and it was probably better and safer to act as though he hadn't noticed.

'Well,' he said, 'what with us taking a one-in-three each day, we're managing to watch over the Baron even now, granted, but –'

'You didn't ask Captain Garnett to assign others to watch his rooms while he slept,' the Swordmaster said, nodding approvingly. 'So, was that being thorough, or a matter of you three never trusting anybody else?'

Kethol shrugged. 'You told us to protect the Baron, and we did.'

'You did a fine job; the Baron is still breathing, and busy at his account books, which is as it should be.' The Swordmaster nodded in approval. 'Which is why I want to keep you on that duty, at least until after he's out of my city, or until the end of the approaching storm, whichever comes last.' He spread his hands. 'I'm sure you're not fool enough to travel in this weather if you didn't have to, and you don't have to. Besides, the Earl might have to hire on more mercenaries before this bloody war's over – and I wouldn't want word to spread that we'd paid off three men and sent them out into the cold to die. Wouldn't help recruitment.'

Kethol shook his head. He knew the Swordmaster jested over the last; mercenaries dying for any reason had little bearing on recruitment, unless it was due to overt stupidity on the part of commanders; gold was the thing, first, last and always. Even so, he responded to the jest as if it was serious. 'We wouldn't say anything, sir. We wouldn't be able to.'

Argent kept his smile in place, but it turned cold. 'The serious concern is when word gets out that you insisted on being paid off, and leaving LaMut now with a storm coming on. Tongues would start to wag, and suspicions could be raised. That could start a whole rush – things could easily get out of hand.' He shook his head. 'All in all, I think it would be better for everybody concerned, yourselves included, if you stay on – at least until both the storm and the Council are over.' He looked over at Kethol. 'Please don't make me insist.'

'You're not saying that we can't get our pay and leave, are you, my lord?'

'No.' The Swordmaster shook his head. 'And I'd best not hear that I suggested any such thing.' His eyes narrowed, and he raised a finger. 'What I am saying is I'm in no mood to put down some pointless insurrection among the mercenaries, and that's just what is likely to happen if the three of you were to sit around the fire at a tavern complaining that the Swordmaster won't pay you off right now.'

'My lord, I –'

Argent's upraised hand cut Kethol off. 'If you get your two friends to go knock on Baron Morray's door and demand your pay, he would open the account books to see what you're owed, and then open the strongroom in the dungeon to pay the three of you every real and every copper you're owed. I'm not saying that you can't do that. But I *am* telling you that I think it would be a very bad idea, right now.'

The Swordmaster's expression was even chillier than the wind leading into the Aerie, despite the fixed smile – or perhaps because of it.

'As to the Baron,' he went on, 'I'll have Captain Perlen assign guards to watch over his rooms in the castle, so the three of you can have some time off, at least while he's sleeping. He shouldn't be in any danger in his bed – but I do want the three of you to stay on to guard him against any mishap the rest of the time. At least until both the Council and the storm have ended.'

Argent poured them each another full glass of wine, and then raised his own in a salute. 'Of course, should we get through this without any mishaps, I'm certain the Earl will not object if I show his appreciation with a significant bonus on top of your agreed pay. Just as I'm sure you'll be inclined to show your loyalty by keeping this entire conversation between you three and myself.' His smile turned especially wicked. 'Do you have a problem with that, Kethol?'

'You said what?' Pirojil closed his eyes and shook his head.

'I said yes, we'd stay on, at least until the end of the Council or the end of the storm,' Kethol said. 'Whichever comes last. I tried to get him to agree to whichever comes first, but he insisted.'

Durine rolled his eyes. 'Which means that we're stuck baby-sitting his baronship, and ready to be blamed if he and Luke Verheyen manage to stick swords in each other.'

Pirojil shook his head. 'It's only for a while longer –'

'You like this?' Durine frowned.

'No. I don't like it. I say we can live with it, at least for now. I don't even blame Kethol, although I'm tempted to.' Durine fixed Pirojil with a questioning expression. 'Sounds to me like Steven Argent didn't give him much choice.'

Kethol said, 'That's true.'

Pirojil shook his head. 'After all, somebody had to go to the Swordmaster and ask for our pay. It could have been any of the three of us. I should have reckoned that Argent wouldn't go for that.'

Durine looked confused. 'So even though we have no choice, it's all right because it's only a while longer?'

Pirojil said, 'No.'

Now Durine was obviously confused. 'What is the problem?'

'The problem is that things are going well, that's the problem.'

'The problem is that there's no problem?'

Pirojil nodded. 'Yeah. As long as things are going well, he's not going to want to make any changes. He's just temporarily sitting in the Earl's chair, after all. It's not like Steven Argent's been made the Earl of LaMut. He just wants Earl Vandros to return to a city in the same condition it was when he left it – and if the time has come to dispense with the mercenaries, Argent is going to want to let the Earl do it, not do it himself.' He shrugged. 'For all he knows – for all we know – the general staff meeting at Yabon will decide to send the body of LaMutian forces north to Stone Mountain, west to Caldara, or to Tith-Onaka only knows where. Be pretty damn embarrassing – for both the Earl and the Swordmaster – if the Duke decides to use the Earl's troops and Vandros then comes back to find that the Swordmaster has paid off all the mercenaries that the Earl of LaMut has just promised to the Duke.'

Pirojil shook his head. 'Don't underestimate the Swordmaster, and don't buy into his I'm-just-a-swordsman talk. He's not just a soldier or duellist, but a politician, as well, and he has to think like one. That's why Vandros left him in charge.'

'I don't like it,' Durine said. 'I'm not sure I believe in any of this assassin stuff, but –'

'But that's not the point.' Pirojil shrugged. 'From what the Swordmaster said, it sounds to me like it was just a load of accidents that didn't quite happen, and I think he and the Earl are finding conspiracies where there aren't any – just as Kethol mistook Baron Morray's little roll in the hay with that serving girl for something else.'

The tips of Kethol's ears burned. That had been embarrassing.

'So what do we do?' Kethol asked. 'We can't leave . . .'

'Not since you said we wouldn't? This whole nobility thing isn't rubbing off on you, is it?'

'No, but . . .'

'Shhh.' Pirojil thought it over for a moment, then shook his head. 'Promises have nothing to do with it. If we decide to leave, we had better quietly take what we have on us and just ride out – bracing the Baron for our full pay wouldn't be wise, not after the Swordmaster's warning. We could probably draw some spending money through Captain Garnett – and we probably should, regardless, or he might start to wonder why we haven't – but that's about all. If we go to the Baron, and if anything bad happens, we get blamed. Either of you like that idea? You want to leave without our money?'

'No.' Durine didn't hesitate. 'I reckon that we leave with our money, when we leave.'

'Or we could just cut our losses and get out of here,' Pirojil said.

'Are you serious about that, or are you just saying it to see if it'll get a rise out of me?'

Pirojil gave one of his rare smiles. 'A little of both, perhaps. Leave?'

'No.' Durine shook his head. 'I already said no – how many times do I have to say it? Kethol?'

'I already told the Swordmaster that we'd stay.'

'Yeah,' Pirojil said, 'but that was him asking. This is me. Leave or stay?'

Kethol didn't like the idea of leaving their pay behind, either. They had managed to accumulate a fair amount of cash, between what they had looted off dead men and what he had been able to win at gambling and snatch up during the tavern fights; not to mention the pouch that Baron Mondegreen had given him, but the Earl of LaMut paid well – and leaving that much gold and silver behind would mean that they would have to find a new employer soon. Besides, there was something about it that just felt wrong.

It wasn't about Morray, either – Kethol didn't feel one way or another about the Baron – but there was the added complication of Lady Mondegreen. He had just about promised her husband that he'd watch out for her, and running out – well, that felt wrong, too.

'Stay,' Kethol said at last. He sighed. 'And there's that bonus, too.'

Damn. Maybe this nobility thing *was* rubbing off on him.

FIVE

Storm

The storm hit hard.

It had started suddenly, shortly after what should have been dawn, with such a deafening crack of unseasonable thunder that it had shaken Durine out of the first decent night's sleep he had had in longer than he cared to remember. While the lightning and the thunder had abated within the next hours, the storm had only grown in its intensity, and Durine had had to bury himself deep into his thickest cloak to make it from the barracks to the keep in the wan grey light, bracing himself against the wind until it felt as if he was almost at a forty-five degree angle.

It felt absurdly warm inside the mud-room off the side entrance to the keep, which was ridiculous. Despite the small cast-iron coal brazier on its tripod, the water bucket there was so frozen that he was able to pick the whole bucket up by the dipper.

He debated bringing his overboots inside – they would freeze solid out here – but decided that going with the crowd was the better part of valour, and left them hung on a hook on the wall over the brazier, hoping that they would at least be kept warm enough that he could put them on over his boots without breaking the frozen canvas. He hung his thick cloak next to them, and tucked his rabbit-fur-lined, bullhide gloves into his belt, and made his way into the foyer, past the shivering guard.

He didn't like leaving his cloak, and the gold hidden in it, but it would probably be safe – and it was definitely best not to seem to be too concerned about an inexpensive cloak, for fear of giving others ideas.

It was less miserable inside than it had been outside, but not much.

Outside, the wind howled like an injured beast that didn't have the decency to go off and die quietly somewhere. It clawed frantically at the walls and windows of the keep, demanding entry. The only small pleasure he could find in the whole situation was the thought that any Tsurani or Bugs out in the forest would probably have frozen themselves stiff by now.

All the castle's shutters had long since been bolted closed. Even so, snow leaked in through every crack and joint that wasn't completely sealed. If the fires in all the castle's hearths – Pirojil had counted two dozen, although Durine was sure that he had missed some – hadn't been kept fully blazing by legions of servants constantly replenishing them with wood, there was no doubt that the wind rushing down the chimneys would have extinguished every one.

Even so, the bitter, snowy wind managed to sneak down the chimneys past the burning fires, leaving behind puddles of water on the floor in front of each hearth, and the carpets had been quickly rolled away so that they didn't get soaked and rot away before spring.

What time the castle's servants had in between trying to seal with mud those cracks between the stones which had previously been invisible – particularly around the window frames – they spent in endlessly mopping up in front of the large fireplaces where the nobles congregated, all the while keeping a steady stream of pots of hot coffee, tea and broth coming.

Durine didn't quite understand that. He would have just kept himself close to the fire, avoiding doing anything that would cause him to have to move. After all, whatever heat you gained from drinking the warm liquid would be quickly lost in the frigid garderobes. The nobles, however, would probably be relieving themselves in thundermugs in their relatively warm quarters, rather than having to unbutton their noble flies – or worse, plonking their naked, shivering, noble buttocks down on a garderobe's frozen seat, and finding that they had stuck to it, more likely than not.

If Durine had had the choice, he wouldn't have ever left his room.

The nobles, on the other hand, were early risers, whether it was from custom, or because of the same thunder that had shaken Durine out of his bed, he couldn't say.

As he passed through the Great Hall, he noticed that Baron Verheyen had commandeered several chairs nearest the larger of the two fireplaces, the one set into the north wall, and busied himself in low murmurings over his steaming mug with the Swordmaster and two other nobles whose names Durine couldn't recall. It was hard to remember them all, and probably not worth the bother. Experience had taught Durine that when you bumped up against one, you merely lowered your gaze, touched your fore-lock, muttered 'm'lord' and shuffled out of the way, unless of course you were killing him, but either way it didn't much matter if you remembered his name or not.

Under other circumstances, though, it would have made sense to spend some time sizing up which of the barons might be worth taking service with, but since the three of them were going to be out of LaMut as soon as they could, why bother?

Baron Erik Folson was easy to remember: with his hard eyes and chiselled chin. When he didn't move – and he seemed to spend much of his time in a pose of some sort – he looked like a painting of a noble lord. He also apparently spent much of his time with his eyes on Lady Mondegreen's cleavage, which was abundantly in evidence despite the cold. His hands also seemed to find their way easily to her arm or shoulder or the swell of her hip; which wasn't really Durine's concern, and since she kept smiling back at him and nodding as he talked, apparently she wasn't concerned, either.

Her eyes caught Durine's for just a moment, and she gave him a quick flash of a smile and a nod before returning to her conversation with Baron Folson.

Berrel Langahan, standing opposite Lady Mondegreen, was noteworthy for reasons quite the opposite of those which made Folson memorable. Langahan was short, fat and bald, his skin browned from years apparently spent mostly outside, looking more like a prosperous farmer than a nobleman. He had that solid toughness under the fat that proclaimed he had gained his girth from muscle-building labour coupled with heavy eating, rather than from sloth and indulgence. He wouldn't have looked at all like a noble – and particularly not like a court baron – if it hadn't been for the jewelled rings that bedecked his stubby fingers, and the slick, knee-length ermine-lined jacket that enabled him to stay away from the fire.

How and why a court baron, a man who supposedly had spent almost his entire adult life in Prince Erland's castle in Krondor, would look like some sort of outdoorsman was something that piqued Durine's interest. But the assembled nobility ignored Durine as he passed, as though he was just another piece of the furniture, and rather than pausing to think how to ask that impertinent question without giving offence, he made his way through the Great Hall and down the hallway to the west wing.

It was morning, after all, and time to relieve the house guard that had watched Baron Morray's door while he slept.

When he got there, there was no guard on the door, and the door itself stood open.

Damn.

Durine plunged in, startling the young housegirl into dropping her armload of wood to the stone floor.

'Where's the Baron?' he asked, gently. There was no point in scaring the poor girl any more than he already had. It was clear that the Baron was gone – his bed had been made, and the remnants of some meal stood on a tray by his bedside. 'Is he at the strongroom already?'

Durine wasn't exactly clear on the details, but some of the account books apparently never left the strongroom in the keep's basement, while the Baron, quite understandably, preferred to work on the others in the relative comfort of his small suite, rather than in the damp cold of the strongroom.

She shook her head. 'I don't know as it's any of your business what his lordship is doing,' she said with a sniff.

Well, so much for being nice. 'Then come with me, and we'll see if the Swordmaster thinks it's any of my concern where the Baron is, and how grateful he'll be to you for keeping the information from me.' He stepped forward to take her by the arm, but stopped when her eyes widened.

'The Swordmaster?'

Durine nodded. 'In case nobody's told you, the Swordmaster himself has detailed Kethol, Pirojil and me to see to the Baron's safety and well-being, and we report directly to him if there's any problem.'

Well, Steven Argent hadn't actually said that, but that had been the implication of his decision to not only keep them on, but to not return them to Tom Garnett's company. Durine wouldn't have liked to have tried to pull rank on the Captain, but this serving girl was another matter.

'I . . . I can't see as how it would do any harm to tell you,' she said, shooting a quick glance toward the door. 'Although maybe I should ask Fath – I could ask the housecarl, first?'

Durine had noticed the light swell of her belly under her blouse, but he had just attributed it to the regular meals in the keep. This apparently was Ereven's daughter, the pregnant one, which began to explain how she felt free to look down on a soldier who wasn't even wearing a LaMutian tabard, much less rank stripes.

'If you wish – if he's close by. Steven Argent is downstairs, in the Great Hall.'

She reached over to the bell rope by the bed, and pulled it quickly three times, then twice, then six times, then once. Durine didn't ask what the code was, but whatever it was, it was effective, because less than a minute later Ereven's glum form came in through the door.

'The Baron,' Durine said, without preamble, 'where is he?'

'Baron Morray?' Ereven's brow furrowed. 'He didn't tell you? I thought you were supposed to be his special bodyguards, the three of you.'

That's what I thought, too, Durine thought. 'Tell me what, if you please?'

Ereven shrugged. 'There was a messenger, just after dawn. There was some problem at the Baron's residence – on Black Swan Road, I think it is? – and he decided to go out and look at it himself.'

'Out in this?'

Wonderful. If the Baron froze to death between here and Black Swan Road, Durine didn't have any real question as to where the blame would fall.

He spun on the ball of his foot and walked out of the room without a word.

It was not starting off to be a very good day.

Pirojil slipped and fell again, trying to hold his cloak shut with both hands, and twisting as he did so that he would fall on his right side – on his dagger, further bruising his right hip, rather than on his left side, on his sword, further bruising his left hip.

Strong hands helped him to his feet, but not before what felt like half a ton of snow had managed to slide down the open front of his cloak and into his tunic. He had wrapped a thick scarf around his neck to try to keep it less cold – warm was impossible – but he hadn't thought to sew the damn scarf to his tunic and wouldn't have had the time to do so even if he had thought of it, and every time he had fallen, the snow had seen an opportunity to worm its way closer to his heart, and taken it.

Snow was like that.

The wind from the west had a personality, and the personality was a cruel one. It had taken the snow and turned every bump in the long road into town into a drift that was at least knee-high, and often came to his waist, and had wickedly packed the snow down with just enough force to make it impossible to wade through easily, but not quite enough to support even Kethol's weight. Pushing straight through the drifts would have worn them out before they had made it halfway to Black Swan Road. Making their way up Black Swan Road was a matter of constantly trying to manoeuvre themselves around drifts, like three warships cruising through shoal waters, avoiding sandbars.

The streets were, not surprisingly, almost empty; though occasionally huddled figures lunged from place to place, all of them bearing bundles, and none of them stopped to try to engage Pirojil, Kethol or Durine in conversation.

Not that he really was up for much conversation at the moment. What was there to say? 'Cold enough for you?'

They pushed on, and then it was Durine's turn to fall, and Kethol and Pirojil's turn to help him up. You didn't want to stretch out your arms to push yourself up; that just guaranteed that you'd load up your sleeves with the snow.

It was good to have friends, even if they were dark, hulking shapes wrapped in their cloaks and scarves, their beards and eyebrows caked with frost and ice and snow.

Kethol pounded the wooden placard at the gate of the next house with his fist, and shook his head when it cleared to reveal a coat of arms that none of them recognized. They probably should have tried to get hold of a local guide – although who would be fool enough to come out in this at anything short of the point of a sword?

Just head up down the road into the city proper, then down High Street until you reach Black Swan Road, the idiot guard had said, *and look for Baron Morray's fox-and-circle crest on the wooden placard on the gate.*

He hadn't said that all the crests on the placards on the eastern side of the street faced toward the west, and that snow had utterly caked each of them, and it was only a sense of fairness that persuaded Pirojil that the guard probably hadn't thought of that any more than he had, although Pirojil did try to keep himself a little warm by vivid thoughts of rubbing the soldier's face into every one of those snow-caked placards.

Besides, they had known that the foot of Black Swan Road was opposite the Broken Tooth Tavern, and Kethol could be counted on to find any place he'd been to – especially any tavern – blindfolded.

Which was close to what this was. The sun should be high in the sky by now, he thought, and it wasn't doing its job. Only a wan, directionless grey light managed to push half-heartedly through the storm, occasionally brightened by a flash of lightning to the east, which was always accompanied by a much-delayed, distant rumble of thunder that sounded like a growling beast.

The crest on the next placard was an unfamiliar three bezants – at least, Pirojil hoped that they were bezants – and the one after that was, thankfully, Morray's rampant fox in its golden circle.

It took all three of them to push the gate open against the mass of snow that had been dumped behind it, and they didn't push it open any more than they had to. The gate had been left unbarred, which made sense, since the guard shack was empty, probably as usual. The walls of a noble's town home were not intended to keep out invading armies, after all, but more to deter thieves and give some privacy from the outside world. This one didn't even have a walkway around the inside of it, and Pirojil wondered if the snow concealed spikes or broken glass embedded along the top of the wall, or if the thieves of LaMut were just too polite to bother a noble's possessions while he slept.

Not that there were many thieves out today, he suspected. It would have been a poor day for burglary, for surely every noble or commoner who had any choice and a lick of sense would be in their homes, trying to stay warm.

The Baron's compound was on the small side, by noble standards: just a single two-storey stone building, flanked on either side by a couple of two-storeyed wattle-and-daub outbuildings. The one beyond the main building was probably the servants' quarters, because the one that they could see dimly through the driving snow had the large doors of a stable, and probably had once housed Morray's personal guard – you could hardly have the earldom's Wartime Bursar travelling about without his own retinue – before most of them had been drafted directly into the Earl's service.

The windows of the main building were tightly shuttered, and what cracks there would have been in the shutters were packed tightly with snow, but the occasional sparks from the chimneys showed that the building was occupied, although the wind and snow quickly snuffed them out, and dispersed any smoke before it had a chance to become visible.

The wooden canopy over the door provided some shelter from the wind; the three of them mounted the steps to the house and crowded into it.

Durine pounded on the thick oaken door. There was no knocker on it; presumably, guests were supposed to be welcomed at the gate, and announced somehow or other before they arrived at the arched doorway.

There was no challenge, no 'who goes there'; the door just suddenly swung inward, and Baron Morray stood there dressed only in a tunic and trousers, a sword in one hand, and a dagger in the other.

'Who is it?' His expression was almost as cold as the temperature outside.

Durine took a step back and held up his hands. 'Be easy, my lord – it's just the three of us.'

Morray lowered both of his weapons, while Pirojil silently cursed himself for his own carelessness. Yes, it had just been Morray, but if it had been somebody else, somebody with ill intentions, he would have been able to skewer Durine while Kethol and Pirojil were drawing their own weapons.

Pirojil was getting sloppy, and that was bad. Well, at least the other two had had more sense; he noticed that Kethol and Durine had their own daggers out, held in a reverse grip along their forearms, keeping the weapons effectively invisible from the Baron or anybody else in front of them.

'Well, don't just stand there, letting the storm in – get inside,' Morray said. He turned and raised his voice. 'No need to worry – it's just the three freebooters that the Earl has inflicted upon me.' His voice was pitched loudly, to carry through the closed door of the mud-room and into the house proper.

They stepped into the mud-room, Pirojil closing the door behind him while Kethol and Durine took the opportunity to sheath their knives discreetly, and the other door swung instantly open.

Morray stepped through, beckoning them to follow. The mud-room opened directly onto what was probably called the Great

Hall, although it wasn't a tenth the size of the one at LaMut Castle.

The hall was filled with close to two dozen men and women, ranging in age from an ancient greybeard in a worker's rough-spun tunic and trousers who was sitting in the big chair in front of the fire half-wrapped in a blanket, to the two sleeping babies he held as he sat, one in the crook of each arm. A vast roast turned on a spit in the main fireplace next to a huge cast-iron pot, attended to by two women in their thirties and a boy of about ten.

'Well, get those thick cloaks off and come on inside. You can take your overboots off after you warm up,' Morray said.

The three of them were soon seated in front of the fire. Pirojil and Durine hung their swordbelts on the backs of their chairs, while Kethol just stretched out his long legs onto a hassock – and steaming cups of Keshian coffee were brought to them without any asking.

Pirojil preferred tea himself, but hot liquid was hot liquid, and the cup warmed his numb hands and didn't quite scorch his throat. Besides, Keshian coffee was rare this far north, and that made the drink more savoury.

Morray was halfway across the room, muttering in a low voice to a pair of thickset men, and only came back to where they were sitting when Pirojil started to rise.

'Sit, man, sit – it's wicked out there, and you look colder than I felt.' Morray frowned down at him. 'What brings you out of the warmth of the castle on a day like this?'

'I was about to ask you the same thing, my lord.'

Morray snorted. 'As if it's any of your concern where I go and what I do.'

'Meaning no offence, my lord,' Pirojil said, 'it is precisely our concern, by order of Earl Vandros, himself. We're supposed to be guarding you –'

'On a day like today, I hardly think that the streets of LaMut are crowded with Tsurani assassins,' Morray said. 'If any such exist, which I very much doubt. Yes, I'm not the only baron who was guided into LaMut by auxiliary troops. You should hear Verheyen complain – and he does complain, to any who will listen – how his own soldiers being put into the Earl's service has meant that he is left with barely a corporal's guard. But I don't see any of the others' guards lounging about their rooms, or . . . interrupting their sleep.' He gave Kethol a quick glare. 'But that discussion is for another time, I suppose – the reason I'm out here is that word was sent to the castle.' He gestured towards the far wall. 'When the storm hit, a bolt of lightning apparently hit the roof of the servants' quarters. Probably would have burned the whole building down if the storm hadn't put the fire out, but as it was, an attic beam fell and broke through into the second storey, and right now the whole building is probably frozen solid.'

Pirojil nodded. 'So your man was asking your permission to move the servants into your – into the main house, because of the storm?'

'Hardly.' The chilly expression was back on Morray's face. 'If he'd been idiot enough to let good servants freeze to death while waiting for permission to bring them out of the cold, I'd have done worse than release him from my service, I can tell you that. No,' he went on, his expression softening as his gaze left Kethol and returned to the two babies sleeping in the old man's arms, 'he was just reporting to me that he had moved them all in here. I felt that it was my duty to at least see that things were well here. As well as can be expected under the circumstances.' He shook his head. 'Which isn't very good – I doubt that we'll be able to move the servants back into their quarters until spring, and we'll probably have to rebuild the whole house before they do. With Enna and her babies installed in my own bedroom here, I'll more than likely have to spend the next months living in the castle and not have a moment of privacy under my own roof until summer, if then.' He shook his head. 'And is that enough information for you? Or should I tell you that I was tempted to curse my own father for pinching the coppers and having the outbuildings built of wattle and daub, instead of good stone, as well?'

There wasn't really any answer for that, and the Baron waited only a moment before grunting his irritation.

'If you three had not rushed out into the worst storm I've ever seen, in another hour or so you would have found me back in the castle, at my account books, where I belong.' He glared. 'And you've done a fine, fine job of delaying my return. I've just sent servants to procure some dry clothes for the three of you, and I'll have to wait until you've warmed yourself and changed before I head back, or you'll come chasing after me and freeze to death, won't you?'

'Well, in truth, when you leave, we will come with you, my lord,' Pirojil said, nodding. 'It's our job, after all, though I'm sorry to put you to so much trouble.'

Morray snorted. 'Oh, just drink your coffee.'

He turned and walked away. Catching the eye of the cook, he gestured towards the three of them, and to the food cooking in the hearth. The cook nodded, and the Baron left the room, his manner as officious as always.

Pirojil just shut up and drank his coffee, and looked from Kethol to Durine, and back to Kethol.

Durine shrugged, and Kethol smiled.

It was just as well, Pirojil decided, that they had been paid to protect Baron Morray's life, rather than, say, killing him.

He would have done it, of course, but he would have been unhappy about it.

Pirojil found, much to his surprise, that he was actually getting to like this baron.

*   *   *

The trip back up the road to the castle was even worse than the trip out had been.

If anything, the storm had intensified. It was impossible to tell how much of the snow was new, and how much was simply being picked up by the wind and thrown at them, although during the few moments that Pirojil stopped to try to catch his breath, he could see the snow banks almost melt and then instantly reform and grow in the wind.

It was dangerous to stop, even for a moment; his toes had long since stopped hurting, and were almost feeling warm now, and that meant that frostbite was only minutes away.

Kethol took the lead, and constantly turned to be sure that the others hadn't got lost. Even when the wind didn't pound directly against the eyes, it was only possible to see a few feet in the storm, and any tracks that they had made on their way to the Baron's residence had long since been shattered and broken in the storm. Durine was next, with Pirojil insisting that Morray follow close behind the big man. For once, the Baron didn't complain, at least not aloud. And with Morray following Durine, the big man's bulk sheltered the Baron from the worst of the storm.

Pirojil brought up the rear, using both hands in the constantly futile battle to hold his cloak close together and keep the storm out. Heating the cloak by the fire had been a mistake; within a few steps of the front door, it had been sodden with melted snow, and had easily tripled its weight with the accumulation of snow and ice.

At least coming out to Morray's residence, they had been mainly moving east, with the storm, no matter how hard it bit and snarled, at their backs. But now they were going into the wind, and it struck them directly in the face, as though it was attempting to stun Pirojil, then peel his cloak away, and freeze him where he stood.

The climb up the hill to the castle was the worst of it, but it didn't feel that way, for although the castle road was totally exposed to the wind, and snowdrifts twisted across it like giant buried snakes, Pirojil could turn his face away from the wind for several steps in a row, and let the cowl of his cloak catch the worst of it.

The best thing about it was the thought of what lay inside: warmth, currently a vague concept as the wind drove ice into every pore it could reach. Each step seemed to take longer, as though Pirojil was trapped in some sort evil spell that let him get ever closer to the shelter of the gate without quite reaching it.

He trudged on.

But, after an eternity of moving first the right foot, then the left, then pausing for a moment to draw a breath, an open door appeared ahead. At last he was running, like the other three, across the courtyard with legs so numb that he would have sworn but moments ago they were barely fit for walking, much less running, revelling. Then they were inside. In the frozen-but-warmer-than-outside mud-room, the four of them sagged down onto the benches, panting like dogs.

'Would you consider doing me a great favour, my lord?' Pirojil finally asked, when he was able to choke out the words between gasps.

'That would depend, I suppose, on the favour you ask of me,' Morray said, gasping almost as much as Pirojil.

He reached down for a moment, as though to unlace his over-boots, then sat back, bracing himself against the wall, looking like a man in his sixties, at least. The wind had sapped all the colour from his face, and left his moustache and beard and even his eyebrows encrusted with ice. He had pulled off his gloves and started to pick at the ice with his fingers, then covered his ears with his hands, and for a moment Pirojil thought that Morray was trying to say that he wouldn't listen, but then realized that the Baron was just trying to warm his frozen ears.

'Well, out with it, man.'

'If there's any further word from your residence – or if anybody suggests that you go outside in this storm – would you be so kind as to say something to the effect of "please deal with it, and I'll come out and see when you've finished with it after the storm has passed"?'

Morray nodded, and almost smiled. 'There's some wisdom in that,' he said, as he finally bent forward to unlace his overboots. His numb fingers gave him trouble with the knots. 'There's some wisdom in that, indeed.'

Lady Mondegreen beckoned Kethol over to where she was standing next to Langahan and Folson, and some other noble that Kethol didn't recognize.

He should have taken another route across the Great Hall, probably. The Great Hall was bisected down the middle by the long table, which had been extended by several smaller tables brought down from the attic.

'Kethol, I hear you had quite an adventure this morning,' she said.

'Well, my lady, I've had better times, and that's a fact.'

The tip of his right ear was still numb – it would be interesting to see if it healed itself, or rotted off – but his full complement of fingers and toes were working, although it was still very painful to walk.

At Morray's insistence, Father Riley, the Astalon priest, had taken a look at the three of them and finally pronounced them fit – but only after insisting that they all spend at least a few minutes with their bare feet in an oaken tub filled with aromatic water that the priest kept hot by repeatedly inserting a red-hot iron poker from the brazier, muttering something as he sprinkled more herbs from a leather pouch.

Whether it was whatever secret preparations that the priest

had added to the water, or just the blessedly hot water itself, colour, which was good, and feeling, a mixed blessing, had quickly returned to Kethol's feet, which were now encased in an absurd-looking pair of rabbit-fur slippers that had been supplied by the housecarl while his boots dried.

The priest was doing a brisk business in cold-related injuries, although Kethol hadn't been able to stop himself from laughing at the way that Father Riley had had to be summoned to the tower when one fool of a servitor had taken another's dare to try to lick the ice off a stone on the east wall, and had got his tongue stuck in place.

The noble whose name Kethol didn't know gave a derisive sniff. 'The lot of you,' he said, 'deserve far worse than you seem to have got. Why would anybody go outside in this if he didn't have to?'

He was a short, slim man, with a carefully trimmed fringe of black beard that suggested that he didn't have much of a chin and had had to carve it out of hair, and a seemingly permanent sneer that suggested it would be unwise to comment upon that – not that Kethol would have.

Lady Mondegreen arched an eyebrow. 'Sergeant Kethol, have you met Baron Edwin of Viztria?'

Once again, Kethol didn't correct her on the nonexistent promotion; he just shook his head. 'No, I haven't had the honour,' he said.

'You were one of the freebooters who went out in the storm after Baron Morray, I take it?' Edwin Viztria said, shaking his head. 'Well, there's a fool born every minute, I've always said to my manservant – the laziest son of a turnip in all of Triagia – and now I can add, truthfully, that there are three other fools born the next minute, who will follow that fool out into a storm that can freeze the bollocks off a bastard!'

Langahan shook his head and gestured toward Lady Monde-green. 'Please.'

'Ah, I'm sorry.' Viztria quickly ducked his head toward the lady 'Begging your pardon, my lady, for my . . . colourful turn of phrase.'

She laughed. She had a nice laugh, one that reminded Kethol of distant bells. 'Oh, I've always found your . . . ah . . . colourful turns of phrase quite charming, Edwin,' she said. 'And I do hope you'll not restrain yourself on my account.'

Baron Viztria turned back toward Kethol. 'I assume that the three of you have had a few words among yourselves about that Morray's folly,' he said, his permanent scowl intensifying for a moment.

'We're not the sort of men to criticize our betters, my lord.'

'Hah! Not while there's noble ears around, I'll warrant, but I don't doubt for a misbegotten moment that you speak more frankly when you're by yourselves, even though you'd be even more of a fool to admit it in polite company than you proved yourself by following Morray out into that,' he said, gesturing toward the outside. He shoved his hands into the pockets of the knee-length jacket, and glared at Kethol, as though daring him to disagree.

Kethol didn't say anything.

'You look as if you have something to say, man, so out with it,' Langahan said.

Folson nodded. 'I'm curious myself – you don't seem to be joining in the general condemnation of Ernest Morray's folly of this morning, and I'm curious as to why. Besides not wanting to criticize a nobleman.'

Well, there was a time for speaking your mind, even in front of nobility, and if this wasn't it, Kethol didn't know what could be.

'Well,' he said, 'the Baron was alerted early this morning that a roof had caved in on one of the outbuildings at his residence –'

'The stables?' Folson nodded. 'I told him, the last time I guested there, that I thought they needed a new roof. Not that anybody ever listens to me.'

'No, my lord, it was the servants' quarters. He felt obliged to go out and see the situation for himself, despite the discomfort of travelling in the –'

'Discomfort?' Viztria raised an eyebrow. 'That seems to me to be a rather weak word for having pounded your way through a blizzard.'

Kethol shrugged. 'It was uncomfortable, and if complaining about it would have warmed me even a little, I promise that I would have cursed my way up Black Swan Road and then sworn my way back down. But my point was that Baron Morray wasn't just haring off out into the cold for no reason. He felt, he said, that he must see to his servants.' It felt strange to be defending Morray.

'And were they well?' Lady Mondegreen asked.

'Everybody was fine, as far as I can tell.' Kethol nodded. 'Some were a bit shaken, I think –'

'Having a roof fall in on me would probably disturb me more than a trifle,' Viztria put in, 'and I'm renowned for my unflappability.'

Langahan snorted derisively. Viztria threw him a black look. Kethol wondered if that was just to convince the locals the two court barons were there to keep an eye on each other or if they honestly disliked each other. Either way, it didn't look like the Viceroy had sent them along to spy on the LaMutian barons. Or did it? Kethol had long been trying to learn to think like Pirojil, even though the effort usually only made his head hurt. His head was starting to hurt.

'Go on, please, Kethol,' Lady Mondegreen said.

'Well, there was probably some frostbite, but when we left the Baron's residence, the servants were well settled in his hall, probably until after the thaw. In fact, I think that it might even be a little warmer in the Baron's hall than it is here.'

'Yes, this LaMutian thaw we keep hearing about but never seem to see,' Viztria said, shivering theatrically. 'I'd rather be back in Krondor, myself, where a man can take a leak in a garderobe without having to worry about a urine icicle spearing some poor sod trying to clean out the dung heap below – again begging your pardon, my lady.'

'Carla, please,' she said. 'I think that I may have asked you as many as a dozen times, just today, to call me by my first name, Edward.'

'Edwin.'

'Well, if you're not going to use my given name, you can hardly expect me to correctly remember yours.' Her smile was playful.

Folson was eyeing Kethol closely. 'So, Baron Morray braves the storm just to be sure that his servants weren't injured? Interesting.'

'Interesting, yes, but what does it tell you?' Viztria said, his sneer still firmly in place. 'If you asked Luke Verheyen, I'll bet my six silver reals to your one bent copper he'd tell you that the only reason that Baron Morray went out into the storm was so that all assembled would hear that he was the sort of man who would go out into the storm to see to the welfare of his servants.'

Langahan cocked his bald head over to one side. 'You believe it's all just an act?' he said, his voice almost dripping with scorn.

Viztria snorted. 'I don't believe one thing or the other, and I'll not be drawn into that feud, as I've enough problems of my own without looking for new ones. But I don't take a story told by a hireling as being graven in stone, either.' He looked over at Kethol. 'You're still here?' he asked. 'Shouldn't you be standing guard, or running some poor sod through, or some other soldierly thing?'

'Please excuse me, my lords and lady.' Kethol bowed, and walked away.

Pirojil made his way carefully down the ice-slickened stone stairs, sometimes squatting to set his lantern down on the step below so that he could use both hands and feet to negotiate a particularly slippery spot. Going back up would be easier, he hoped.

The flickering light from the lantern he carried showed that the barred cells were empty. Pirojil didn't have the slightest idea what the cells' normal state was, or why a noble would ever throw somebody into a dungeon rather than just have that somebody's throat cut. Still, there was something that seemed more than passing strange about the prison and the strongroom sharing the same part of the castle.

The oil lamps hung from the naked beams were all lit, and their smoke hovered in a cloudy haze near the ceiling as Pirojil made his way past racks of barrels, towards the rear of the dungeon. He started at a scurrying sound, but decided that it was just a rat, and if the Swordmaster or Tom Garnett wanted the rats here killed, they could order somebody else to do it.

The only thing Pirojil planned on killing today was a bottle of wine he would retrieve from a bin on his way up when Kethol came down to relieve him, as he was now relieving Durine down in the dungeon. Not one of the good bottles on the racks that stretched from one wall to the other – those were likely fully accounted for – and he had no intention of finding himself caught carrying a rare bottle of some fine red that the Earl would want on his table when he returned from Yabon, but he didn't think that anybody would object to him hooking himself a bottle of ordinary plonk from one of the bins, and drinking himself to sleep with it.

He made a mental note to put on his thickest socks – perhaps two pairs of them – and then his boots, before he drank himself asleep. His boots would take at least a full day to dry properly, and if he didn't make sure that they stretched as they dried, they would shrink, and it was a certainty that a pair of aching feet were far cheaper than a new pair of boots would have been.

He made his way to the far end of the dark basement, where

the door to the room outside the strongroom was closed, and when he pounded on it, it took a few moments before the barred view port slid quickly open, although no face appeared in it.

'Greetings, Durine,' he said. 'It's just me.'

Durine's broad face appeared in the window, and he gave a quick glance before the door swung open and Pirojil was admitted inside.

Morray didn't seem to notice them; he was bent over some papers on his desk on the far side of the room, right next to the iron door that led to the strongroom proper. An intricately-embossed brass oil lantern flickered on the lefthand side of the desk, too close, in Pirojil's opinion, to the stacked leatherbound books, and a handful of quills stood in a very plain wooden box next to the mottled green inkjar on the right. Near Morray's right hand rested a steaming mug of what smelled like tea, rather than the ubiquitous coffee.

The hearth in the wall next to the Baron had a good fire built up in it. Durine stooped to throw another log on, then poked at it with the poker.

'Pirojil is here, my lord,' he said, when Morray didn't look up.

'Who? Oh – fine.' Morray looked up with a frown. 'Well, be off with you, then.' His voice dropped to a barely audible mutter. 'As though some assassin is going to sneak down the chimney and knife me while I'm working on the books.' Then he bent back over his work.

Pirojil handed his lantern to Durine. 'Watch out for the stairs.'

Durine nodded, and left; Pirojil bolted the door behind him. Pirojil pulled on the thick leather glove by the hearth to pour himself a mug of hot tea from the cast-iron teapot that lay on the stones in front of it.

The Baron ignored him as his eyes glanced from one large, leatherbound book that he seemed to be reading out of, to the long piece of carefully ruled parchment on which he was completing a column of figures, and then back again. Look, think, write, again and again – it seemed to be awfully boring work, but at least it wasn't Pirojil's work.

Exactly what was involved in 'working on the books', Pirojil didn't know. The other part of taxes seemed simple enough to him – the barons collected taxes, sent some to the Earl, who kept some and conveyed the rest to the Duke, who probably did the same thing and passed along a bit to King Rodric or Prince Erland.

The Baron glanced up in irritation. 'Well, is there some reason that you're just standing there?' He gestured toward the large chair next to the hearth. 'If you'll just sit down, I won't keep seeing you out of the corner of my eye, and you won't distract me. I'd like to finish this before dinner, so that I can spend at least a little time dispelling some of Verheyen's lies about me.' His tone was less irritated than his words suggested. 'Just sit, and drink your tea, and I'll be done shortly.'

There wasn't anything else to do, so Pirojil just sat and drank his tea: it might be an unusual situation to be sitting drinking tea while standing guard, but it wasn't bad. He probably should make an effort to learn about all this bookkeeping stuff, even if his needs would never be as complicated as an earldom's Wartime Bursar's. Pirojil could add a column of figures, albeit slowly and with some errors – though if he tried enough times, it finally added up – but there had to be more to it than that, if he wanted to do it right. If the three of them ever did save up enough to buy that tavern, it would be Pirojil who would be counted upon to handle the money, after all.

It was something they talked about, from time to time. Pirojil would run the business side of the tavern. He had negotiated with military paymasters from Salador to Crydee; he should be able to out-negotiate winemakers and brewmasters, shepherds and cattle ranchers, and never mind getting the whores upstairs – and they would want to be sure to have whores upstairs; it was always good to be able to sell one thing that never ran out.

There would, undoubtedly, be some new tricks to learn, but Pirojil could manage that part of it.

Durine could keep the peace, as long as he had a little bit of help when needed. Anybody drunk enough to want to face off against the big man would be more than drunk enough not to notice him or Kethol coming up behind him with a truncheon. It would probably be best to have Durine fight the first few by himself, by way of letting him establish a reputation, and letting it be known that the Three Swords Tavern – that did have a nice ring to it, didn't it? – was the sort of place a man could have a few beers, a hot meal and a quick poke, without being bothered, as long as he behaved himself.

It could happen.

They might even find themselves some women – regular women, not just an occasional whore. Particularly after the war. War had a way of shaking things up, and it might be that he could find a nice-enough looking, biddable-enough woman, who would decide that exchanging regular meals and a safe place to sleep was worth having to put up with him mounting her in the night or even the daytime – she could always close her eyes – or even of having to look at his ugly face every morning. He might even make a few concessions to her, like, say, having a regular bath.

That would be a good end, indeed, for the likes of the three of them, and it was a nice dream, and it gave them something to plan and save for.

Of course, they'd likely all be dead long before that dream came true.

He found himself looking at the heavy iron door to the strong-room beyond. There was, undoubtedly, more than enough gold behind that door to buy a hundred taverns, although probably not enough to buy off those who would be sent after them, if they somehow or other managed to get out of the city with that gold.

It would be worth considering, though.

He noticed that Morray was looking at him, smiling strangely.

'You seem to be eyeing the door with some interest,' the Baron said.

Pirojil kept his expression blank. 'Just staring off and thinking, my lord. No offence was intended.'

Morray nodded. 'Well, go ahead – just open the door, and take what you want, if you can.'

His tone of voice wasn't threatening, and he made no move towards either the swordbelt hung on the back of his chair or toward any other weapon, at least as far as Pirojil could see.

Pirojil shook his head. 'I've no intention of robbing the Earl,' he said. 'Bad for my business, and much worse for my health.'

Morray chuckled. 'Don't worry about your business, or your health – there's more than enough in there for a legion of you to retire on, I assure you. Tell you what, if you can open the door, right here and now, you will be allowed to leave, healthy and alive, with all the gold that you can carry. You have my word on that. Go ahead; try to open the door.' His expression grew stern. 'I'm not much used to giving a command twice, man, and I'd like not to ever have to do so a third time.'

Pirojil didn't know what the Baron's game was, but it was probably just as well to go along with it. He set down his teacup and walked across the soft carpet to the closed iron door.

It was a solid-looking piece of metal, rimmed along the edge with a riveted band of blued iron, thick as a finger. There was no lock on it that Pirojil could see; just a plain metal handle. He set his hand on it, but hesitated, until Morray's nod and gesture made it clear that the Baron really did intend him to open it.

He pushed down, at first gently, but then harder.

It didn't budge.

He set his whole weight on it, but the handle might as well have been welded in place. He pushed harder, and thought that the handle itself gave, just a trifle, perhaps, but it didn't even begin to turn.

Perhaps there was some trick with the rivets? They looked solid, and as Pirojil ran his fingers up and down them, they all felt solid enough to the touch.

What was he missing?

'It was an honest offer,' Morray said, 'but I had no doubt that you'd be unable to open the door.' Morray rose to his feet and tucked the thick leatherbound book under his arm, then with his free hand gestured Pirojil to move out of the way.

'Get the light, would you?' he asked.

Pirojil lifted the lamp from the desk, as Morray set his hand on the door handle, closed his eyes for a moment, and gently pressed down on it, not touching the heads of the rivets, or anything else.

Morray muttered something, barely vocalizing the words.

The handle turned, silently and easily. Morray muttered something more under his breath as he swung the heavy door open on its hidden hinges.

He accepted the lantern from Pirojil, and stepped inside. Pirojil didn't follow him in, but he could see that the small room beyond was filled with racks sagging beneath the weight of hundreds of muslin sacks. Morray ignored these and stepped to a bookcase, crowded with leatherbound volumes of various sizes, and replaced the one he held there.

He smiled at the way Pirojil was eyeing the sacks. 'Pick one of the sacks,' Morray said. 'Let's see what's in it, shall we?'

'But –'

'Please.'

'If you insist, my lord.' Pirojil shrugged. 'I'll choose the right-hand rack, second shelf from the bottom, the sack behind the second one from the right.'

'Very well.' Morray nodded. He retrieved the sack that Pirojil had indicated, untied the slipknot that held the sack closed, and spread it open.

Buttery gold coins gleamed in the lantern light; Morray dipped his hand in, and let them run through his fingers and back into the bag, before closing it and putting it back in its place.

'I don't often show anybody the inside of the strongroom, but when I do, I always make a point to show them some of the gold.' He grinned. 'I would not want anybody to get the idea that it had become filled with bags of rocks under my stewardship of the Earl's Purse, eh?' He closed the door, and turned the handle. 'Would you care to try it again?' he asked.

'Only if you insist.'

There was obviously some trick to opening the door, and Pirojil didn't really want to know what that trick was – or, at least, he didn't want anybody to know that he knew what the trick was.

If there turned out to be some gold missing, ignorance was a good defence.

'Oh, there's no harm,' Morray said. 'There's a spell on the lock – it will only turn for those who know the words to unlock the spell, and you can imagine that those words are not widely distributed, and there's some magical ... penalty involved if someone were to come close to but not quite saying the right words.'

Pirojil shuddered. He could imagine what those magical penalties might be, and the truth was probably much worse than he was imagining. One thing the years had taught him: if it involves magic, it was better to be far away than near by.

Besides, if Pirojil were to try to break into the vault, he probably wouldn't go through the front door. He considered, then discarded, half a dozen foolish plans involving tunnels, holes-in-the-wall, odd mining devices he had once seen outside Dorgin, and the possibility of the gods granting him a wish out of boredom; then decided to return to the bleak reality he knew: it was not terribly comfortable, but it was familiar.

Morray frowned down at the ink on his fingers.

'Well, now that that's done, I'd best wash these clerk-stains from my hands, change into something more festive, and get back up to the Great Hall. The first official meeting of the Baronial Council is tonight, but things have already well started, I'd guess.' He raised an eyebrow. 'Are you coming along, or would you prefer to stay here and try the door some more?' He smiled. 'If you listened very closely, you might even have heard the lock's key spell almost well enough.'

Almost. Pirojil shuddered at the implications of that 'almost'.

'I'm at your service, of course, my lord.'

The fight was just starting when Kethol walked into the barracks, shivering and shaking his cloak, intending to get some much-needed sleep.

Six or seven Verheyen men had squared off against Morray's men over by the door to the stables, and pushing and shoving had already turned to blows and kicks, although no weapons were drawn, as far as Kethol could see. At least he assumed the men were all Verheyen and Morray's men; the barracks had only two small hearths, one at each end of the room, so most of the soldiers were bundled up in their cloaks; for all Kethol knew, a couple of rockheads from another baron's company might have joined in just for the hell of it. Once again he found himself dwelling on the idiocy of fighting when no one was paying you to do so.

It looked more like a tavern fight than real combat, so far, which was just as well. If someone drew a blade it could turn ugly faster than a mountebank could part a farm boy from his coppers on market day.

One thickset Mut went down, and another one leapt on him, thick fists pummelling his chest more than his face, and then another joined in. A sergeant in a Verheyen tabard tried to hold one of his comrades back, but that just gave one of the Morrays a chance to whack him over the back of the head. The sergeant instantly forgot his role as peacemaker, turned and delivered a thunderous wallop that sent the Morray man sliding backwards across the stone floor. He was impressed; the sergeant wasn't all that big, but he'd served up a blow that Kethol would have been proud to call his own.

Soldiers from other baronies, quite a few of those from both Morray and Verheyen, were staying out of the way, and all of the mercenaries were either lying on their bunks or sitting at the tables, watching with interest but not even raising a voice, much less a hand. It wasn't their fight, any more than it was Kethol's.

The only exception was the mad dwarf Mackin. Mackin was counted mad for three reasons, his first being his preference to fight for pay, which made him rare among his kind, and the second being his proclivity for bedding human women, which marked him as unique among his kind, and last his tendency to speak to the thin air, as if someone was standing there holding a conversation with him, which hardly made him unusual among mercenaries in Kethol's judgment. The crazed dwarf leapt from his bunk and landed on his improbably large bare feet on the hard stone floor, cheering at each punch and kick as though he was watching some sort of sporting match.

Kethol was, of course, moving backwards out of the door. It hardly looked a good time to try to join the dice players in the corner, who had barely paused in their game. By now the fight – and he had seen enough of them to count himself an expert – was only moments away from becoming a full-on brawl, complete with broken heads, swollen jaws and missing teeth. He had almost made good his exit when he backed into the Swordmaster, who had just come in from the outside, shaking his cloak to clear the snow off it.

Steven Argent unceremoniously shoved him aside and stalked into the barracks.

'Stop!' he shouted, punctuating the word by snatching up a bottle and smashing it on the floor.

There must have been something to this voice of command thing, Kethol judged, because to his surprise, the fighting stopped immediately. The men who had moments ago been beating each other slowly began to pull themselves apart and rise to their feet.

Steven Argent stood in the middle of the barracks for a long minute, looking from one face to another.

There was no sound at all, save for the wind howling outside.

'You – and you, and you, you and you,' he said, pointing out men who had been fighting, and then at two of the sergeants who had stood by and watched. 'I've got a little job for you. We need another cask of beer hauled up from the Broken Tooth – good dwarvish beer, if you please – and I'm sending the lot of you out in the storm to get it.'

He stood silently, his hands still on his hips, a look of utter contempt written across his face; then he turned and swept out of the room.

Kethol shrugged, and spread his cloak over his bed. He unbuckled his sword and hung it on the hook nearby and lay down to get some sleep which, as usual, quickly overtook him.

The last things he heard before the warm darkness closed about him were the comfortable, familiar rattling of dice and the clinking of coins on stone.

Durine dumped another armload of wood into the bin next to the hearth, and brushed himself off before throwing another log on the fire. The servants weren't quite ignoring this particular hearth, but they seemed to be giving higher priority to the one across the Great Hall, and it was easier to just go out into the cold and retrieve some wood from the woodpile than to annoy some servant about it.

That was the thing about cold – as long as there was warmth nearby, a few moments of it really weren't all that bad.

The log hissed quietly at him, and then slowly began to burn around the edges.

Close to a score of the nobles had gathered themselves at the larger hearth at the far end of the Great Hall, with a few hangers-on. Pirojil was at Morray's elbow, standing just outside the small circle of barons and noble ladies who were engaged in some intense conversation.

The soldiers – mostly captains, except for a few odds and ends like himself – had understandably gravitated to the opposite side of the hall, so that the table down the middle of the hall acted as a social buffer. Durine didn't know if gathering in the Great Hall was standard practice for visiting captains or just some sort of special dispensation given out under the circumstances. Either way, the captains appeared at ease, and none of the nobles spared them a glance.

Visiting captains were usually housed in one of the barracks buildings, at the far side of the inner bailey, and if Durine had been in their boots he would have found a quiet corner there and kept out of the way of his betters in the keep. But that was probably one of the many reasons that he wasn't an officer.

Besides, over in the barracks, there were certainly games of dice and bones, and drinking, and doubtless other things going on that were probably considered to be prejudicial to good order and discipline. It was a wise captain who neither tolerated too much of such distractions, nor made too much of an effort to quash them. Too much order and discipline was bad for order and discipline, after all. You needed a balance to maintain morale, and with the storm locking up a load of soldiers, things were going to be getting more tense each day without additional irritations.

It had been bad enough in LaMut before, in that dimly-remembered time, just a few days ago, when winter was just making things cold and muddy, instead of clawing at everything like some ravening beast.

Tom Garnett was just finishing the story about the Night of the Bugs. Pirojil hadn't paid enough attention to know if the Captain had got the details right, and probably wouldn't have, even if he had listened closely since he and the other two had been too busy with their little piece of the battle to pay much attention to what others were doing.

Another captain – maybe one of Verheyen's – plopped himself down in a well-upholstered chair and leaned back, stretching his legs out. 'The one good thing I can think of about all this,' he said, closing his eyes and folding his hands over his flat stomach, 'is that we don't have to worry, at least for the moment, about a Tsurani attack.'

'Which,' Tom Garnett said, 'would make this a perfect time for such an attack.'

'Time?' The captain let his hands drop to his sides, and sat up, visibly irritated. 'Certainly. Opportunity?' He shrugged. 'I think not. If there are any out there stupid enough to venture out in the storm, the blizzard would do our work for us. If we haven't driven every one of the bastards out of LaMut –'

'Which we haven't, or my men killed a whole group of non-existent Tsurani the other day,' Tom Garnett said.

The Captain nodded, conceding the point with good grace. 'Yes, and you did yourself proud, from what I hear, but that was less than a company in strength, wasn't it?'

Garnett nodded. 'True enough.'

'And if there've been sightings of more anywhere near LaMut, I surely hope they'd have been reported to me. Far as I can tell, the nearest Tsurani are somewhere east of the Free Cities borders, and not much east at that. Few if any left in Yabon Province, I'm glad to say.'

'Yes,' Tom Garnett said with a quick nod. 'I'm just as happy that it wasn't more. Wish it had been less. But they were real enough, I can tell you that.'

'Well, yes.' The Captain sipped at his coffee. 'But, apart from a few stragglers trying for their own lines, I think it's over – for now. Later? Elsewhere? I doubt it – I've heard rumours about things heating up around Crydee, and even rumours about the Tsurani departing back to wherever they came from.' His mouth twitched. 'Which, even if it's true, I'd still want to know if and how they can come back, and where.'

'Yes, there are a lots of rumours,' another captain said, nodding. He was a man of around fifty, with a bristle of moustache under his sharp nose, and a way of biting off the end of each word. He sipped at his wine as he stared at the fire, and huddled more deeply into his jacket. 'I don't much care for the ones I hear regarding what's going on in Krondor.'

Tom Garnett glanced over at the nobles across the room, then looked back at the Captain, frowning. 'And if spreading these rumours more widely is liable to serve us all well, then let's all get to it, and do it thoroughly, and not waste any more of this lovely day, Captain Karris, shall we?'

Karris bristled, but settled himself back down, and raised a spread hand in surrender and apology. 'A good point, Tom, a good point indeed – and it's one I flatter myself I would have made if another had been fool enough to speak as I just did. A man can't help wondering, no, but it's another matter entirely to fail to keep your tongue in check, eh?'

Garnett nodded. 'I've always thought so.' His mouth twitched. 'You can't fight the whole war yourself; I always reckoned watching out for my own little piece of it was more than enough for me and my company, and that I'm best off leaving the bigger pieces to the men with the titles and responsibilities.'

'Well, then you do better than I,' another captain said. 'I can't help thinking about a lot of things. Worrisome time; I don't know about the rest of you lads, but I haven't slept through the night in longer than I care to think about.'

'Sleep through the night?' Karris laughed bitterly. 'That's an ancient myth, or so it feels. I've spent so long worrying about what's over the next hill that my mind tends to spin out of control when I'm in four walls. I feel like a horse that can't help galloping despite his lead being tied to a post; all I'm doing is going in circles.'

He grunted as he pushed himself to his feet. 'And since I've nothing better to do right now, I think I'll make sure that my little boys and your little boys are playing nicely. I don't need the Swordmaster to break things up again just because the lot of them feel as head-tied as I do. Most of them don't have the sense the gods gave turnips, so they're unlikely to listen to gentle words of wisdom like yours. They might need sterner words, though. Like, say, "take an extra watch"?' He brightened. 'Come to think of it, standing just a single extra watch on the walls, right now, would do just fine for some serious punishment, wouldn't it?'

Outside, the wind howled, as though in agreement with Karris.

Tom Garnett chuckled. 'That it would.'

He watched Karris stalk away towards the mud-room, then got up from his chair to fumble a small briar pipe out of a pocket. He patted at his trouser pockets for a moment, and was reaching for the leather bag that lay on the floor next to him when another captain tossed him a small pouch.

'I thank you, Willem,' he said. He filled the pipe with tabac, lit it with a long taper, and puffed furiously on it until he was satisfied with the smoke. 'Might as well enjoy what you can, while you can, eh?' He gestured toward the mud-room with the pipe's stem. 'That's what I missed out there, the most. I got the feeling that the Tsurani could smell the smoke for miles and miles, and I never did see any need to let them know where we were when I didn't have to.' He puffed away strongly. 'Missed my pipe, I did.'

Another of the captains chuckled. 'I missed . . . softer things than a good pipe,' he said. 'And I suspect I will, again, come spring. I'm just glad to be out of the storm – and off the line for the moment.'

At that, a sudden gust of wind came down the chimney, sending a rush of sparks and ashes flying from the hearth. The Captain slapped at where one bit of burning ash was threatening to set his trousers on fire.

'Though spring seems far away. You think that we'll be moved west, to Crydee? Or north? Or kept here, lest the Tsurani move towards Krondor?'

Tom Garnett puffed at his pipe. 'Probably all of that, and more. That's what our betters are working out in Yabon right now. But for here and now, as I was saying, if there are any Tsurani stragglers out there, they're too busy freezing to worry about attacking anything. I expect we'll find a few corpses scattered about come spring.'

The other captain nodded. 'Father Winter, as I'm told that they say on the steppes of Thunderhell, can be a powerful ally – and we can use all the allies we can get.' He looked over at Durine with distaste. 'Even if we have to pay some of them for the privilege of their alliance.' He had been silent until Karris had left, and had watched him walk away with barely-concealed hostility.

Tom Garnett looked up at Durine, who just stared blankly back. 'Durine,' he said, 'have you had the pleasure of meeting Captain Ben Kelly of Barony Folson?'

'No.' Durine shook his head. 'No, I haven't.'

Kelly nodded coldly. 'No, we haven't been introduced, and I've not sought out an introduction, either. I've little use for freebooters, myself, by and large, but I suppose we must make allowances in these times.'

Durine didn't say anything, and Kelly apparently took that as a sign of weakness, rather than restraint. 'Nothing to say, eh? You've a fair collection of scars – but your tongue seems to work, and –'

'Please, Captain,' Tom Garnett said. 'If you've got some grievance against the man, bring it up with me, not with him – he's in my company, and he's my responsibility.'

'Excuse me, Captain,' Durine shook his head. 'No, sir – meaning no disrespect. At the moment, I'm not under your orders ... Captain.'

Kethol would probably have gone along just for the sake of getting along, and Pirojil would have found some way of changing the subject or of giving the Captain the same message in some indirect way, but that wasn't Durine's nature.

'Right now, I'm not in any company,' he said. 'The three of us have been given a task, on orders of the Earl, and we're not under the command of anybody save the Swordmaster,' he said slowly and carefully. He drew himself up parade-ground straight, and stared straight ahead, not meeting Tom Garnett's eyes. 'Meaning no disrespect to your rank or to your person, Captain.'

Kelly didn't like that. 'Which is why you feel so free to join a gathering of officers, eh? And what's all this about a special task? I've been hearing rumours –'

'I thought we'd agreed not to involve ourselves in rumour-mongering,' Tom Garnett said quietly.

'Well, it's one thing not to talk about matters at court and nobody here knows the truth. But it's another matter when we've got a man right here – and a freebooter, at that – who claims some sort of special status. What is that all about?'

Durine didn't answer, and after a moment Tom Garnett leaned

forward. 'There was some concern about the safety of Baron Morray, and the Earl thought it best that he should have his own bodyguard, for the time being. It's not as though he's the only baron to be brought into council with extra security, and I don't think –'

'Concern?' Kelly's brow furrowed. 'You think that Tsurani attack in Mondegreen was aimed at Baron Morray personally?'

'No, not really.' Tom Garnett shook his head. 'It wouldn't make much sense. I can't see how any Tsurani would know that Baron Morray would be with that patrol.' He got a distant look for a moment. 'We don't know how they think, or if they understand what a calamitous turn it would be for us if we lost the Military Bursar for the army. Or how they'd know, if they did.' Realizing he was digressing, he said, 'But even if they did understand, for one thing, his going along on this was a last-moment decision by the Earl, just before he left for Yabon. And for another, it didn't look that way to me. My guess is that if Morray was the target, they'd have killed him first, rather than spring the ambush as early as they did. I trusted Durine and his two friends to see to the Baron while I chased off the Tsurani. As they did, as they certainly did,' he said. He looked up at Durine. 'Did it seem to you that they were specifically hunting the Baron?'

Durine shook his head slowly. 'No, although the bastards did make for him first – but I reckoned that was just because they assumed that he was an officer, rather than anything . . . personal. To be honest, Captain, I didn't spend a lot of time thinking about it, not then.'

Or later, for that matter – it had seemed to him to be an ordinary, even clumsy, sort of ambush. But trying to work out the purpose of an attack during a war always seemed to Durine to be like trying to work out which part of the body was getting wet when you plunged into a river.

Besides, how could the Tsurani have come by the information? Who would they ask?

The Tsurani captain, or Force Leader, or whatever the bastards called him – Durine just thought of him as the Tsurani captain – had been killed during the battle. Durine was sure that the captured Tsurani had been thoroughly questioned, and even more sure that they hadn't been told anything. From what they had learned about the Tsurani since the invasion began, the common soldiers didn't ask questions and their officers didn't volunteer information. Besides, you could slowly feed most of them into a fire feet first and they'd just keep staring at you with hatred in their eyes until they died, without saying a word. Say what you would about the Tsurani, but they were tough bastards, Durine grudgingly was forced to admit. And those slaves of theirs had even less useful things to say, regardless of how docile or co-operative they were.

Being told nothing beyond the immediate job at hand was a familiar feeling for Durine, until fairly lately, come to think of it. Not that he minded, not really; Durine liked to keep things simple. He wasn't a strategist, and logistics and such just made his head spin. He preferred to leave such things to others, and do the one thing that he was good at: killing people.

'But no,' he said at last, shaking his head, 'it didn't seem that way.'

Kelly wasn't satisfied. 'Then why all these rumours? And why the extra guards for Baron Morray?'

Tom Garnett dismissed it with a wave of his hand. 'I'm sure it's nothing to be concerned about, not really. But with the Earl gone to Yabon, and the Hereditary Bursar ill, I can think of a few thousand small, golden reasons why it's best to take extra precautions with the health of the Military Bursar, eh?' He gestured toward the mud-room. 'LaMut is already filled with baronial soldiers who don't, at the moment, have the Tsurani around to remind them that we're all on the same side, and forget about rivalries between their liege lords. And when you add the mercenaries, just about the worst thing I can think could happen would be the inability of the Earl of LaMut to actually pay his debts, even temporarily.' He shook his head. 'Damn lousy day when you'd want an attack by the Bugs and Tsurani to distract the men of Morray and Verheyen from the fact that one group of them are likely to be soldiers of the Earl within a few years, living the high life in LaMut, while others are going to go back to their baronies, sooner rather than later.'

'The Earl?' The words were out of Durine's mouth before he had a chance to stop them.

Tom Garnett nodded. 'I don't think it's any secret that Earl Vandros is likely to marry Felina and end up as the Duke, do you? Any of you?' He grinned as he looked from face to face, from nod to nod. 'And no matter how energetic their wedding night might be, I doubt that they'd be able to produce an heir quickly enough.' He shook his head. 'If you ask me, the next Earl of LaMut is likely in this castle right now – probably in conversation just across the room – and I'd not care to wager who it might be, although if I had to guess, I'd guess either Morray or Verheyen.'

Kelly shook his head. 'I would have guessed that Mondegreen was the obvious choice myself, particularly as he's childless – he could hold the office until Vandros has sons – although he wouldn't be my favourite candidate.'

Most of the other captains frowned at that, but Tom Garnett just smiled. 'You'd prefer, say, Baron Erik Folson as the Earl, I take it?'

Kelly spread his hands. 'Well, of course I would, given my own position, but I can honestly swear that there would be far worse choices.' He stared at the fire and sipped at his coffee. 'But, alas, I think it unlikely, given that the Baron has two adult sons – and both battle-proven, I'm proud to say, having trained them myself. Either of them would do as Baron, or, eventually, as Earl.'

'And you think that would disqualify Baron Folson?' Tom Garnett's brow furrowed.

'I think it might. When he's Duke, Vandros might like to have a few years to produce a ducal heir, and then perhaps a younger brother to take the earldom, and might choose to put in Mondegreen as Earl, as sort of a place-holder. He couldn't do that so easily with my baron, more's the pity.'

'Well, that's not going to happen. Mondegreen will not be around long enough for that sort of thing.' Tom Garnett shook his head. 'Even if the marriage were to take place in Yabon today, Brucal to abdicate in Vandros's favour tomorrow, and some wizard caused Felina to pop out twin sons the day after, Mondegreen is out of it. Which is a pity – he's a good man, with a sharp mind, a steady hand and a very slow temper. He reminds me of the old Earl even more than Earl Vandros does; given they're cousins, that's not surprising.'

Kelly puffed on his pipe. 'Does anybody else think it more than passing strange that we've a couple of court barons here, as well? Could it be that, say, Viztria is being primed for the earldom?'

'Viztria?' Another captain snickered. 'Not unless the main weapon of state of the new Earl of LaMut were to be a thorough tongue-lashing.'

Several captains laughed, including Tom Garnett.

'Harsh language has started more than one war, though.' Tom stopped laughing and added, 'Probably not him, no, but it might make sense for the new Duke to sweep the slate clean, so to speak, and appoint an earl from outside Yabon. There's some precedent for that.'

Kelly shook his head. 'Precedent, perhaps, but I find myself not liking that idea at all, particularly considering the other court baron here. Langahan, I hear, is just a stalking-horse for the

Viceroy, and there's reason enough to believe that Guy du Bas-Tyra views the Western Realm of the Kingdom as just a reluctant cow to be milked, then left to forage for itself until it's ready to be milked dry again.'

'Yes, there is.' Tom Garnett nodded. 'Milked dry at best – if not bled utterly white to feed the East. But Guy du Bas-Tyra doesn't rule in Yabon –'

'Thankfully.'

'– and I know Earl Vandros. I served under him, when he was the senior captain in rank, though not in age, when his father was Earl. I can't see Duke Vandros appointing an earl from the East, no matter what the pressure from the Viceroy. As long as Duke Borric is in place in Crydee, Vandros would have a powerful ally in opposing any of Guy's plots.'

That made sense, actually. In some ways, Yabon was caught between the enmity of Borric conDoin, Duke of Crydee, and Guy du Bas-Tyra, and while there were dangers inherent in that, it also would make it more than a little difficult for the Viceroy, even if he were to succeed Prince Erland – even though he had already succeeded Prince Erland in fact if not in law, since being named Viceroy – to bring much pressure to bear on the Duke of Yabon, be it Brucal or Vandros. For while Guy had the King's ear as his favourite advisor, Borric could count on the support of most of the lords of the West, and some in the East who were not kindly disposed to Guy, or who viewed any usurpation of ducal prerogative as a threat to their own rule. The King might rule, but the Congress of Lords was a force even the most reckless king could not long ignore. No, Guy might plot, but in the end, Vandros would appoint his own successor in LaMut.

Tom Garnett puffed thoughtfully on his pipe. 'But an outsider to LaMut – a reliable, Western outsider, not some effete Eastern sock-puppet who can't speak without Guy du Bas-Tyra's hairy arm up his arse – as the new Earl? That might make sense, and

I can tell you that Vandros, earl or duke, will be more concerned about doing what makes sense than he will be in courting favour with anybody, including the Viceroy. Perhaps Alfren of Tyr-Sog's second son . . . ? You'll forgive me if I can't quite recall his name at the moment –'

'Elfred,' Kelly said. 'Met him once. I wasn't overly impressed.'

'– and choosing an outsider would have the advantage of the new Earl not coming into his estate with ancient enmities and rivalries, at least none here.'

Durine didn't think that Tom Garnett had forgotten about the accidents, but he had to admire how the Captain had neatly changed the subject, even though he had diverted the others into the sort of political gossip that they had disavowed, but which Durine had thought inevitable, given the situation. He wondered if the others were really distracted by talk of politics and succession. Durine wasn't. Whether they were real accidents or just failed assassination attempts against Morray was another matter, but the point was that these accidents had caused the Earl to have the three of them assigned to protect Morray. The politics were, perhaps, interesting to others, but the job was what mattered to Durine. But if the Captain wasn't going to mention it, neither was Durine.

Still, it was something to think about. The only thing that could be construed as a near-accident while they were on the road had been the Tsurani ambush, after all.

Unless, he thought, grinning to himself, that serving girl in Mondegreen had chosen a most unlikely way to drain the life from a man. Durine wouldn't have minded that sort of attempt being repeatedly made on his own life by a woman so nicely shaped, as long as he had some time to rest up between attempts.

'Yes, I can see the need for extra care.' Kelly eyed Durine unblinkingly. 'Particularly when there are men about who fight only for gold . . . and don't fight all that well, so I've been told.'

Durine waited for Tom Garnett to confront the other captain, but Garnett just smiled at Durine over the rim of his pipe, as though to say, *Well, man, you've said you're not under my command, so you're not my responsibility, are you?*

Which was, after all, entirely fair. Durine would have preferred generosity to fairness, but he would settle for fairness, and be glad of the bargain.

'I've fought well enough, Captain,' Durine said. 'Proof of that is that I'm still alive, isn't it?'

'Well, the only thing it proves is that you're lucky, as are we all.' Kelly pushed himself out of his chair. 'But, yes, that's some evidence. But I can't imagine that you'd mind providing a little more evidence, enough that might stack up to actual proof – with practice blades, say, on the training floor?'

The parade ground next to the barracks was the usual place for training, but it didn't make a lot of sense to Durine for them to go out into the storm, not for something like sword practice.

Tom Garnett chuckled. 'It seems to me that it's rather brisk outside to be making any use of the parade ground, and I'm not sure that practising with snow up to your waist would do much more than freeze your privates.'

'In which sense did you mean that?' another captain added, with a smile.

'Well, both, actually.'

'We don't need the parade ground,' Kelly said. He gave a quick gesture to one of the other captains, who nodded, rose and walked from the room. 'Let's see how he does, here and now,' he said, turning back to Tom Garnett. 'Shall we?'

Garnett thought it over for a moment, then looked up at Durine. The Captain nodded, the stem of his pipe still clamped between his teeth. 'I can't see why we can't, at that.'

Tom Garnett had taken the initiative in asking permission of the assembled nobles, and while Baron Viztria had made some disparaging comment about boys playing with swords, most of the others had either nodded in assent or, in the case of Lady Mondegreen, been openly enthusiastic at the idea, as had the Swordmaster, who had dispatched a boy to retrieve his own practice equipment.

Nobody quite said why, but Durine wondered if the enthusiasm was really for some distraction from matters of state and the monotonous discomfort of being trapped indoors in a large, draughty castle that seemed more cramped and crowded by the hour. Durine wasn't really sure about why someone might want relief from the former – as a soldier, he strongly preferred boredom to terror – but he was already beginning to feel as if the castle was, minute by minute, shrinking around him.

Durine slipped the white, oversized practice trousers over his own and let Kethol tie them off at his ankles. He donned the white canvas practice jacket and belted it tightly around his thick waist.

Captain Kelly had quickly donned his own practice gear and stood with his bulbous mesh helmet tucked under one arm, tapping his foot while another captain finished blackening his practice sword over a candle flame.

Durine eyed the unfamiliar wire mesh helmet with scepticism. He was more used to the usual wooden masks, the narrow slit in them preventing the wide, blunt point of the practice sword from taking out an eye, and the way the wire flexed made him nervous.

He poked at the mask with a thick finger. It gave a little, but not sharply; it would probably protect him. Blunted or not, a thrust from a practice sword could take out an eye almost as easily as a real weapon could; just as a vigorous enough blow to the skull could crack it.

The best thing to do, of course, would be to block a thrust to the head and not have to worry about protection, but it was best not to dwell too long on protecting one part of your body over another. Durine had seen more than his share of men lying on the ground with unmarked faces, too dead to be concerned about their untouched eyes any more than they were about the yellowy, blood-covered snakes of intestines dirtying themselves on the ground. Besides, one could no more expect to come out of practice unbruised than one could count on coming out of a fight uncut. Best to not worry overly much about this or that, and just get on with it.

He unbuckled his own sword, and handed the swordbelt to Kethol, accepting the practice blade in return.

He hefted the mock broadsword. It fit his hand nicely, the brass-wound grip cold against his skin. Other than the fact that it couldn't cut or stab, it looked and felt like a real sword, and was probably made from a blank by at least a journeyman sword maker. Nobles clearly got better practice weapons than ordinary soldiers did. The blade was every bit as wide as Durine's own thumb, and heavy enough to cut to bone, had the edges been properly sharpened, instead of being carefully rounded. Still, applied correctly, it could raise a healthy welt.

He slid his thumb down the smooth surface, feeling at the shallow dents and slight nicks, then gave a quick tug at the bell-shaped guard, which held solidly. The point was blunt: capped with a concave steel bulb that even Durine's fingers couldn't loosen; it had been thoroughly welded on. Durine hoped that Kelly had made sure that his own weapon was as safe. It balanced a little too much to the hilt, but was only off by a little.

Durine had faced a rapier before, but never in battle. His own preference was for the broadsword, longsword or, occasionally, the hand-and-a-half, which he considered an unusually versatile weapon. A rapier was a duelling weapon, and not all that effective against armour, but it was deadly from the point, which made it particularly nasty in the hands of someone who knew what he was doing. A broadsword's point would hang up on a small bit of armour where a rapier's point could seek out a small gap and rid you of an annoying opponent. But if you had to parry a two-handed sword, a rapier was about as useful as a kitchen broom.

Pirojil had been busy blackening the practice dagger that Durine was going to use. He swapped it for the sword, and blackened that, handed it over, then settled the mesh helmet over Durine's head.

Durine walked over to the open area, and kicked off his borrowed slippers. While they definitely slowed him down, he would have preferred wearing his boots, but they were still drying out. The soft leather soles slipping and sliding on the dark marble had little appeal.

The stone was bitterly cold beneath his feet.

'Dagger, too, eh?' Kelly more said than asked, taking up a ready stance.

Durine nodded. 'It's what I'm used to,' he said. 'If you've no objection.'

'No, not at all; go with what you prefer, man. I can hardly take the measure of you if you feel yourself half-armed, eh?'

Sparring was one thing, but Durine had yet to be in a real fight where he hadn't wanted to be able to lash out in more than one direction, or protect himself from more than one enemy. A shield was a fine thing, yes, but by personal philosophy, Durine preferred something in his left hand that could cut, and shields were most useful in a full battle line where you had men on all sides of you whom you could trust to hold fast as long as they lived. The three of them preferred skirmisher work for just that reason, which was how most of the mercenaries were used, at least most of the time.

He dropped back into a ready stance, his chest angled only slightly away from Kelly, who took up a more conventional duellist's stance, almost sideways to Durine, leaving most of his body protected by his sword.

They closed slowly, Kelly making a tentative move in a high line, which Durine blocked, then stepped back a pace rather than riposting.

Sparring was, no matter how you tried to do it, different from the real thing. In a real battle, you almost never had time to feel out an enemy's defences; you had to dispatch the one in front of you before another was on your back, and any time you retreated, even a foot, the odds were all too good that you'd retreat into somebody, or stumble over something. Even on the rare occasions that it was one on one, in real life, one party rarely had time to set himself – which was how Durine preferred it, as long as he was the one surprising the other, rather than the other way around.

They closed again, and this time Durine was able to catch the other's blade with his dagger, and whip it aside for what should have been long enough for him to slash Kelly with the edge of his sword, but Kelly was faster than he appeared. A quick step back took him out of range long enough for him to bring his sword around and block the dagger when Durine advanced a careful half step.

Parry and counter; thrust and block; the sparring continued, in its tentative, unnatural way.

Durine had the stronger wrist, but Kelly had the better feeling of the blade, which is why Durine refused to let him 'have the blade', to let him feel what Durine was about to do next by the subtle pressures and movements of the two swords against one another just before or after a blow. Instead, he met every attack with a parry or counter, or disengaged. Durine had sparred against swordsmen who had had extensive training in the rapier before, and their ability to feel through the blade what their opponent was going to do could be easily countered simply by refusing to let them take the blade.

Some other problems weren't nearly so easy for Durine to dispense with.

Kelly was a trifle faster, and his sideways stance perhaps gave him an extra inch of reach, but Durine was fast enough that it was always a danger that he would get past Kelly's sword and close, and with his dagger, if he ever managed to get within the arc of Kelly's sword, it would be all over in an instant, whether it was practice or a real fight.

Durine let his swordtip drop just a little too much, and when Kelly feinted high, he took a half-step back while blocking. Kelly closed the distance in a lunge, a low-to-high line attack that Durine slipped, batting Kelly's sword aside, then hacking down, hard, on his vulnerable arm, hard enough that Kelly dropped his sword.

Reflexively, Durine slashed the air to his left with his dagger, then slashed Kelly once again, across the midsection, before taking two quick steps back.

That wasn't just sparring protocol – Durine had twice been cut by men who hadn't quite yet realized that they were dead, and didn't care to repeat that, not even in practice.

Kelly scooped up his sword . . .

'Halt!' a firm voice called out.

The Swordmaster stepped between them. Steven Argent had slipped into a practice tunic, but not yet donned his leggings, and he had a practice sword of his own tucked under one arm, careless of the way that it blackened his tunic there, as though he had no doubt that he would emerge from any bout unmarked.

'Nicely done,' he said, smiling thinly. 'Run through that last sequence again, please. Slowly, if you will.'

Durine and Kelly squared off again. They re-enacted their duel with Argent making comments, as if critiquing two students. It was now apparent he was fascinated with Durine's style, ignoring duelling tradition and fighting the bout as if it were a combat situation. When Durine reached the point where he had marked the Captain's tunic, Argent cried 'Hold!'

Turning to Kelly, he said, 'Here's where you made your mistake, Captain. He was already moving forwards when you lunged, and by the time you committed yourself to it, he was ready to parry in passing, and leave you open from guzzle to zorch.' He frowned. 'Neither fish nor fowl, as they say in Rillanon – you're halfway between duelling and combat, both of you.'

Baron Viztria gave a derisive sniff. ''Tis easy enough to impale oneself upon that flailing oaf's blades, if one's skill is no match for one's opinion of oneself. That broadsword is otherwise useless.'

The Swordmaster spun on him, white-lipped. 'Practice bouts and duelling etiquette are one thing, while combat in the field is quite another.'

Viztria made a dismissive gesture with a white lace handkerchief, muttering even lower, 'If you say so, Swordmaster.'

'If you think there's no difference, Baron, go find five others who agree with you. I can line up with five of my soldiers with those broadswords you mock, and we'll set them against the lot of you with your rapiers. We'll soon see how clumsy and useless a heavy sword is when you're not given either the time or space to execute a delicate crossover and riposte, sir.'

He held Viztria's gaze for a long time, until the Baron smiled and shrugged an apology.

'I, of course, bow to your greater knowledge of such matters, Swordmaster,' he said, and the way he ran a finger across the duelling scar over his left cheekbone was only vaguely insolent. 'I proffer my most sincere apologies if I have in any way offended any of the noble company here.'

Steven Argent blinked a couple of times, then nodded and let his jaw unclench. 'Then let's say no more about it ... my lord,' he said, turning back to Durine and Kelly. He had gone as far as his rank would permit in dressing down the Baron in public, and they both knew it. Another remark and Argent would face a displeased

Vandros when he returned, as Viztria would no doubt lodge a complaint over the Swordmaster's lack of manners in public. The Baron's manner showed he too recognized this was a situation that could only get worse if he spoke, so he made a gesture of acquiescence, a flourish of his handkerchief, a slight bow of his head, then a practised turn and a stately walk away, clearing showing his back to the Swordmaster as he crossed to a chair, then slowly sat down.

Argent watched him the entire way, locked eyes with him a moment, then turned to Kelly and Durine. 'As I said, what you were doing was neither duelling nor combat. Let's try it a little bit differently, this time. Back up, both of you – more, more, give yourselves some room. Fine.'

A solid two score feet separated the two men. Not exactly what Durine would have called practice range. Argent instructed them both to make a charging run, as if in the line.

Now, this was more familiar to Durine, despite his preference to avoid line-against-line; he set off in a slow run, his sword over his right shoulder, as though Kethol was in his usual place to the left, and Pirojil on the right, where he belonged.

The obvious trick was to use a little robbed time at the end, to let the rest of the line clash first – and it was such an obvious trick that it was why a line attack required the trust of the men on both sides, because that move would probably save the life of the man who tried it, but cost the lives of the men on both sides of him, as the three of them simultaneously making that move together had indeed cost the lives of men to the left of Pirojil and to the right of Durine, all three times that Tom Garnett had ordered them into the line.

As they closed, Durine slashed down and then up, catching Kelly's blade and sweeping it out of the way. Almost – Kelly slashed back down at him, catching Durine on the right side, moments before Durine's slash scored the Captain's back, leaving behind a dark stripe from the blackened edge of the blade.

Durine kept his feet, but Kelly tumbled to the ground, coming up quickly, on guard.

'Halt!' instructed Argent. He moved to stand between the two combatants, and motioned for them to approach. 'Very nice,' the Swordmaster said. 'I'd call that a draw, and score the two of you as injured. Which means, of course, both sides lose a useful soldier – the winning side at least for several weeks, the losing side for the rest of his life, which would last until the end of battle, if that.' He gestured toward a pair of nearby chairs. 'Have a seat, you two – and Baron Viztria, would you honour me with a quick bout?'

Viztria looked as if there were at least a hundred other places he'd rather be at that moment, but there was no graceful way he could decline after his arch remarks. With a feigned air of amusement, he consented and donned the practice jacket.

Durine gratefully slumped into a chair, surprised at how he had to stop himself from trembling. Pirojil was quickly at his side, proffering a warm mug of mulled wine, and Durine drank it greedily, while he watched Steven Argent give a quick lesson in sabre work to Viztria. The Baron never came close to laying a blade on the Swordmaster. Then they switched from practice sabres to practice rapiers, and he dispatched the Baron every bit as quickly with the lighter, edgeless weapon.

Viztria made a feeble attempt at a humorous remark about it being a bit of an off day as he withdrew from the practice floor with a less than graceful exit. Then, one by one, Steven Argent had a quick practice rapier bout with three of the other barons, including Morray.

As Morray retired, Baron Verheyen said, 'I'll have a try with you, Swordmaster.'

Argent nodded politely, but Durine could see a shadow pass across the Swordmaster's features. By reputation, Verheyen was the finest swordsman in the region, perhaps in the Western Realm.

The look of quiet confidence that had marked Argent throughout the preceding four bouts was replaced with focused intensity as Verheyen quickly donned the practice tunic and helm.

They took their places and the room fell quiet, for every captain and baron present sensed that this match would be far more serious than the previous ones. Upon the command to commence, Verheyen launched a furious attack, seeking to take the fatigued Swordmaster before he could marshal his defences. Argent might not have been Verheyen's match in speed, but he was as practised a swordsman as lived in the Kingdom and he responded with studied efficiency.

Durine watched closely with interest. He rarely saw this sort of swordwork – most of his experience involved dispatching someone as quickly as possible, by any means possible, including gouging eyes, kicks to the groin, or throwing dirt in the eyes. The form of the duel was alien to him, yet the artistry of the blade-work was seductive. Both men were masters of the rapier, and both knew every drill and exercise taught by the finest teachers from the Imperial School in Great Kesh to the Masters' Court in Roldem.

It was a thing of beauty, thought Durine. Verheyen held the edge in speed and footwork, but Argent knew more combinations and counters, so they stood evenly matched. Minutes seemed to drag on, as anticipation of a victory made the observers study every move, counter, and feigned attack. The room remained silent, save for the popping of wood in the hearth, and the sound of scuffling feet and steel upon steel.

Back and forth the duel went, no man gaining a clear advantage. Durine considered it likely Verheyen would eventually win; his sword was faster and he was fresher than Argent.

Even so, he was not prepared for the end, when it came. Verheyen launched a furious running attack that left him open to Argent's counter, but when the Swordmaster moved to counter,

Verheyen switched his blade and struck low, taking Argent hard across the knee.

Grimacing, Steven Argent pulled off his sparring mask. 'The match is yours, my lord.'

Verheyen turned and removed his own mask. 'Well fought, Swordmaster. I've not had such a test in years. You do honour to your office.'

Argent nodded in acknowledgement. Then he crossed to sit down next to Durine, and nodded to him. The Swordmaster's face gleamed in the flickering firelight, and his black hair was sweat-slickened against his head, but he was smiling.

Durine sympathized with him. When in doubt, 'do what you do well' was not a bad rule to live by, and the Swordmaster was indeed a master with the blade. Durine thought that in an equal rematch, should Steven Argent be fresh or Verheyen fatigued, Argent stood a fair chance of winning.

Talk burbled about Durine, and outside the storm howled. After a while, the Swordmaster removed his practice tunic, stood up and went to speak with the nobles, leaving the mercenary alone. Durine sat back, closed his eyes and just let the heat from the hearth wash over him, while the wine warmed his belly and his soul.

All in all, he had had worse days.

SIX

Aftermath

The storm had broken.

The sky above the castle was a clear and royal blue, with only a distant trace of grey clouds near the horizon to the east, and just a wisp of distant, cottony whiteness in the west to mar the vista. In the wake of the storm, as though it had spent all its energy lashing LaMut, the cold air lay across the land exhausted, barely able to move.

Dark columns of smoke rose from hundreds of chimneys throughout the city below, snaking crookedly into the air, nudged along by a breeze that was softer than a baby's breath, although even more certainly colder than a paymaster's heart. It drove the heat out of Kethol as he stood on the ramparts of the castle wall, careful not to snicker at the panting of the soldiers who were stamping down the snow on the walkway with the pointed farming spades that were, at best, ill-suited to the task. There were, of course, better tools for the purposes of clearing deep snow, but no one seemed to have them in LaMut. He had overheard several of the staff remark this blizzard had been a once-in-a-lifetime event. It had certainly been more than enough for *his* lifetime.

A steady clang-clang-clang from the smithy over by the far wall probably spoke of the need for more snow shovels being remedied, Kethol guessed. It shouldn't take the castle blacksmith long to hammer out a few broad-bladed, flat shovels, even with the necessity of additional mounts being reshoed with the clawed LaMutian horseshoes that Kethol had never seen anywhere else, and hoped never to see again.

Below, the men of Tom Garnett's company shivered in their cloaks as they saddled up for the morning patrol. Gouts of steam spurted from the horses' nostrils as they whinnied their complaints at being forced out into snow that was currently up to their knees. That snow was quickly being packed down into something more firm by all the feet and hooves involved, and the only major snow removal operation in the inner keep had been accomplished with the clearing of enough snow from around the main gate to let it swing open, enabling the patrol to depart. The preparations were, unsurprisingly, taking much longer than usual.

The riders worked in pairs to keep the horses steady long enough to saddle the mulish creatures, one man holding firmly onto the reins, while the other tightened the saddle girth, then tied down the rest of the gear even more carefully than usual.

It would likely be a difficult patrol, although Kethol judged that the chances of combat were nearly non-existent – even if they managed to get beyond the city below, which was problematic at best. There was ice lurking beneath the soft-looking snow, and even a clawed horseshoe might slip on it. While a falling horse would not of necessity always break its leg, Tith-Onaka, the soldiers' god, had a cruel sense of humour. Kethol decided that must explain the presence of a dozen unsaddled horses that were being led out of the stable. You normally didn't take remounts with you on patrol, unless you expected to be gone for a long while and anticipated a horse going lame or having to be put down.

It also explained the low curses from the stocky Horsemaster, Benjamin Deven, which Kethol couldn't quite make out, but probably amounted to additional if unnecessary cautions to the riders to be careful with their mounts, as though the horses were the Horsemaster's own children, and the soldiers merely unreliable nannies.

The preparations for the patrol had been preceded, he knew, by a confrontation between Steven Argent and the Horsemaster. Kethol had gone up to the Aerie to speak with the Swordmaster, and perhaps pay a quick visit to Fantus – the little firedrake seemed to actually like him, for some reason or other – and had quickly retreated at the sound of voices inside, in a surprisingly loud argument over the question of even sending out a patrol right now.

It was not Kethol's problem, thankfully, but he could see both sides of the issue.

The only good thing about the present situation that he could think of was that any enemy activity would be marked indelibly in the deep snow. Even if the Tsurani knew the old trick of a company marching single-file, while dragging branches behind them to obscure a trail – and they probably did – they weren't stupid and this was their fourth winter: it was all so pristine and virgin white out there that it would be impossible to move unnoticed anywhere within tens of miles of LaMut. A force of any significant size would leave a trail even a city man could see.

And while Kethol doubted there were any Tsurani closer than the Free Cities border, he did rather hope there were actually legions of Tsurani and Bugs out there . . .

. . . and that their rotting carcasses would be found come the thaw.

Not that he would be around to see them. For a moment he thought of a snug little inn somewhere . . . somewhere warm.

The sound of soft footsteps crunching on the packed snow behind him drew him from his momentary reverie and he turned.

Grodan, the leader of the Natalese Rangers, walked up, his grey cloak wrapped tightly about his long, lean frame. 'Hail and good morning, Kethol of wherever-you-happen-to-be-at-the-moment,' he said.

'Hail and a good morning to you, as well, Grodan of Natal.' Kethol nodded. 'I didn't see you or the other two Rangers during the storm. You weren't actually out in it, were you?'

'Hardly.' Grodan's mouth twitched. 'I've heard that you went out into it, to rescue Baron Morray.'

Kethol shrugged. 'It wasn't much of a rescue, really.' Why he was coming to Morray's defence he didn't quite know, but it would have seemed disloyal to let the Ranger's implication stand unanswered, despite the fact that Kethol himself thought Morray an idiot to have willingly ventured out into the belly of the storm.

Grodan was idly watching the city below, when a man, huddled deeply in a cloak, climbed out of a second-storey window from a half-buried row house on High Street, just the other side of the north gate. The man lost his grip on the windowsill and slid down the snowdrift, tumbling and rolling until he reached the bottom.

Kethol could imagine the curses being uttered as the man got to his feet and tried to slap the snow from himself, but he was too far off for the sound to carry, despite the still air.

The Ranger laughed. 'Well, that's quicker than digging himself out, eh?' He sobered as he watched the people moving about on the streets below, making their way through the deep snow. 'I hope there's enough meat stored in the city; it'll be weeks before there are any animals brought in to market.'

That wasn't one of Kethol's worries. Any castle had to have enough preserved food in its storehouses not just to weather a winter, but to weather a siege, and Father Winter's siege could not possibly go on long enough for him to be missing any meals, although he might quickly grow tired of a diet of pickled beef, if it took too long for livestock to reach LaMut from neighbouring farms and ranches. And given the severity of this last storm, it probably would take a while.

'So where were you? During the storm, that is. If you don't mind me asking,' Kethol said.

It was unlikely that the Ranger had sought him out just to make conversation, but Kethol was willing to wait until Grodan got to the point. The Baron was up and about, with Pirojil at his side, and Kethol wasn't due to take over bodyguard duties until noon.

'Don't mind.' The Ranger shrugged. 'My father used to tell me, when there's nothing to do, it's best to do nothing. Beldan and Short Sam and I were simply holed up in our rooms, with some food and wine to keep us company, and just caught up on some much-needed sleep.' He gave a thin smile, and then yawned broadly. 'And the three of us have had so much of that, in fact, that we find ourselves tired of sleep and eager not to be so rested, if that makes any sense to you.'

'It does, at that.' Kethol nodded. 'I'm feeling the same way, although I don't mind missing the daily patrol –' he let his gaze sweep the white snowscape below as the patrol mounted up and the horses stamped their hooves '– if truth be told, it bothers me not a bit that my own duties keep me right here.'

Grodan's mouth twitched. 'Perhaps that could be changed?'

'Oh?'

'The other day, Captain Garnett boasted of your tracking abilities. I was going to invite you to accompany me on my own sweep to the north. I'd welcome the company.' Grodan frowned at the assembling patrol below. 'Somebody needs to go and see what's out there. That lot will be lucky to get a mile.' His expression remained impassive, but Kethol detected a slight change around the mouth that he took to be disdain.

'I was thinking the same thing. I doubt anybody could get far.'

'On that, I disagree.' Grodan produced a piece of jerky and took a thoughtful bite. 'I thought to see if there's anything interesting stirring between here and Mondegreen – perhaps some more of those Tsurani you ran into last week.' He eyed the unmarked snow. 'Not that tracking is as much of a challenge as moving is, at the moment.'

'You think your ponies can move any faster than those horses can?'

Grodan shook his head. 'No, I'd not try to ride out. I thought we'd go on foot.'

'Walking?'

From the castle walls, Kethol could see drifts of snow that had reached the second storey of some of the houses along High Street, and the small, dark tunnels through the bases of the drifts that the occupants, had, dwarflike, dug to get themselves out of the snowy prison.

And into a somewhat larger snowy prison.

It was no more likely that the Ranger could make his way any significant distance on foot than Tom Garnett's company would be able to on horseback, and Kethol wouldn't have been surprised if the patrol found itself unable to make its way out of LaMut, much less push out into the countryside.

'Yes, walking.' Grodan nodded. 'Rangers have their ways, Kethol.'

Kethol had heard legends about the Natalese Rangers, about their almost supernatural ability to move through the forest quickly and silently, leaving no trace. He'd heard the same of the Royal Krondorian Pathfinders down south, too, and of the Imperial Keshian Guides even farther south, and rumour had it they all were somehow related, by blood or magic or some such. But Kethol was by nature and disposition suspicious of legends, and aware that his own abilities seemed magical to those who hadn't been raised in the wild.

'Well,' he said, 'if you expect to make it to Mondegreen I guess you must have your ways, indeed.'

'You sound doubtful.'

'A little, perhaps.' Kethol nodded. 'No offence meant, but I don't see how you'd be able to do much more than anybody else, not in this. I can't imagine you've tried to make your away across such ground before.'

'You'd be wrong.' Grodan smiled slightly. 'It gets fairly . . . interesting around the Grey Tower come winter, particularly in the high meadows.' He shrugged. 'And it's a matter of some pride to my people to be able to scout anywhere, no matter what the conditions. Not that I'd have wished to be scouting last night in the storm. But I'd have managed.'

Calling the Ranger a liar or braggart didn't seem to be the thing to do, so Kethol just asked, 'So how do you do it? Move across the snow, that is. Some sort of magic, is it?'

'No magic involved.' Grodan seemed vaguely amused at the suggestion. The Ranger thought it over for a moment. 'Well, I guess there's no harm in telling you, since you'll be able to see, if you just watch.

'Travelling across deep snow is just a matter of spreading your weight across enough of the snow that it will bear you. We make large shoes by bending a hoop of birch into a oval frame, and cover that hoop with a latticework of leather thongs, then strap it to our boots. We call them *brezeneden*, from a phrase for "clumsy walking" in the Old Tongue. It takes some practice. It can be pretty amusing watching someone get around on them the first time.' He looked out across the castle wall. 'Making a set of brezeneden is just a matter of an hour's work or so, and Short Sam has probably finished making several sets – he's quicker with his fingers than Beldan and I, and I've left that to him.'

Kethol nodded. It seemed to be an interesting idea, and something to think about were he ever stuck in a snowy hell like this again. 'Birch for the frame?'

'Any flexible wood will do.' Grodan shrugged. 'Moving on these things is slow going, but I should be able to complete my circuit to the north within a few days. Beldan and Short Sam will cover their own areas, as well.' He cocked his head. 'Are you sure that you won't accompany me?'

Kethol shook his head. 'As I said, my own duties prevent that.'

'But you would accompany me, if your duties didn't make that impossible?'

'Of course.' Kethol nodded, then forced himself to smile. 'I'd do so at swordpoint – and it would have to be a *very* sharp sword.'

Grodan laughed, and patted at his cloak, over where his sword lay hidden, only its dragonhide hilt visible. 'I happen to have a very sharp sword, but I'd not use it to force my company upon you,' he said, still smiling.

'Then I wish you well,' Kethol said. 'And if there is an extra pair of these brezeneden available, I'd count it a favour if you would leave those behind for me to try out.' While Kethol had no desire to try to stamp his way through – no, on top of – the snow, it would be interesting to see how well these things worked. Just another trick to add to his bag, one that probably wouldn't be of any use.

But you could never tell.

Grodan nodded. 'I see no harm in that.'

He clapped a comradely hand on Kethol's shoulder, then drew himself up straight. 'Well, then, Kethol of wherever-it-is-you-happen-to-be-at-the-moment, I'll bid you a good day, and look forward to another opportunity, perhaps, to see your performance in the wild. Farewell.'

'Farewell, Grodan of Natal.' Kethol watched the Ranger walk away. It would have been nice to know what that all had been about, though it was just possible that it was about just what it seemed.

Maybe.

Durine turned the corner close to the wall of the keep. The overhanging buttresses above had kept the lee side of the fortress relatively free of the huge drifts which made progress anywhere else almost impossible. He walked along the entire side of the keep, attempting to keep snow out of his boots, determined to reach the barracks by the shortest route possible without having to dig his way through shoulder-high drifts.

He was about to turn a corner which would bring him within sight of the marshalling yard and the barracks when a beefy soldier in a heavy cloak came into view, with three others marching single file behind him. Barely enough room for one man to pass meant that someone was going to have to back up.

The soldier stopped and said, 'Make way, freebooter.'

Durine knew what was coming next, but he thought he should at least make some attempt to resolve this matter without having to risk breaking the man's head or his own knuckles. 'You're but a half-dozen steps from the sally port you just walked through; it would be far less difficult for me if you'd back up to let me pass.'

'Less difficult for you?' said the soldier, rubbing his red-bearded chin as if considering the request. 'But then, I have no concerns for what is more or less difficult for you. There are four of us and only one of you. It would be better for you to turn around and make way for us.'

Durine looked at the other three men, who were watching the big soldier and Durine with some amusement. 'There is that,' said Durine as if considering the matter. Then with speed unexpected in so big a man, Durine took one quick step forward and unleashed a thunderous blow at the man's head. He hit the large soldier so hard he spun around, allowing Durine to catch him under the arms. With a quick lift, Durine picked up the man, and slung him across his shoulders in the same sort of way as Kethol might hoist a stag he had taken in a hunt. Then Durine moved forward till he was looking down at the next soldier in line and said, 'I think we should get your friend back inside, don't you?'

This short soldier went pale and nodded. Then he pushed his way past his two companions who quickly seized upon the wisdom of retreating before the huge mercenary. The three of them swiftly made their way back to the sally port and one of them opened the door. Durine dumped the huge soldier unceremoniously at the threshold and turned him over. He rummaged through the man's belt purse and withdrew a pair of silver coins.

One of the soldiers said, 'What do you think you're doing?'

Durine looked at the man with his brows furrowed and said loudly, 'I don't fight for free!' He pocketed the coins and turned his back on the men, then focused on breasting his way through the snow, across the marshalling yard, to the barracks.

Pirojil had been sleeping in the barracks when the storm had hit, and now it was his turn to guard Baron Morray. Kethol was with the Baron and would head to the kitchen for a meal when Pirojil got there. Durine silently cursed the luck that made him the one to have to plough through heavy, wet snow. He might well be the one best suited for the task, but he didn't relish it for that fact.

Halfway between the keep and barracks, he encountered two soldiers with broad shovels clearing the way. Feeling lucky to have been spared some of the labour of getting to the barracks door, he crossed the marshalling yard and entered the barracks.

There he found Pirojil dressing, in anticipation of his shift approaching, half-listening to some tale or another being spun by the mad dwarf, Mackin. 'And then she says, "tall enough where it counts!"' He exploded into laughter.

Durine saw Pirojil's brow flicker and realized the ugly man had found the dwarf's story amusing. 'Your turn with the Baron,' he said, moving to his own bunk.

Pirojil nodded and stood up. 'Any trouble?'

'None to speak of,' said Durine, pulling off his boots.

Pirojil nodded and departed without comment.

Mackin asked, 'Have they cleared the snow down into town?'

'Not yet.'

'Too bad. I could use an ale and a woman.'

Durine glanced around the room and saw a lot of men sitting on their bunks, staring at the ceiling or walls, lost in their thoughts. He could smell the tension in the room. To the dwarf he said, 'You're not the only one.'

Pirojil leaned back against the wall as the nobles took their places around the table in the Great Hall, with the Swordmaster at the head. Surprisingly, Lady Mondegreen sat at the position of honour to Steven Argent's right. It was apparently not just a surprise to Pirojil, either: Folson passed a quick comment to Langahan, making a small gesture towards the head of the table.

The rest of the barons and nobles were scattered along both sides of the table according to some plan that Pirojil couldn't quite work out, but he was sure wasn't accidental, if only because it put Verheyen at the foot of the table, while Morray, presumably because of his post as Wartime Bursar, sat to the Swordmaster's left.

The long table was covered with fresh linen tablecloths, overlapping in places, and the only objects on its pristine white surface were the swords and daggers of the assembled nobles, bared and sheathless as though – unlikely as it seemed – they were expecting to have to use them.

Pirojil hoped it was unlikely. He was far too many paces away to get to Morray's side in what he trusted was the improbable event of Baron Viztria suddenly picking up the sword in front of him and running Morray through. Should that improbability come to pass, the best Pirojil could do was to help pick up the body. After he had killed Viztria, of course; assuming Steven Argent didn't beat him to it. Pirojil kept his face impassive, but smiled inside remembering how the Swordmaster had embarrassed the pompous little baron in front of his peers.

Plates of food, mugs of coffee, and a few bottles and wineglasses were being served to the guests by a squad of servants from side tables around the room, indicating to Pirojil that the Council would probably be going on for several hours at least, although nobody had explicitly said as much, not in Pirojil's hearing.

'By order of the Earl of LaMut,' the Swordmaster said, as he rose, while the others remained seated, 'this Baronial Council in the Earldom of LaMut is now called to assemble. Let any of the assembled who cannot now freely swear their allegiance to Earl Vandros, to Duke Brucal, to Prince Erland, and to the Kingdom itself now either absent themselves without fear of retribution or penalty, or explain to the satisfaction of this noble company why they cannot so swear.'

Pirojil wondered about the omission of the King or the Eastern Realm's Viceroy, Guy du Bas-Tyra – by name or rank, although Steven Argent had mentioned the Kingdom in the vaguest possible generality – but he didn't know what that meant, although it was clearly something unpalatable to two men from the way that Baron Langahan and Baron Viztria, both from Krondor, were scowling.

Well, Langahan's scowl probably meant something. As to Viztria, the fox-faced little court baron always seemed to have either a scowl or a sneer pasted on his face, and neither expression necessarily meant anything more than that his face was in the room with him.

Several pairs of eyes turned to Berrel Langahan, the improbably sun-browned, improbably common-looking balding court baron, who frowned and quickly shuffled to his feet, waiting until Steven Argent sat before he spoke.

'As you all know,' Langahan said, 'I am from the court in Krondor, and am not fealty-bound to the Earldom of LaMut, nor to the Duchy of Yabon; the same is true of my friend, Baron Viztria. While I hold Duke Brucal of Yabon and Earl Vandros of LaMut in the highest esteem, I cannot swear my allegiance to either the earldom or the duchy.' His expression grew stern. 'Although I can and do freely swear my allegiance to the King, and obedience to his chosen Viceroy, may the gods grant him great health and deep wisdom in these most difficult of times.'

It was probably not the most politically delicate thing to say, given the feud between Guy du Bas-Tyra and Borric of Crydee. Duke Brucal of Yabon was probably too closely allied to Borric for the taste of Guy du Bas-Tyra's supporters – which surely included any court barons who were permitted out of Krondor without a short leash, much less dispatched to a council of any kind in Yabon.

'Health and wisdom to the Viceroy – and to the Prince,' Steven Argent said, as though agreeing. His face was set in a friendly mask, but his eyes showed a darkness Pirojil would not particularly have liked to have seen directed at him.

'Health and wisdom to the Prince!' the rest repeated, some more quickly than others.

'Health and wisdom to the Prince,' Verheyen said, the last of the barons to repeat the words, in a voice that was just a trifle louder than necessary.

'Yes, of course – health and wisdom to the Prince,' Langahan said, almost immediately, and was echoed by the rest of the table.

Langahan had a long look at Verheyen, then blinked and went on: 'I cannot, as I have said, in good conscience, by word or silence, claim allegiance to the Earl or the earldom, save as part of this realm, this kingdom.' He looked from face to face. 'I think it best to have that out in the open at the beginning, and if there is any man – if there is any man among you, who feels that I should absent myself from these deliberations because of that, I beg of him – or her –' he said, bowing towards Lady Mondegreen as he corrected himself, 'to speak now, and I'll sadly absent myself from these proceedings, and swear to hold no grudge or grievance against any here for that.'

And, probably, count on Baron Viztria to report every word to him, or at least to Guy of Bas-Tyra.

There was silence at the table, and after looking from face to face, Steven Argent nodded. 'Your presence here is welcome, Baron Langahan.'

Langahan bowed, more gracefully than Pirojil would have thought such a stocky man could, and seated himself.

Viztria rose. 'I'm not a man who claims to be of few words,' he said, with a snort, 'as is my friend Baron Langahan, but I'll try to make an exception. I fully confess that my fealty is to the realm as a whole, and the Kingdom beyond that, and not to some muddy pit of –' He paused, then forced a pained smile as he continued. 'To some important barony that itself is a part of an equally important duchy. If anybody objects to my presence here, let him – or her, my lady – let him speak now, and I'll repair to my room and catch up on some correspondence.'

He might as well have come out and said that if he was excluded, a messenger would be quickly making his way to Guy du Bas-Tyra, but Steven Argent nodded gently, as though accepting his words at face value.

The declaration of what amounted to a tentative alliance if not quite allegiance was received with a silent assent and nods by the rest, as well.

Pirojil read that as a good sign. The estrangement if not

hostility between the East and the West, represented here by the LaMutian barons on one side and by these two court barons on the other, was not going to be mended here, but it would be ignored for the time being, at least publicly.

Steven Argent sat back in his chair. 'Very well. There are many matters to discuss, from the taxes to be collected and disbursed, and to the rebuilding of what's been let go in the war, and our brief from the Earl is that we are to come up with recommendations on all matters touching the earldom, save for the conduct of the war, which is the province of the general staff, presently meeting in Yabon.' He smiled thinly. 'I am sure that the Earl, and the dukes, would all like our advice on such things, but I see little point in this noble company spending its time and efforts on issues that are being decided by others with greater knowledge and responsibilities for them.'

'And never mind,' Baron Viztria added, with his usual sneer under his thin moustache, 'that giving even good advice that comes too late to take it is about as worthwhile as paying stud fees for the services of a gelding, eh?'

The Swordmaster's smile was broad, but chilly. 'Precisely,' he said, giving a quick, jerky nod. 'Normally, the Earl would preside over the Council. In his absence, custom dictates he choose a senior baron to sit in his place – the most likely choice would be Baron Mondegreen, as the discussions here will certainly involve matters that involve him as the Hereditary Bursar of the Earldom.'

Pirojil followed him so far. Mondegreen had long been too frail for frequent trips into LaMut during the war, which is why Morray had been appointed by the Earl's father, and confirmed by Earl Vandros, as the Military Bursar, and from what Pirojil could see, that had meant, in practice, that he was also holding down Mondegreen's more general bursarial duties on behalf of the earldom, as well.

But if getting along well was going to be the theme of the day, and it clearly was, substituting Morray for Mondegreen to preside over the Council was guaranteed trouble, and there was trouble enough as it was. The castle barracks were filled with soldiers who, in the absence of Tsurani to kill or anywhere to go, were close enough to murdering each other right and left at the best of times, and with the storm having kept everyone penned up inside for days, it wasn't remotely close to being the best of times.

So Pirojil just leaned back and waited for Steven Argent to announce that he would continue to preside over the Baronial Council.

'I'm not going to preside over the Council,' the Swordmaster said.

Eh?

'It hasn't passed my notice that some people habitually refer to me as "that Eastern Swordmaster", or "that ex-captain from Rillanon", despite my having served the Earl of LaMut these last dozen years.

'Besides, I'm a soldier and the Swordmaster, and that's all I want to be. The recommendations here need to be made by the Council, and not be influenced by somebody like me.'

It was all Morray could do not to strut sitting down. He smiled and preened himself, and Verheyen wasn't the only other baron who glowered at him.

'Which is why,' the Swordmaster continued, standing as he spoke, 'I ask Lady Mondegreen to take this chair, and I shall excuse myself and leave you, my lords and lady, to your deliberations – unless I hear an objection.' He held up a peremptory hand. 'Let me say first that I would take any objection to my selection of her as an insult not only to the house of Mondegreen, but to my own honour, as well, and a gentleman of Rillanon would know quite well how to deal with that, as would a swordmaster of LaMut,' he said, his voice threatening in its casualness.

Verheyen was the first to react. He nodded and smiled. 'I think that Lady Mondegreen is a fine choice, and I can think of none better, and many worse, myself included. Wouldn't you agree, Baron Morray?'

Morray was caught, and fairly. It was all he could do to nod. 'Of course I'm happy to let our deliberations be guided by the lady, who is perhaps even more wise than she is fair.'

'Hear, hear,' several of the other barons cried out, and Steven Argent walked from the room, beckoning Pirojil to follow him.

SEVEN

Promotions

The Swordmaster opened the door.

Pirojil assumed he had something on his mind, as he didn't wait upon protocol and let Pirojil open the door for him. Steven Argent had seemed content to keep his thoughts to himself on the walk from the Council chamber to his own quarters, though he did mention he had sent for Durine and Kethol to be waiting for them, just prior to the start of the Council.

Durine was, as he had been instructed by the messenger, already up in the Aerie with Kethol when Pirojil and the Swordmaster strolled in, looking for all the world like a couple of old friends, if you didn't look too closely at the scowl on Pirojil's ugly face.

Kethol, having beaten Durine to the Aerie, had taken the chair next to the hearth, and was busily scratching at the fire-drake's eye-ridges, using the hilt of his knife. It looked to be less than gentle, at least to Durine's eyes, but Fantus arched his back and preened himself like a reptilian cat, his wings spread either in pleasure, or simply to soak up the heat radiating from the fire.

Durine had parked his bulk on a wooden bench by the fire,

and was staring at Kethol playing with the little dragon, not quite sure what to make of it.

'I think he likes me,' Kethol had said.

'Oh.'

As Pirojil and the Swordmaster walked in, Steven Argent made a stay-seated gesture and waved Pirojil towards a chair, before seating himself across from Kethol. Then he stretched his long legs out and folded his hands behind his head. He seemed insufferably pleased with himself. 'Well, that went better than I had expected, eh?'

Eh?

Pirojil turned to Durine. 'The Swordmaster put Lady Mondegreen in charge of the Baronial Council.' He nodded. 'Which came as something of a surprise to some others, I'll wager.'

The Swordmaster grinned. 'It did that.' He gave them a shrug, and a look of total innocence. 'And truth be told, I think it's defensible, and I'm prepared to make my case for it to Earl Vandros – since Baron Mondegreen did, after all, send his lady to represent him, and since he was the obvious candidate.' He sobered. 'How well the rest of it will go, I can't say – there's much work to do, and the Earl will have to judge how well they set priorities and budgets.' He shook his head. 'My life is weapons and martial arts, but I've been around long enough to know that we could empty the Earl's treasury with loans to the barons for repairs come spring, and still not fix all the damage done in the war.' He stifled a yawn. 'I've no doubt that the presence of quick money and more work than workers will bring a flood of daubers, carpenters and stonemasons north from Krondor Province.'

Pirojil almost smiled. Only an Easterner would call the Principality 'Krondor Province'. After twelve years, the Swordmaster was still, 'that ex-captain from Rillanon'. He had been right in removing himself from the head of the Council.

Argent shook his head wearily, as if issues of finance and

governance were far more fatiguing than any combat. 'That's sure to drive up the prices of everything from the cost of a chicken in the market to the price of a yard of dry goods.' He uncorked a bottle on the table at his elbow and poured himself a glass of wine. 'But, thankfully, it's not my problem, and I can get back to matters for which I've a better feel.' He sipped his wine. 'Which is why I've sent for you.' He looked over at Kethol. 'You told your companions about that unseemliness in the barracks – that fight between Morray's and Verheyen's men that you and I walked in on?'

'Well, no.' Kethol shook his head. 'It seemed more of a scuffle than a fight, and it didn't seem worth mentioning.'

Argent snorted.

Kethol shrugged. 'There were no deaths, only a few broken bones, and not even a stab wound –'

'We have hundreds of soldiers from a dozen rival baronies, trapped here in LaMut, all of them war-weary, irritable, bored and looking for something to keep themselves amused, and you think that a fight isn't worth mentioning?'

The dozen rival baronies was a slight overstatement, but the scope of the problem was as the Swordmaster indicated, Kethol thought to himself, probably worse.

Still, save for the barons' personal guards, the vast bulk of the baronial troops were billeted separately in nearby towns and villages, and whatever problems Baron Folson's men might have with, say, Baron Benteen's, were entirely academic; the storm had isolated the companies, one from the other.

But there were far more than enough of the feuding Verheyens and Morrays in the city to cause serious trouble – and they were hardly the only example.

The Swordmaster shook his head. 'The captains tell me that they've already had to break up a few other *scuffles*, as well –'

That was to be expected. It was one of the reasons that Durine was pleased their own assignment kept them in the castle, rather than stuck in the barracks with the rest. In such squabbles, neutrality was difficult; people had a way of resenting a man who refused to take sides – or rather they resented a man who wouldn't take *their* side.

'– and Captain Kelly and a couple of sergeants had to carry a soldier to Father Riley – the private with a knife wound to his side. A curious kind of knife wound that nobody, apparently, if you believe the soldiers in the barracks, either gave or witnessed.'

'I hadn't heard that,' Pirojil said.

Durine shook his head as well.

'You will, one way or another,' Argent said. 'And you will, I trust, when you do, be careful to mention that the soldier in question – one of Verheyen's – had a very small wound. He'll recover fully, and have nothing but a scar, memories and a few days' bed rest to show for it.'

The three of them nodded.

'In the meantime, I've had the captains order their off-duty men out of the barracks and out into the city, to stretch their legs, if nothing else. It's either that or put a captain on watch in each of the barracks rooms and hope that things hold together, and I'm –' he stopped himself, then shrugged and went on '– and while I can trust my own captains, I'm not sure that some of the barons' officers aren't as much of a problem as their men. These baronial feuds often last generations and involve all manner of grudges, down to enlisted soldiers whose grandfather was insulted by some other common soldier's grandfather.'

Steven Argent looked from face to face, as though challenging them either to agree or disagree, and Durine didn't have to look at his companions to know that they were keeping their expressions utterly blank and noncommittal, just as he was.

Steven Argent shook his head and went on: 'But there's going to be some trouble, of that I'm sure, and I want somebody besides the City Watch taking a quick look around for me. The Constable seems to be far more eager to tell me that all is well than anything else – not to mention he's ill equipped to take on a force of trained soldiers with his small company of men – and while I've already got a company of my regulars backing the Watch, and have as much faith in Captain Stirling as I do in Tom Garnett, should a full-scale conflict erupt, my men would as likely be overrun by one side as the other; most of my troops are up with the Earl in Yabon or still out on the line, dug in.' For a moment it looked as if he wished those men were back in the city, for more reasons than just keeping things tranquil. He glanced from Durine to Kethol to Pirojil, and said, 'I'd just as soon have another three sets of eyes and ears out in the city today. And not just eyes and ears – mouths, as well.'

Durine nodded, slowly, regretfully. 'Which is where we come in, my lord?'

'Enough of that "my lord" nonsense, please – and yes, that is where you come in.' He shook his head. 'I'd rather have Tom Garnett and some of his top sergeants, but they're the ones most familiar with the nearby environs, and I need them on the patrol. I could have sent out a company of Verheyen's men, which would have at least kept them away from Morray's, but they'd probably try to push too far out, just to prove that they are the equal or better of anybody else, and get themselves lost.' His mouth twitched. 'I may live to regret that I didn't send them.' He sighed. 'It would have been nice to have the Rangers as guides, but they, perhaps properly, seem to think that they're needed for wider scouting.' He scowled. 'Not that they'd take my orders, anyway – that would be too easy, eh?

'So I've got to use most of the regulars left me in the city for patrol, and that means I need you three.' He got up from his chair and rummaged around in his desk. 'Draw some regulars' LaMutian tabards from the quartermaster, and wear those under your cloaks, and if you run into any problem that needs sorting out, you show your tabard and sort it – with threats of any fights being seen as a rebellion against the Earl's reign. But, mainly, I want you back at table with me tonight, able to give me some real feel for how things are going, eh?'

'Understood, sir,' Pirojil said with a nod.

'Individually, that is.' The Swordmaster scowled. 'The three of you tend to clump together, and while that's fine for a battle, that's not what I have in mind here. Spread out, look around, help keep things quiet, and report back. Understood?'

'I understand, sir,' Pirojil said. 'And as to the looking-around part, I see no problem. But in terms of stopping any trouble, I'm not sure that will work, my lor— er, Swordmaster.' He shook his head. 'Regardless of what tabards we happen to be wearing, I don't think that a bunch of baronial soldiers are going to pay much attention to orders from any of us, not unless . . .'

'Unless they're not privates, but sergeants, at least. And even that's a dicey matter, at best, if they aren't their own sergeants,' finished the Swordmaster. Steven Argent nodded as if in agreement with himself, then reached into his desk drawer and produced a small packet of shoulder tabs. 'Which is why, as of now, you're brevetted to captain, each of you; I've already informed the other captains, and the City Watch of that – draw some whistles from the quartermaster, too, and don't be afraid to blow for the Watch. Don't get over-eager, now; your rank reverts when this council is over, the roads are open, and we can clear some of these troops out of the city, and keep them out.' He eyed them levelly. 'If not before.'

Pirojil raised an eyebrow. 'Again, meaning no offence, sir, is that a threat or a promise?'

Steven Argent's laughter didn't sound forced. 'It's some of both, eh?'

Pirojil looked over at Durine, and then at Kethol. 'When the roads are open, we'll be on our way south, in any case, with our pay warm in our pouches.'

'Yes, yes, yes – well, what are you waiting for?'

Pirojil cleared his throat. 'I'm sure that brevetted captains get full captains' pay – and –'

'Yes, yes, you can have captains' pay, and I'll inform the paymaster. Will that be all, or is there anything else you need to bother me with?'

The three of them rose, but Pirojil stopped at the door and turned back.

'Well?' the Swordmaster looked up in irritation. 'What else?'

'Well, there is the matter of Baron Morray.'

'The three of you have been loafing on that duty long enough.' The Swordmaster snorted. 'I don't think anything's going to happen while he's sitting at the council table, nor while everybody and his brother is trapped in the keep – but I'll think about that. You can let me worry about the Baron for today; you just get out into the city and do what you can to keep the peace.'

Durine said. 'We'll do what we can.'

The Swordmaster nodded. 'As will we all, eh?'

'Yes, sir.' Durine said.

It seemed like the right thing to say.

Durine made his way through the narrow path down the middle of the street towards the smithy on what he had once been told was, officially, the Street Named in Honour of King Rodric, but which everybody always seemed to call Dog Street. Whether that was because that was its name before the change, or a manifestation of the hostility between West and East, he didn't know.

LaMut was coming back from its storm-driven hibernation, if not quite digging out.

While only a few deep imprints of horses' hooves – well, their whole legs, more than just their hooves – could be seen, paths made by boots crisscrossed the narrow street in great profusion, as though they were the imprint of a huge, vanished web that had, overnight, been woven by some huge, imaginary spider.

He sniffed the air. Maybe it was a trifle warmer, although not nearly warm enough to stop him from shivering, much less to melt the snow. Possibly it was just the stillness of the air that made it seem less bitter. Nothing short of the miraculous appearance of the hot summer winds that blew across the Jal-Pur desert could melt the snow quickly enough to open up the city of LaMut and stop things from falling apart.

A miracle would be nice.

Where was the goddess Killian when you needed her? Probably stretched out on a blanket spread on the warm sand at some beach outside of Durbin, sipping a tall, cold drink, and chuckling, from a great distance, at what she had done to LaMut. Tith-Onaka was probably on the next blanket along, and whether he was laughing with her or scowling at her was something that Durine wouldn't have wanted to guess; the soldiers' god had a mean sense of humour.

A commotion from the smithy down the street caused Durine to hurry his pace.

Flashes of easily half a dozen different tabards – including, he noticed with some relief, the grey tabards of LaMutian regulars – showed in the gaps between the cloaks of the soldiers gathered around the open door. There seemed to be a little pushing and shoving, but nothing violent, not yet.

Durine had some sympathy with the soldiers' eagerness to get inside. If you absolutely had to be out in the city on such a cold day, and were trying to avoid a tavern out of a reluctance to be part of a throng of too many soldiers crowded together drinking too much beer, one of the obviously warm places to find yourself was a smithy. A soldier could always conjure up a reason to visit a smith; a belt to be mended, a dagger to be sharpened, a new binding needed on a sword hilt. Anything would do to keep a man warm before the forge's fire for half an hour or so.

A fight inside a smithy, though, was likely to be rather worse than one in the Dangling Keshian Tavern next door. Tavernkeepers were used to such things, at least as far as not providing a plethora of heavy metal objects that could easily come to hand as improvised clubs. Blacksmiths had different expectations, and different priorities.

He pulled back his cloak to expose his rank tabs, and gently elbowed his way through the crowd of soldiers, and through the door.

Damn. Karris, the bristle-moustached captain belonging to barony Benteen, was facing off Captain Kelly, of Folson Company. Beyond the workbench that served as a sales counter for the smithy stood the smith, watching carefully, his ropy-muscled arms flexing slightly as he waited, his hair and loose shirt soaked with sweat, his hammer resting on a massive anvil. Both apprentices continued to work the bellows on the forge, kicking sparks out of the forge and onto the rough-hewn floor of the shop with each alternating down stroke, pausing only occasionally to feed another chunk of scrap iron into the stone vat half-buried in the coals. Work would go on – on whatever it was that the smith was about to cast in the boxy mould that waited next to the forge – while the captains argued. To Durine's practised eye it looked as though the smith would pick up that hammer and return to work, as soon as the metal was ready. He might use it on whichever captain came across the workbench, but otherwise he wouldn't intervene in the argument. Unlike your average inn or crockery shop, there weren't a lot of breakables in a smithy. And, moreover, at this point the two captains were merely talking.

It hadn't passed Durine's notice, the night before, that the two captains didn't like each other much, and Durine didn't know if the problem was personal, or a projection of the rivalry between their respective barons.

It could have been both, of course.

'Please,' Kelly said, an unnatural-looking smile threatening to strain little-used facial muscles to the point of spasm, 'I'll be more than happy see that my own needs are met after yours, my good friend, Captain Karris.'

His voice was too loud, but he wasn't quite shouting.

'Only if you insist, Captain Kelly,' Karris said, every bit as loudly, 'although I hope you don't.' He fingered his moustache. 'My only need is to have my broken stirrup rebrazed, and while I'll need it for the next patrol – and the saddler will need an hour, perhaps, to stitch it back into place – my next patrol will have to wait until the roads are open, and I think the need for a working poker for the hearth in Barracks One is greater, at the moment, than mine is for a stirrup.'

The poker in question lay, bent almost double, on the counter, next to the broken brass stirrup, but Durine was more interested in the way that the various soldiers in the shop were watching the two captains argue, though there was something more than a little strange about the argument.

For one thing, this discussion was taking place at this smithy down in the city, and not at the smithy in the castle courtyard, where the needs of both officers and enlisted men were typically seen to. Perhaps the castle smith was too busy with other things, although what they might be, Durine couldn't imagine.

For another thing, this argument-that-sounded-more-like-foreplay was taking place in front of a crowd of soldiers. Durine could count on the thumbs of one hand the number of times he had heard officers willingly try to openly settle even minor differences in front of the rank and file. An officer might fight a duel at sunrise with other officers as seconds and witnesses, but most would rather be trampled by incontinent cattle before they'd break discipline in front of their men.

Kelly noticed Durine, and gave him a quick, chilly nod before turning back to Karris with his painfully-forced smile. 'My friend, if I don't let you go first, I'm not sure I'll be able to forgive myself.'

Karris gave a very theatrical shrug. 'No, please. After you, my dear Ben.'

Kelly raised a finger. 'You know, if I were to go first some people might think that you'd chosen to go second merely for the pleasure of lingering in the comfortable warmth of the smithy.'

Karris nodded at that. 'Yes, some people might be so foolish as to think that.' An idea seemed to occur to him. 'Perhaps,' he said, 'what you and I should do is to take ourselves to the Dangling Keshian, and talk about old times over a mug or two of good dwarven ale until both of our projects are complete.' He turned to one of the nearby soldiers. 'Silback, stay here, please, with, with . . .'

'Haas,' Kelly said, indicating one of the Folson soldiers. 'Haas will wait with him.'

'. . . stay here with Private Haas, until the stirrup and the poker are mended, and then the two of you can come and fetch us from the Keshian.'

'Sir.' Silback drew himself up straight, his face utterly expressionless.

Kelly turned to Durine. 'Ah. Captain Durine. Congratulations on your much-deserved brevet,' he said.

Karris joined him in the nod. They were all chums now. 'Yes, yes, yes, congratulations, indeed. Would you care to join us?'

Durine nodded, and the crowd of soldiers parted as the three of them made their way out into the cold.

'Well,' Kelly murmured to Karris, his genial smile frozen in place, 'I think the point has been made, you treacherous son of an unknown father.'

Karris nodded and clapped a hand – just a bit too hard to be really friendly – upon Kelly's shoulder. 'I can only hope it has,' he replied softly, 'you catamite. Let's put an end to this charade; I know you're eager to drop your trousers and bend over for anybody who can put the word "lord" in front of his name.' Still smiling, he clapped his other hand on Durine's shoulder. 'And what do you think, you oversized pile of shit in an undersized bag?'

Durine forced a smile to his own face. 'I think the lesson has been taken, here and now,' he said. 'How long it will hold is another matter.'

Both captains nodded in unison, then Ben Kelly sighed. 'We do what we can, eh?' The three moved along the street, away from any soldiers who might hear. Kelly continued, 'If his baron ends up as Earl, I'll be finding another earldom to seek service in, or take up a freebooter's life, anything rather than serving for one day under this bastard as Swordmaster –'

'The feeling is mutual,' Karris said. 'And not just because of the way that the left flank of the line collapsed in the Battle of the Forest because you insisted on keeping your company in reserve.' The tone was still even, but there was more than a little heat buried beneath it. 'But for now, orders are orders, and we've too many men with as much cause to hate each other, so we will do the best we can to keep things quiet. Even if it means turning my back on this Kelly in the tavern, knowing that he'd spit in my beer.'

Kelly nodded. 'Only if I didn't have time to unbutton my trousers,' he said with a humourless smile. He preceded the other two up the snow-packed steps to the front door of the tavern, not quite banging his head on the sign that displayed a cartoon of a Keshian dangling from a gallows.

'After you, my dear Captain Karris.'

'No, after you, my friend, Captain Kelly.'

Durine just walked through the door and let the two of them work out which would follow.

Here and now, things were holding together, and they probably would at least long enough for the captains to share a mug of ale and have their smithing done, and while some of the soldiers would perhaps find it even stranger than he did as to how a fireplace poker had found itself suddenly bent almost double, or a brass stirrup had been broken during a time when its owner wasn't going anywhere near a horse, he could at least hope that, for now, they would take the point of this little charade, and model their own behaviour on that of their captains.

Beyond that?

Durine shook his head. The captains couldn't be everywhere at once, even if all of the rest had got the point, just as these two had.

Just a matter of time, was his guess.

EIGHT

Confrontation

The tavern smelled bad.

Exactly how, Pirojil couldn't quite say. Certainly it didn't smell bad in any objective sense; quite the contrary: the scent of the lamb leg simultaneously being unfrozen and cooked on the spit in the hearth filled the tavern with an absolutely mouth-watering, savoury aroma. It got better every time the thick-set woman tending it turned the spit, and then immediately splashed the upper surface of the meat with a couple of spoonfuls of the garlic-laden wine-and-spices mix from the wooden bowl on the stool beside her.

Despite her nervous glances over her shoulder towards the clumps of soldiers, it seemed peaceful enough, though, if you just looked at it. But it smelled wrong.

The group of Morray soldiers gathered around three tables at one end of the Broken Tooth pointedly ignored the Verheyens at the other end, without even a muttered comment or glare at how their positions put the Verheyens nearer the warmth of the hearth.

Half a dozen of the mercenaries had also taken their orders to 'go down into the city proper' as meaning 'go down to the nearest tavern and eat and drink', and both the puffy-faced Milo and the mad dwarf Mackin had been at it for a couple of hours, judging from the pile of gnawed chicken bones on the table in front of them, and the way that Mackin's eyes seemed to have trouble focusing.

Pirojil picked an empty table in the strikingly unoccupied centre of the room. When Milo gave him a quick nod of greeting, Pirojil beckoned him and Mackin to join him. The unlikely pair rose and staggered over, Mackin splashing more ale on the floor than probably remained in the huge earthenware mug that he clutched in his thick-knuckled fist.

'Greetings, Pirojil,' Milo said. 'Joining with the common ruck for a quick beer?'

'Yeah.' Mackin laughed and more collapsed into the stool than sat down on it. 'Didn't think we'd be seeing much of the three of you, now that you've got yourselves such cushy billets.' His improbably large mouth twisted into a leer. 'You seem to be spending as much time with that Lady Mondegreen as with the Baron, eh?'

Well, that wasn't true, and why that should matter to Mackin was something that Pirojil didn't want to know any more about than he had to, although Mackin's frequent patronage of the human whores upstairs was a matter of some ugly barracks humour among the other mercenaries – as long as the dwarf wasn't present. Most of the time, you could rely on a mercenary not to get involved in a fight when there wasn't any pay in it, but there were always exceptions, and Mackin very definitely was one: he was known to take more than a little umbrage when his unusual preferences were made a matter of jest. He was probably the only dwarf between Dorgin and Stone Mountain who preferred serving as a mercenary to living with his own kind, and he was probably the only dwarf on the entire world of Midkemia who thought human women were attractive to look at, let alone bed. Then again, Pirojil considered, they didn't call him 'Mad' Mackin out of whim.

'I've spent a little time around her, yes, although that's just been a matter of orders and duty.'

'She is easy on the eye, though.'

Pirojil shrugged, though for a brief instant he tried to imagine what it must be like to be Mackin. For an even briefer instant he tried to imagine himself with a dwarf female, then, when his stomach began to get queasy, pushed aside the thought. Like most men, he preferred to bed with his own species. He was beginning to wonder if he had cursed himself with an image he might never lose, when the tavernkeeper poked his bald head out of the back room. Pirojil caught his eye and signalled for beer, wondering idly whether it was going to be the horrid local brew or the much better dwarven ale.

Mackin said, 'Your new duties must be keeping you busy. Haven't seen much of you since the brevet.'

'I've been busy, and that's a fact,' he said.

He thought about it for a moment, and decided not to go into detail that was none of their business, and would sound like bragging, anyway, despite the fact that his one wish, right now, was that the snow outside would melt and that the three of them could just ride out of this city.

'It seems quiet here,' he said.

Milo smiled over his beer. 'Too quiet.' He jerked his chin towards the stairway to the cribs upstairs. 'I don't hear any squeaking floorboards and haven't seen much of anybody going upstairs to blow off some steam. They all just keep drinking,' he said, leaning forward and lowering his voice, 'and I'm not too drunk to notice that a couple of the Verheyen men keep looking toward the door.'

'Like they're expecting somebody, maybe?' added the dwarf.

That possibility hadn't occurred to Pirojil, and it should have.

The fact that he wasn't used to this sort of thing was only an explanation, not an excuse, and Steven Argent was the sort much more interested in results than either explanations or excuses. Pirojil raised an eyebrow at the dwarf.

'Yeah.' Mackin grinned, revealing a missing tooth. 'You're right!'

Pirojil was glad the dwarf understood the significance of the raised eyebrow, so now maybe he'd explain it to Pirojil. There were times when Mackin assumed scratching your backside was a signal or a sneeze was a message, just as there were times he'd start up a conversation with empty air.

The dwarf nodded as he said, 'They're probably waiting for enough others to arrive so that they can settle some business with a nice little advantage – say two-to-one, or three-to-one.' He drained his mug and pounded it on the table, shouting for more. With evil glee he whispered, 'It should be a good show.' Then he lost his smile and indicated some other mercenaries at the far end of the room. 'At least, it should be a good show from that table over there where Filt and them others are, near enough the back door to get out if things get too interesting, rather than right here, in the middle, where we're likely to get trampled under-foot.'

Milo nodded agreement. 'Best to be ready to find a table to crawl under.'

Pirojil would agree with that under normal circumstances, but as he was now an officer of the Earl's court, the circumstances were anything but normal. He had to figure out how to keep this brawl from erupting. The best thing to do was to get one or the other side to leave, to find some other place to drink. There were at least nine taverns in lowertown, after all . . .

Pirojil's head was beginning to ache. This business of having to think about more than himself and his two companions was turning into a brain-twisting business. Yes, there were nine other taverns, and every one of them was almost certainly filled to the rafters with equally twitchy soldiers from all the different baronies. Pirojil wasn't idiot enough to think that the Verheyen-Morray feud was the only one around. Although he didn't have the details on what the issues were between Folson and Benteen, or Morray and Mondegreen or any of the other pairs of baronies you could name might be about. Issues were issues, and rivalries were about whatever you decided they were about when you decided to pull a blade and cut someone up, and the only thing Pirojil knew was he could do nothing about the issues, but he was supposed to try to keep people from cutting up one another.

Until things had quietened down, the urgency of all those rivalries had been suppressed by the immediate matter of fighting the Tsurani and the Bug; besides, most of the troops spent most of their time in the field, with ample space between them, not crammed together into the same city, let alone the same barracks buildings.

Finding some sort of overall solution was the responsibility of the officers, and if the officers had any better idea to ease tensions than sending off-duty troops out into the city, they surely would have done that, rather than –

Oh. *He* was an officer now, at least in theory, although his cloak concealed his new rank tabs at the moment.

Bloody hell.

He thought about it for a moment. 'Stay here.'

'You giving orders now?' asked Milo.

'Just do it, Milo; we'll argue about it later.'

The balding, watery-eyed man blinked several times, then nodded as he reached for his mug. 'That we surely will, Pirojil. That we surely will.'

Pirojil rose and walked over to the table of Morray men. Two of them nodded, and one of them frowned.

'Aren't you one of those freebooter privates who are supposed to be watching the Baron, so that that asshole Verheyen doesn't have him killed?' the man asked. He was a barrel-chested man, with little hair on his head besides his thick black beard, although his neck and forearms were covered with a thick mat of the stuff. The sergeant's stripes on his tabard were weathered and faded.

'I'm one of the mercenaries, yes,' Pirojil said, gesturing toward a chair in an unvoiced question, and seating himself at the sergeant's nod. 'My name is Pirojil.'

'Gardell,' the sergeant said, introducing himself. 'Glennen, Darnell, Roland, Garden, and Spotteswold,' he said, pointing to each man as he named them in turn. 'But you didn't quite answer my question, Pirojil – shouldn't you be watching our lord's back?'

Pirojil spread his hands on the table in front of him. 'I don't know what you've heard, but if there's any reason why Baron Verheyen should try to have your baron killed, it hasn't reached me.'

Gardell snorted at that. 'Then you haven't been listening much, have you?'

There was only so much you could do to try to persuade men who wouldn't be persuaded, and Pirojil was tempted to let it all go. However . . .

'I was just at the Baronial Council this morning, and both barons – and all the rest – made it clear that they think that there are other, more pressing, issues right now than whatever disagreements –'

'Disagreements, bollocks.' Roland spat on the floor beside him. He was a big man, perhaps a finger's-width taller and broader even than Durine, but his voice was surprisingly high-pitched – enough so that Pirojil wondered if some battle wound hadn't gelded him, not that there was an easy way to ask such a question.

'Yes, disagreements.' Pirojil raised a finger. 'Disagreements that won't be improved any if, say, a bunch of you go at it with the bunch of Verheyens over there. And never mind for the moment that I think they're waiting for more of their own people to arrive.'

Gardell nodded slightly, and seemed to relax in his chair. 'Well, then,' he said, 'maybe we ought to go over and . . . discuss things with them while it's just six-on-five, eh?' He started to push back from his chair, and didn't even pause when Pirojil raised his hand.

Then the others started getting out of their chairs, which didn't go unnoticed by the Verheyens across the room, judging from the sound of scraping chairs behind him.

'Sit,' Pirojil said, throwing back his cloak to expose the captain's tabs on his right shoulder. 'Now.'

Gardell thought about it for a long moment – too long a moment – then sat down suddenly, visibly wincing at the laughter that erupted from the other side of the room when he did. 'Captain, eh? Those wouldn't be counterfeit rank tabs, by any chance?'

Pirojil allowed himself a smile. 'You can ask the Swordmaster himself about that, if you'd like,' he said.

Gardell grunted. 'Remind me never to play pa-kir with you . . . Captain. I can't tell if you're bluffing or not.' He thought about it a moment, the added, 'As I'm sure you do know, here in the Kingdom they hang men for impersonating officers, so putting that into the centre of the table against my getting a tongue-lashing from the Swordmaster seems to be overbetting the pot. I'll take your word for it. Captain.'

Pirojil said, 'I have a suggestion: when you get back to the castle, you might also want to ask your own captain what he thinks about you fighting with Verheyen men –'

'I can swear that Captain Martin has as little love for Verheyen and his gang as any of the rest of us do,' Gardell said. 'Only reason he broke up the fight in Barracks Three last night is because he wanted us to save it all for another time – like now.'

Gardell's words sounded sincere, and Pirojil was torn between wondering if this Captain Martin was an utter idiot for not having just stamped on the idea of internecine fighting, or whether he was a real genius for having found a formula that had quickly ended a fight, at least for the night, no matter what it threatened for the all-too-near future.

Pirojil turned back to Roland.

'Very well, then, I'll make that suggestion an order: ask him about brawling in the city. And tell this Captain Martin of yours that the Swordmaster might be asking him, later this afternoon, about whether or not he understands that there's to be no fighting at all, and what the responsibilities are for captains loyal to the Earl of LaMut in enforcing his commands.'

None of the others said anything in response to that. Which he couldn't let stand.

Pirojil wasn't much used to giving orders – whether they were liked or not – but he had taken more orders that he hadn't liked than he cared to try to estimate, much less count, and he remembered how Baron Morray had phrased it, just the other day.

'I'm not much used to giving an order twice, Private Roland,' he said, 'and I wouldn't like to have to do so a third time.'

He eyed Roland levelly, unblinkingly, until the big man nodded and Pirojil carefully avoiding taking notice that Roland's nod was itself preceded by a quick nod from Gardell – there was no point in being a stickler for detail – and rose, gathering his cloak about him.

'Yes, sir,' Roland said, drawing himself stiffly to attention, though not removing the sneer from his face. Then he walked towards the front of the tavern.

As he did, three of the Verheyens pushed their chairs back from the table.

'Hey, why the rush?' one said.

'Kind of cold out,' added another.

'You sure you don't want to hang around and play for a while?' a third asked, as two of his colleagues moved to block the doorway.

'Don't move a muscle – that's another order,' Pirojil said quietly to the Morrays.

Pirojil was already on his feet. He shrugged out of his cloak and dropped it to the floor, revealing his new rank tabs, then strode over towards the Verheyens, more hoping than believing that Gardell would keep his men in place.

'Is there some problem here?' he asked as loudly as he could without, he hoped, seeming to shout.

The Verheyens had been ignoring him, but their eyes widened when they saw the rank tabs.

'Sir,' one of them said, and was followed by the others.

Grudgingly, the six Verheyen men drew themselves up to attention, and Pirojil gave them a long stare, as did a pair of men who had been blocking Roland's way, ignoring the manner in which he ungently elbowed his way between them.

'I'm in need of six volunteers to haul some ale up to the keep,' Pirojil said. 'You're them.'

'Captain, we –'

'Is the discipline in Baron Luke Verheyen's troops so bad that they don't understand how to obey a simple order?' he roared.

He didn't quite know how it would break – he was sure how it would have broken if he'd had only sergeant's stripes on his sleeve rather than captain's tabs on his shoulder – but if it broke the wrong way, he would kick the table towards three of them, knock down a fourth, and hope he would be able to make his own escape after triggering the very fight he was trying to prevent.

How he would explain that to the Swordmaster later, would have to be a problem he saved for later.

'No, sir. We know how to obey orders, sir,' one of the privates said, his eyes fixed on Pirojil, although the glowering expressions on the faces of the other men served as well as a mirror to reflect the smirks of Gardell and the other Morrays.

Some people, it seemed, didn't know when to keep smiles off their faces.

'Very well, then,' Pirojil said, accepting the concession with a nod. 'Innkeeper – *Innkeeper!* Get out here, now, if you please.'

The tavernkeeper was so quickly out of the door from the kitchen and into the room that Pirojil felt sure he must have been watching the whole scene through the beaded curtain.

'Yes – *Captain* Pirojil,' he said, with only a slight overemphasis on Pirojil's new rank. 'Is there something I can do?'

'The Earl is requisitioning three hogsheads of ale. These men will carry them up to the castle, and this one – what's your name, soldier?'

'Garrick, sir.'

'– and Private Garrick will carry your bill to his captain, Captain . . . ?'

'Captain Ben Everet, sir.'

'Captain Ben Everet, who will present it to the paymaster. Captain Ben Everet will, I hope, meet me at Barracks One in an hour; please convey my request to him, Private Garrick.'

'Yessir.'

The tavernkeeper simply nodded and successfully repressed a smile. The casks would probably contain the local human-brewed swill while the bill would be for the more expensive dwarven ale. A regular provisioning officer would have been specific, but Pirojil not only had no idea what a hogshead of either human or dwarven ale would normally cost the Earl and he had other far more pressing concerns at the moment than the Earl's kitchen being overcharged by a few coppers.

Sullenly, pretending to ignore the chuckles of the Morrays, the Verheyens shuffled towards the kitchen and the access to the cellar beyond.

Pirojil reclaimed his cloak from the floor, and folded it carefully on the stool before sitting back down with Mackin and Milo.

'Captain Pirojil, eh?' Milo didn't meet his eyes; rather, he seemed to focus on running the tip of his index finger through a small puddle of spilled beer.

Pirojil shrugged. 'As you said, there are some advantages to my present billet, all in all.' Not to mention the disadvantage of being held responsible for things that he couldn't control, but there was no reason to go into that, not at the moment.

'Giving orders seems to become you,' Milo said.

Mackin snickered. 'Yeah, it did, this time.' He frowned. 'And cost me some coppers: I bet Milo that the Verheyens were going to jump you, and not just go meekly down the stairs then out into the cold, just because you'd asked, er *ordered* them to do so.' He carefully counted out six copper coins and slid them across the table to Milo, who looked for a moment as if he was going to say something, but instead just shrugged and pocketed them.

'I take it that you and the others in the corner would just have found some other place to be,' Pirojil said.

'I would have.' Milo nodded. 'And as quickly as my dainty little feet could carry me, at that.'

'Me, I would have stayed and watched,' Mackin said, taking a thoughtful sip of his beer. 'But, no, it wouldn't have been my fight, Captain.'

Pirojil didn't blame him, but it was the first time in a long time that it had occurred to him that making some sort of connection with anybody other than Kethol and Durine would have had its advantages, rather than just the obvious disadvantages. The trouble with people was that if you expected them to get involved in your problems, you had better be willing to get involved in theirs.

Pirojil probably could have got Mackin and Milo involved in the fight on his side, lessening the odds that Pirojil was beaten to death, but that still wouldn't have done any good. Once a fight of any kind started, every baronial soldier in the tavern would be going at it. Even if the Watch arrived quickly enough, to put the fire out here, once any blood was drawn, those two baronies would be fighting on sight. And as everyone was happily snowed in together in a small part of town, they'd be seeing one another frequently.

Pirojil dug the Watch whistle out of his pouch, and held it in the palm of his hand. 'Do you have a problem taking orders?' he asked.

Milo's face didn't change expression. 'Not usually. As I think you've seen, from time to time. Depends, I guess, on what the orders are.'

Pirojil slid the whistle across the table to Milo. 'Consider this tavern as your post. Keep the peace here – blow for the Watch if there's any problem.'

A quick look passed between Milo and Mackin, and Pirojil recalled how Milo tended to make himself absent when the Constable was around. Pirojil didn't know what that was all about – it wasn't any of his business – and now was definitely not a good time to bother asking for details.

Heavy footsteps sounded on the floor, and the three pairs of Verheyen men walked out in single file through the wooden-beaded curtain from the kitchen, each pair carrying a hogshead.

The snickers from the Morrays were cut off even as Pirojil turned towards Gardell, although the smiles remained, some of them hidden behind mugs of ale raised in a sarcastic salute to the departing Verheyens.

Shit. That wasn't going to be enough.

In fact, Pirojil had just probably made things worse in the long run, even though he had been successful in preventing a fight breaking out right here and now. The Morray men might hold their derision in check now, but, later? Would they avoid snickering here, or in the barracks, or avoid moving to another tavern and bragging to anyone who'd listen that the newly-breveted, ugly

captain had taken their side in the Verheyen-Morray feud and
sent the cowardly Verheyens stumbling meekly out into the cold?

Not bloody likely. All Pirojil had done was to dump more wood
on top of an already-smouldering pile. It might take some time
for that fire to break into flame, but the fire would just burn
brighter and hotter, later on.

'Halt,' he called out to the Verheyens, just as the first pair of
men was just about to step out into the mud-room. 'Just stand
there for a moment.

'Everybody,' he said, addressing the whole room, unsurprised
to find that all eyes were on him. 'Listen up. It seems like I made
a mistake – the Earl is going to need another three hogsheads of
ale, and I know that everybody just heard the men from Barony
Morray volunteer to move the next three hogsheads up to the
castle, just as soon as the nice folks from Verheyen get back from
their own labours.'

He walked over to the Verheyens, and spoke softly: 'So I'm sure
you men will want to take your time, set your burden down and
rest every few feet, if you like, and be sure not to tire yourselves
out speeding up to the castle, so that your friends from Morray
will have plenty of time to rest and fortify themselves with food
and drink before it's their turn to stagger out into the cold. You
can –' he stopped himself. 'No; just wait here for a moment. I've
got one more thing to say, and it's for all of you.'

He walked back to the centre of the room, halfway between
the two parties.

'Although I know the Swordmaster's made his feelings clear to
the captains, and that the captains have already made it all clear
to anybody with two ears who is capable of listening, I'll repeat
the message, just in case anybody here failed to get it,' he said.
'There are to be no problems. There are to be no fights. It doesn't
matter who starts it, or why. Any brawls will get people tossed
into the city jail. Any bloodletting will get people sent to the

labour-gangs in the mines. Any killings will get people hung. So, it's just not going to happen. Understood?'

There was silence in the room. 'Is that understood?'

Murmurs of *yessir* echoed through the room, and Pirojil gestured towards the Verheyen men that they could go.

The Verheyens moved through the mud-room and out of the front door of the Broken Tooth Tavern almost as quickly as they could have walked unburdened, and Pirojil returned to his seat next to Milo and the dwarf, ignoring the glares from Gardell and his companions.

Yes, it was unfair – from the Morray men's point of view. It was the Verheyens who had set a trap for them here, after all, and the fight would have been the Verheyens' fault, not theirs – even though they could have just walked out when the Verheyens walked in.

If Pirojil had let it lie as he had first intended to, he would have only earned the enmity of one side.

Now, he had both sides hating him. On the benefit side of the ledger, however, maybe it would distract some of them from the fact that they hated each other even more, at least for a few hours, maybe even a day, and the only cost would be that Pirojil had another dozen or so men that he would not want at his back on a dark night.

A captain's pay was starting to look like awfully cheap coin for this.

'Well, that was probably a better way to handle it,' Mackin said, quietly. 'I was thinking that, myself, even before you decided to speak up.'

'Then why didn't you say anything?' Pirojil regretted the words the moment they were out of his mouth.

'Not my job.' The dwarf shrugged. 'As I said, *Captain* Pirojil, it's none of my business how my betters conduct themselves. You may remember that feeling, from when you were a lowly soldier . . . what was it? Yesterday, eh?'

'Be still, Mackin,' Milo said, frowning. 'The man's doing the best he can.'

'Still none of our concern.'

'Maybe not. Maybe so.' He turned back to Pirojil. 'Okay, Pirojil – I'll do what I can,' Milo said. 'No promises about how successful I'll be.'

'Be successful,' Pirojil said, as though ordering something done would make it done, something he had always despised when officers had done it to him. No matter what the legend was, when an officer told you 'jump,' asking him 'how high' on the way up was utterly pointless.

Milo made a face. He was probably thinking the same thing.

'Please,' Pirojil added. It seemed to be the thing to say, officer or not.

Milo nodded. 'I'll do my best. Until when?'

Pirojil hadn't thought about that, although if he had been on the other end of the order, he certainly would have done.

'Until you're relieved, that's until when,' he said at last, trying to work out who, exactly, he could get to relieve them. He jerked his head towards the other mercenaries off in the corner, who were watching the three of them far too intently for Pirojil's taste. 'Enlist some help, or your own replacement, if you need to. Find someone reliable, and I'll see they're paid, same as you.'

And how a group of mercenaries were supposed to keep the peace between the feuding factions, even in the cramped confines of the Broken Tooth Tavern, was another matter. They would have to improvise, just as Pirojil had.

'Easier said than done,' Milo said. 'Maybe if I was a sergeant?'

Pirojil had to laugh. 'You want me to bring that up with Steven Argent?'

'Probably not.' Milo shook his head, and smiled ruefully. 'No, come to think of it, definitely not. Take a promotion and the next thing I know I'll find myself an officer having to help keep the peace throughout LaMut, and having to conscript a bunch of others to help me hold back the sea with a fork.'

He slid the whistle over to Mackin, who nodded and tucked it into his tunic.

Mackin smiled up at Pirojil. 'Shouldn't you be making sure those Verheyens don't get themselves lost on the way to the castle?'

Pirojil didn't think that they would be taking their time, and he really didn't much care if they went directly up to the castle or wandered around in the city, tiring themselves out while they carried heavy hogsheads – but he did have to go have a talk with the Verheyen captain. Not that Pirojil's words would do any good if the Swordmaster's had already failed. Pirojil knew that Steven Argent had already talked to the captains, and from what Pirojil knew of the Swordmaster he had no doubt that Argent had made his feelings crystal clear.

Which began to explain why the Swordmaster had gone to the extremity of brevetting the three of them – he wasn't just, as he had admitted, unsure of the reliability of some of the baronial captains, he was sure of their *un*reliability, at least under the present circumstances of close confinement, and couldn't count on the ones he could trust to keep the lid firmly on the pot.

He was right to worry, Pirojil decided. Even if all of the captains were utterly reliable, incredibly competent and on top of the situation around them, LaMut was both too large and increasingly too small.

It was, he decided, a lousy day.

A particularly lousy day when you were wearing a pair of fresh new captain's tabs as heavy as lead weights that somebody had nailed to your shoulders.

A lousy day when you looked back at the more active periods of the war, when the castle's barracks were almost empty instead of crowded from floor to rafters, and when even the baronial soldiers in the Earl's service were far more concerned about where the nearest Blues and Bugs were than they were with how much they hated their traditional local enemies.

Pirojil pulled his cloak about him as he rose. Then he walked out of the Broken Tooth Tavern into the stark, frozen whiteness of the lousy day.

It really was a lousy day when a man actually found himself happy to be outside in the cold.

NINE

Plotting

Kethol stopped.

The only sound he could hear was his own breathing as stopped to look around the white-covered landscape. Old habits die hard, and he forced himself to listen to the sounds of the woods between breaths. He considered the absurdity of the moment, and reflected on the past as he listened to the breaking of ice in the distance and the faint sounds of a light breeze in the bare branches of birches and pines, oaks and elms.

Kethol had once, uncharacteristically, a long time ago, befriended a juggler.

The juggler had been a travelling performer who had been pressed into service in Lord Sutherland's forces during one of the cycles of wars with Keshians and rebellions from the locals that seemed to never stop in the Vale of Dreams. Said cycles of wars and rebellions in the Vale of Dreams being one of the reasons that Kethol, Durine and Pirojil always had the Vale as a fallback destination; there was always employment in the Vale, though if Kethol never had to face a load of battle-crazed Keshian Dog Soldiers again, that would be more than fine with him.

The juggler had been brought into service by one of Lord Sutherland's roving press gangs during a break of a few weeks between rebel attacks – the Kingdom had effectively outlawed slavery decades earlier, but labour gangs at the Keshian front were still a common thing; fortifications had to be rebuilt and men without convincing stories as to why they were trying to cross the border were considered renegades. Some were just unlucky, and a few of those might be cut loose when a company sergeant or captain was convinced the labourer was harmless. Kethol had always thought it a strange system; if he had been a Keshian spy, he would have been the most cheerful worker on the line, and been everyone's best friend. Eventually, he'd have been turned loose to do whatever it was he was to do. Those who attempted to escape and were killed in the process were idiots, solid proof they couldn't be Keshian agents. They were too stupid.

This time, however, the press gang wasn't bringing in labourers, but wall-fodder.

The juggler was obviously not a spy, but he hadn't had a compelling reason as to why he was hiking along a dusty trail in the foothills of the Vale, rather than travelling with a caravan or, at least, a band of entertainers. So, into the work gang he went. After a month, the sergeant in charge had cut him loose and against any reasonable logic, the juggler had decided to hang around. Perhaps he had grown to love camp food.

Kethol's company was manning a defence at the time, which meant guarding the work gang as much as looking for Dog Soldiers. He had come to know the juggler and when the young man had remained after being released from the work gang, Kethol had, for reasons he could never quite explain to himself, taken Kami under his wing. He had been enrolled in the ranks of the mercenary company Kethol was serving in, by a dubious sergeant who owed Kethol a favour.

Between sessions of Kethol trying to play swordmaster to the poor, manifestly doomed sod – you would think that a man so dexterous while juggling could not possibly be so clumsy with a sword – the man had explained his own personal philosophy, such as it was, which amounted to, 'when you don't know what to do, do what you *do* know what to do.'

Which sounded sensible, on the face of it.

Until he had discovered that, for Kami, that had meant that when he found himself frustrated with his inability to use a sword and shield he would take a few minutes and go off by himself or out into the night to juggle with whatever there was around – rocks and pebbles, if his juggling kit was not nearby – while he thought things out.

He had always come back relaxed, and ready to do his best during another lesson, and while he never did quite master even the most basic rudiments of sword work, he at least had good-naturedly put in a lot of hours working at it, and Kethol had found himself admiring the do-what-you-know philosophy, even if he wondered about its practicality.

Granted, it hadn't worked very well in the end for poor Kami, when the first Dog Soldier Kami went up against had feinted low and then slashed high, leaving his sword dropping from his fingers while his severed head tumbled through the air to land preposterously upright, a surprised expression on his dead face . . .

But at least it had given him some comfort and pleasure in the interim. If you did what you knew – or pushed what you knew just a little further – you could ignore, for the moment, that you were in over your head.

Which, perhaps, was why Kethol now found himself on a set of brezeneden, making his way – thanks be to Grodan, may his tribe increase! – more across than through the snow to the north of LaMut, a canvas bag over his shoulder.

Moving across snow on these brezeneden was something new to Kethol, but following tracks across the landscape was something familiar, even when they were as deep as the horse tracks from Tom Garnett's departing patrol, and a trail that a blind man could, quite literally, have followed by touch.

He had left his money-cloak in his footlocker in the barracks, hoping any thief would find other, more inviting opportunities than his footlocker. He had half-concealed a small leather pouch of reals in a corner of the locker, hoping that a barracks thief would just take that and look no further; and then had donned his solid white, winter cloak.

When he crouched down with his cowl up, even if he didn't spread his cloak over himself and the dark canvas bag wrapped in a sheet almost as white as the fresh snow – he would look like a small drift that had accumulated over a rock, or a tree stump, or a fencepost.

Perhaps it was spending time with Grodan or looking at the brilliant reflection of the sun upon the snow, but he was coming to the judgment that those grey cloaks the Rangers preferred did make a sort of sense in this countryside. Most winter days were not blindingly white as it was today, but overcast, grey, cloudy, or snowing, and the landscape rarely stood in this stark relief of absolute white and black shadows under the trees. The neutral grey would be good camouflage in all manner of circumstances. For a moment he wondered if he might find such a cloak, then decided carrying a third cloak around was just too much to bear; besides, explaining to Durine and Pirojil why he'd taken to this new fashion might entail more talking than he had patience for.

After he had found himself beyond the first stand of windbreak trees, which had now acquired a mammoth windbreak snowdrift with a few green strands of pine needles sticking through on the leeward side, he had spread out his cloak on the snow and lain down upon it to rest for a few minutes – moving through thigh-high snow was hard and sweaty work – and when he finally stopped panting, he had strapped the brezeneden to his overboots, and started to walk.

He now understood the origin of the brezeneden's name: 'clumsy feet'.

It made sense.

Sure enough, after the first few dozen steps – during which he had carefully watched his feet – he had become cocky, and picked up his pace. Immediately after which, he had stepped his left brezeneden down on top of his right, and when he had lifted his right foot, his boot had worked loose from the leather bindings and he had plunged face first into the snow. Even after he had got back to his feet and perched himself on the brezeneden again – a struggle in itself – it had taken several long, cold minutes to remove his thick gloves, retie his right boot to the brezeneden, and slip his hands back into the blessed warmth of his gloves and move on.

It went better, after that – until the next time that he had stepped on his own, suddenly-broadened, feet and while this time the lacings had held, he had still fallen down in the snow. But after a while he thought he had the knack of it, although he suspected that there were some subtleties to using these things that Grodan knew, and wished the Ranger had shared with him.

He wondered, for a moment, whether to attribute those omissions to malice or to stupidity, and decided that Rangers weren't stupid. The Ranger didn't strike him as particularly malicious, either. It must have been the inability to explain it all in one quick talk. Or, it could merely have been the Ranger's odd sense of playfulness. He'd known men who found a great deal stranger things than this amusing.

Still, after a while, his feet started to learn how to avoid each other, and he was able to move at a preposterously fast pace, under the circumstances. The marks that his brezeneden made would probably be erased by the first decent wind, but even in the absence of a stiff wind, the branch that he was dragging behind him would obscure them from all but somebody with the observations skills of a Natalese Ranger.

At a bend, he came upon the carcass of a horse, blood from the long sword wound in its neck having stained the snow a dark red.

The impressions in the snow made it clear what had happened: the horse had slipped on a patch of ice hidden beneath the snow, exposed by everyone riding the trail-breaker's path. The rider had been thrown into a nearby snow bank which had half-buried him.

Kethol shuddered. In his mind he could hear the sound of the cannon bone breaking, and nodded in approval at the footsteps that showed that the rider had braved the animal's undoubtedly desperately flailing hooves to cut its throat, quickly ending the doomed creature's pain. Retrieving the saddle had taken the work of at least a dozen men, judging from the footprints – the stirrups had probably got themselves caught beneath the horse, and several men had been required to lift enough of its bulk to slide it out.

They hadn't been disturbed during all this either.

The smoke puffing into the lazy air far in the distance suggested that the nearest farmhouse was probably more than a mile away, and the likelihood of any peasant having heard this relatively minor commotion was even smaller than one having been fool enough to venture out to see what had happened.

Which was fine with Kethol.

He drew his knife and set his gear aside and knelt in the packed-down snow next to the dead animal. It was small for a horse, which meant that it easily weighed six or more times what the largest buck deer that Kethol had ever taken had, and probably half again the size of that huge buck elk that had fed the company for a solid week up in Thunderhell.

A full field dressing would require more than one man's strength: he could break the breastbone, with enough effort; but it would take two or more men working together to spread the ribcage.

Still, the horse hadn't yet quite frozen. Even though he was panting and sweating with exertion when he had finished, he was quickly able to cut through the hide and flesh to expose the left rear hipbone. He wished he had thought to bring a small camp hatchet to break the bone free of the socket, but it was the matter of only a few minutes until he was staggering through the waist-deep snow, dragging the leg across the snow behind him towards a stand of birches that had managed to remain mostly unburied in the storm.

The storm had washed itself out around the stand of trees, leaving a small eastern hollow with barely a foot of snow in it, where he quickly cleared a spot to the icy ground. One of the long-fallen trees provided branches that snapped off in his hands and, with the aid of his dulled knife, chunks of wood, out of which he quickly built a fire.

Starting the fire took only a few moments – he didn't have to use the sheet of birch bark folded over in his rucksack, since the nearby birches provided plenty of that material, and he peeled a large strip off a wide bole, and with a few strokes from his flint-and-steel kit quickly built up a smouldering blaze. Then he ran back to the carcass to retrieve the rest of his gear, as well as leave more footprints.

He hacked off a hunk of horsemeat from the leg he had salvaged, and roasted it on the point of his knife over the fire, nibbling at it from time to time, rather than waiting for it to cook all the way through, out of impatience, rather than the pressure of time. Even if the patrol was unable to make a full circuit around the city, the breeze would blow the smoke away and even if they had to double back – as he expected they would – he would hear them coming long before they saw the clumsily-butchered carcass, and make his escape with the bulk of the windbreak between him and any observation.

It wasn't bad, although Kethol had never really cared for horsemeat. A man who much cared what he ate should probably have picked a better profession than mercenary soldier, but he was surprised to find that he had worked up a serious appetite. He ate quickly at least a couple of pounds of the meat. The rest he threw in the fire.

He dumped more wood on the fire, then went back to the carcass and hacked off as much meat as he could at speed and buried the pieces in the snow at the far end of the hollow. Then he pissed on the snow nearby in several places.

He opened the canvas bag and took the pieces of Tsurani armour that he had stolen from the storeroom in the keep's basement – early on in the war, the Muts had apparently been as interested as everybody else in collecting and examining this curious armour – and scattered them about the clearing.

The Tsurani sword, removed from its black sheath, snapped satisfyingly when he set the point on the ground and bore down on the flat of the blade with his foot, and he tossed the body of the sword aside, scooping up the few inches of the point and tucking it into his pouch.

He peered out from the hollow, and listened.

Nothing. Nothing but a slight wind, and the far-off chittering of some bird, a feathery braggart that apparently wanted to let the whole world know that it, too, had survived the storm.

Dragging the branch behind him, he set off on his brezeneden, pausing only for a moment to drop the sword point next to the horse's corpse, then quickly making his way across the ridge, back towards the city. It would probably be a good idea to wait outside the city until dark. The cover of night would serve him well when he staggered back in.

He would have to bury the brezeneden in the snow outside the city, though. Pity. But now that he knew the trick, he would be able to make another set if the need for them ever arose, as he devoutly hoped it never would.

You do what you can, the long-dead Kami had said.

When you don't know quite what to do, you do what you can do.

Not a bad philosophy.

Kethol didn't know how to prevent a fight from starting, much less how to end one without leaving everybody on the other side dead or dying – at least, everybody who hadn't fled. And the Swordmaster's ordering him to do it hadn't magically conferred upon him that ability.

Like Pirojil and Durine, he could have settled for going out into the city and looking and trying, but it didn't take any more than two eyes to see that there were problems, and that things were only going to get worse while a dozen feuding factions were trapped in the city.

What to do about that was beyond Kethol.

It wasn't beyond precedent for Kingdom nobility to yank subordinate incompetent nobles from their estates. Or even less than incompetent, no matter how lofty their station; as Guy du Bas-Tyra had apparently been able to do to Prince Erland in Krondor, using Prince Erland's supposed failing health as an excuse, if not a reason.

If the Earl had been here, the obvious solution would be for the Earl to explain to the feuding barons that he viewed the present situation as a test of their own leadership abilities, and that he would remove any who flunked that test. And the question of who the next Earl of LaMut was going to be could also be touched on.

But if the Swordmaster took that approach he could easily touch off the very situation he was trying to prevent. As he kept truthfully pointing out, he was not the Earl, after all, and nobles often would listen to one thing and agree when the point was being made by their betters, yet bristle when told it by an inferior, even if it was the same damn thing.

The winners would write the history, as usual, and the history would say that the losers had started the fight, and had been put down by a combination of loyal baronial troops and a few regulars, and anybody who could swear otherwise would be rotting in the ground somewhere, unable to make their dead voices heard.

Blame the war, as usual; if it wasn't for the war, the bulk of the LaMutian regulars wouldn't have been off fighting Tsurani: they would be here in LaMut, and barons at a council in LaMut would have had only their own personal guard, so any hostility between the various elements would have been a minor problem, rather than a serious threat. At worse, a duel might be called out, most likely it would have come down to nothing more troubling than a couple of lackeys getting into a scuffle in the stabling yard.

Now, it could be a full-scale riot, or worse, city fighting between armed men with years of battle experience and less sense than the gods gave a salamander. At the moment it looked as if even a scuffle between lackeys might trigger a battle between the barons.

Kethol didn't know how to handle that.

But Kethol did know how to do a few things.

He knew how to make his way across the land without drawing attention to himself. He knew how to field-dress an animal – or quickly hack off a leg in the absence of time to do a proper job – and he knew how to let the other players in a game distract themselves while he kept his eye on the main chance.

It would look for all the world as though some Tsurani scout had been hiding in that clump of trees, and had observed the LaMutian patrol passing by, leaving behind the dead horse. The Tsurani had been unable to resist supplementing whatever meagre rations he had with some fresh horsemeat, then made his escape, avoiding leaving footprints by hiding his tracks among those of the patrol's horses. Who knows: the man might even be a trail-breaker for a raiding party. The Tsurani were clever when it came to war, and might be clever enough to attack when the Kingdom least expected, in the dead of winter.

It might not work, but the thought of some Tsurani lurking about might well give the baronial troops something else to think about besides killing one another.

One could always hope.

TEN

Rumours

Steven Argent didn't like it.

He forced himself to sit back in his chair in the Aerie, ignoring the glass of wine on the side table at his elbow, the better to glare at the fragment of blue ceramic in his hand – if only to avoid glaring at Tom Garnett, who sat across from him, petting Fantus, and waiting for the Swordmaster's response to his report.

Why everybody *else* – even that freebooter, Kethol – seemed to be taking to the firedrake was a recurring, if relatively minor, irritation. Steven Argent was still frustrated at his ongoing inability to keep Fantus out of the Aerie, and momentarily, from time to time, used that minor frustration as a welcome distraction from more important and far more frustrating matters.

Like this bit of sharp blue ceramic that he held in his hand, the other armour piled next to his chair, and Tom Garnett's report about how and where it had been found.

Steven Argent had not been surprised that snowdrifts from the storm had made it impossible for Garnett's patrol to make even a complete circuit of the city, even on the closest roads. That was expected, but the effort had had to be made, if only to confirm

how thoroughly they were all snowed in. His only surprise was
that the patrol had cost only two horses – one slipping on ice,
and another gone lame on the return leg of the patrol – he had
anticipated losing as many as four. And any surprise irritated him.
There was a rule about soldiering and warfare that he had learned
long ago: all surprises are bad.

Another rule: all rules were broken, upon occasion.

But he could count on the fingers of one hand the number of
times that he had had anything resembling a good surprise during
the years of this war with the Tsurani, and the more than a dozen
years soldiering before them. Surprises were always things like
the relief column being a day late and of half the strength that
you were counting on, rather than arriving a day early or at twice
the strength. Or the enemy over the next ridge was an army
instead of a company, never a patrol instead of a company.

It was widely known that ever since the war had started the
Tsurani, come winter, retreated behind their lines to await the
coming of spring and the resumption of the war, and from what
Steven Argent thought he knew about the number and quality
of soldiers that they had fielded, their fear or religious avoidance
of combat during winter was one of the few reasons that they
hadn't swept across Midkemia from north to the Great Northern
Mountains, south to the Bitter Sea. All reports indicated that the
Tsurani homeworld harboured armies many times greater than
what they were throwing at the Kingdom. A report to the Earl
from Prince Arutha at Crydee on what they had been told by a
Tsurani captive indicated that this war was merely an aspect of
some massive political struggle on the Tsurani homeworld.

Argent found politics even more irritating than surprises.

He had never heard of the Tsurani deliberately leaving scouts
behind Kingdom lines during their winter retreat, or about
stranded Tsurani turning scout, rather than turning tail for their
own lines. If that had happened now, that would be a surprise.

And not a good one. And if it happened because of Tsurani politics, it would be a doubly irritating surprise.

'So?' he asked. 'What do you think? Just another straggler?'

'No.' Tom Garnett shook his head. 'Unlikely. Not that it's impossible – but living off the land well enough to survive in winter isn't something that I'd expect a lot of the Tsurani to be good at, and those few, desperate ones who jumped us last week were in the worst state I've ever seen any of them in.

'This one was in good enough shape, apparently, even after having survived outside in the storm – he picked himself a very good spot for that, and from how suddenly and hard that blizzard hit, that he survived at all tells me that he's both good and lucky. He had probably been hiding out in that very stand of trees, watching the comings and goings of the city.

'Watching and waiting from a stand of trees, then quickly taking advantage of the situation to provide himself not only with a quick meal, but as much meat as he could carry – that speaks more of skill than desperation. And he was smart enough not to return to that spot.'

The Swordmaster half-seriously believed that the test of a man's intelligence was how much that man agreed with the views of one Steven Argent, and he had always considered Tom Garnett to be particularly intelligent, although no doubt he had certain disagreements with him, but kept them to himself. Loyalty and sycophancy were two entirely different things, in Argent's estimation.

'Yes,' he said at last. 'It's bad enough to think of Tsurani scouts helping to prepare the way for their spring offensive, but if that means the Tsurani have changed their ways of avoiding combat over the winter, that's a very bad sign.'

Tom Garnett nodded. 'Wouldn't be the first time they've learned a new trick.'

'There are a few they seem reluctant to learn, though,' said Argent.

'Cavalry.' Tom Garnett nodded, agreeing. 'By all reports, they seem to have some odd sense of honour about not riding, for which I'm grateful. They've certainly captured enough of our horses to have taken it up, should they be so inclined. And I can't imagine too many things a Tsurani isn't brave enough to try.'

Argent nodded in agreement. No man who had faced the Tsurani would gainsay their bravery.

'But they do seem to have learned a few things from us. Still, even concluding that they've adopted winter scouting ahead of the spring re-engagement is a lot to read from this one incident, and it wouldn't necessarily mean that –'

'How the hell do you *know* it's just one incident?' Argent snapped, then held up a palm in an instant apology at the harshness of his words. 'I'm sorry, Tom; it seems that holding down the Earl's chair under these absurd conditions has tightened me like a bow string.' Steven Argent had never believed in the old saw, 'never apologize, never explain'. When you made a mistake, you apologized, lest the men who served under you thought you were an idiot who never noticed that he had erred.

Tom Garnett nodded, accepting both the correction and the apology. 'I don't know it's only one incident, at that. How quickly can we get a message to Yabon?'

Relaying the intelligence to their superior was the obvious thing to do, but Steven Argent shook his head. 'I'll check with the birder, but I doubt that we have any Yabon-homing messenger pigeons – the Earl is due to bring some back with him.' He shrugged. 'I did receive one, a few days ago, announcing his safe arrival there, but I can hardly tell it to turn around and fly back, eh?'

Earl Vandros had always gently mocked Steven Argent's concern about the paucity of messenger pigeons in LaMut, and it gave Steven Argent no joy at all to have been proven right. With dozens of messages quite literally flying back and forth in advance of the general staff meeting in Yabon and the Baronial Council in LaMut, the stock of pigeons was far too low for his taste.

'So, what do we do?' Tom Garnett frowned and drew himself up straight. 'My apologies, sir – what I meant is: what are your orders?'

Steven Argent forced a smile. 'Well, my first order is to give me the evening to think about what to do next, and let's keep this matter to ourselves for the –'

'Er.' Tom Garnett blinked. 'I'm afraid it's too late for that. The only way I could have stopped my men from talking was to lock them all in the barracks, with guards outside, and even then I'm not sure that the secret would have held.'

And, he didn't have to add, *I wasn't under any orders to lock up the very men you need out and among the rest, trying to keep the peace.*

Steven Argent nodded, accepting the explanation. 'Well, it's out, and I suppose word will have reached the barons soon, if it hasn't already. I'd better go answer their questions before they tear the Great Hall apart, eh?' He forced himself to chuckle. 'That last was just a figure of speech, and an ill-chosen one, under the circumstances.'

He rose, and the Captain set his glass down and quickly got to his feet as well, but he gestured at Tom Garnett to sit back down. 'Oh, don't get up. Stay and finish your wine, man; you certainly deserve it, and it's a shame to waste even half a glass of such a fine Rillanon red. I can't imagine when we'll be getting more in.'

The Captain reseated himself, and gave the Swordmaster a quick salute with his wine glass. 'Thank you, sir; I'm no judge of wine, but I've rarely had better. But as to the barons having heard, I'm sure that's so. I've found that gossip always travels faster than the most speedy crossbow bolt.'

'So I'd best get out and about,' the Swordmaster said. 'You wouldn't have any good news for me, would you?'

'My apologies; no, I don't.' Tom Garnett shook his head. 'Good news seems to be in as short supply as fresh produce, right about now. Although . . .'

'Yes?'

'Well, when we were coming back in to the city, the air definitely did seem to be warming a little, and I don't think that's just from all the exercise and the way that finding this armour had my heart pounding in my chest. I suppose any change in the weather is good news.' He reached over and scratched at the fire-drake's eye-ridges, and smiled as the lizardlike creature preened himself. 'And I think that Fantus likes me.'

Steven Argent laughed. It wasn't much of a laugh – the times didn't seem to be terribly funny, all things considered – but it was real enough.

Pirojil, with Durine in tow, intercepted the Swordmaster coming down the stairs, just as they were walking up the winding stair-case to the Aerie to report to him.

From their own discussion, it was clear that their reports to the Swordmaster would be similar, and would inevitably lead Argent to the same conclusion that both of them had independently drawn: things were barely holding together in the city, and with the way that the regulars, the Watch and the baronial captains were keeping a lid on the pot, it would likely continue to simmer a little while longer before, sooner or later, it boiled over.

It hadn't been much of a coincidence that they had encountered each other on the way back up the hill to the castle. They both knew that the Swordmaster dined early, by himself; and because they both had understood that when he said he wanted to get their report 'at table', he had meant that they were to join him in his rooms and report privately, rather than later, when he joined the nobility in the Great Hall.

Pirojil hoped that they wouldn't have to persuade Steven

Argent that they hadn't disobeyed his very explicit orders to split up when they went down into the city, although he found himself worrying about having to do just that, and gathering names of witnesses in his mind.

At least it gave him something minor to worry about – what could Steven Argent do, after all? Take away all three sets of their captains' tabs and simultaneously relieve them of the responsibility of trying to keep a lid on things? A full-scale bloodbath would be a relief after the tension he experienced trying to act like an officer. This leader-of-men stuff was nerve-wracking, to say the least.

No, getting relieved of duty was the least of their worries. Where, for example, was Kethol?

Kethol had, it seemed, understood Steven Argent's instructions differently – Kethol wasn't always the brightest of men, in Pirojil's studied opinion, particularly when he was out of his element, and a snowed-in city was most assuredly not Kethol's element. On the other hand, perhaps he was just a few minutes behind them.

Or perhaps Kethol was just lying dead in some back alley, having tried too hard to break up a fight, and finally run into either too good a swordsman, or too many of them.

Steven Argent paused a few steps above them, looked down, and nodded. 'There you are. It's always been my policy to dine with newly-made captains, but there's been a sighting of a possible Tsurani scout, and –' he stopped himself. 'No, what's happening in the city is likely to be more important, at least at the moment.'

Pirojil suppressed a derisive sniff. Yes, it was very bloody likely to be more important. Whatever this 'interesting development' was, it couldn't be more important than open warfare being one shoving match away from breaking out among the factions in the city.

'I'd better hear your report now, and we will dine later,' Steven Argent said, 'but quickly, if you please.'

From what snatches of conversation Durine could hear, from across the barrier of the table and most of the width of the Great Hall, the after-dinner concerns of the assembled nobles were more about the Tsurani scout than they were about problems of taxes and succession, and were decidedly more friendly.

Even Morray and Verheyen were too busy listening to the Swordmaster holding forth, as he had been through the nobles' dinner and for the past hour after, to spend time glaring at each other, although Edwin of Viztria couldn't keep the usual alternating sneer and scowl from his face, or avoid dropping an occasional comment that Durine was just as glad he couldn't entirely make out. Baron Edwin was one of the few men Durine had met that he felt deserved to be throttled merely for being annoying.

Whoever this Tsurani scout was, he had provided a useful distraction. Durine was inclined to lift a glass in toast to him, as long as his presence this far south didn't presage some sort of huge Tsurani troop movement. Looking at the other captains gathered around the hearth, Durine judged he wasn't the only one of the captains who would have been happy to buy the poor freezing sod the drink of his choice. Those who had taken a turn through the suddenly peaceful barracks reported that the men were now anticipating combat with the Tsurani, not one another. Yes, he'd gladly buy that Tsurani scout a drink.

Before cutting his throat, of course. Gratitude could only go so far.

Durine was finishing his second glass of wine, and deciding whether he had better switch to coffee or tea, when Haskell the Birdmaster came down the steps from the loft above the Aerie, and handed something – a message, presumably – to the Swordmaster, who accepted it with a quick, dismissive nod, then finished what he was saying to Edwin of Viztria before stepping under a lantern to read the note.

If the message had any effect on the Swordmaster at all, it didn't show on Steven Argent's increasingly-lined face; and it didn't show in his actions, either, for he just tucked the message into his belt pouch and resumed his conversation with Viztria.

Probably nothing important, even though, a few minutes later, when Durine looked over towards where the nobles were, Steven Argent, Lady Mondegreen and Baron Morray were gone, leaving Barons Folson and Langahan to rejoin the other nobles on the far side of the room.

The talk was mainly of the scout, and what that portended for the spring, and if Durine hadn't switched to coffee after a couple of glasses of wine, he would have been thoroughly drunk by the time Kethol had staggered in, well after dark, and joined the rest of the small cluster of soldiers around the smaller hearth in the Great Hall.

He had, uncharacteristically, been almost entirely silent, which was very unusual for Kethol, who habitually talked in crowds enough to blend in, and didn't like drawing attention to himself by silence any more than by loquaciousness.

Durine shrugged. He could ask about it later, and probably would.

Captain Karris came in out of the cold, stamping his boots on the marble floor to clear the snow from them, apparently disdaining the idea of doing so out in the cold of the mud-room.

'Hail, Karl Karris,' Tom Garnett said. 'Any word?'

'Word?' Karris sniffed, scooping up a mug. He squatted in front of the coffee pot next to the hearth, wrapping his hand with his cloak to grip the handle, disdaining the nearby leather glove.

'There are plenty of words – but they're fairly quiet words at the moment, at least out in the barracks. Lots of men getting some sleep, even though a few have had to drink themselves to sleep, and the rest seem to be spending an unusual amount of time seeing to their gear.' He chuckled to himself as he plopped down into the empty chair between Durine and Garnett. 'There're some swords out there that are now more than sharp enough to shave with.'

Kelly nodded. 'But those that aren't asleep seem to be spending their time looking at the windows, rather than at each others' throats, as though they can see Tsurani storming over the castle walls through the bloody shutters.' He grinned. 'Lousy day when the best thing that happens is a rumour of a Tsurani winter troop movement.'

'You don't think it's so?'

'Me, I hope it's so – I hope that there's a legion of them frozen out in some fields, ten miles to the west, but I don't believe it. Not that it would matter much if it was so – they seem to be in endless supply, like sewage flowing through a pipe, and that pipe pours out in the Grey Towers. They could afford to lose a legion to a bone-headed move like trying to marshal an army in a blizzard. But they're not stupid enough to try that. No, my guess is that the Tsurani have just added another string to their bow –'

'Winter scouting?' Karris scowled. 'I don't much like that thought, but . . .'

'Yes, if it's just that, that's bad enough, certainly, but it's not the end of the world. Still, if I were at the general staff in Yabon City, I'd be carefully rethinking how early things are going to heat up, come spring.'

'In more ways than one, eh?' Tom Garnett grimaced at his own weak joke.

'Yes.' Karris thought it over for a moment. 'LaMut – Yabon itself, for that matter – has been, thankfully, more of a sideshow these days, with the real action at Crydee and Stone Mountain, and I'm pretty glad of that, but if that's about to change, I hope

our betters will stop stripping the defences in Yabon down to a
bare minimum, to reinforce the West.'

'Which could, of course, be just what the Tsurani want us to
do,' Kethol said, quietly, speaking more than a monosyllable for
the first time since he had sat down. 'And then they just redouble
their efforts against a less well-defended Crydee, and go through
the dwarves at Stone Mountain like a toe through a well-worn
sock, and –'

'"Us", you say?' Kelly raised an eyebrow. 'Us? Since when is
there an *us*? From what I hear, you and your friends are still
southbound, the moment that it's thawed enough, with most of
the mercenaries with you.'

Durine didn't know about most of the mercenaries – he
thought some would stay, as long as there was pay to be had, and
that some would go, as he and Kethol and Pirojil surely would.
These rank tabs were a temporary breveting, and if this news
presaged some new major Tsurani movement into Yabon, the idea
of getting out of LaMut had even more appeal than it had before.

Not that it needed much more appeal.

Kethol just blinked. 'I'm just saying that it might be a bad idea
to make too much of this one incident, as surprising as it is.' He
shrugged. 'Grodan of Natal said that he and the other two Rangers
would be back in a few days, and I doubt even the most talented
Tsurani scout could make his way through LaMut without leaving
some tracks that a Natalese Ranger would notice.'

There was general agreement and widespread nods at that.

The abilities of the Rangers were widely respected – although
Durine wondered how even they would be able to make any
progress across the land right now. Kethol at least seemed sure
that they would, but that was probably just Kethol having bought
into their legend; Durine was more sceptical by nature.

'Rangers?' Durine started at the way that Morray spoke up: he
hadn't heard the Baron approach. 'What's this about the Rangers?'

Tom Garnett pointed his pipe-stem at Kethol. 'Captain Kethol was just explaining that the Rangers are scouting the surrounding area. He was urging calm, and suggesting that we wait to see what their report is before leaping to conclusions about Tsurani late-winter campaigns and such.'

'I couldn't agree more.' Morray nodded. 'Sound counsel, that.' He looked from face to face, and the side conversations cut off abruptly. 'I'm just but a lowly land-baron, and all,' he said, his voice tinged with bitterness, then quickly went on, 'but it seems to me that there'll be time aplenty to panic later on, if there's anything to panic about.'

His voice and even his posture were soothing, too soothing and relaxed to be natural, but that was the only clue as to how tightly the Baron was keeping himself under control.

Morray beckoned to Kethol. 'Might I have a private word with you, Captain Kethol?' he more asked than commanded. 'There's a matter or two we need to discuss.'

Kethol gave a quick glance at Durine, then rose and left the Great Hall with the Baron.

Durine wondered what that was all about, and from the looks at him from the other soldiers it seemed he wasn't the only one wondering; however, he kept his face carefully blank, and Kelly went on, after a few awkward moments of silence: 'Yes,' he said, 'panic won't serve us at all, but there's more than enough to worry about. It gets worse all the time, as it is. Each year, the Tsurani are more secure in the Grey Towers and the surrounding areas. Each spring, they have the choice whether or where to strike out – west to Crydee, or south to the Bitter Sea, or south and west through the fringes of the Green Heart to Carse and Jonril. Or east to LaMut, for that matter. They picked their entry point cleverly – if they had entered this world at Crydee, we'd have them bottled up against the Far Coast, or if they had chosen the High Wold, we could bring the forces of both the East and West realms together against them, and smash them flat.' He punctuated the words by clapping his hands together, as though smashing a fly.

That would, of course, have been easier said than done; the Tsurani would have made an awfully large fly, and Durine wasn't at all sure that even collectively the Realms had enough force to smash them flat. But he was more than a little amused by the notion that the only places deemed useful for the Tsurani to have invaded through were in the Kingdom, although the fact of the invasion happening through some sort of rift near the Grey Towers spoke of good planning or better luck on their part.

It would have been nice, say, if the rift to Midkemia had been created a few feet below the Bitter Sea, and drowned every cursed Tsurani and his kin on Kelewan. That was a fine wish, but then again, Durine had always felt that if you put a pile of wishes in your left hand, and the hilt of a sword in your right, it was what was in your right hand that was likely to affect what happened around you.

'What we need to do is to carry the battle to them,' Karris said. He drank deeply from his goblet – he had quickly switched to wine after draining his mug of coffee – and reflexively wiped his wine-soaked moustache on the back of his hand.

Tom Garnett nodded. 'A sound enough idea, but how?'

'If I had some real idea as to how,' Karris said, glaring, 'I can swear I'd be doing something more useful than sitting around the fire drinking and smoking with you lot.' He pulled his pipe out of his pocket and began to puff on it, careless of the fact that it wasn't lit.

'I like the idea, myself, but it's the how that matters.' Karris sighed. 'And as to how to carry the war to the Tsurani, rather than letting them deliver it to us, I've no useful notion, but some hope that those at Yabon will have better than an inkling. We could try to plan out the whole war here, I guess, over our pipes and coffee, but we don't know what Duke Brucal and his advisers know.'

The rest let that go by with nods and mutters of agreement, although Durine doubted that, say, a captain serving Duke Borric of Crydee would have considered the general staff meeting at Yabon City to be simply *Duke Brucal and his advisers*, nor would a dwarf fealty-bound to Dolgan of the Grey Towers or to Harthorn of Stone Mountain, or whomever Queen Aglaranna of Elvandar had dispatched to represent her and elfkind, for that matter.

Just a matter of perspective, he supposed.

He leaned back in his chair and closed his eyes. It had been a long day, but tomorrow would likely be easier, and, he hoped, better.

What was going on with Kethol and Morray, though?

ELEVEN

Suspicion

Kethol followed silently.

Morray led Kethol up the stairs and down the hall to his suite of rooms. Once through the door, he gestured for Kethol to take a seat. They were in the room called 'the sitting room' for some reason, although every room in the baron's suite had chairs suitable for sitting. Morray seated himself across the table from Kethol before pulling on the bell-rope at his right hand.

'I find myself in need of a glass of wine,' he said. 'Or several, perhaps.'

Emma, the daughter of Ereven, the housecarl, was in the doorway almost before Morray had let go of the bell rope.

'Yes, my lord?' she asked, smiling.

'A bottle of good red, please, and two glasses – unless you find yourself hungry, as well, Captain Kethol?'

Kethol shook his head. 'I ate earlier,' he said. The pounds of horsemeat were still weighing heavy on his belly; just as trying to work out how to tell Pirojil and Durine what he had done to distract the feuding factions was weighing on his mind, and whether to just keep his mouth shut was weighing on his conscience, or what there was of it.

'Then just the wine, please,' Morray said, smiling gently at the girl.

'At once, my lord.' She departed the room as quickly as she could. As usual, the nobility got far better service than the common ruck. Prettier service, at that, despite the fact that the serving girl was far enough along in her pregnancy that her walk out of the room was more of a fast waddle.

Morray looked at Kethol carefully, as though searching for something in his face, though Kethol didn't know what that something could be.

He hoped that the Baron wasn't searching for some hint that Kethol had created this whole Tsurani scout rumour out of some captured armour, a dead horse, a set of brezeneden and a need to distract the local factions. Kethol was starting to wonder if that had been, after all, such a clever idea, all things considered, with open talk about the Tsurani having dramatically changed their habits, and the necessity of Kingdom strategy adapting to that change.

Surely, one nonexistent-but-believed-in wintertime Tsurani scout in LaMut couldn't cause the nobles in Yabon City seriously to revise their strategy, could it?

He hoped not, and thought not, but . . .

But, it wasn't really his problem. When the thaw came, he and Durine and Pirojil would be gone for quieter places and times somewhere else – anywhere else that there weren't Tsurani and Bugs – and what happened in the Kingdom in general or even in LaMut in particular would no longer be any of their concern. And even if he felt a little guilty – although he wasn't really familiar with that emotion – he was enough of a gambler not to let that show in his face.

'There's a matter that I need to discuss with you,' the Baron said. His expression was sombre as he produced a small piece of paper from his pouch.

'This just arrived tonight, by messenger pigeon from Monde-green City. Baron Mondegreen died late last night,' he said, his words flat and level, as though commenting on the weather. 'Which was expected, although . . .' he shook his head, as if finding words was a task. He paused, then repeated, 'Which was expected.'

Kethol nodded. 'I know that he was expecting it, and he seemed to face it with courage and good grace.' It seemed like the thing to say; that it was true was almost irrelevant. 'I only met him the once, but he seemed to be a kindly man.'

Morray nodded. 'That he was. He and I had our differences, but he was always a gentleman about them, and I have no doubt he would have been the same had Carla married me, rather than him.'

Kethol controlled his own shock. As far as Kethol had been aware, Lady Mondegreen had always been Lady Mondegreen. The thought of her as a young girl engaged in a romance with even one man beside her husband seemed . . . both obviously reason-able and utterly preposterous, at the same time, although, looking back, he had seen hints of it. Morray wasn't a recent conquest, a comfort to a lady robbed of her husband's vigour by illness; rather, he was an old suitor, perhaps one who had claimed her heart even while her father gave her hand to Mondegreen.

'His lady knows,' Morray said. 'She's taken to her rooms, and Father Finty has given her a draught which may help her sleep, although she resisted it.' His jaw clenched for a moment, then he went on: 'Father Kelly's note was short.'

Kethol understood the brevity of what a pigeon could carry.

'But the note says that a long letter, dictated by the Baron himself, is to follow, and I have my expectations as to what the letter will say, given the last letters that he sent to LaMut.'

Emma came back with a bottle of wine and a set of glasses on a tray that she held clumsily in front of her belly. She set the tray down on the table. 'Shall I serve, my lord?' she asked.

He shook his head. 'No. I'll take care of it.' He looked up at her, and after a moment she forced a smile and nodded.

'Just ring if you want me, my lord.'

'I shall,' he said, dismissing her. He uncorked the bottle and poured a glass of wine first for himself, and then for Kethol.

'I give you George, Baron Mondegreen,' Morray said, raising his glass. 'May he long be remembered for his kindness, wisdom and honour, with gratitude and appreciation.'

He waited.

The toasts that Kethol, Pirojil and Durine gave their own dead comrades were shorter and not at all suited for polite company. Kethol struggled for the right words, as the usual ones quite likely wouldn't have gone over very well. 'The poor sod,' didn't seem right, and neither did 'And we've got his pouch!' nor 'And if nobody else buries him, he can rot where he lies.'

'Baron Mondegreen,' he said, finally.

They drank.

'Now . . . on to other matters, which may or may not concern you.' He cocked his head to one side. 'I have to ask: what *did* you say to Baron Mondegreen when you met him?'

Kethol shrugged. 'Nothing terribly much, my lord. It was most "yes, my lord", and "of course, my lord", and the usual sort of thing one says to a noble.'

'Strange.' The Baron seemed puzzled, even if the puzzle didn't seem terribly urgent. 'You clearly impressed him, and he is . . . was not easily impressed. Wasn't there some conversation about a stand of oaks? About hoping to meet him or his son there, some twenty years from now?'

Oaks? The only conversation Kethol had had about a stand of oaks had been with –

Oh.

'Not that I could say, sir.' His conversation about a stand of oaks had been with Lady Mondegreen, not her husband or her child. How and why that story had been changed he couldn't imagine, although he did have more than a good guess as to one of the people who had been involved in that.

Morray scowled. 'I'm not sure whether to be impressed with your honour or angry with you for keeping a secret when there's obviously no need.' He shrugged. 'But be that as it may I'd like you, the three of you, or any of you, to take service with me, and see to it that Baron Mondegreen's son – if it is a son – lives to see that stand of oaks, some twenty years from now.'

Kethol didn't understand. He said as much.

'I'll make it simple for you, then: Lady Mondegreen is with child. It is her late husband's child – is that *clearly* understood?'

'Yes, my lord.'

'If it's a boy, as I hope it is, that child will need a legal guardian until he reaches his majority and can become Baron Mondegreen in practice, as well as in law.' He tapped his chest with a thumb, then gulped down the rest of his wine and poured himself some more. 'That guardian will be me.' He stopped himself, then shrugged and went on: 'And there's no point in trying to keep secret what will be apparent to all, sooner than later: I'll be withdrawing myself from consideration as Earl of LaMut, once Vandros becomes Duke of Yabon, and I'll support the choice of Luke Verheyen as Earl.

'While it will still be Duke Vandros's choice, of course, as to who to appoint as his successor, with Verheyen having my support along with the support from his faction, Vandros would be a fool to choose anybody but Verheyen, and he is no fool.' His jaw clenched for a moment. 'In return, Verheyen has agreed, as Baron or Earl, to support my guardianship of Barony Mondegreen – both to and as the Earl – and to . . . other matters.'

'Your marriage to the lady?'

'Yes.' Morray nodded. 'Of course, we'll wait a decent interval, but . . . yes. Baron Mondegreen's boy, if it is a boy, will come into his estate in difficult times, and I want his son – *his* son, do you hear? – I want his son to be able to handle whatever comes his way. Baron Mondegreen was impressed with the three of you, and you're to be the boy's tutors in martial matters, as well as his bodyguards. He's to be able to fight like an angry bear – and, if necessary, slit a enemy's throat without a moment's hesitation or regret, then spit in his face in anger for the way that the blood dirties his boots.' His expression softened. 'And, truth to tell, if it's a girl, it will do her no harm to know how to fight, as well, in these times.' Morray studied Kethol's blank expression. 'A traditional swordmaster, like Steven Argent, can train a noble son to be an officer, to fight duels and to command men in the field. The boy will have that. But I also want someone with the child who'll teach him how to deal with a blade in an alley or . . . treachery from a friend.

'You've no other local loyalties.' He paused to consider his words. 'The men of Mondegreen will be loyal to the child, because he will be the next Baron Mondegreen. I want more. If you swore to protect the child's life – not just with your skills and your bodies, but your forethought – and vowed to kill anybody who would harm that child, it would be a different thing. Do you see?'

Kethol didn't understand all of what was going on, but he knew he didn't like either idea: signing himself up for a lifetime of service or flatly turning the Baron down, not to mention that he couldn't speak for Durine and Pirojil, no matter what Morray thought.

There was only one thing to do: stall, until he could get Pirojil to work it out.

'I'm flattered, and honoured, my lord.'

'So you accept?'

'I'll have to speak to the others before I can commit them –

or even myself. We long ago agreed that we'd decide matters of where we go and what we do together, and I can't bind them by my promise, nor make it without at least giving them fair notice.'

What I really want to do, my lord, he thought, *is to make utterly sure that I never spend another minute I don't have to around the twisted, flowing politics of LaMut, much less embedded in it, up to my nostrils, with the tide coming in.*

But there was another side to it.

Yes, this whole offer suggested a conspiracy – not just between Barons Morray and Verheyen, trading off Morray's chance at the earldom for Verheyen's support in his marriage to Mondegreen's widow – but it also suggested that something strange had gone on between Baron Mondegreen and his lady, and Kethol would leave it to Pirojil to work it out, as trying just made Kethol's head ache.

He was a simpler man, all in all.

And Kethol remembered a kind-eyed, dying man, gasping in his deathbed in his stinking room. He could never forget the way the dying man had put his wife's safety in Kethol's hands. Kethol wasn't sure that he could decline the request that came not just from Baron Morray, but from that kind-eyed dying man who had – and this was such a minor thing that he didn't understand quite why it seemed to mean so much to him – offered him a cup of tea and looked up at Kethol with trust.

Trust – except from Durine and Pirojil – wasn't something Kethol was any more used to than guilt. He didn't quite know how to deal with it. It was there, lodged in his chest, or up in his throat, or maybe the pit of his stomach. It lingered and reminded him of that old man every minute. No matter how much he wished it wasn't there, he couldn't pretend that trust hadn't passed between them, any more than he could just privately dismiss it as indigestion.

Morray nodded. 'In the morning, then.'

He refilled both their glasses, and they drank, as though they were a pair of merchants who had just sealed a bargain.

'He said *what*?'

The emphasis on the last word was the only sign that Durine was furious. The three of them had gone outside, onto the packed snow of the parade ground, where they could have a private discussion without worrying about being overheard. Breath from his nostrils turned to steam in the cold night air – but it looked rather as if Durine was so angry that he was suddenly producing smoke, and the effect only further emphasized his obvious displeasure at what Kethol had just told him.

'And you said what?' Pirojil shook his head in disgust, and dug at the snow with the toe of his boot. 'Tell me, *please* tell me that you're just fooling with me, that you really said, "I'm sorry, my lord, but we've got an urgent engagement somewhere else, anywhere else".'

Kethol just repeated what the Baron had told him, and that he had agreed to talk it over with Pirojil and Durine, and give the Baron an answer in the morning.

Pirojil swore under his breath, both at Kethol, and at himself, then tried to calm himself down. It was important to keep your eye on the goal, and while Kethol apparently couldn't, that only made it more important that somebody else be able to think clearly – or think at all, since Kethol clearly wasn't going to do that – for all of them.

They had to detach themselves from LaMut, to get away.

Pirojil started with that. If you didn't know what you wanted to do or where you wanted to go, you had no chance of doing that or getting there.

So, start from the beginning: the three of them wanted to get away.

What they *should* be doing, right now, was sewing up their pay

– which was still lingering in the vault in the castle basement, awaiting the imminent conclusion of the Baronial Council and what Pirojil hoped was immediate disbursement after its conclusion – into their cloaks or the coin vests that they wore under their tunics, preparatory to getting out of town the moment it became possible.

Very well. That was impossible at the moment, so forget about that. Forget about getting out of LaMut at the moment, too, though right now, if there had been some way to get out of here without the coin, Pirojil would have taken it in a moment.

He said as much.

Durine nodded. 'Yes, I would, as well. If there was a way. When the ship's sinking it's time to get overboard and not worry about what you've got stored in the hold, eh? But right now, we're locked in the hold ourselves, and we'd best hope that the crew can keep it afloat until we can break the door down, and then dive over the side.'

'And quickly.'

Kethol didn't do what he should have done, which was to nod vigorously in agreement.

Instead he just stood silent for a moment, then shrugged.

'Well,' he said, 'it doesn't much matter what we want to do, not at the moment, not unless you want to leave our pay behind *and* you think that we can make our way across deep snow like a trio of Natalese Rangers?'

'Which we can't,' Pirojil said.

'Well, even if we could, there's the matter of the money, and I don't like giving up our pay.' Kethol spread his hands. 'So we're not leaving for the moment –'

'You, Kethol, have a keen eye for the obvious,' Pirojil said.

'– and that means that we can at least think about Morray's offer, doesn't it?'

'What's there to think about? How far down the path you've

taken us without our knowledge?' Pirojil tried to calm himself. What they should be doing was separating themselves from this war. Instead, with every passing minute, it seemed that they were getting further intertwined in local affairs that were none of a mercenary soldier's proper business, and should have been none of their concern.

First there was bodyguarding Morray against the threat of this apparently mythical assassin, and then being detailed by the Swordmaster to help keep the peace among the feuding factions, and now . . .

'No.' Pirojil shook his head. 'Make that: shit, no. I'll tell you right now, my answer is no.'

Durine nodded. 'Mine, as well. I'm not at all sure that this Tsurani scout does presage a Tsurani drive to the east, much less a late-winter one, but if it does, given their numbers and the number of the Muts standing in their way, they could run through LaMut and not slow down until they reached Loriel.'

'Or the Dimwood, for that matter,' Pirojil said. Which was probably an exaggeration, but not much of one. There was not a lot of anything between Loriel and the Dimwood.

'And more to the point, it doesn't much matter what cushy billet you think you've procured for us if that billet is crushed beneath Tsurani sandals – along with us, eh?' Durine said. He frowned and shook his head.

'Would you just please think it over for a moment?' Kethol pleaded. 'Please?'

'This stupid idea of yours –'

'Hey.' Kethol held up a hand. 'It *wasn't* my idea. I wouldn't have brought the subject up at all, not without discussing it with the two of you –'

'And somebody had better learn to keep his mouth shut, and work harder at staying invisible at other times than when we're hiding in a forest, eh?' Pirojil shivered. Maybe it was a little warmer

– well, no maybe about it; it was starting to warm up – but that didn't make it comfortable outside.

'I don't know what it is that you think I did,' Kethol said. 'Other than not telling the Baron no right away. All I agreed to –'

'You *should* have said "thank you, my lord, for your very gracious offer, but no, no, no, no", not left him to think that we might take him up on the offer, if the price is right or if pressure is applied. He might up the price and apply the pressure, eh?' Pirojil wasn't disposed to accept excuses. 'As to what else you did, you flirted with the Baroness, that's what you did, apparently.'

That was unfair, but Pirojil wasn't disposed to be overly fair at the moment.

Durine shrugged his broad shoulders. 'Which shouldn't have had such dramatic results. Then again, a little nick over the artery in your neck shouldn't cause the blood to spurt out until you lie dead on the ground, either, but it does! Little things can have large effects!'

'Just think about it,' Kethol said, insisting. 'I promised we'd think about it.'

'I can't *help* thinking about it,' Pirojil said, his mind racing.

'Well, then.' Kethol gave a happy nod.

'He said he was *thinking* about it, not that he was seriously *considering* it,' Durine said.

Assuming that Kethol was telling the truth about his brief conversation with Baron Mondegreen, and Pirojil didn't have any reason to doubt that – even Kethol could not be stupid enough to lie to him, not right now – Pirojil didn't believe for one misbegotten moment that the origin of this idea lay with either of the barons, Morray or Mondegreen.

Lady Mondegreen was obviously behind it, and every indication was that she was terribly dangerous.

All roads led to her – from her husband having gained an

inflated view of their abilities as warriors, right up to Morray giving up his campaign for the earldom.

Pirojil wouldn't have been surprised if the idea of breveting the three of them to help keep peace in the city had originated with her, and Steven Argent didn't even know that the seeds had been planted in his mind – perhaps while he was busy trying to plant the seeds of what would officially be Mondegreen's son in her belly, although if she had manipulated the Swordmaster, she had probably been somewhat more subtle than to whisper suggestions while they coupled in the night.

No; that was wrong.

She had been pregnant for some time – that was clear from her trip to Mondegreen, to spend one last night with her husband and establish the child's paternity. But the rest of the idea held up, and there was no reason to believe that her apparently effective dalliances had ceased upon her return to LaMut, and quite a lot of reason to believe otherwise.

It seemed that she wanted some reliable outsiders to watch over the upbringing of the child growing in her belly, the child that had apparently been put into her belly by one of the nobles with whom she had been cuckolding her dying husband, a child planted there quite probably with that husband's knowledge and blessing.

Which meant either that she didn't trust anybody around her, not even Morray, even though he had apparently been her childhood sweetheart; *or* that she, as a matter of policy, believed in coppering all bets.

Or both, of course.

That she was capable of being bloody-minded was no surprise to Pirojil, now that he had a moment to think about it. She had, after all, married Mondegreen rather than Morray, and it was clear that she had had the choice between the two of them.

Was that because she had had her eye on being the wife of the

Earl of LaMut and hitched her wagon to Mondegreen's star? She certainly would have noted Vandros's unavailability because of his longstanding attachment to Felina, and his likely ascension to the dukedom. Logic argued against her setting her cap at the younger earl. If she wanted to rule in LaMut it would have to be as the wife of the man to follow young Vandros.

Had she really worked all that out and calculated that Baron Mondegreen was likely to become the Earl – before anybody else had?

Or was it just that she had expected to outlive Mondegreen, and had her eye on both baronies?

It even could have been that she just preferred the man she had chosen to the man she had passed over. Call it affection, or love: call it anything you liked. It hadn't stopped her from manipulating other barons and soldiers with an ease and ability that terrified Pirojil, who didn't think of himself as a man easily frightened.

Pirojil always preferred to have a high opinion of the opposition, even if it usually made sense to keep that opinion to himself. He had to admire the enemy here, because the enemy was clearly Lady Mondegreen, and she was good at what she was doing, and capable of laying plans that would take years to complete, promptly adjusting her tactics as things changed on the ground – what with her husband's inability to get her with child, and the wasting disease that had, finally, killed him.

Pirojil thought he had had great respect for the political abilities of Kingdom nobility, but this woman . . . It was a shame that she wasn't born a man, or Pirojil knew who would be running the staff meeting in Yabon City at this moment, if not presiding at the table of the Viceroy in Krondor.

She was probably good at some other things, as well. She had managed to persuade Morray to make a deal with his enemy, Verheyen, with Morray's only payment being herself and the appointment as regent of Barony Mondegreen in return for Morray giving up his claim on the earldom.

Had that been the plan all along? It seemed likely, although there was no way to know for certain.

Morray didn't seem to be the sort to take a sure small profit over a large speculative one, and the word was that he had possessed a more-than-average chance at being the next Earl of LaMut. Yet, in the space of a few hours, he had given up on that. Pirojil nodded. *Very nicely done, Lady Mondegreen,* he thought. From what Kethol said, while it was clear that Morray was dedicated to the notion of raising Lady Mondegreen's child as though it was her freshly-dead husband's, it was also clear that Morray thought the child was his.

As it might well be.

He could blame the Swordmaster, as well, come to think of it. Steven Argent had apparently, although probably unintentionally, planted in Lady Mondegreen's serpentine mind the notion of the value of outsider bodyguards with everything to lose if something happened to whoever they were supposed to protect: so it wasn't surprising that she would want a set of bodyguards like that – or those specific bodyguards – for her own child.

And he could blame himself and Durine and Kethol, too, for that matter, for the quick and effective way that they had protected Baron Morray during the Tsurani ambush that had only been a few days before, but was already starting to feel like ancient history. That had apparently impressed Lady Mondegreen, for whom combat had been a nebulous thing until the Tsurani had dragged it into her lap.

So Pirojil could blame the three of them for that. He chuckled to himself. As long as he was diverting himself by blaming, he could blame the Tsurani, the King, Prince, and Regent and the gods themselves, and probably be more right than wrong.

Not that laying the blame would do any good.

'Well,' he said at last, 'my careful, considered, thoughtful answer is the same one as my offhand, reflexive, instinctive answer: no.' He shook his head. 'I like things just a *leetle* more straightforward than they are here, and this Lady Mondegreen scares the shit out of me.'

'Lady Mondegreen?' Kethol hadn't worked it out, yet. Pirojil would have to explain it to him slowly, later.

Using very small words. One. At. A. Time.

'Yes. Her.' Durine was nodding. 'Yeah. I'd much rather have her as a friend than an enemy, but . . .'

'Shit, yes. I'd rather be in a death duel with Steven Argent than that. At least with the Swordmaster you've got a chance to see the blade coming your way.'

Durine nodded again. 'Or run away from it, without knowing that you were just running into some other blade, put in place against just that eventuality.'

'Enough chance of that if you're a friend, eh?'

'Yeah.'

She hadn't done anything to harm them – save for wrapping them more and more tightly in local politics, and politics was a dangerous sport, and not to Pirojil's taste.

Protecting yourself was one thing. Spending twenty or more years protecting not just one baron for one little patrol, but a baby baron, through to his majority, was something else entirely. And knowing that you had been picked precisely because you had no local connections, that you understood that if anything, ever, happened to the baby, the boy, the man, it would be your fault . . .

That would certainly compel whatever fool agreed to that to take great pains with the safety of the baby, the boy, the man.

But Pirojil wasn't that kind of fool, and he really did want to be able to sleep some time over the next twenty years, and on better than a one-in-three.

'So,' Pirojil said, 'we have to decide. Yes or no? Do we decide that we enjoy the taste of LaMutian conspiracy, and ask for more, with a helping of intrigue on the side? Or do what any sensible man would, and run the moment we can? And if that means leaving our pay behind, so be it.'

Durine chuckled. 'I think your position on it is clear. As is mine.'

'But –'

'Shut up, Kethol. It's my turn to speak.' Durine shook his head. 'I'll be clear about my choice: I am leaving. If it's with one or both of you, that's fine. If you want to stay behind and take service here, Kethol, I'll wish you well, bid you goodbye, and make sure that the gold is properly divided before I go. I don't like things complicated, and the more we get involved with this northern nobility, the more complicated things get. Not for me.'

Pirojil nodded. 'I agree. Two of us say no to the Baron's kind offer. If you want to say yes, you're on your own.'

Kethol stood silently for a moment, and then his shoulders slumped. 'You're right, I guess. I just wanted to think about it.'

'We've thought. We've talked. Decide.'

Kethol raised both palms in surrender. 'Oh, never mind. I'm with the two of you.' He sighed. 'And if you choose to think me a fool for having considered staying, then you can just go ahead and do so.'

Pirojil clapped a hand on Kethol's shoulder. 'Well, what I think is that there are no other men I'd rather have watching my back, and that's a fact. We're agreed, then?'

'I already said so.'

'Good.' Durine nodded.

A thought occurred to Pirojil, but he dismissed it, or at least tried to.

Manipulation was one thing; murder another.

It was unlikely that Lady Mondegreen had poisoned her

husband so that she could marry her lover. Wasn't it? The Astalon priest treating the Baron would probably have been able to discern the existence of the poison, if not necessarily find a cure.

No, he decided, she hadn't murdered her husband. If she was willing to leave dead bodies in her wake in order to advance herself, there was no reason why she would have waited this long to rid herself of a troublesome husband, and the trail of bodies would have been long. Besides, Durine had known his share of cold-blooded killers and he relied on twenty years' experience that she wasn't such a one.

In any case, it was almost over.

The air was warming, peace had been made between the two most hostile of the feuding barons, and all they had to do was politely turn down Baron Morray's and Lady Mondegreen's generous offer, get their pay, and head south as quickly as possible, leaving LaMut behind them. Assuming that they could get their pay before they had to leave.

He shivered.

It might be warmer outside than it had been, but he felt colder.

TWELVE

Morning

Everything appeared peaceful.

The golden morning sun had just barely breached the eastern walls, so that it shone in through the now-unshuttered windows, splashing golden morning sunlight into Lady Mondegreen's bedroom on the second floor of the castle. Tapestries covering the stone walls opposite the windows blazed with unexpected vibrancy, made brilliant by the golden light playing across them. An array of jars and bottles resting on her personal table glimmered like jewellery as the sunbeams reflected off their glass and porcelain surfaces, sending sparkling motes into the gloomy corners of the room. As the sun rose, the reflected light seemed to move, alive, shimmering and changing colour from golden, to silver, to white.

An obviously empty bottle of fine Ravensburgh red lay on its side on the bedside table next to two glasses, one empty, one with a thimbleful of wine remaining at the bottom. Some delicacies lying on a tray beside the wine – shelled nuts, sweetmeats, and a bit of cheese – had dried during the night.

On a chair beside the bed, a man's clothing and a woman's nightgown lay neatly folded.

The bedside lantern had long since burned itself out of oil, or been quietly, peacefully extinguished.

The bedclothes had been disturbed no more than bedclothes would normally have been disturbed in sleep by the two forms that lay there, intertwined, beneath the covers.

It was all peaceful.

The lovers lay facing one another, as if they had been gazing into one another's eyes as they succumbed to slumber. Even what seemed to be a veritable sea of blood from their cut throats had soaked into the sheets and clotted, leaving Baron Morray and Lady Mondegreen lying together, unmoving in death.

THIRTEEN

Investigation

The guard had fallen asleep.

White-faced, still shaking, he admitted as much.

Steven Argent believed him.

The Swordmaster gestured him into a chair while Tom Garnett looked on. There was no point in keeping a dead man at attention, after all, and clapping him in the dungeon could wait for a few minutes, until Steven Argent worked out what questions, if any, he ought to ask him right now.

He found himself possessed of a bizarre sense of utter calm. He didn't even ask the man when he fell asleep, or how long. How would he know?

How could the idiot have been so sloppy? How could Tom Garnett have picked a sergeant who would have picked a soldier to stand guard over Morray's suite who would have been so sloppy? How could Steven Argent have picked –

Damn!

'Are you certain that you didn't see Baron Morray go to Lady Mondegreen's room?' he asked, quietly.

'Nossir. I mean, yessir. I mean, yessir, I did.' The soldier was staring straight ahead, not meeting the Swordmaster's gaze. 'It was none of my concern, I thought, and the Baron didn't need to tell me that. I just stood my post – I could see the lady's door, down the hall, and I didn't think that the Baron would have wanted me to move over to a post in front of her door while he was inside.'

That made sense.

Not that it would have made any difference if he had fallen asleep while standing next to Lady Mondegreen's door, or had just gone down to the barracks and abandoned his post.

First things first, he thought, *first things first.*

The obvious suspect was Verheyen – at least, that would be the obvious suspect to Morray's men.

Tom Garnett nodded, as though he was reading the Swordmaster's thoughts. 'I've got the Morrays, with Karris's company, on a quick march to the north, with the Verheyens and Kelly's men to the south.' His mouth twitched. 'I know it's not my prerogative, but –'

'But it seemed more important to separate them, even for a few hours, than it was to take the few extra minutes to get my orders on the subject.'

Garnett agreed with a nod. It would have seemed that way to Karris and Kelly, as well.

Not that Steven Argent thought that it was Verheyen, not given the arrangements that Verheyen and Morray had made between them the night before, which amounted to Morray's surrender. Yes, Verheyen might have hated Morray, but part of that was just rivalry over the earldom, and as of last night, that rivalry had ended, with Morray's surrender. Whatever animus remained would be set aside once the larger prize was won.

But if not Verheyen, then who?

And why?

Steven Argent shook his head. That sort of question wasn't

going to be answered by an idiot of a swordmaster, who apparently couldn't keep his mind on the simple task his earl had given him of keeping one land baron alive, and who had such slack discipline among his troops that soldiers fell asleep on watch.

He shook his head. There would be no excuses. He had always emphasized such basics, and any one of his sergeants would have kicked a man bloody if he'd found him sleeping on watch, even what was supposedly a perfunctory watch as that on the Baron's suite in the castle had been. And yes, it had been important to separate the factions of these fractious barons in this once-in-a-lifetime combination of too many of the wrong troops in LaMut, too few of the right ones, and a blizzard locking them all in the city.

He would present his resignation to the Earl, immediately upon Vandros's return, and in the unlikely event that the Earl would have such a useless fool as a private, Steven Argent would expiate his guilt with a sword and pike in the line.

He pointed at the soldier who sat in the chair, and then at the door. 'Get him down to the dungeon, Tom, and put three men on the door, watching him. He looked down at the ashen face. 'You are not to hang yourself in your cell; you're to await the Earl's justice, and suffer it like a man.'

The soldier nodded.

'As will I, I suppose,' the Swordmaster said. If only he hadn't gotten clever, if only he hadn't let Lady Mondegreen persuade him that Kethol and his men would be far more useful keeping things quiet in the city while she brokered a peace between Morray and Verheyen, rather than worrying about some unlikely assassin that had agents not only in LaMut, but among the Tsurani.

But she had been persuasive, as had the facts – this hypothetical assassin had been just that – hypothetical – up until this morning, and had looked less and less unlikely to exist as the days had gone by. Neither she nor he were easily impressed, but the three freebooters had impressed both of them.

Yes, he thought, disgusted with himself, *blame the dead.*

But it *had* seemed to be a good idea at the time, and if the idiot soldier now departed for the dungeon hadn't fallen asleep, it would *still* have seemed like a good idea. The immediate danger had been warfare breaking out among the factions, and if that had happened . . .

As it still could, and probably would.

He glanced over at Tom Garnett. 'This one can't wait upon the Earl's return, can it? I don't see much other choice, do you?'

The Captain shook his head. 'Somebody has to find out who murdered Baron Morray and Lady Mondegreen – somebody with credibility, that credibility backed up by the authority of the Earl of LaMut. And quickly, before everything falls apart around us. It can't be you or me,' he said, holding up one finger, then adding another, 'as we're the incompetent idiots who let the Baron get murdered on their watch.'

Steven Argent forced himself not to wince, but instead just nodded.

'It could be Viztria or Langahan,' Tom Garnett added another two fingers, 'but to choose them is tantamount to turning over LaMut to Guy du Bas-Tyra, one way or the other. Besides,' he said, shrugging, 'you've spent time at the court in Rillanon, and those of the court in Krondor are only a little less devious. I wouldn't at all put it past Guy to have sent his barons here just to make trouble –'

'Of course not, but . . . murder?'

'And what could be more trouble than this?'

'You think that one of them is the killer?'

'I don't think so, but I don't *know,*' Tom Garnett said. '*You* don't know. I know it's not me, and I know it's not you. But you don't know that it's not *me.*'

'You?'

Tom Garnett threw up his hands. 'It was my man who fell asleep on watch – maybe you should have Kelly or Karris keep an eye on me, down in the dungeon. I surely would, if our situations were reversed. I'm not even sure that it's not Erlic, who –'

'Erlic?'

'The guard.' Tom Garnett frowned. 'He might have done it. I don't have the vaguest idea as to *why* he might want to murder the Baron and Lady Mondegreen, but I can swear that falling asleep on guard isn't *his* custom. Or that of any of my men – which is why I've got three men on his cell, and intend to go down to the dungeon and supervise them myself, lest we find that he's hanged himself in that very cell . . . with or without some help.'

'You think he may be a dupe?'

Garnett shrugged. 'At this point, anything is possible. More likely, he might have seen something he doesn't know he saw; talking to him may draw out a clue as to who's behind this bloody-handed business. You might want to send someone to watch me.'

'I trust you, Tom.'

'Well, then maybe I need someone to keep me safe, as well as to keep Erlic safe.'

'You don't trust your men.'

'Up until this morning, I would have trusted any of them, in any combination, with my life, and with things that I value more than my life.' Tom Garnett's hands actually shook; he knotted his fingers together in rage to stop the trembling. 'But I've just been given reason to reconsider, haven't I?'

He spread his hands, and stared at them until his traitor fingers stopped trembling. 'And you can't put any of the landed barons in charge of the investigation. All of them have something to gain with Morray dead, especially if suspicion falls on Verheyen.'

Steven Argent nodded. 'There are only three men in this castle who we *know* have everything to lose, and nothing to gain, by these murders.'

'Yes. Three men who don't want anything out of LaMut except to be *out* of LaMut, with the money that they're owed – money that will now remain in the vault until Earl Vandros gets back – unless somebody else knows the spell that will open the vault. Do you?'

Steven Argent shook his head. 'No. I'm a soldier, not a clerk. At least, I was a soldier, up until this morning. But I take your point. Still, they could have accepted the offer to watch over Baron Mondegreen's child, and if they did, that hardly makes them uninvolved.'

It had been an unlikely possibility, but the lady had been very persuasive, and –

No. No, he wasn't thinking clearly at all. Agree to watch over the baby, then kill it in the womb – along with its mother and its father?

When they could just have said no?

Stupid, stupid, stupid. His only excuse was that this wasn't the sort of thing that he was used to.

Either way . . .

Tom Garnett spoke what should have been obvious to Steven Argent: 'With respect, if it does, it makes them involved only innocently.' Garnett shrugged. 'They'd hardly accept the offer, and then kill the Baron and his lady, when simply saying no would have done, would they?'

Argent nodded. 'I was just thinking that.' He fell silent for a moment, considering his options. Then he said, 'There's an old saying, "you've a willing horse, so flog him another mile". Send for them.'

Tom Garnett smiled as he got up. 'I already did, sir. They should be waiting outside the door. And if I know Pirojil, he's probably been eavesdropping just outside.' He drew himself to attention. 'Unless you have other orders for me, sir, I'll be in the dungeon, watching the prisoner.'

'Yes, you're dismissed, Captain. Send them in. And may Tith-Onaka watch over us all.'

Kethol shook his head.

The Aerie was filled with glares. The midmorning sun glared in through the window, and Durine and Pirojil were glaring at Kethol, if only because he was petting Fantus, rather than paying attention to anything else.

Well, what was Kethol to do? Steven Argent had just laid this matter in their hands, and gone downstairs to gather the remaining barons together for an impromptu council, and to announce that he had chosen Captains Kethol, Pirojil and Durine to investigate the murder of Baron Morray and Lady Mondegreen.

The Swordmaster's latest orders made sense, sort of, in a way, but . . .

Pirojil put it into words for him.

'There's only one problem with this latest set of orders,' Pirojil said. 'I don't have the vaguest idea *how* to find out who did this.'

Durine nodded. 'Usually, after a battle, if I've wanted to know who killed somebody, I just asked – although I swear that Mackin is lying about having done that Bug all by himself.'

'The one in the forest or the one near the Grey Towers?'

Durine raised an eyebrow. 'He claims two? I thought he was just talking about that little mishap in the Yabon Forest last autumn.'

'Could you two please, please keep to the matter at hand?' Kethol pleaded. 'I don't know how we can do this either and as you know, thinking things out isn't my specialty.'

'Apparently.' Pirojil frowned.

Kethol repressed a protest. His most recent attempt to think things out seemed to have gone well – it had distracted the baronial troops, after all, and perhaps it had even given Lady Mondegreen the arguments she had apparently needed to get

Verheyen and Morray to come to terms with each other. He would
have liked the opportunity to ask her that.

On the other hand, if that was so – and Durine and Pirojil
would think it was so – that very distraction had also triggered
the offer from Baron Morray, and Pirojil and Durine were still
angry with Kethol for having not simply spurned that offer.

So it was best to keep his own counsel on whether or not he
had been clever or a fool. He didn't have the slightest doubt how
the other two would see it.

In the meantime. . . 'How long do you think we have?'

'Hours,' Pirojil said. 'Unless we get awfully lucky. Baron Morray's
troops are loyal to him: and there are too many Mondegreens
about; their lady is lying dead in her room, and the perpetrator
of both crimes must be sitting downstairs in the Great Hall.'

'Tom Garnett sending the Morrays and Mondegreens to try to
break through to the closest villages made sense.'

'Yeah. That's why we've got hours, rather than a battle raging
in the streets.'

It wouldn't be the first time that feuding between local factions
had turned into outright war – Pirojil could have asked the resi-
dents of Traitor's Cove about that.

'I'm hoping,' he said, 'that one group can push through to
Kernat Village to the north or Vendros to the south, but they're
miles away, and I doubt that they can make it, especially through
waist-deep snow, when they probably can't even find the roads.'
His eyes seemed to lose focus for a moment. 'Probably the best
thing to do is to send out Tom Garnett's and Kelly's companies
to slaughter one or the other side without warning – but I don't
think the Swordmaster is going to order that.'

'Bad precedent, that,' Durine said. 'It just might run to slaugh-
tering some mercenaries, rather than paying them off.'

'Yeah, there is that. The story about Morray and Verheyen
making peace between them isn't going to sell very well –'

'You don't believe it?'

'I do believe it, but I don't think that it's going to be very persuasive, not to the Morray and Mondegreen men, and it's only a matter of time before they take matters into their own hands, or the regulars stamp on them a little too hard.' Starting a fight was easy; stopping it before it started was difficult; crying halt after it had started was next to impossible.

Kethol nodded. 'So we'd better do what we've been told to do – find out who did it, and quickly.'

Durine nodded. 'Which brings us back to the question of how?'

Kethol turned to Pirojil. 'How is usually your specialty.'

Pirojil threw up his hands. 'In this? This isn't my specialty. This isn't anybody's specialty.' He closed his eyes for a moment. After a while he said: 'One place to start is with information.'

'Like, for example,' Durine asked, 'going around and asking everybody in the castle, "Excuse me, my lord, but did you happen to cut a couple of throats last night?"?'

Kethol didn't think it funny at all, but Pirojil nodded. 'Like that. Let's see if we can work out how the barons – and the captains and guards, who also have free run of the castle – spent last night and evening.'

'And you think they're going to tell us?' Kethol didn't understand.

'No, you idiot – but if, say, Baron Viztria says that he was up until dawn chewing the fat with Baron Langahan, and Langahan says he went to bed early, we know that one of them is lying.'

Kethol nodded. 'Somebody was watching the hall, and took advantage of the guard falling asleep.'

'Or maybe not falling asleep. Maybe he's in on it, too. Somebody had better ask him.' Pirojil turned to Durine. 'Ask him. Thoroughly. Then find me.'

'And you'll be?'

'I'll be down in the Great Hall, interviewing the nobles and the captains – somewhat more gently than you'll be talking to that idiot Erlic.'

Durine nodded.

'And me?' Kethol asked. 'I'd be useless at that, idiot that I am.'

'If you can restrain your sensitivity over the fact that you're a dolt for a moment, maybe you can be of some value.' Pirojil grinned. 'You can scout the terrain.'

'Terrain?'

'Yes, terrain. You were raised as a forester, son of a forester, yes?'

Kethol didn't like to talk about it, or about the destruction of his boyhood home that had sent him out to make his living with bow and sword, but it was true, and he nodded.

'Well, what does a forester do if he finds the guts of a poached deer out in the forest?'

Kethol shrugged. 'That's not hard. You see if you can track the poacher from it, try to get some idea of the direction he came from. If you get really lucky, you'll find the arrow that took the deer.'

'That happens?'

'Sure. If it goes right through the neck, an arrow can hide itself pretty well, and poachers are sometimes sloppy. If you find an arrow, even though it'll probably be unmarked – poachers aren't usually considerate enough to mark their arrows for you – you can usually get some sort of clue from the fletching and the arrowhead as to where it came from, and that gives you a clue as to –'

'*Clue*, yes. That's the word. We're looking for clues. Check out the lady's room – and see if you can find some sort of clue.'

Kethol's forehead wrinkled. 'I don't think that there are going to be any arrowheads in there, and I doubt even more that I'll be able to track somebody across the carpet.'

Pirojil spread his hands. 'I don't know what *kind* of clue. Maybe the weapon that cut their throats? It could have been left there, I guess,' he said, sceptically. 'If it's distinctive . . .'

It didn't sound likely. Indeed, it sounded just this side of impossible.

'And search Baron Morray's rooms,' Durine said.

'Again: for what?'

'And, again: I don't know,' Durine said.

'I do,' Pirojil said. 'For something – a slip of paper, maybe, or a notation in a book. Neither too easy or too difficult to find, but it'll have some sort of short incantation written on it, the spell that will allow somebody to open the strongroom in the dungeon.'

Worrying about getting paid at a time like this shouldn't have disgusted Kethol, but it did, and he let his disgust show on his face.

Pirojil just shook his head. 'Really gone native, haven't you?'

'Shit, Pirojil –'

'Well,' Pirojil said, the ghost of a smile flickering across his ugly face, 'I suppose I must have gone native, too, because I wasn't thinking about our pay, not at the moment. But right now we've got to worry not just about a band of Morray's men, ready to avenge their murdered baron, but a band of mercenaries, some of whom will work out that they don't get paid until somebody can open the strongbox, and I don't think the Swordmaster is going to appoint one of the barons as even a temporary bursar until we've discovered the murderer; and even if he does, it won't much matter if the Bursar can't open the strongroom safe.'

Durine nodded. 'Best thing the Swordmaster can do, assuming things don't break into open warfare, is just pay off the mercenaries – and the regulars, for that matter. Money tends to settle people down.'

'That's what I thought.' Pirojil looked from Kethol to Durine.

'Any volunteers to mutter something that sounds like a spell while trying to work the safe?' He shook his head before answering his own question. 'No.' His mouth twitched. 'Come to think of it—' He walked to the door, and leaned outside. 'Send for Milo and Mackin, two mercenaries down at the Broken Tooth. Tell them to report to me, in the Great Hall, now.'

'But—' the guard outside started to protest; Pirojil silenced him with a pointed finger.

'If you've got any objections to my orders, go and ask the Swordmaster. He's put the three of us in charge of this, this, investigation, and I suspect that he means it.'

Retreating footsteps sounded in the hall, and Pirojil turned, grinning. 'I'm getting to like this being in charge thing.'

Durine shook his head. 'I'd like it a lot more if I knew what we were doing.'

'Me, too,' Kethol said.

On that the three of them could agree.

Still, the rule of 'when you don't know what to do, do what you know how to do' did make sense, and Kethol had looked at dead bodies before. This talking to people was another thing – what did Pirojil expect, that the murderer would jump up and say, *I did it*, if Pirojil just looked at him sideways?

'Well, we'd all better do our best to look like we know what we're doing.'

Durine grinned. 'Is that what officers and nobles do all the time?'

'Probably. But let's get to it.' Pirojil clapped his hands together, and gestured the other two to their feet. 'Durine to the dungeon; Kethol to Lady Mondegreen's room; and I get the assembled barons and captains. We meet back here, at noon.' He grinned. 'I'll have Ereven bring us lunch.'

Durine made his way down to the dungeon, balancing carefully on the gritty stone steps.

Tom Garnett and three of his soldiers were gathered in front of the nearest of the cells. A huge brass key that Durine assumed was the key to the cells hung on a hook next to an oil lantern hanging from an overhead beam – on the opposite side from the cells. A man locked in a dungeon cell might be able to get at it, if he had a long enough stick with a hook on it, but presumably there were no long, hooked sticks as standard equipment in the Earl's cells.

All four men – no, five, including Erlic – drew themselves up, not quite to attention, as Durine approached, but one indicating respect for his rank, if not for the man. They all looked familiar, and so did this Erlic.

Durine shook his head. A week ago, or less, an age ago or more, two of these four men had been the ones that Tom Garnett had sent to bring Durine to the Swordmaster, to be assigned, along with Pirojil and Kethol, to protect Baron Morray.

'Disgusted with me, eh?' Tom Garnett said, apparently misreading Durine's expression.

'No, Captain. Disgusted, certainly, but not sure who with, except for Erlic.' Durine shrugged. 'But enough of that. I'll need to talk to Erlic, privately.'

'Can't do that, Captain,' one of the others said, shaking his head. 'We're on orders not to take our eyes off him. Some people think that he might decide to avoid the Earl's justice, and I'm one of those people, and never mind for the moment that orders are orders.'

How Erlic would do that was an interesting question, Durine thought. He had been stripped of his tabard and trousers and boots. He had dropped the thin blanket that he had had wrapped about him when he had come to attention, and now he stood shivering in a tunic that reached to his knees.

Well, maybe he could tear the blanket into strips, braid the strips into a rope, tie one end of the rope to the bars and the other around his neck, and then make a flying leap and break his neck, but Durine reckoned he would notice Erlic trying to do that, and could probably stop him.

But Durine didn't say anything; he just looked at Tom Garnett, who quickly nodded.

'We can lock you in with him, I suppose, and remain within shouting range.' His lips were white as he turned to the soldier who had spoken. 'Captain Durine isn't sure that we're not involved,' he said, quietly, casually, as though commenting upon the weather.

'Shit,' one of the men said, as he walked over to the beam and retrieved the key. 'You want to hand over your swordbelt, and maybe that extra knife you've got strapped to your back, under your tunic?'

Durine was unaccountably irritated. He thought he had kept that knife a secret, and didn't know when or how the man had spotted it. He didn't like the idea of having stayed in place so long that that sort of thing became a possibility. But he unbuckled his swordbelt, and gave it to another of the soldiers, then drew the knife and handed it, properly hilt-first, to the one who had asked for it, then gestured at Erlic to back away.

He went into the cell quickly, half expecting that Erlic would try to jump him, and looking forward to beating him, just to get discussions off on the right foot . . .

But Erlic just moved to the back of the cell, and slumped down on the overlarge shelf stuck into the wall that served as a prisoner's bed. A few moments later the two of them were locked in, and Tom Garnett and the guards moved out of sight, and either out of hearing or silent, although Durine wouldn't have wanted to guess which.

It probably didn't much matter, unless all four of them were involved in the murder, and while Durine wasn't willing to throw any possibility out, that didn't seem to be likely.

He hoped.

Of course, there would be a simple way to find out. If he pasted a satisfied look on his face after he had finished talking with Erlic and they were part of some sort of conspiracy to murder Baron Morray and Lady Mondegreen, they would quickly kill Durine in the cell, rather than allowing him out. If so, one of them was probably going for a crossbow right now, just to make it easy.

That thought warmed him as he turned to Erlic. 'So,' he said. 'I don't have much to bargain with, and you've got less, but let's see if we can work a deal.' Working a deal was more Pirojil's thing than Durine's, but Durine had watched him many times. 'I could start by, say, breaking a couple of your fingers and promising to stop if you tell me everything you know.'

Erlic looked up at him, and shook his head. 'But I don't know anything, except that I fell asleep at my post.'

'Nobody asked you to look the other way while they went into Lady Mondegreen's room, say, just to have a quick talk with her?' Durine didn't think that it would be that easy, but it wouldn't hurt to ask. It still left the question of why Erlic hadn't noticed that somebody had exited the room covered with blood, or heard the sounds of a struggle, but one thing at a time.

Erlic shook his head. 'Nobody asked me to do anything. Baron Morray went to her room, but –'

'But he's done that before.'

Erlic nodded. 'I had the watch on that hall last night, too, and the night before.' He shrugged. 'He just ignored me, and I pretended not to see him.'

'Who is in the next room?'

'From Lady Mondegreen?'

'No,' Durine said. 'From Prince Erland.'

Erlic just looked confused; sarcasm, apparently, didn't work for him.

'Yes, from Lady Mondegreen.'

'Verheyen on the near side – the side nearest me – between her suite and Baron Morray's suite. Viztria and Langahan share the suite beyond her room.'

And if this castle was as lousy with secret passages between rooms as Castle Mondegreen was, there were three more people who could have done it, and if it was Verheyen or any combination of them, then maybe it wasn't this poor sod's fault, after all.

That might save his neck.

Durine paused for a moment to consider: it could have . . . no, should have taken two people or more to kill both Baron Morray and Lady Mondegreen without raising an outcry that would have awakened this idiot, or somebody else. Maybe one man who was awfully quick with a knife –

Damn. Servants. He hadn't thought about servants, although why. . .

He could think about why later. 'Any of the serving staff go in or out?'

Erlic shook his head. 'Not that I saw. Not there. Emma, the housecarl's daughter, brought Baron Morray a bottle of wine, but that was to his suite, and she brought a tray to Baron Folson's room, just before she brought me my own dinner, and another to Viztria's just after the clock struck two, I remember that, but –'

'Which he shares with Langahan.'

'Yes, but –'

'But nobody went into Lady Mondegreen's room, that you saw.'

'Except for Baron Morray, which I already said.'

'Yeah, but I don't think he slit her throat, and then his own.' Durine shook his head. 'You wouldn't happen to know if Baron Verheyen usually stays in that room when he visits the Earl, do you?'

Erlic shook his head. 'No, I don't know, but . . .'

'But what, man? Out with it.'

'But usually, there's only one or two barons staying in the castle, at the most, and when they don't stay at their own residence in town – though I don't think Baron Verheyen has one – they're usually put up in the big suite, at the end of the hall. There was some grumbling, the other night, about the court barons getting the good suite.'

As though the fractious barons didn't have more important matters on their mind.

'Is there anything else you can tell me?' Durine asked. 'Anything at all.'

Erlic shook his head. 'Just that I swear I've never fallen asleep on watch before.' He looked as if he was about to cry.

'Well, you certainly picked a great time to lose your virginity in that, eh?' Durine rose. 'Look: it may – *may* – not have made any difference. I want your word that you'll wait for the Earl's justice.'

Erlic nodded slowly. 'I deserve that.'

'I'm not asking what you deserve. I'm asking you for your word.'

'You'd accept my word?'

'Yes,' Durine said, lying. It seemed to be the best way to get agreement from Erlic.

'You have my word, sir. I'll not take my own life.'

Durine nodded. 'Good.'

He rose, and drew the other hidden knife from under his left armpit, then beat it against the bars until he heard feet pounding on the stone floor.

He pasted a satisfied look on his face.

'You found out something?'

Durine nodded wisely. 'Yes,' he said. 'It's quite possible that I found out the most important thing. Let me out of here, please,' he said, resheathing the knife. 'And do keep an eye on Erlic.'

Tom Garnett seemed to relax, and one of the other men went for the key.

Nobody tried to stab Durine as he stepped out of the cell and quite deliberately turned his back on them to speak to Erlic one more time. Durine didn't know whether he was happy or sad about it – it would, at least, have been a clue, and despite his protestations to the contrary, he didn't have a clue – or, to be more accurate, he either had none, or far too many.

'We'll be watching him,' Tom Garnett said.

Durine nodded. 'Yes, you will.' If Erlic turned up dead, that would, perhaps, be another one of these clues they were looking for.

Kethol didn't know what to look for.

The two bodies that lay in the bed were dead, and the killer hadn't shot them with a marked arrow, or any kind of arrow at all. Unsurprisingly, there were no bloody bootprints across the deep carpet, and what impressions of feet and shoes there were, were indistinct and useless.

He had looked at the bodies, just because that was something he knew how to do.

There was obviously some dust in the air, although where it had come from, he didn't know, but he did have to keep wiping his eyes, particularly when he looked down at Lady Mondegreen. He had opened the window to let the stink clear out of the air, but that didn't seem to help as much as it should have, at least with the dust.

He turned back to the bodies on the bed. It was important to remember that these were just bodies, just dead meat, not two people, each of whom had treated him, all in all, better than a mercenary soldier had any right to expect.

Death was, as always, utterly undignified, although these two had escaped the worst of that. If you ignored the blood and the death stink, you could have imagined them to be sleeping. After staring at Lady Mondegreen for a few moments, he knew he couldn't ignore the simple fact of death. The colour in her cheeks, present when she laughed, or when tweaked by the cold wind while they were riding to her estates, was gone, replaced by a near-parchment pallor that could not be mistaken for anything other than what it was.

He pushed aside any feelings of regret; he had seen death transform someone he knew from a living person into a lifeless thing too many times. He had found the Lady Mondegreen fetching, and she had been kind to him, but she was now a lifeless thing, and the faster he looked for those clues, the faster he could put this behind him.

He glanced around, as if seeking some sign, something out of place, something he would recognize: as he would a bent twig where one didn't belong, or crushed grass or mud from a boot on the side of a rock. Jars of face powder and scented creams made no sense to him. Lady's fineries provided no recognizable answers.

Think, he ordered himself. *When you find a poached deer, the first thing you do is examine the deer.* He tried to ignore the blood and the stink. With the cold wind blowing in through the window, it really wasn't too bad.

He bent over them.

A sharp blade had slit the throats both deeply and neatly, although he had no way of telling whether the wounds had been made with a dagger or a sword – except that the awkwardness of wielding a sword mitigated against it.

It was not impossible, mind. There had been that guardsman, outside Dungaran . . .

He shook his head. No. It had been one thing to sneak up behind someone, and grip him by the hair while he whipped the man's sword around to slice through his throat, his own sword not being available, having stuck itself too firmly into the spine of the previous guardsman. It was quite another to hack down on somebody lying asleep in the bed.

But had they been sleeping? Had they perhaps experienced a moment of awareness of what was upon them?

Probably not, or they would have raised an outcry. But he had to know, and he couldn't ask them.

Or maybe he could, come to think of it.

He forced himself to pull down the sheets and examine the bodies.

They were covered with blood, and the room stank from the way that both the Baron and his lady had voided themselves in death, but there were no wounds on their hands or arms, just on their necks.

Kethol rubbed at an old scar on his left hand. If you didn't have anything else to put in the way of a blade, you would use your hand, by reflex, particularly if the blade was going for your face. He had done just that, twice, and had become devout about always keeping a spare knife or two handy, after that time in Dungaran.

But no: from all the evidence, somebody – or somebodies – had simply crept into the room while the two were sleeping, and suddenly slit their throats right at the base of the neck, either both at the same time, or so quickly that neither had had the time to awaken and try to hold off the attacker. Kethol was puzzled. He didn't think a man could strike one victim fast enough to silence her – and he presumed that she was killed first to keep her from waking up shrieking – then kill her lover without him stirring. It would take speed few men possessed.

Kethol found himself thinking, speed to match what Durine had told him he had seen in Baron Verheyen when he crossed blades with the Swordmaster. He moved to the head of the bed. Yes, a flick with the tip of the sword, starting at the base of the Lady's neck and an upward thrust, then a downward jab with the point of the blade into the Baron's throat, slicing outward. Yes, it was possible one man alone could do this if he were fast enough.

Very professional. Kethol could admire the workmanship with part of his mind, even while the other part wanted to get a rag to clear the caked blood from Lady Mondegreen's chin. He pulled up the sheet to cover both of them, as it didn't seem right for him to be looking down at a naked noblewoman, not even in death.

It probably hadn't hurt much, or long. Kethol didn't quite understand it, but there were some wounds, even fairly deep ones, that just oozed blood out, and were, if you could get attention quickly enough, usually survivable, although if you got even an oozing belly wound, it would fester and kill, and it would usually be over in a matter of days.

Others spurted blood in a short fountain, and could kill a man in a few heartbeats. Or a horse, for that matter – it had been only yesterday that he had admired the way that Tom Garnett's soldier had dispatched his broken-legged horse with a similar, clean wound.

It would be interesting to know that man's name, although it probably didn't mean much.

He searched the floor of the room, unsurprised to find that the knife wasn't there. It almost certainly wasn't in the room at all, although he would search carefully for it, just in case.

Or was it? Was it there in plain sight? Could the killer have used Baron Morray's own knife?

No. The folded clothes on the chair were just clothes. The killer couldn't have used Baron Morray's belt-knife, because it was undoubtedly on his swordbelt in his own suite of rooms, along with his sword. The Baron, of course, hadn't thought to bring along a weapon when he had come to drink a late-night toast with his lady, just a bottle and two glasses.

It was hard to tell how much of the wine had splashed on the floor when the bottle had been overturned, but when Kethol carefully lifted it up from its side, there was still a small amount remaining in it.

Kethol wanted a drink as badly as he had ever wanted one, but he corked the bottle and set it aside.

Baron Morray hadn't seemed to be an overly sentimental man, and Kethol certainly wasn't, but Kethol hoped that the Baron wouldn't mind if Kethol drank a toast to him, later.

Later.

A bell-rope hung near the bed, and Kethol pulled it. He wasn't sure exactly how the system worked, although he had been down in the kitchens, once, and had seen the rack of bells mounted on the wall, each one with a slightly different sound. It didn't matter – whichever servant appeared, Kethol would just have him or her send for the housecarl.

Ereven, the housecarl, was at the door in just a matter of a few moments, his eyes locked on Kethol's, as though if he stared hard enough at the soldier, he could ignore the bodies on the bed.

'Yes, Captain?'

Some things never changed. The housecarl's normal glum expression was firmly in place.

But his schedule had been out. The dampness of his face and the bleeding nick at the point of his jaw showed that he had put off shaving until mid-morning, which wasn't his usual habit. Kethol had never paid the housecarl much attention, but he had never seen him other than freshly shaved, and Kethol assumed that he had had to do that both day and night.

'How long have you been housecarl here?'

Ask questions, Pirojil had said. The obvious question – who murdered these two people? – didn't exactly seem worth asking. If he knew the answer to that, Ereven would surely have mentioned it.

'I've served Earl Vandros and his father for all of my life, Captain, as did my father before me. I started off as a boy in the kitchen, washing dishes, and I have held every position on the Earl's household staff, save for pastry cook and nursemaid.' He smiled and shook his head. 'I never could manage egg whites well enough to get a popover to loft well enough, and –'

'Enough.' If Kethol didn't stop the housecarl, he would probably go on for the whole day. It was often that way with taciturn people – once you got them talking, you could hardly make them stop. 'But housecarl – chief servitor – how long?'

'Six years, Captain. Ever since Old Thomas died.'

'Then you would, presumably, know about any secret passages in the castle?'

Ereven blinked. 'There aren't any –'

'This isn't the time for discretion,' Kethol said. 'Normally, I'd be more than happy for LaMut Castle to keep its own secrets, but if the murderer came in through one of those secret passages, it would be sort of nice to know where they are, wouldn't it?'

Ereven nodded. 'I'm sure that that's so, Captain, and there used to be secret passages, but the old earl had them all sealed up – at least, all of them that I know of.' He stood silent for a moment, then shrugged and went on. 'I think that there may be a secret exit from the Earl's own chambers, still, and from the way that Fantus has been snaking himself down from the loft to the Aerie, I'm fairly sure that there's some hidden way there.' He shook his head. 'But not in the guest wing.'

He walked past the bed, towards the door to the garderobe, Kethol following.

The garderobe itself was covered with a wooden seat, and Kethol idly wondered if it was at least theoretically possible for somebody to have made his way up the wall of the keep and into the room that way, through the open bottom of the garderobe.

He lifted up the seat and looked down at the frozen midden heap on the snow below. No, the hole cut through the stone, which permitted the user to dump his wastes below, was barely large enough to admit a child, and certainly not a full-grown man, even if he had been able to climb the side of the wall.

And he wouldn't have been able to do that without leaving some marks on the ice-slickened outside wall, he decided: the dust that had covered the seat showed that it hadn't been moved in some time. The nobles would, understandably, given the cold outside, prefer to use one of the thundermugs sitting on the stone floor next to the garderobe, instead, rather than exposing their private parts to the cold air.

It was the wall opposite the fixture to which Ereven drew Kethol's attention. He pulled back on an old tapestry – faded deer fadedly frolicking in a faded meadow – to reveal a wall of bricks set into the stone, the bricks apparently solidly mortared into place.

'This was a small cabinet, with a wooden inset in the back, when I was a boy,' Ereven said, 'and if you pushed up on the shelf that was *here*, and pushed on the moulding *there*,' he said, touching his fingers to two spots on the bricks, 'it would open into the back of the wardrobe in the Green Suite.'

Kethol shoved on the bricks, and carefully examined the juncture of wall and ceiling, then of wall and floor. It wasn't impossible, he guessed, that the whole bricked wall could swing on some hidden hinge – or even some part of it – but a close examination of the mortar revealed none of the hairline cracks that would surely have been there.

'I can ask permission from Baron Viztria and Baron Langahan for you to examine it from the other side,' Ereven said. 'It's still the wardrobe, but –'

'We'll skip asking anybody permission, but I will take a look.'

There was none of the expected protest, either in word or on Ereven's lined face. He simply nodded, accepting the necessity of it.

And he'd take a close look at the other walls, too. And the wardrobe in Lady Mondegreen's room; and at the walls behind every tapestry in the hall.

It probably wouldn't do any good, mind, but at least it was something he could do.

'You can go back to your duties now,' Kethol said.

'Yes, Captain.' Ereven's face was impassive as always. 'Father Kelly has asked me to tell him when he may prepare the bodies for the funerals.'

'Is that something you've done, too?'

'Yes, Captain,' Ereven said. 'Helping with it, that is. I wrapped the old earl in his cremation shroud with my own two hands, since you ask.'

Was there a flash of anger behind the flat speech and the expressionless face?

'Is that something that I should ask of the Swordmaster, or is this part of your . . . authority, sir?'

Kethol didn't know, but he didn't want to admit it. Admitting ignorance was a luxury, right now. Pirojil had said that they had to look and act as if they knew what they were doing, and an honest admission that he didn't have any real idea where his authority began and ended didn't seem sensible, any more than making an honest admission that he didn't have the slightest idea what he was looking for.

'Yes,' he said. 'But not until sundown, just in case my colleagues need to see what I've seen here.'

'Yes, Captain.' If Ereven wanted to know what Kethol had seen, or if the two bodies lying on the bed in death had affected him, he made no attempt to ask. Without another word, he turned and left the room, leaving Kethol alone with the dead.

He took a last long look at the Lady Mondegreen, her pale face looking serene in death. How could she feel the pain of the blade yet remain asleep? She should have been lying there with eyes wide in pain, her features contorted with fear, not looking as if she but slumbered.

Kethol wiped at the tears forming in his eyes as he said a silent farewell to the Lady.

Damn, but this dust was getting to be annoying.

FOURTEEN

Plans

The nobles turned to watch.

Milo and the dwarf entered the Great Hall reluctantly, gingerly, with quick side glances at the nobles gathered along the far side, and halted under the archway. They looked for all the world as though they would rather have been anywhere else than here.

Pirojil share that feeling more than a little.

Rising, Pirojil gestured to Baron Viztria to say seated where he was, in the only other occupied chair next to the small hearth, and walked over to where Milo and the dwarf waited, shuffling nervously.

For once, Viztria didn't complain, although all throughout Pirojil's interview with him he had been emitting an almost non-stop series of complaints, combined with, as far as Pirojil could tell, no useful information.

Viztria claimed he had spent the entire evening – including dinner, 'which was adequate, under the circumstances, although the meat had been decidedly overdone, and there wasn't enough garlic in the world to hide the gamy taste of a boy-lamb that had been slaughtered months past its prime,' he had observed – in pleasant conversation with the others in the Great Hall. That lasted until the celebration over the mid-evening announcement of Morray and Verheyen's decision to put their difficulties behind them had led to a great many toasts, and much relief. 'Despite the inadequate training and supervision of the castle's bumbling servants that led the thumb-fingered clods always to neglect to properly air a wine before serving it – and never mind the fact that the Earl's cellars were poorly stocked in the first place, although a gentleman had to make allowances here, out in the middle of nowhere, after all,' he had added. Viztria then went on to explain to Pirojil that later, in the company of Langahan, he had walked up the stairs to the guest rooms – past the entirely awake guard, and since Viztria now knew that guards in LaMut habitually fell asleep on duty, that failure would surely be of great interest to some in Krondor! – and gone up the provincially uncarpeted stone steps, then down the hall into the suite that he shared with Baron Langahan. Viztria had then proceeded into his own bedroom after using the garderobe for one of its intended purposes and, since a certain impudent breveted captain apparently wanted to know all the details of matters that were none of his concern, Baron Viztria had, indeed, pissed like a racing horse. Then, without any prompting on Pirojil's part, Viztria added, 'And if the Captain needed further information, the name "Viztria" is a contraction of an ancient Delkian phrase meaning "dark snake" or "black serpent", a nickname of the founder of the line, which referred both to the relatively swarthy complexion that I, the present Baron Viztria, have not entirely inherited, and to other, rather more impressive, anatomical characteristics which I most certainly have inherited, thank you very much, which is why I've petitioned the Royal Heraldry Guild to add a Black Python to my family's coat of arms!'

Pirojil nodded and said nothing. After relieving himself, Viztria had gone back into his sleeping chamber and stripped off his clothes quicker than a fifteen-year-old nobleman's daughter from Rillanon could shuck her first ballgown in the back seat of a closed carriage, and was fast asleep before his head hit the pillow, and if there were no further insulting questions, he would just as soon let the Captain get on to insulting somebody else . . .

Pirojil found himself relieved to leave Viztria behind him, and joined Milo and the dwarf, beckoning them to follow him into an alcove off the Great Hall. The alcove contained a table which was used by servants when the Earl held a gala in the hall, but currently it was empty.

'You sent for us, Captain?' Milo asked, as though there was any question of it.

'If he didn't, there's a regular who's going to be missing a few teeth,' Mackin said.

'Yes, I sent for you,' Pirojil said as he leaned back against the table. 'I've got until noon to finish questioning the nobles –'

'About the murder?' asked the dwarf.

'No, about their preference in linen and flowers.' Milo shut his companion up with a quick slap to the back of the head.

Mackin was about to object to the rude treatment, when Pirojil said, 'Yes, about the murder. You've heard?'

'Shit, captain,' Mackin said, 'everybody has heard, including those poor bastards out marching in the snow, from what I was hearing as Kelly and his men were chivvying one bunch out of the gates this morning.'

Milo nodded. 'Yeah. We've even heard that you and the other two have been put in charge of finding out who did the two of them.' His smile seemed almost genuine. 'Better you than me, eh?'

'Yes, you've heard right.'

'Well, it seems to me that you'd better come up with the killer quickly, because the Morrays already have their candidate, and the Verheyens are looking halfway between scared shitless and furious.' He rubbed his thumb and first two fingers together. 'And some of the others have been able to add one dead lady and one dead bursar, and start worrying about whether our noble employers are going to decide that it's easier to kill the help than pay it off.'

Pirojil held up a hand. 'You can relax about that,' he said. 'It's being seen to.'

An officer had to be able to lie to the men, and tell them everything was fine. How it was being handled and by whom wasn't what Pirojil was trying to concentrate on at the moment, although it would be handy if Kethol happened to find the magical passphrase to the strongroom in Baron Morray's suite of rooms. The Earl of LaMut and his predecessor hadn't been fools, and would surely have allowed for the possibility of all of the few possessors of that secret being killed, and put in place some scheme to deal with that eventuality.

Pirojil liked his own theory about the pass-phrase being hidden somewhere in Baron Morray's rooms, although he probably wouldn't have known what it was if he was looking right at it, and wouldn't have wanted to test it out, even if he was pretty sure that he had the right one.

It was likely that the Swordmaster would know where it was, or at least know how to get to it, but it was even more likely that Steven Argent would very much not appreciate being nagged about such – to him – trivial matters as paying the men, not at the moment.

And he would have had a point.

Pirojil turned to the dwarf. 'Mackin, what I want you to do is get the captains together – all of them – and get a moment-by-moment description of everything they did last evening.'

'Can't do it.' Mackin shook his head. 'Four of them are out with the marchers.'

'Then get all the rest, on my authority – any who object, send them straight to the Swordmaster. I think that'll convince them to behave. They can meet you down in the dungeon. Tom Garnett is busy keeping an eye on Erlic, and I'd like them all there.'

'Giving orders to captains, eh?' the dwarf smiled too broadly. 'I could get used to that.'

'Better not.' Milo cocked his head to one side. 'And for me?'

'Just a moment. Mackin, why are you still just standing there?'

The dwarf gave Pirojil a long look that as much as shouted that they'd discuss this later, privately, and that Pirojil wouldn't much like the form or results of the discussion. Pirojil had heard enough empty threats to not react. Mackin shrugged, then stalked away.

There was an idea flittering around the back of Pirojil's mind, but first things first.

'Well?' Milo asked, when the dwarf had gone.

'Can Mackin handle the captains alone?'

'Hell if I know.' Milo shook his head. 'This isn't the sort of thing that he knows anything about, Pirojil. That goes for me, too, and –'

'And it goes for me, and Durine and Kethol, as well, and Steven Argent has given us about as much choice as I'm giving you.'

Milo smiled. 'Which is none.'

'You have a keen eye for the obvious. For one thing, you can go after Mackin and get him started with the captains, and make sure he doesn't start a fight! Get them talking about their activities last night. When you think he's got the hang of it, I want you to get back up here and help me with the nobles – see if you can get anything useful out of Viztria; I didn't.'

The mercenary's mouth twitched. 'Very well. Not that I know what to ask about.'

'You think I do?'

Milo smiled. 'One can always hope.' The smile thinned. 'You said there was one thing. Which suggests that there's another.'

Pirojil nodded. 'I . . . I have a question to ask you.'

'I don't know as I like the hesitation. You've not been so shy, of late.'

'I'll be blunt, then: what are you wanted for?'

Milo's face went totally blank. 'I don't know what you're talking about.'

'I think you do. I think you've got a price on your head, and a local one, and I want to know what it's for.'

He sniffed. 'It wouldn't be for murder, that I can tell you. If there were such a thing as a price on my head, here or anywhere else. Which there isn't.'

'Very well: there's no price on your head here, and I promise to give you fair warning when I next see the Constable – who, by the way, is presumably still snowed in in Kernat Village. But if there was such a thing, what might it be for?'

'I couldn't say.' Milo shrugged. 'But if I had to guess about how somebody *else* might have gotten himself in such a . . . predicament . . .'

Pirojil nodded. 'Of course. Somebody else.'

'Well, it might be that this somebody else had a different, er, profession, when he was younger and more foolish. One that paid a damn sight better than soldiering, at that – thievery, say. Maybe somebody got out of town, just in time, some years ago, having to leave too quickly to take the evidence with him. And maybe he found that his profession paid just as well in other places, too, and picked up a few other tricks of another trade, along the way. It could happen.'

'Yes, it could.' Pirojil nodded. 'But why would he ever come back?'

'I don't know.' Milo's shrug was too casual. 'Probably he wouldn't come back. I know that I wouldn't.'

'But we're not talking about you; we're talking about this other fellow.'

'Well . . . maybe when the war broke out, just maybe he would remember that he'd had a home, and a homeland, once.' Milo swallowed hard, although his calm expression never changed. 'Maybe he remembered those things, even though it was long ago, and just possibly he might want to, oh, kill one, or two, or maybe even a few dozen of the bastards that had invaded his home and his homeland.

'But maybe he couldn't quite just show up and enlist in the regulars, and find himself garrisoning the very town that he had left so . . . hurriedly.'

'No, I can see that he wouldn't be able to do that.'

Milo's eyes went all vague and unfocussed. 'But still, he might really want to do something about the Tsurani invasion, even if he couldn't do much – after all, he was just one man, and the one thing he was really good at couldn't do a damn thing to help the war effort.' He shrugged again. 'But I wouldn't know anything about that.'

'Of course not,' Pirojil said. 'Not that it would matter much, given that the Constable is out of town, and there's probably nobody like that in LaMut, anyway.'

'I hoped you'd see it that way, Captain,' Milo said with more threat than hope in his voice.

'This non-existent person – I wonder which baron might he have been fealty-bound to . . . not to Baron Morray, or to any other baron, I'd hope?'

Milo shook his head. 'None, I'd guess, if I had to guess – I'd think of this fellow as a townsman, born and raised in LaMut or a nearby town, and not beholden to any baron.' He looked up at Pirojil. 'No more so than you or me, eh?'

Pirojil nodded. 'I'd imagine so. You'd better go help Mackin gather the captains and get him started with them, then I'll want you back up here to see what you can get out of Viztria while I take on Langahan.'

'That sounds like more fun than talking about somebody else, eh?' Milo brightened. 'The dungeon, you say,' he said, his mouth twitching. 'I've never much cared for jails, for some reason or other, but this time, I'll be on the right side of the bars, I suppose. You think that the captains will know anything useful?'

'Nah.' Pirojil shook his head. 'I very much doubt it, and even if they did, they'd be no more likely to tell me than to tell you. But you never know – and I might have something else for you to do, later on.'

'You know. . .' Milo sighed. 'I was afraid you were going to say that.'

Durine caught up with Kethol in what had been Baron Morray's suite.

His desk in the sitting room here might have been the twin of the one in the dungeon. The books stacked on it looked to be the same ones that Durine had seen sitting on the Baron's desk downstairs – they probably were the same ones, come to think of it; it was unlikely that the Baron maintained two sets of books – and they were stacked in the same position at the front right corner.

Durine didn't *think* that the pen and mottled green inkwell had been carried up from the dungeon, and they, too, were in precisely the same place as their counterparts below, and either the finely embossed glass-and-brass oil lamp was identical to the one that stood on the desk in that small office outside the strongroom, or it had been brought up here, and the first seemed much more likely. Even the straight-backed wooden chair was identical.

Durine nodded. Baron Morray had liked things his own precise way, and it made sense that he would want his working environment to be identical in the dungeon and his suite. It wasn't exactly a surprise that he had, as usual, got his way.

In the end, though, had he got his way? Had he really been willing to trade his chance at the earldom for the certainty of Lady Mondegreen?

It was possible. If so, he had certainly not had the best of the bargain, at least not from Durine's point of view.

Then again, if somebody was going to kill him anyway, he had at least had one last night with his lady, rather than one last night of hoping some day to be the Earl of LaMut, so maybe he hadn't been cheated quite as badly as it had first seemed.

'Have you found anything interesting?' Durine asked.

'Interesting? You mean, like some note that says, "I killed Baron Morray and Lady Mondegreen, ha ha ha ha", with a signature and seal at the bottom?'

'Well, that would be interesting, but I was thinking about something a little more subtle.'

Kethol was clearly shaken; sarcasm wasn't usually part of his repertoire.

Durine didn't quite understand it. It was just another couple of deaths, when you finally came down to it, and Durine was used to being around death, after all, as were Pirojil and Kethol.

That was the trouble with caring about people. They were, every bit as much as horses and cows and pigs, sacks of meat; and meat spoiled and rotted, sooner or later. If you were going to rely on something, metal was always a better choice than meat, whether that metal was gold or steel.

Kethol plonked himself down in the Baron's chair, and began going through the drawers. 'No, I haven't found anything interesting.' He pulled out a small, bulging leather pouch, and upended it. Silver reals and a few small golden coins rang down onto the wooden surface. Kethol scooped them back into the bag, and put it back in the drawer.

Durine walked to the bookcase, and pulled down a volume. He riffled through the pages but didn't recognize the language, although the glyphs looked vaguely Elvish. Carefully, he placed the book on the carpet, then pulled down the next.

'What are you doing?'

Durine shrugged. 'Well, it could be that the pass-phrase is on a piece of paper stuck in one of the books.'

'Do you really have to do that now?'

Durine ignored Kethol. There really wasn't any point in arguing, and there was nothing else useful he could do. Pirojil had intended for him to beat the truth out of Erlic, but the man was already limp with shame and self-disgust, and it was clear the only thing that Durine could have got out of the poor sod was some new bruises on his own knuckles, and the same story.

Durine didn't have any objection to hurting people, but he didn't need the exercise. While he wouldn't have minded trying that technique out on some of the nobles – that Baron Viztria would, he thought, look a bit better with fewer teeth – he didn't think that even with his present authority he could get away with that, and trying to work out the truth of something from what somebody was saying was Pirojil's specialty, not his or Kethol's.

He supposed that he could have taken a look at the bodies, but he had seen bodies before, and it seemed even more unlikely that his eyes would catch anything that Kethol's eyes missed than it did that there was anything useful to see at all. The assassin had, after all, probably not carved his name into the flesh of his victims, any more than he had left a confessional note here.

There was probably more wealth in this room than in some of the bags in the strongroom below, although it was difficult to work out an easy way that they could be converted into cash, and Durine couldn't quite see the three of them strapping bags of books to their horses before they rode out of town.

Though the sooner they did, the better.

Nevertheless, he kept working his way down the bookcase. If

the pass-phrase was hidden in one of the books, it might have been written into the book itself.

And even that was unlikely.

If Pirojil had organized it, it would have been something clever – like, say, cutting the pass-phrase into a dozen parts, and giving each of the barons some of those parts, so that any three or four of them could reassemble the complete pass-phrase – and there was no reason to think that the LaMutian nobility was any less clever than Pirojil, or would simply leave such a valuable thing lying about for the easy perusal of some servant cleaning the Baron's rooms.

He was halfway through the shelves when he noticed that Kethol was glaring at him.

'Is there any chance you could actually do something useful?' Kethol asked.

Durine shrugged. 'Sure. Just give some idea as to what that something useful could be.'

'Well, you could help me with the desk.'

Durine spread his hands. 'I'll be happy to help you look through the Baron's desk, or go through his wardrobe, or anything else – but I don't know what I'm looking for even if I see it.'

Then again ... Baron Morray's swordbelt, complete with dagger, was hanging from a hook on the wall. Durine didn't *think* that the Baron had cut his own throat, and then Lady Mondegreen's, but ...

He drew the sword. A nice rapier, he decided, although the grip was definitely too small for Durine's oversized fingers, and he would have preferred a larger bell-guard, and a polished one, rather than the deeply-inscribed curlicues that covered the surface of this one. Tastes varied, and Durine preferred things simple: he would have rather known that a sword tip would bounce off, and in which direction, rather than unreliably stick some times and bounce off at others, but that probably didn't make much of a difference to the defender, and it might throw off an opponent's timing, just a trifle, which could be more than enough.

Each to his own.

The light, narrow blade was well-oiled, without a hint of rust, and the tip was sharp enough to dig out a splinter. When he gripped the blade with his left hand, covering the blade with his sleeve to protect it more from the moisture of his finger than to protect his fingers from the edge, it flexed nicely, then sprang back straight. Not the sort of weapon Durine would have wanted to take into battle – even if you sharpened the edge, the light blade didn't have enough weight behind it to cut to bone; but it was a fine duelling weapon.

He replaced the sword and drew the companion dagger. The hilt was covered with the same greenish dragonhide, and the brass hilt was inscribed with curlicues in complement to the bell-guard of the rapier.

But the dagger was heavy, balanced nicely at the hilt, and sharp enough to shave the hairs off Durine's arm.

And utterly devoid of any blood, fresh or dried.

He hefted it in his hand. 'Could the killer have used this?'

Kethol looked up from rummaging through the desk drawer, and his irritated glare quickly faded. 'Possibly. Sharp?'

'Very.' Durine used the tip of the dagger to point to the now-bare patch on his forearm. He ran his thumbnail down the edge of the blade, and while the steel bit slightly into the nail, there weren't any fine nicks that Durine could feel, much less coarser ones that he could have seen. 'Hasn't been used to chop at anything.'

Kethol shook his head. 'Which doesn't mean anything. The killer slit the throats very neatly.'

'No wounds on the arms? Seems strange – you'd think that the killing of the first would have awakened the second.'

Kethol nodded. 'I took out a guard, once, while his partner was sleeping nearby, just a few feet away, and –'

'Dungaran?'

'No. Semrick, I think, or it may have been Maladon. They all blur together after a while. But as I was saying, I'm pretty good, and he didn't make a move until the knife was through his throat, but he did thrash around enough to wake up the second one, and I kind of had to rush with him.'

'Maybe Lady Mondegreen or the Baron were heavy sleepers?'

'I suppose so.' Kethol sounded doubtful. 'Either there were two killers, and they timed it well, or the killer was very, very fast. One of them thrashing around in their death throes wouldn't have made much of a difference if the other already had a cut throat. Takes some speed, though.' He thought about it for a moment. 'Of the barons, I'd say that Verheyen and Langahan are the fastest, having watched them spar with Steven Argent the other night. Verheyen might even be a touch faster than the Swordmaster.'

'Well, he is younger.' Not that that had made a difference in their sparring. Speed was a fine thing, but Steven Argent had more decades of training in his wrist than Verheyen, and the Baron hadn't laid a practice blade on him.

Which suggested an ugly possibility. 'You don't think it could be the Swordmaster, do you?'

'No.' Kethol sat back. 'I hadn't thought about it. Why would he want to?'

'Well, there are rumours that he was having his way with Lady Mondegreen, too.'

'There are lots of rumours.' Kethol shook his head. 'If you believe the *rumours*, the Lady was spreading her legs for every noble in the earldom. I don't.'

'Neither do I.' Durine nodded. There was no way to be sure of anything, but he liked Pirojil's theory that Lady Mondegreen had carefully been picking her paramours for the dark hair and grey eyes of the husband who couldn't get her with child – which helped to explain her affairs with Morray and Argent, and if she had been willing to lower herself to commoners, added more additional local candidates than Durine could count.

But ... 'Everybody and his brother's rooms haven't been reeking of patchouli and myrrh. Argent might have decided that if he couldn't have her, nobody else would.'

Durine didn't really believe that, but he was with Kethol, and didn't have to restrict himself to speaking carefully. And, besides, it was a possibility.

Kethol thought about it for a moment – the effort apparently was a strain – and then shook his head. 'And do it in a way that could set off the very uprising that he's been working hard to prevent?'

Durine put the knife back in its sheath. 'I guess not.' He paused, thoughtful. 'Throat cut?'

Kethol shook his head in surprise at the question. 'I already *told* you –'

'No. Not here. That time in Semrick or Maladon or wherever it was.'

Kethol nodded, understanding the change of topic. 'Yes. Pumped out a lot of blood, and fast, but he still kicked and thrashed like a stuck pig, even though I got through the windpipe and he couldn't get a sound out of his mouth.'

Durine nodded. Having had some experience in such matters himself, he preferred a stab into the kidney – the shock of the pain usually froze the victim into paralysis – or a hacking blow into the base of the neck, hoping to sever the spine, but these were the sorts of things that professionals could have honest differences of opinions on and, by and large, Kethol's results were better than Durine's on this sort of thing.

Which suggested another, really ugly, possibility.

'Yeah. You still prefer cutting a throat to stabbing from behind?' He tried to make it sound like just a typical bit of shop talk, but Kethol didn't take it that way. 'Last night you were awfully quiet.'

Kethol pushed himself away from the desk and stood. 'If you've got something to say, get it out. If you think I . . . I did that, then –'

Durine held up a hand. He wasn't any more afraid of Kethol than he was of anybody else, but even so . . .

'No, not really. I've never known you to kill anybody without a reason, and I can't think what the reason would be. Jealousy? Anyone can see you were half-smitten with the Lady, but that's no reason to kill her, and I was getting the impression that you liked Morray.'

'Respected him, at least, sure.' Kethol nodded. 'So if you're not accusing me of the murders, what are you saying?'

'Nothing much. Just seems to me that you were awfully quiet last night, and that isn't usual, and I'm wondering if there's something you haven't told me.'

'And if there is?'

'Then either tell me now, or don't. Your call.'

Kethol swallowed, sat down, and started to talk.

Durine's expression never changed while Kethol, keeping his voice low, explained about how he had created the mythical Tsurani scout from some old Blue armour, a dead horse, and a pair of brezeneden.

When he finished, Durine just nodded.

'Too clever by half, but it seems to have worked.' He almost smiled. 'Sounds more like Pirojil's sort of thing than yours. He didn't have a hand in it?'

Kethol shook his head. 'I didn't have time to talk it over with either of you. The idea only occurred to me when both of you were on your way into lowertown, and I realized that I didn't have the vaguest idea of how to stop a fight, except by killing everybody involved. The two of you might be able to impersonate officers, but that's not my way. So I did what I could.'

He had done that, although Durine thought that Kethol's worries about one mythical winter scout completely disrupting the Kingdom's strategy were overblown. The captains had chewed it over, but the nobles running the war were used to reports from the lower echelons that overstated things – like a squad reporting heavy opposition usually meaning that there were another couple of squads of Tsurani over the next ridge, or maybe a company, rather than a legion.

The report about the scout had startled the captains, and Durine, as well, but the dukes and their senior officers would just add that report to the mix, and even if they believed it, they'd not blindly commit the entire forces of two dukedoms to prepare for an attack towards LaMut just because of this one report. If the Kingdom's rulers were that easy to distract, they wouldn't have stood up to the Tsurani this long.

'These brezeneden, though,' Durine said. 'They sounded interesting. You think you could find where you buried your set?'

Kethol nodded. Of course he could. Nobody else would have noticed just another hump in the snow, but he had deliberately chosen a place halfway between two trees, just in case he wanted to retrieve them later, and Kethol could remember a tree as well as he could remember a face.

'Any possibility that you could make another couple of sets?'

Kethol nodded. 'But –'

The noon bell rang. 'We'd better get up to the Aerie, and see what Pirojil's found out. Unless you think we'll find any more of these "clues" here, or know somebody that I can try to beat some information out of?'

Kethol shook his head. 'No.'

'On your way, then,' Durine said, making a brushing-away motion with his fingers. 'I've got to use the garderobe, and then I'll be right up.' He raised a cautionary finger. 'You can tell Pirojil about the brezeneden, but don't talk about the other matter,' he said. 'He's got enough on his mind, and we know that there are secret passages up there – the walls may have ears, eh?'

Kethol didn't mention the Tsurani scout ploy, but he might as well have done, the moment he explained about the brezeneden.

Pirojil sat back in his chair, his hands folded over his belly, and then nodded.

Very clever, he mouthed, rather than said. Then, quietly, 'When we're done here, can you go make another three sets? And how long would it take?'

Durine had asked the same thing. Kethol nodded. 'Not long. Several hours, probably.'

There was ample wood and leather, among the several score other things that the castle might need during a siege, stored on the racks down in the dungeon, and if he couldn't find suitable thongs he could cut them himself out of a cowhide. The room they shared in the barracks had a hearth, and the teapot would serve to produce steam. Probably they wouldn't be as elegant as those that the Ranger had made, but it could be done. Just a matter of cutting the strips, bending them into shape, and then weaving on the latticework of leather thongs.

'Why?'

'For the obvious reason.' Pirojil nodded. 'I think it might be handy to get out of LaMut before the snow melts, now that it's warming up enough that we can, and –' He waved it away. 'But I'm letting myself get distracted. What did you see in Lady Mondegreen's room?'

Kethol told him, in as much detail as he could. Pirojil didn't interrupt, except to ask him to clarify a point or two. Not that there was much to clarify: the two dead people were dead; they had been sliced by somebody fast and good; and there was nothing at all that Kethol had found that resembled a clue.

Fantus seemed to enjoy the recitation, though; he had appeared moments after Kethol had, and Kethol hadn't seen where the fire-drake had come from.

Not that it mattered much; Kethol just drew his knife, and scratched at the drake's eye-ridges while he talked, and Fantus arched his neck and preened himself, as usual. A firedrake was actually kind of a pleasant companion, although he had never heard of another tame one. If the three of them ever did manage the Three Swords Inn, he might see if there was a way to catch and tame one.

But thoughts of that long-off day didn't stop his recitation. A knock on the door did.

'Yes?'

Ereven, the housecarl walked in, bearing a tray. How he had turned the knob with his hands occupied was something that Kethol wondered about, but didn't ask. Every profession was enti-tled to its little trade secrets, after all.

'You asked to be served lunch, here, sir?' Ereven asked, only a trace of a sniff suggesting his irritation at these interlopers treating the Swordmaster's rooms as though they were their own.

'Yes, and I also sent for Mackin —'

'The dwarf, sir?'

'Yes, the dwarf. Make sure he finds his way up here, please.'

'Yes, sir.'

Durine walked in as the housecarl walked out, and sat himself down in a chair next to the hearth. 'I could get used to these accommodations,' he said. 'Pity.'

'Yeah.' Pirojil seemed to force a smile. 'A real pity, that.' He scooped a meatroll up off the plate and chewed thoughtfully for a moment. 'Very well, I —'

There was another knock on the door, and Mackin walked in without waiting to be given permission to enter. He nodded curtly at Kethol and Durine, then planted himself in front of Pirojil.

'I take it,' Pirojil said, 'that the Swordmaster is still downstairs with the rest?'

Mackin nodded. 'Well, you can see that he isn't here, so that doesn't make you all *that* clever.'

'No, what makes me clever is that I know that *you* know where he is, or you wouldn't have pushed your way into his quarters without so much as a by-your-leave.' With Pirojil seated, he and the dwarf were almost eye to eye. 'Milo is still talking with the nobles?'

Mackin nodded. 'Yeah. He is – last I saw, he was deep in conversation with Folson, who seems to be less indignant about being questioned than the others were. Although nerves are tight. When Milo dropped a wine glass, every last one of the nobles was on his feet, and half the house guard came running.' The dwarf smiled. He was clearly enjoying the nobles' discomfiture.

'Did you find anything useful from the captains?'

'No. Although I don't know what I was supposed to be asking about, other than "did you happen to go slicing a couple of throats last night?" Were you really expecting something?'

Pirojil shook his head. 'Not really. I've got one more job for you, though. Something I'm sure you can do.'

'Yes?'

'Get a shovel, and check the midden heaps under each of the garderobes. You don't have to dig terribly deep.'

'Is this some sort of joke?' the dwarf was not happy. 'What am I supposed to be looking for?'

'What you're supposed to be looking for is a bloody rag, or a kerchief – maybe a shirt. Some piece of cloth with a few long streaks of blood on it.'

'And you think I'm going to find it there?'

Pirojil shook his head. 'No, I think you're not going to. But you are going to look, and you're going to be able to say that you looked. When you finish looking, come back up here and report to me.' He paused a second, then quickly added, 'And have a bit of a wash, before you do.'

'And then?'

'And then, you and Milo are going to back the three of us, when we gather all of the assembled nobles around the table in the Great Hall, and . . .'

'And?'

'And then I expose the murderer,' Pirojil said.

Mackin looked as if he wanted to say something, but he just stood staring at Pirojil for a moment, and then grinned. 'All because there isn't a bloody rag in the middens?'

'Perhaps,' Pirojil said.

'You going to tell me about this?'

Pirojil shook his head. 'No. I'm not even going to tell Kethol and Durine. They find out at the same time you do.'

Another pause. 'I can live with that, I guess. A shovel, eh?'

'Go.'

Mackin went. As he neared the door, Pirojil said, 'And wash off that filth before you come back!'

Over his shoulder, Mackin shouted back, 'I washed a bit before I reported!' then he disappeared through the door.

Pirojil regarded the dwarf as he left the room and wondered what his definition of 'washed a bit' entailed. He still looked as if he'd rolled down a coal bin and stank like a sewer. Then with a slight sniff, Pirojil decided he must have washed up some, as he didn't reek any more than usual.

Pirojil took another bite of the meatroll, then turned to Durine. 'I want you and Kethol to head over to our quarters, and work on those . . . snowshoe devices he talked about. At least three sets – five would be better. My guess is that things are going to be a little uncomfortable for us, come the morning, and I think we'd best be out of here, pay or no. Agreed?'

'Shit, yes,' Durine said. 'Shame to leave any money behind, but . . .' He reached into his tunic and produced a familiar-looking leather pouch. 'I collected our pay from the Bursar, anyway, and a little extra for our troubles. Maybe Steven Argent will think that we got shorted a bit, but I'm not disposed to hang around to pick up the change, are you?'

Pirojil's ugly face split into a grin, but Kethol found himself more than vaguely disgusted.

He didn't quite know why. It wouldn't have been the first time, or the fifty-first time, that they had taken money off a dead body. Which was less theft than this was, technically, but it had seemed different. You had to look at the man lying there when you went through his pouch . . . there was something almost nauseatingly clean about having pilfered it from the Baron's desk.

But a man who made his living as a mercenary soldier couldn't afford compunction, and if Kethol had fallen prey to an awkward sentimentality, he could keep it to himself.

So he just nodded. 'Sure,' he said.

Durine nodded. 'One last round of ale at the Broken Tooth tonight?'

Pirojil nodded. 'Fine with me.'

Kethol shook his head. 'One last drink, tonight, yes. That's been our tradition every time we leave a place behind us –'

'Except when we've had to take to our heels,' Pirojil said, nodding in agreement. 'I'm not a stickler for tradition, though. Still, it seems to have brought us luck before, and I'd be loath to –'

'There's enough wine left in the last bottle that the Baron and his lady drank for a short toast, and I'd . . . I'd like to drink to them, in my last night in LaMut. And I'd like the two of you to join me.'

Both of the others stared blankly at him, and finally, Durine spoke. 'Very well, Kethol. We'll do it your way.' He turned to Pirojil. 'Just how sure are you?'

Pirojil opened his mouth, closed it, then opened it again. 'I'd say the chances of things working out as I think they will are, maybe, sixty-sixty. Less if I talk too much about it, in advance. Even to the two of you.'

'So?' Durine raised an eyebrow. 'You shut up, and do what you have to do, and I'll take sixty-sixty on it working,' he said, rising.

Kethol nodded. 'Me, too.'

FIFTEEN

Answers

The room was quiet.

Too quiet.

At least, that was what Steven Argent thought, although he kept his thoughts to himself, as usual.

'I'll ask you all to take seats at the table, my lords,' Pirojil said. 'There will be another request in a moment, and I'll ask that everybody bear with me.'

'If you know something, then out with it, and enough of this shilly-shallying,' Viztria snarled, taking one quick step toward Pirojil.

Steven Argent stepped in front of the Baron. 'I think, Baron Viztria, that it would be wisest if we all do as Captain Pirojil requests – if only because, at the moment, his request is my order – and until Earl Vandros returns, my orders in this castle are law.'

Viztria looked as if he was going to say something, and Steven Argent hadn't decided how he was going to handle it, but he didn't have to cross that bridge, because the weasel-faced little man just closed his mouth and sat.

The only sound that broke the silence was the crackling of the logs in the hearth, and the shuffling of chairs as the assembled nobles took their seats at the long table, as Pirojil had directed.

Steven Argent looked from face to face, silently mocking himself for thinking that there would be some sign of guilt written there.

Pirojil seated himself at the head of the table, beckoning to the Swordmaster to take a position to his right. Baron Langahan started to seat himself on Pirojil's left, but the ugly man shook his head. 'I'd prefer you sit further down, my lord. If you don't mind.'

There was nobody in the Great Hall except for Pirojil and the nobles. His companions were off elsewhere – Pirojil had been vague about that – and the dwarf and the watery-eyed mercenary that Pirojil had pressed into service were down in the dungeon with the captains and those soldiers of the guard with posts inside the castle itself, although the watchmen on the walls had been left in place.

Even the servants had been dismissed and sent to the kitchens under the eye of the housecarl, with orders to keep them there until they were sent for.

Steven Argent didn't know precisely what Pirojil was up to, but whatever it was, he thought it would be a good thing if word of it didn't leak beyond this room until he had had a chance to make up his mind about what needed to be said, and to whom.

'The next item...' Pirojil turned to Steven Argent. 'Swordmaster, if you would be kind enough, please draw your sword. I fear there may be an attempt to interrupt me, and I'll trust to your authority and skills to decide both whether that's to be tolerated, and how to handle it.'

'I'm sure –' Viztria started, but Argent stopped him.

'I'm sure that I'm perfectly capable of handling any sort of interruption,' Steven Argent said, as he rose and drew his rapier. 'And if somebody were foolish enough to get out of his chair and make for Captain Pirojil, I'm also sure that I could cut him down before he took three steps.'

'Interesting phrase, "cut him down",' Pirojil said, nodding. 'Not the easiest thing to do with a rapier – although I've never seen a finer swordsman than yourself, sir, and I've no doubt that you could spit anybody in this room on your blade before he took one step."

Argent nodded agreement.

'Thank you, Swordmaster,' Pirojil said, then turned back to the assembled barons. 'We're going to be a while, and I'd like everybody to make themselves comfortable, although I believe there's one here who won't be able to be comfortable, and for that reason, I would be more comfortable if each and every one of you would take off your own swordbelts, and place them on the table in front of you. Right now, if you please – or even if you don't please.'

Several of the barons looked to Steven Argent, but most were already unbuckling their belts, and in a few moments, there were a dozen swordbelts on the rough-hewn surface of the old oaken table.

'Thank you,' Pirojil said. 'I'm going to have to spend some time talking – I think you'll all understand why shortly – and things will go faster if I'm not interrupted, although, of course, the Swordmaster is in charge here, and I'm lecturing you only through his sufferance.

'Let's begin at the end, and skip quickly back to the beginning. The end: last night, somebody murdered Baron Morray and Lady Mondegreen.

'The beginning: a little more than a week ago, in the wake of some strange accidents that a suspicious man might think constituted a series of attempts at assassination, Earl Vandros of LaMut assigned three mercenaries – myself, and my long-time companions, Durine and Kethol – to watch over the Baron's safety. Which we did, with nothing unusual happening – except for the ambush in Mondegreen.

'I think that the suspicions were reasonable, but they turned out not to amount to anything. During the war, Baron Morray spent a lot of time in LaMut, and I reckon if somebody here really wanted him dead, he would have been killed then. I don't believe in some conspiracy that not only involves a few abortive attempts here – a pot falling from a window, which could have been caused by the wind; ice on the steps, not uncommon in winter; even the girth of his saddle wearing through – and a Tsurani attack. So I conclude that the attack was unrelated, and the accidents were just, well, accidents. Such things do happen, after all. Although the accidents, and the suspicions that they raised, apparently did give somebody an idea.

'Somebody very clever, and very fast.'

'Enough of this, man. If you've something to say, come right out and say it.' Verheyen's lips were white as he leaned forward.

Before Steven Argent could say anything, Pirojil nodded. 'Oh, I have a great deal to say, my lord, and I can get to it if I'm interrupted less. Be that as it may, this room is filled with clever people, many who might well find themselves better situated with Baron Morray dead.' He turned to Baron Folson. 'Just as an example, take yourself, my lord. One of your captains – Captain Ben Kelly, I believe is your man? – thinks that you might make a very good Earl for LaMut, once Earl Vandros becomes Duke; and until Baron Morray and Baron Verheyen made a peace between them last night, there still was a chance for you.' He raised a palm to preempt an objection, although Argent noted that Folson just sat silently, and did not object. 'Which is true enough for Baron Benteen, and the rest of the local land barons, any of whom, I trust, feels that his noble rump would grace the Earl's chair quite adequately – and, perhaps, with good reason in many cases.'

'That doesn't make me a murderer,' Benteen said.

'No, my lord, of course it doesn't. It may, however, make you the *beneficiary* of a murder, and it's not unreasonable, it seems to me, to suggest that while many here might have had a reason to murder and not carry out that desire, the murderer certainly did have his reason, and didn't simply wake up in the middle of the night and decide to slit a couple of throats for the simple exercise of it. If I might go on?'

Hearing no objection, Pirojil went on: 'Baron Verheyen would seem to be the only one of the local barons who has no motive – at least, no longer. After all, as we all know, he and Baron Morray reached an accommodation last night, and I, for one, think that Baron Morray was as good as his word, and would have thrown his full support behind his former enemy, as he had sworn he would.'

Verheyen sat back in his chair and nodded. 'Yes, he was a man of his word, and that's a fact that none will dispute.'

Pirojil smiled. 'Which is perhaps more self-serving than generous of you to say, my lord. After all, if you thought that Baron Morray might quietly whisper to the Earl anything other than what he proclaimed in public . . . well, that could leave you somewhat discommoded, my lord.

'Or, if you believed that Lady Mondegreen might think that her husband-to-be would be a more suitable choice – let's not ignore that the Baron was found dead in her bed, please – she might have exercised her very considerable powers of persuasion on Earl Vandros, and not to your benefit.' He pursed his lips for a moment. 'I think that we all can agree that Lady Mondegreen was, among other things, terribly persuasive.'

Steven Argent hoped that the tips of his ears didn't look as hot and red as they felt, but all eyes were on Pirojil, anyway, and not on him.

'So let's not dismiss you, quite yet, my lord Verheyen, while we turn to the court barons, Barons Viztria and Langahan. Or should we deal with the Swordmaster first?' He nodded to himself, and turned to Steven Argent. 'Let's do that. You've all heard the rumours that Steven Argent was having an affair with Lady Mondegreen, and I'll not embarrass the Swordmaster by asking if the rumours were true. A denial might not be believed, under the circumstances, as we could reliably expect someone who murdered to lie; and an acknowledgment would humiliate him. A gentleman, as I understand it, does not speak of these things.'

'You can't believe the Swordmaster did it, or you're even more a fool than you are a pompous twit,' Viztria snickered. 'If you think that Steven Argent is the murderer, then you're an ass to leave him as the only armed man in the room.'

Pirojil shrugged. 'Or I could be attempting to draw him into attacking me, thereby proving his guilt. I'm perfectly capable of that sort of deviousness,' he said, 'and as to him being the only armed man in the room, I'm not certain that that's true.'

Where it had come from Steven Argent couldn't have said, but Pirojil suddenly had a knife in his hands, and from the looks of it, it was a throwing knife.

'Be that as it may,' he said, looking down and running the tip of the blade under his thumbnail, as though to clean it, 'let's not be distracted, and turn to Barons Viztria and Langahan, who have every reason to wish every baron in LaMut discredited – and the Earl himself, for that matter – to further augment the influence and authority of the Viceroy, Guy du Bas-Tyra, at the expense of the Duke of Yabon, who is, by the Viceroy's reckoning, too closely allied with Duke Borric of Crydee, of whom Guy du Bas-Tyra is known to be more than passingly unfond.

'If one of Earl Vandros's barons is murdered by another baron, under his own roof, and the murderer is never caught, doesn't that argue that he's not competent to be Duke, regardless of whom he marries? It's not unknown for a duke to remove an incompetent baron from office, and while I know that a prince or his viceroy would be reluctant to remove a duke, it's not at all unlikely that Guy du Bas-Tyra would never permit Earl Vandros of LaMut ever to become Duke Vandros of Yabon, if one of his subordinate barons is believed to have got away with murder, is it?'

Langahan's face was unmoving. 'Sometime later, Captain Pirojil, you and I may have occasion to discuss your show of disrespect for the Viceroy, who would never countenance such an action.'

Pirojil shrugged, his eyes never leaving the tip of his knife, which was working its way down his fingers. 'Perhaps he wouldn't. If he knew about it. But he'd be a strange ruler, indeed, who didn't take an opportunity that presented itself to him, wouldn't he?' He looked up. 'So. We know that everyone in this room has at least some reason to think himself better off with Baron Morray dead, and we don't even have to consider the possibility, for the moment, that the real target was Lady Mondegreen, and that one of her other lovers – if indeed she had other lovers – decided that he'd rather she be dead than warm and alive in another man's bed, eh?'

Argent didn't say anything, didn't do anything.

Yes, his affair with Carla had had its intense moments, but he had always known that he was not the only one, and as fond of her as he was, he had no cause to resent her having chosen Morray, as he had known that she would. He hadn't even been sure that their own relationship would have ended with her marriage to Morray; Carla Mondegreen had had a very Eastern view of the bounds of marriage being more of a guide than a border.

And even if he had missed her, even if he never again smelled her perfume as she lay warm in his arms, even if the image of her in another man's bed had haunted him (though it wouldn't) would he kill her for that?

Never.

'So let's move along and consider the question of opportunity and, just for the sake of argument, let's consider that it was the Swordmaster himself who decided to kill the two of them, and stalked down from his quarters in the Aerie, a hidden knife on his person and murder on his mind.

'It seems a rather strange coincidence that he would see the watchman asleep, doesn't it? Unless, of course, he arranged it himself with the watchman, and this talk of Erlic falling asleep was merely a conspiracy between the two of them. Which wasn't the case.' Pirojil shook his head. 'My friend Durine is capable of being very persuasive in his own way, and he's certain that Erlic, who now is locked up down in the dungeon, is as shocked as anybody else about these two murders.

'No. It was the sleeping watchman that turned a desire into an opportunity, and the murderer had to be in a position to see that sleeping watchman, and quickly – very quickly; I'll get to that in a moment – take advantage of that rare opportunity.

'Steven Argent, maybe? He's in charge of the castle and the entire earldom while Earl Vandros is away, but that doesn't mean that he wouldn't seem out of place prowling the hall outside the guest quarters, for any reason, much less waiting for a once-in-a-lifetime chance to find the watchman asleep.

'Baron Viztria was quite right – I know it wasn't the Swordmaster, and indeed I'm more than slightly gratified that he is the only other man in the room beside myself with a naked blade in his hand.

'No, the killer was one of you barons, residing in the guest wing, somebody whose presence in itself would not have drawn any particular attention to him, simply because he – like the rest of you – belonged there.' He nodded. 'In my own profession, I've always thought it important to take advantage of surprising opportunities, and in a way, I've got to admire how the killer did that. He couldn't be sure that the sleeping watchman would remain asleep, mind you, so he had to be ready to kill him, too

– and quickly, before his outcries could summon anybody, and then disappear back into his own room, only to reappear with the rest of the barons who had gone to bed, apparently every bit as surprised as the rest.' Pirojil looked up. 'Visualize it yourself, my lords, as I've been spending the afternoon doing. The killer hears Morray in the hall and glances out of the door. He sees the Baron enter the Baroness's chamber. He ponders his choices. He has the two of them alone and vulnerable. He waits. Later that night he looks out of the door again and he notices that the watchman is asleep. Seizing the moment, he quickly dresses himself –'

'Dresses himself?'

Pirojil nodded. 'He can't stalk across the hall in his nightclothes, after all, not with a knife in one hand and a sword in the other – he might need the sword, after all, to kill the guard quickly on his way back to his room, should the guard awaken or be awakened. If, before the murders, he's seen in such a strange condition, it's going to be clear to all that his intentions were bloody, although perhaps not quite clear what those intentions were, and why risk anything prematurely? He's a vile piece of shit, begging the pardon of all but one of you, but he's not an idiot.

'So, as I was saying, he dresses himself, and takes the opportunity to go over and open the door to Lady Mondegreen's room, perhaps having spent a moment listening outside, for sounds of sleep or – well, or for other sounds.

'And then he opens the door, sees them asleep on the bed, and steps inside, then closes the door behind him. From this point on, he's committed, and while he's fast with a knife – he's about to demonstrate that as he stands over their bed, he can't quite be sure to slit first one throat and then another without the thrashing about of his first victim awakening his second.

'So he draws his sword, and holds it back, the point over, perhaps, the eye of his second victim, ready to run the point of that sword through and into the brain to silence his second victim, if the first one's death is a little more violent and dramatic than he hopes for.

'But he's lucky, as well as fast and good at what he does, and his knife is very sharp and his hand very steady, and a few seconds later, blood is fountaining from the throats of both Baron Morray and Lady Mondegreen.

'And now, he's in a rush, and his heart is pounding, thumping in his chest. He's done his deed, and he has to get out, and back to his room.

'He blows out the lantern – if somebody has heard something and walks in, he wants that somebody to walk into darkness, and his sword point; besides, he wants the room dark when he opens the door, for the obvious reason – and then he's back at the door, pulling it open only a crack to see if the watchman is still asleep, which he is.

'So he goes down the corridor, with his sword already drawn – remember, the guard could wake up suddenly, even at his quiet footfalls – and back to his room.' Pirojil finally looked up. 'But I've left something out, haven't I?' he asked, smiling.

He turned to Baron Langahan. 'Excuse me, my lord, but would you be so kind as to slide over your swordbelt?'

Langahan did just that, with no more than the slightest of hesitations, and with the hint of a scowl.

'What are you leaving out, Pirojil?' Steven Argent asked.

'Why, the knife, my lord,' Pirojil said, extracting the knife from Langahan's belt. He held it up. It was a usual sort of belt-knife, its stacked-wood grip fancier than Steven Argent would have preferred, and its single-edged blade gleamed from both polish and oil. 'When a throat is cut – and I can tell you that I've cut a few throats in my time – blood doesn't just ooze out. It spurts. He would have been lucky if the blood didn't coat the whole blade, and perhaps his hand as well.

'He could hardly go out into the hall with a blade dripping blood, could he?

'Now, if he wasn't rushing, he could have spent a few minutes carefully cleaning the knife off – perhaps using the sheet from the bed, or tearing off a piece of the sheet, although that would have made a loud noise.

'But my friend Kethol examined the room very closely, and he reported that there were no bloody rags left – just some spots on the sheet, where, perhaps, he quickly cleaned his blade as well as he could in a few seconds. Did he stand in the light of the oil lamp and clean the blade carefully, thoroughly, being sure to get at all the cracks, then bring the bloody cloth along with him?' Pirojil shook his head. 'I don't think so. I don't think that he went across the hall with the knife held behind his back, or along the flat of his arm, either, as that would have indelibly marked his clothes with blood, and with his sword in his right hand, as he crossed the hall. He would want to keep his left hand free.

'I think he simply made two quick swipes on the bedsheet, in the dark, and then sheathed his knife, and later thoroughly – very thoroughly, my lords – cleaned that knife in his own room, down to the last spot of blood, perhaps burning the rags afterwards, or more likely simply using his water pitcher, and pouring the bloody water down the garderobe – or perhaps even drinking it, as disgusting as it sounds, to hide the evidence.

'Blood is so . . . so messy, my lords.'

Steven Argent shook his head. 'But . . .'

Pirojil took the knife and began to cut away at its sheath. 'My apologies, Baron Langahan, for ruining your sheath.' He spread the leather out. 'If it had been Baron Langahan, we would have seen signs of the blood here. In fact, if you look at those brown stains there –'

'That's an old stain,' Langahan said. 'Hasn't everybody at some time put away a knife when it wasn't clean?' He shrugged. 'I can remember once when I was hunting with the Viceroy, years ago, when we took a boar, and –'

'Yes, my lord, it is indeed old blood, or at least old something.' Pirojil turned to Viztria. 'I think I'll ruin your sheath next, my lord. Unless you have some objection?'

For once, Viztria was speechless, but he simply slid his sword-belt across the table, and Pirojil repeated the process.

'No stains here, my lord. Baron Verheyen next, I think.'

Verheyen snorted as he did the same, and Pirojil cut his sheath open as he had the others.

'Interesting, Baron Verheyen,' he said, as he spread the leather for all to see. These stains appear rather . . . fresh.' A sneer curled itself across Pirojil's thick lips. 'You murdering pig.'

Verheyen was on his feet, snatching the sword from Folson's sheath. 'You lying sack of –'

'Stop right there, Verheyen,' Steven Argent commanded. 'You're under arrest, in the name of the Earl of LaMut.'

Verheyen shook his head, his face red with rage. 'I'm innocent,' he bellowed. 'I'm not sure what your man is up to, Argent, but I'll find out after I've stuck him a few times!'

He lunged for Pirojil, who was quickly out of his chair and around the table.

Steven Argent moved between them, and struck the Baron's rapier aside with his own rapier.

Pirojil watched the two men confront one another, waiting for an opportunity to bolt for the door. It wasn't fear that motivated him, but caution, for he had heard Durine's recounting of the practice bout between Argent and Verheyen and knew the Swordmaster would be fortunate to emerge from this conflict alive. Once to the door, Pirojil would shout for guardsmen to overpower the furious baron.

The only problem with the plan was that several barons were standing in a knot between Pirojil and the door. To try to move around them would bring him within a thrust of Verheyen's sword.

While he pondered his next move, the struggle commenced.

Pirojil was impressed. He had seen many a fight, from barroom to battlement, and with every sort of blade imaginable, but Baron Verheyen was as fast a swordsman as he had ever seen. Pirojil was certain that had *he* stood to face the Baron alone, he'd now be dead upon the floor of the Great Hall. He wasn't even sure he could confront him with Durine and Kethol standing behind him with their swords at the ready.

Argent and Verheyen were now exchanging blows faster than Pirojil thought possible. The look of concentration on the Swordmaster's face revealed the fact that he knew himself overmatched. Yet he continued to press on. He might not be quite as fast as the Baron nor as deft with the blade, but he was far more practised, and experience counted for a great deal when death was on the line.

Back and forth they lunged and parried, yet they hardly moved from their original positions, taking only a step or two in either direction, and Pirojil kept watching for an opportune moment to run to fetch the guards.

Three high attacks from Verheyen were countered by Argent, who riposted twice and found his opponent ready. Then the Swordmaster launched a seemingly frantic attack of his own, only to be repulsed by the nimble footwork of the Baron.

Then Pirojil sensed a change in Argent.

It seemed that the Swordmaster had spotted something that Pirojil hadn't seen. There was a pattern emerging, and suddenly Pirojil forgot about seeking the guardsmen, instead becoming entranced by the display of swordsmanship before him.

Both men were drenched in their own perspiration, despite the cold, and the only sound in the room was the stamp of leather boots upon the cold stone floor, the ring of steel upon steel and the heavy breathing of the two combatants. Blow, parry, riposte, parry; the contest wore on.

Then Pirojil saw it. Argent was laying a trap. Each time the two men crossed swords, the blades lingered in contact a tiny bit longer, with a little more pressure upon the opponent's blade. Argent almost fell into a pattern, three high strikes and a low strike, lulling Verheyen into studying it for an opportunity. He changed to two strikes, then three again, causing the Baron to hesitate in his riposte.

Then Argent offered Verheyen the blade. He took a block and pressed forward, and for an instant Verheyen took the blade, resisting the pressure. Then Argent moved left, allowing his blade to fall away and Verheyen found himself over-extended and exposed for just an instant.

And then Steven Argent was standing over a dead man, and Verheyen's blood was running down the length of his sword. The Swordmaster looked down at the dead baron then very slowly and very deliberately he produced a handkerchief from his tunic, and cleaned the blade very carefully before putting it back into its scabbard.

'You thought it would turn out this way, Pirojil,' Argent said.

The ugly man nodded. 'It seemed possible. Corner a rat and he'll fight; and I wanted this rat cornered, my lord. He deserved that. And I'd just as soon I not be known as one who killed a nobleman, no matter what the justification or cause. Baron Verheyen has relatives, and he has some friends, I'm told, and I'm sure that some will blame me as much for exposing him as they will blame him for the murders.'

'So you put me in harm's way to protect you from retribution?'

Pirojil shook his head. 'To tell the truth, my lord, I wasn't thinking that far down the road.' He shrugged. 'As to why, well, in the field, I'll put myself and my friends up against almost anybody – we've done that enough times – but I know I'm no match for a nobleman in a duel, and you were the only man here with a chance to stand against the Baron.' He looked down at the body on the floor and added, 'I'll tell you it doesn't bother me at all that a murderer met his reward.'

Lord Viztria looked down at Verheyen's still form. Blood was soaking into the thick carpet covering the cold stones. 'But why?' he asked.

'My lord?' said Pirojil.

'Why kill Morray and Lady Mondegreen? Morray had agreed to step aside in Verheyen's favour.'

Pirojil shrugged. 'Just because Morray said a thing, doesn't mean it's true. Is any agreement made here between the barons binding upon the Earl? Or the Duke of Yabon? Or the King?'

'Well, no,' said Lord Viztria. 'But it seemed logical.'

'A combined Mondegreen and Morray makes the most powerful barony in the duchy,' added Argent. 'And the very self-less act of stepping aside for the greater good might be just the thing that would cause Earl Vandros to recommend Morray to the Duke as his successor.'

Pirojil said, 'Seeming to have no reason to murder a rival, Verheyen now could ensure beyond a doubt Morray would not become again a rival for the earldom. He's got no motive, so no one thinks he did it.'

Steven Argent said, 'It sounds so simple.'

Pirojil arched an eyebrow. 'Swordmaster, if I may?'

'May what?'

'Address the barons, once more, for just another moment?'

Steven Argent nodded. 'Please.'

Pirojil turned to the others. 'I just wanted to thank you for your kind attention, and bid you all farewell. As I said, I'm not entirely sure that some won't blame me and my friends for exposing the murderer more than the murderer himself, so we're withdrawing ourselves from the service of the Earl of LaMut, and we shall be on our way in the morning.'

'In the snow?' said Lord Viztria, with his usual raised eyebrows and sneer.

'Snow melts, my lord Viztria. We'll manage.' He turned back to the Swordmaster. 'May we keep our room in the barracks for the night, my lord? Or should we seek accommodations in town?'

Steven Argent didn't understand.

Why?

These men had proven their worth, under the most trying of circumstances, and he had been about to offer them permanent commissions, subject to the confirmation of the Earl. Maybe they weren't exactly what he thought of as officer material, but competence and loyalty should have a reward.

But, before the barons, with Verheyen lying dead on the floor, he didn't quite know what to say, so he said nothing, and simply nodded.

'A good day to you all,' the preposterously ugly man said. Then he turned on the balls of his feet and walked out of the hall.

He didn't look back.

SIXTEEN

Truth

It was dark outside.

But that was outside, and they were, thankfully, inside, and the oil lamps made the room comfortably bright.

The sounds from the barracks common room were more muted than usual. Pirojil could just make out the sounds of distant conversation over the rattling of dice.

They gathered around the hearth in their quarters, the bottle of wine from Lady Mondegreen's room on a side table next to Kethol, who was busying himself, weaving leather thongs in and out of each other across a wooden frame.

What few possessions they had seemed to have grown in their time in LaMut, and they had had to procure four extra rucksacks from the castle dungeon in order to keep what they didn't want to throw out. A packhorse would have been good, but Pirojil couldn't quite see how to get a horse on brezeneden.

Durine had been sceptical, and was ready to make another run, throwing out some of their collection, but Kethol had quickly improvised a sort of sled from an old door, some extra strips of wood, and a piece of rope, which should be easy enough to pull across the snow, until the snow melted, which it showed every sign of doing quickly.

A few days of hobbling along on these awkward-looking brezeneden, and then . . .

After that, they'd have to procure some horses in the next town, though that might be difficult. Well, if they had to walk all the way to Zun to get mounts, at least they had enough money for it. They could even afford to be a bit picky –

No, any horses would do. They would have to sell them in Ylith anyway, and men who were about to take ship away – far away, as far away as they could get – were hardly in the best bargaining position. They'd need five horses, most likely . . .

Kethol had already finished another set of brezeneden and was working on one more, when there was a knock at the door. It opened without a word being spoken, and Mackin's improbably broad face peered through.

'Come in,' Kethol said. 'We were just talking about you.'

'Milo says we're going with you,' he said.

'You're welcome to leave town with us,' Durine said slowly, carefully. 'Although if you are going to come with the three of us, there're some things we'll have to get straight –'

'Yeah.' The dwarf's grin broadened, and he stretched out his thick hands and cracked his knuckles. 'Looking forward to it, I am.'

'– by talking it out. We settle things by discussion and vote, the three of us, and not by beating each other up. We save that for when we get paid.'

Mackin shrugged. 'Well, we can talk about it. If it doesn't work out, you three can go your way, and Milo and me, we can go ours. Long as I don't have to keep calling you "captain", and saying "yes, sir" all the time, that might happen. Or it might not. You never know.'

'I'm not a captain,' Kethol said. He had been the first to get out of his grey officer's tabard. It, like the others, still had the rank tabs on the shoulders, but all now lay neatly folded on a chair by the door. 'Never was much of one.'

'Me, neither.' Durine nodded. 'Just three men who kill people for money,' he said, then shrugged his massive shoulders and looked over at Kethol and Pirojil.

Maybe they had enough money now to find a place for the Three Swords Tavern?

Or would it have to be the Five Swords?

Mackin nodded. 'Then we'll see. We leave at first light?'

'Wolf's tail,' Pirojil said. That's what they called it down in the Vale, that grey light before dawn that was certainly good enough for their purpose, since leaving was their purpose.

Mackin nodded. 'Then I'd better get a few pints of ale in me, and get some sleep, eh?'

He left without waiting for an answer.

'You think it'll work out?' Kethol asked. 'Why bring in another two?'

'We can find work for five as easy as three,' Pirojil said. 'And I think that Milo needs to leave LaMut, for a few reasons. We can talk about those tomorrow, eh?'

Kethol bent back over his work. 'Fair enough.'

Pirojil wouldn't cut Milo and the dwarf in, not without them buying their share with blood and money over time, but you never did know how much money a mercenary soldier had on him, not unless you searched him very carefully, and it was entirely possible that the other two had enough for their share.

And there had been some blood involved, already, although he didn't even want to think about that, not right now, and wouldn't want to talk about it, ever.

But cutting them in would be something to discuss. Even if it was only a way to avoid discussing other things.

Secrets, he thought.

Shit.

He and Milo had a secret.

Pirojil had been sure that the murderer was Verheyen, and thought he might be able to corner the Baron, forcing him – he was known to be short of temper – to do something that would reveal his guilt.

But he hadn't been sure of it, and Pirojil liked a sure thing.

He could blame the Swordmaster for having put them in an impossible position. Or he could blame himself for not trusting his own instincts and reasoning.

Or he could just try to forget about it.

There was another knock on the door and this time whoever it was waited long enough for Durine to say, 'Come in.'

It was Milo, with an impassive expression on his face, and five small leather pouches held in his cupped hands. 'The Swordmaster sent me, with your pay.'

'Our pay?' Kethol looked puzzled. 'How did they get into the strongroom?'

'I don't much like asking about strongrooms,' Milo said, grinning for a moment. 'But as I understand it, Steven Argent took up a collection among the barons, to be repaid when the Earl gets back. Not enough on them to pay everybody off, mind, but enough for the five of us, so let's not let anybody else know about it, eh?' He pocketed the two smaller ones, and handed over the other three. 'You might want to count the money, and check with him, just in case you think some of it might have fallen out on the way over.'

Durine nodded. 'We'll certainly count it. Be a shame for us to get off on the wrong foot, and all, since you and the dwarf are going to be travelling with us, I'm told.'

'Yeah,' Milo said, looking at Pirojil, not at Durine. 'It would be a shame if there were any misunderstandings, so let's be sure that that doesn't happen.'

'Easy.' Pirojil raised a hand. 'We won't have any problems. Or if we do, you just go your way, and we'll just go ours.'

Milo nodded, and left, closing the door behind him.

Kethol laid the final one of the brezeneden on the pile with the others, then stretched. 'Well, if we're moving out in the morning, let's get some sleep tonight. Bar the door, stand a one in three, or both?'

'Both,' Durine said.

Pirojil nodded. It only made sense. Word would get around quickly, with the barons all talking to their captains, which meant that they were known to have a fair amount of money on them – although not nearly as much as they actually had – and you could never be sure about thieves and such.

'I'll take the first one, then wake you,' he said to Durine, who nodded.

Back to normal, at least in that.

'I dunno.' Kethol looked at the door longingly. 'I'd sort of like to go up to the Aerie and say goodbye to Fantus.'

Durine laughed. 'That wouldn't be a good idea. The Swordmaster would probably talk you into the three of us staying on, which would mean, as far as I'm concerned, that it would mean *you* staying on, because I need to get out of here.'

Pirojil nodded. 'Me, as well. Besides, I've never been very much for goodbyes, and neither have you.'

'Yeah, but that's with *people*,' Kethol said, as though it made some sort of difference. 'Dragons are different. In another world, maybe I might have liked to get to know one, you know?'

'In *this* world, if you walk out, don't come back and tell us we're staying,' Durine said, firmly.

Kethol gave up with a bad imitation of good grace. 'One more thing . . .' he said, pouring what remained of the wine in the bottle into their three mugs. He passed out the mugs, and looked expectantly at Pirojil.

'Your turn, I think,' he said.

'We all knew the Baron about as well, but Lady Mondegreen seemed to have taken a particular fancy to you,' Pirojil said. She had also played him like a lute, but she had probably liked him, too. And Kethol had certainly taken quite a shine to her, as well. As had Pirojil, in his own way. Just because she scared the shit out of him didn't mean that he hadn't liked her – he just would have preferred to like her from a distance, given her penchant for manipulation, combined with her abilities at manipulation . . .

Which, in the long run, hadn't made her throat any less resistant to being cut, though.

Kethol thought it over for a moment. 'Baron Morray and Lady Mondegreen: a true gentleman, and a great lady,' he said, then downed his wine with a quick gulp, as did Durine.

Pirojil sipped at his own wine, making it last.

Not the worst he had ever had, although it was a bit bitter and tannic for his taste. Not that a man in his line of work should be fussy about such things. Still, it might be that the Three Swords – or the Five Swords, now, perhaps – would have a wine cellar, as well as good dwarven ale and a decent human brew, and maybe he ought to acquire some knowledge about such things, even if he probably couldn't ever afford fastidiousness.

Kethol blew out the oil lamps, and he and Durine lay down on their bunks, and were almost instantly asleep.

Pirojil took his chair, and leaned it back against the barred door, and let his eyes sag shut for a moment.

Yes, there would be a lot to think about, and a few things to talk about, eventually. But give it a while. He sipped some more of the wine. Too bitter, really. Maybe there was something about all this that he was missing.

He hadn't missed much, he was sure. Verheyen probably would have got away with the murder, although, in the long run, he wouldn't have ended up as Earl of LaMut, not if the murder had gone unsolved, and with everybody still under permanent suspicion. It wouldn't have been either of the two Bas-Tyra stalking horses, either, although Guy du Bas-Tyra might have ended up profiting by having some other vassal of his put into the earldom. Vandros would hardly be in a position to resist the pressure from the Viceroy, not under the circumstances.

Pity that he had been right.

He had been hoping that there would have been a sign of fresh blood in Langahan's sheath. Viztria was too much of a popinjay to be a murderer, but Langahan was a quieter sort, and probably more dangerous.

He sipped at some more wine. Not much of it, but he might as well enjoy it.

No, it had been Verheyen. Verheyen had had, in his own way, just as much respect for Lady Mondegreen as Pirojil did. It would have been nice to have had a look at Verheyen's sheath before, but that wouldn't have had the same impact.

Having Milo lift Verheyen's knife, cut his own finger, and rub it on the inside of Verheyen's sheath before replacing the knife had been the right thing to do, and if Pirojil would never know for certain if Milo's blood had covered Lady Mondegreen's and Baron Morray's, he could live with that. Maybe Verheyen had been just a little more fastidious than Pirojil had thought he was.

Maybe not.

Best to make sure that the problem was solved, and he had done that. Steven Argent wouldn't have liked knowing how he had solved it, but . . .

To hell with him.

Tell a soldier to solve a problem for you, and he would do just that, and he'd do it with steel and blood, and do his best to be sure that it wasn't his blood, and Pirojil's betters were best off not knowing just how he had solved the problem. That was true for Kethol and Durine, too, at least for now, although he would tell them, eventually, when they were all far enough away.

Far away sounded good.

The next thing Pirojil knew, Kethol was shaking him awake, as the grey light of pre-dawn filtered weakly in through the mottled glass of the window.

And as soon as he awoke he knew that he had been horribly wrong.

He caught up with the murderer in the kitchen. Even at this hour, it was crowded with cooks and assistants, and the smell of the baking bread was overpowering.

'Good morning, Ereven,' he said.

'And a good morning to you, Captain Pirojil,' the housecarl said, his face as glum as usual, no more, and no less. 'I understand you're leaving – did you want me to pack some provisions for your journey?'

'No. We're fine.' Pirojil shook his head. 'No. What I wanted was a few moments of your time – I thought I should say goodbye to you. And I'm not a captain any more, nor would I wish to be.'

Ereven nodded. 'My time is yours, of course, Captain,' he said. 'A word about what?'

'Step outside with me, for just a few moments.'

The parade ground was still packed with snow, but it was starting to melt, and it was slippery beneath their feet.

'I know,' Pirojil said.

Ereven's expression didn't change. 'Know what, Captain?'

'I know that the bottle of wine you gave to Baron Morray was drugged. As was, I assume, poor Erlic's supper.'

'I don't have any idea what you're talking about, sir.'

'Oh, I think you know exactly what I'm talking about, Ereven. I could even hazard a guess as to why, rather than how, but the how is clear enough. And as to the who, I'm tempted to say the people who conspired with the late Baron Verheyen were you *and* your daughter, Emma.'

That got to Ereven. He paled. 'Captain, I –'

'But I don't even know if Verheyen was involved, not really. He hated Morray, and he was probably smart enough to see through Lady Mondegreen's negotiated settlement, but was he the murderer, along with you?' Pirojil shrugged. 'That I don't know. And I want to.

'And if I don't get an answer right now, the note that I've left – never mind with whom – will be put in the hands of the Swordmaster, a few days from now. Then he'll be asking you the same question. Unless . . .'

'Unless?'

'Unless you explain to me, right now, why. The "how" part is easy, and I should have seen it before. A guard falling asleep on watch? A reliable man, up until the night before last. And then he suddenly fell asleep on watch. Very convenient.

'A strange coincidence. Unless, of course, his food was drugged, as was the bottle of wine, which explains how you were able to slice their throats without waking them. A fine kitchen knife, well-sharpened, as all good kitchen knives should be, left their room on a covered tray, with you, after you brought it in on a covered tray, to slice their throats while they lay drugged. It wouldn't be at all strange for the housecarl to be washing a knife down in the kitchen, would it?' Pirojil nodded. 'I think your daughter helped.'

'She doesn't know anything about it. Please don't bring her into this. It's not –'

'It's not right? You mean, in the sense that slitting two people's throats isn't right? Or –'

'He treated her like a plaything,' Ereven said, with no change in his inflection. A lifetime of keeping his expression and tone under control hadn't abandoned him, even now. 'He lured her into his bed, and made all sorts of promises to her – it's not totally unknown for a noble to take a common wife, and a gentleman who sires a bastard acknowledges him.'

'But Baron Morray didn't do that.'

'No, he didn't. He lied to her and she thought he loved her. She was a good girl, and had never known a man before the Baron. I hoped to marry her to the son of Grigsby, the grain merchant. He's a man of means and his son will take over the business one day. But a "kitchen wench" with the bastard of a noble in her arms? My girl thought herself in love with Morray, but he said nothing to her as her belly swelled with his baby, sir. I think . . .' his voice faltered. After a moment he carried on: 'Then to marry a woman who carries his baby – it's no secret that Mondegreen was ill and his lady was with Morray many times.' Ereven's voice turned bitter. 'What sort of man would deny his own? Not admit he fathered my daughter's child, and then let another man claim a second child with the woman he was to wed? He and Lady Mondegreen were evil.'

Pirojil nodded. 'And this was your last chance to punish them for that, eh? Verheyen wouldn't have him as Bursar, and wouldn't want his fingers on the Purse in advance of coming into the earldom. Morray and Lady Mondegreen were going away to become a country baron and lady and do their best never to set foot in LaMut again, for fear that Verheyen might think they were gathering support against him, no matter what Morray had sworn.'

'Yes, sir.'

Pirojil nodded. 'That drug that you put in the wine, and the food. Do you have more of it?'

Ereven hesitated for a moment. 'Yes, sir.'

'Then I've a suggestion. It won't save you, but . . .'

'But my daughter?'

Pirojil nodded. 'I'll leave her out of this, if you'll take your-self out of it. Swallow all of that drug that you have, and if you think that may not be enough to kill you for certain, find some-thing else that will, and swallow it, too. Wash it down with a bottle of the Earl's finest wine – but before you do that, write a note saying that it was you who drugged Erlic's food – you can say that you did it at Verheyen's behest, if you'd like, but if you say that you did it at *mine*,' he added quickly, 'all of it will come out, you can count on that. *All* of it – about how your daughter prevailed upon you to murder the father of her baby.'

'But she *didn't*. She doesn't even *know*.'

'So what? The daughter of a self-confessed murderer's word against that of the captain who solved the riddle of who killed Mondegreen and Morray? Who will the Earl believe? They *might* wait until the child is born before they hang your daughter. Make your choice, housecarl. But make it now, and make it wisely. You won't have another opportunity.'

The impassive expression was back on Ereven's face. 'Your offer is acceptable, Captain.' He nodded, once. Then, for a moment, just a moment, the mask dropped from his face. 'You can have my blood on your hands, too, to go along with Baron Verheyen's.'

Pirojil shrugged. 'I've had a lot of blood on my hands, Ereven. I'm used to it.'

Ereven wasn't the only one who could control his expression, after all.

Pirojil could try to justify it to himself. After all, despite the peace they had made Verheyen was Morray's enemy, and Baron Morray would not have minded at all Verheyen being dead, and never becoming the Earl of LaMut. He could blame Steven Argent for putting him in a situation that was more than he had been able to manage. Pirojil was a soldier, dammit, and not some sort of constable, nor judge.

But that wouldn't work. And if there was a way to put blood

back in a dead body, Pirojil would have used it many times before.

However, Erlic's blood was still in his body, and at least Pirojil could limit the damage.

Ereven nodded. 'I'll see to it directly, sir. And if you'll promise to put in a good word for my daughter, I'll say that it was Verheyen.'

Pirojil shook his head. 'No promises. If I come back this way – unlikely, but you never know – I'll look in on her, though. That's the best I can do.'

'It's good enough, sir.' Ereven drew himself up straight. 'If there's nothing more . . .'

'No. There's nothing more.'

'Then I've got some writing to do, and a bottle of wine to find with which to wash down the powder, and I'd best be getting to it before you change your mind.'

'Yes,' Pirojil said.

The housecarl turned and walked back into the kitchen.

Pirojil turned and walked away.

He had a great deal to do and wanted it done before they found the housecarl's body and the note. If Durine's description of the – whatever he called them, the snowshoes – was correct, they would take some getting used to as they made their way out of LaMut. And given the realization that a perfectly innocent baron – or at least as innocent as any baron could be given their nature – had died needlessly, Pirojil would rather not be around for the incessant chatter about the murders that was certain to be the table-talk of every noble in the duchy for weeks to come. He would prefer to be remembered as 'that really hideous captain' than have too many people recall his name. Even if no one ever discovered the truth, Verheyen had friends who would think it some sort of justice to see Pirojil vanish.

Pirojil wanted to vanish from LaMut, but on his own terms,

and he wanted to find himself somewhere warm, but not in a funeral pyre.

They should be on their way, the five of them, as soon as possible. As he hurried down a corridor and climbed the stairs, Pirojil stole a look out of a window over the City of LaMut. Not a bad place as cities go. He'd been in far worse and few better. The sun was getting ready to rise, and the city was coming to life. Then he turned to leave the room, wondering absently how many other things they had got wrong. Not that it mattered. In a few years everything would be forgotten with a new earl in LaMut and Vandros in Yabon.

The one question that nagged at him a bit was how that firedrake, Fantus, had continually managed to get into the Swordmaster's office. There had to be a secret passage somewhere in this castle that even the housecarl didn't know of. Still, life was full of unsolved mysteries and as such went, that was a minor one.

Pirojil glanced out of the window at the new day, glad he was alive to enjoy it.

And somewhere, outside, a dog was barking.

Available August 2008 in trade paperback from Eos Books

JIMMY THE HAND

Legends of the Riftwar: Book III

by Raymond E. Feist and S.M. Stirling

Jimmy the Hand, the gifted boy thief of Krondor, was just a nimble street urchin, until the day he met Prince Arutha. Helping the prince rescue Princess Anita from Duke Guy du Bas-Tyra, Jimmy runs afoul of Black Guy's secret police—a situation made worse when he blatantly refuses to lie low to rescue his fellow Mockers from the cruel reprisal of the Duke's henchmen. Given the choice of disappearing on his own, or with a little professional help—in a weighted barrel at the bottom of Krondor's harbor—Jimmy flees the only home he's ever known, and ventures south to Land's End. But this rural enclave isn't the haven Jimmy hopes, and soon, his youthful bravado and courage lead him into the hands of a dangerous presence . . . and plunge him deep into the maw of chaos and death.

Turn the page for a sneak preview!

Men cursed as they grappled.

Jimmy the Hand slipped eel-like between knots of fighting men on the darkened quayside. Steel glittered in torch- and lantern-light, shining in ruddy-red arcs as horsemen slashed at the elusive Mockers who strove to hold them back. Only seconds more were needed for Prince Arutha and Princess Anita to make their escape, and the fight had reached the frenzied violence of desperation. Screams of rage and pain split the night, accompanied by the iron hammering of shod hooves throwing up sparks as they smashed down on stone, to the counterpoint of the clangour of steel on steel.

Bravos and street-toughs struggled against trained soldiers, but the soldiers' horses slipped and slithered on the slick boards and stones of the docks and the flickering light was even more uncertain than the footing. Knives stabbed upward and horses shied as hands gripped booted feet and heaved Bas-Tyran men-at-arms out of the saddle. The harsh iron-and-salt smell of blood was strong even against the garbage stink of the harbor, and a horse screamed piteously as it collapsed, hamstrung. The rider's leg was caught in the stirrup, crushed beneath his mount, and he screamed as the horse thrashed, then fell silent as ragged figures swarmed over him.

Jimmy fell flat under the slash of a sword, rolled unscathed between the flailing hooves of a war-horse scrabbling to find better footing, tripped one of the men-at-arms who was fighting dismounted against three Mockers, then dashed down the length of the dock, his feet light on the boards.

At the end of the quay he threw himself flat on the rough splintery wood to hail the longboat below:

'Farewell!' he called to the Princess Anita.

She turned toward his voice, her lovely face little more than a pale blur in the pre-dawn light. But he knew that her sea-green eyes would be wide with astonishment.

I'm glad I came to say goodbye, he thought, an unfamiliar sensation squeezing at his chest below the breastbone. *It's worth a little risk to life and limb.*

He grinned at her, but nervously; the fight with Jocko Radburn's men was heating up and his back felt very exposed. It wouldn't be long before the Mockers broke and ran; stand-up fights weren't their style.

Another, taller figure stood in the longboat. 'Here,' Prince Arutha called. 'Use it in good health!'

A rapier in its scabbard flew up to his hand. He snatched it out of the air and rolled over, just in time to avoid a kick from one of Radburn's bully-boys. Jimmy rolled again as the man pursued him, heavy-booted foot raised to stamp on him like an insect. Letting the sword go he reached up and grabbed toe and heel with crossed hands, giving it a vicious twist that set the bully roaring and twisting to keep it from being broken. That put him off-balance, and a kick placed with vicious precision toppled him screaming into the water. His gear dragged him under before the echoes of his scream could die.

'Time to go!' Jimmy panted.

Rolling up to his feet, Jimmy yanked the rapier from its scabbard and looked about for a worthy target—preferably one blocking the best escape route. Below, he could just make out the rhythmic splashing of the oars counterpoint the chaos of the battle all around him. Farewell, he said

again in his heart. Then, as a pile of baled cloth blazed up:
Oops!

Lanterns began to appear on the boats around them, and
watchmen from the surrounding warehouses came running,
while from all around men called out: 'What passes?' and
'Who goes there?' And a growing shout: 'Fire! Fire!'

A man in the black and gold of Bas-Tyra snatched a
lantern from one of the watchmen and marched toward the
end of the dock, giving Jimmy an idea of whom to attack.
The soldier grinned at the sight of the thin, ragged boy
before him.

'Brought me a new sword, have you?' he said. 'Looks
like a good one. Too good for gutter-scum whose whiskers
haven't yet seen a razor. My thanks.'

He swung a backhand cut at Jimmy, a lazy stroke with
more strength than style. No doubt he imagined that he
could easily smash the rapier from the young thief's hand
and then hack him down.

The finely-made blade was alive in Jimmy's hand; heavy,
but perfectly balanced, limber as a striking snake. It flashed
up almost of itself and turned the clumsy stroke away with a
long *scringgg* of metal on metal. The guardsman grunted in
astonishment as the redirected force of his own stroke spun
him around, then shouted in pain as Jimmy danced nimbly
aside and slashed at him.

More by luck than skill, the sharp steel caught the
guardsman on the wrist, parting the tough leather of his
gauntlet and cutting a shallow groove in the flesh beneath.
With a gasp, the man shook his wrist and took a step
back, disbelief visible on his coarse features even in the
darkness.

Jimmy laughed in delighted surprise. Clearly not
everyone had Arutha's skill with the blade. The hours he'd
spent training with the Prince while waiting for Trevor

Hull's smugglers to find a ship for Arutha and that old pirate, Amos Trask, to steal for their escape had paid off. Jimmy felt as if the soldier moved at half Prince Arutha's speed. He laughed again.

That laugh galvanized the solider into action and he struck out at the young thief with blow after powerful blow.

Like a peasant threshing grain, Jimmy thought—he had little experience of matters rural, but a deep contempt for rubes.

The blows were hard and fast, but each was a copy of the one before. Instinct led him to raise the rapier, and the cuts flowed off steel blade and intricate swept guard; he had to put his left palm on his right wrist more than once, lest sheer force knock the weapon out of his hand. But he knew he was moments away from dodging to his left, thrusting hard and taking the soldier in the stomach. Arutha had always cautioned patience in judging an opponent.

An instant later Jimmy's back met the side of a bale; glancing to either side he realized he'd been neatly trapped in a short, dead-end passage of piled cargo. The man before him grinned and made teasing thrusts with his sword.

'Caught like the little sewer rat you are,' he growled.

The man raised his sword and Jimmy readied himself to execute his move, confident he would be through with the soldier in another moment. Then, suddenly, a pair of grappling bodies hurtled by, each man with a hand on the wrist of the other's knife-hand, stamping and cursing as they whirled in a circle like a fast and deadly country dance. They tumbled into the Bas-Tyran man-at-arms, throwing him forward with a cry of surprise. Jimmy didn't hesitate. He felt a mild instant of regret that he couldn't execute his fancy passing thrust, but he couldn't ignore such an easily acquired target. Jimmy stabbed out, and felt the needle point of his rapier sink through the muscle and jar on bone, the strange sensation flowing up through the steel and hilt to shiver in his shoulder and lower back.

The man dropped his lantern with a cry that turned into a screamed curse as the glass shattered. The splattered oil blazed high, driving the wounded soldier back. He dropped his weapon and began to beat at spots of flame on his clothes, while Jimmy climbed the pile of bales like a monkey.

'You should know better than to corner a rat!' he called over his shoulder as he bounded down the back of the pile and struck the ground running.

He heard someone whistle the code to withdraw and saw Mockers streaming into alleys and side-streets like wisps of fog scattering before a high wind. Jimmy raced to join them, but before he ducked into an alley he turned to look out into the bay. Trevor Hull and his smugglers were diving into the water, some swimming under the docks while others made for long-boats standing by in the water. Beyond them, Jimmy could make out the form of the *Sea Swift* turning toward the broken blockade line, canvas fluttering free and catching the light like ghost-clouds in the dark; he raised his arm to wave. He knew it was useless; the Princess would have been hurried below to safety as soon as she'd been brought aboard. But he could no more have resisted that wave than he could have not spoken that one last word to her.

The young thief turned and ran down the alley, as light on his feet as a cat and almost as keenly aware of his surroundings. He might not be a great swordsmen—yet— but fleeing through the darkened alleys of Krondor was a skill he'd mastered thoroughly long before he reached the ripe old age of thirteen.

As he dodged through the byways of the city, his thoughts turned to the time he had spent with the Princess and Prince during the last few weeks. The Princess Anita was what girls were supposed to be and in his experience never were. For a boy raised in the company of whores, barmaids and pickpockets, she was . . . something rare, something fine, a minstrel's tale come to breathing life. When he was near her he wanted to be better than he was.

It's well she's gone, then, he thought. A lad in his position couldn't afford such noble notions.

Besides, he thought with a wry grin, she would one day marry Prince Arutha—even though he didn't know it yet— so Jimmy had no business having such feelings for her. Not that having no business doing things had ever stopped him.

I suppose if she has to marry, and princesses do, he's the one I'd want her to.

Jimmy liked Arutha, but it was more than that. He respected him and . . . yes, trusted him. The Prince made him see why men would follow a leader, follow him to war on his bare word, something he'd never thought to understand. Jimmy's experience had been solely with men who commanded through fear or because they could deliver an advantage to those who followed. And Jimmy served at the pleasure of the Upright Man, who did both those things

Jimmy ran his hand along the scabbard of Arutha's rapier, his now, and smiled. Then he grew suddenly solemn. Being with them had brought something special into his life, and now it was over. But then, how many people in the Kingdom got this close to princes and princesses? And of those, how many were thieves?

Jimmy grinned. He'd done better than well in his acquaintance with royalty: two hundred in gold, a fine sword, including lessons on how to use it, and a girl to dream about. And if he missed the Princess Anita, well, at least he'd got to know her.

He headed for Mother's with a jaunty step, ready for a light meal and a long sleep.

Best to sleep until Radburn cools off, he thought. Though that might mean he'd have to sleep until he was an old man.

Jimmy neared the large hall called Mother's, or Mocker's Rest, carved out among the tunnels of the sewers. To a citizen of the upper city it would have looked gloomy enough: the drip of water and the glisten of nitre on ancient stone. But it would have been little more than another junction of tunnels in the city's sewer system, a bit larger than usual, but nothing remarkable. To the average citizen of the upper city, the eyes watching Jimmy approach the entrance to Mother's would have gone unseen, and the daggers clutched in ready hands would have been undetected , unless at the last, fatal instant, they were driven home to protect the secret of Mocker's Rest.

To Jimmy it was home and safety and a chance to rest. He pushed on a stone, and a loud click preceded the appearance of a small opening, as a door fashioned of canvas and wood, cleverly painted to look like rock, swung wide. He was short enough that he could walk hunched over while a taller man would have to crawl, and he quickly traversed the short passage to enter the hidden basement. A Basher stood watch and as Jimmy appeared, nodded. Jimmy was thus spared a lethal welcome. Any unknown head coming through that passage had roughly a second to intone the password, 'There's a party tonight at Mother's' before finding his brains splattered all over the stone floor.

The room was huge, carved out of three basements, all with stairs leading up to three buildings owned by the Upright Man. A whorehouse, an inn and a merchant of cheap trade-goods provided a variety of escape routes, and Jimmy could find all of them blindfolded, as could every other Mocker. The light was kept dim at all hours of the day or night, so that a quick exit into the sewers wouldn't leave a Mocker without sight.

Jimmy nodded greetings to a few of the beggars and urchins who were awake; most slept soundly, for there were still many hours until dawn. They would all be in the market minutes after sunrise on a normal day. But today would be anything but normal. With the Prince and Princess safely away, reprisals would be the first order of business. The City Constables and the Royal Household Guard had been easy enough to cope with over the years, but this secret police installed by Guy du Bas-Tyra since he took the office of Viceroy was another story. More than one Mocker had been turned snitch to them and the mood of the room reflected it. While there was a quiet sense of triumph at having aided Princess Anita's escape, the benefit was long term; the Upright Man thought about things that way, Jimmy understood. Some day Princess Anita would return to Krondor—or at least Jimmy hoped so—and those who supported her and her father, Prince Erland, now had a debt to the Upright Man that he would contrive to collect in the most beneficial fashion.

But that was all for the future, for the Upright Man; for the common thief, pickpocket, or whore, there was no benefit this day. Instead, the city above would be crawling with angry spies and informants, looking to identify those who had embarrassed Jocko Radburn, head of the secret police. And he was not a man to embarrass without repercussions, Jimmy understood.